OOGIE BOOGIE BOUNCE

M. Stephen Lukac

First Paperback Edition: February 2008
ISBN 978-1-929653-92-8

Published by:
Delirium Books
P.O. Box 338
North Webster, IN 46555
sales@deliriumbooks.com
www.deliriumbooks.com

Copy Editors: David Marty & Steve Souza

Author's Note:

No actual shoplifters, rednecks, bookstore employees, discorporate souls, mages, or psychics (headless or otherwise) were harmed in the creation of this novel.

For my own, personal Colony:
Nathaniel, Zachary and Alexys.

You may not live in my head,
But I carry you all in my heart.

ACKNOWLEDGEMENTS

It's been a long time since I've had the opportunity to do this, so there's a completely new list of people to thank:

To Shane at Delirium: If my plumbing was still connected, I'd offer my next-born, but it isn't, so you'll have to settle for this, for no other reason than giving me the ability to answer the oft-asked "When's you next book coming out?" with more than a pathetic shrug.

To Janet Jr.: You know why. I'll never be able to repay your kind generosity, although I haven't forgotten how much I still owe you.

To Brian: Although I understand why you've had to batten down the hatches, I'm happy to still be permitted to come aboard. I have to thank you for having the opportunity to thank you, so…thank you.

To J. A.: The initials aren't fooling anyone that counts bro. You're a man, baby, and I tell everyone exactly what that means.

To Andrew: What I thought was the end of the fight was just the minute between rounds. Thanks for working my corner; I wouldn't have any other cut man but you.

To Drew: My partner in crime, my sounding board, my marinating amigo. Who knew I'd find another brother so late in life?

To Vince: *Oogie Boogie Bounce* may not turn your crank as far as titles go, but I think you'll like where Keith winds up by the end (and you never did provide an alternative to *Bounce*, so everyone's stuck with it).

To all my fans: God, that still sounds strange. Thanks for waiting so long for the next chapter in Milo's saga (and yes, it is a saga, if only because of the interminable intervals between installments). Hopefully, you won't have to wait as long to find out what happens next, and will still want to after reading this (I know what happens next and trust me, you're going to want to find out).

To everyone I share DNA with: No, the sick and twisted material that precedes and follows is not a product of damaged genetics, so sleep in peace. You shouldn't be afraid just because I turned out this way.

Probably.

Finally, to Rhonda: I can wax as eloquently as the next guy, but when it comes to you, words still fail me. So, let that which is known remain unwritten, but understand it will never change.

Be careful what you wish for; you may receive it.
— Anonymous

PROLOGUE

The first cut is the most important.

Ken Chesterton begins his incision just above the genitals and stops at the sternum. He's careful to control his cut, only going deep enough to penetrate the stomach muscles. Burying his knife to its hilt and tearing with all his strength might satisfy the deepest recesses of his reptilian brain, but the resulting smell of punctured intestine and ruptured bladder will stay in his nostrils for days.

Arlie Garrison twists his beer can until it rips in two, satisfying his own R-Complex in a less visceral manner. He sends the aluminum halves sailing into the darkness beyond the circle of their lantern, where they clang against the other severed castoffs of the evening. Ken whirls at the sound, fixing Arlie with a ferocious stare.

"Do you have to make so much goddamned noise?" he asks, turning back to his butchery.

"Calm down," Arlie says, opening another beer. "Who's gonna hear us out here in the woods?" He sucks foam from the top of the can. He doesn't mind these late-night excursions with Ken; in fact, he looks forward to anything that takes him away from the missus and their mewling brats. Beer and guns wins over bitch and brood every time. Ken's a bachelor, so Arlie figures he can't truly appreciate the joys of escaping hearth and home for a night of drinking and killing.

Ken sheathes his knife in the soft earth and turns the body on its side. As the guts begin to spill out, Ken retrieves his knife and slices at the fat holding the intestines in. After several deft cuts with the large blade, a pile of steaming viscera lies next to the hollowed carcass.

"That's gonna be some good eatin'," Arlie says, toasting Ken's expertise. His eyes shine from reflected lantern light as he wipes his tongue across his lips. Thoughts of fresh meat sizzling in a pan compete with the buzz generated by eight cans of Old Milwaukee.

"Don't start drooling," Ken replies. "This one's not for eating; not by us."

"How's that?" Arlie nearly chokes on his beer, struggling to deal with this unexpected case of *appetitus interruptus*.

"We're not eatin' this one." Ken cleans the blood from his knife. "I got us a buyer for it."

"A buyer?"

"That's what I said."

"I heard what you said; I just don't understand it," Arlie mutters.

"What's not to understand?" Ken asks. "I found us a feller willing to pay cash money for this. Don't worry; you'll still get a full belly out of the deal. You'll just get to fill it with something different this time."

"What about Hiram?"

"What about Hiram? What's any of this got to do with him?"

"You know how he feels about freelancing," Arlie says, hiding a frown with the aluminum can. "If it don't benefit the community, it shouldn't benefit anybody."

Ken looks up from his cleaning. "Don't go getting all converted on me Arlie. We were doing this long before we hooked up with The Brotherhood, and we'll be doing it long after we're gone."

"Sure, sure," Arlie says, avoiding Ken's stare. "I'm just saying; we don't want to wind up on Hiram's bad side."

"I'm not sure Hiram has a good side," Ken muses,

returning his attention to his blade. "I'm starting to re-think this whole Brotherhood nonsense."

Arlie nods. "That's fine. Whatever you think is best. I'm with you Ken. You think we need to get gone, then we're gone."

"I haven't decided yet."

"Well, you just let me know." Arlie drains beer nine without further comment.

Ken wants to quit The Brotherhood? Arlie likes that idea just fine. The missus has been bitching lately about living in the compound, so he'll go along with anything that'll shut her up. Ken wants to go back into business for themselves? Well, all right then. Wads of cash collected from some city boy lazy or stupid enough to pay for what's free for the taking? That suits him just fine too, so long as the city boy don't start asking questions.

Arlie doesn't like folks asking him about his business.

Neither does Ken, so Arlie isn't too worried. Ken tends to answer pesky questions with the point of his Spyderco, so if Ken's buyer gets too curious, Arlie figures they'll have new merchandise for a new customer.

Dancing dollar signs distract Arlie so much that he throws his empty can into the brush without ripping it in half first. He cringes as the missile flies, knowing Ken's gonna yell about the noise when it hits the other cans.

But there's no metallic crash, only a dull thud.

Followed by: "Ouch!"

Ken crosses the clearing to stand beside Arlie, now holding his Colt Peacemaker. Arlie's not quite as fast with his Remington, but after fumbling a bit, has the rifle trained at the same spot as Ken.

"Who's gonna hear us out here in the woods?" Ken mocks, sighting down the pistol barrel. "Is that what you asked me?"

"Shut up," Arlie says, trying to remember if he still has a round chambered.

Ken swivels his head to work out the kinks in his neck and steps forward. "All right whoever you are. Get your ass on out here where we can see you."

"Yeah," Arlie chimes in, setting the stock against his shoulder. "Let's get a look at you."

The brush in front of them crackles and shudders as one gloved hand pushes through, then another. Ken and Arlie get several seconds to examine the hands as their owner attempts to pry the thicket apart. The lavender cloth offers little protection against the thorns and stickers covering the interlocked branches. Brambles stick to the small straps fastened across the backs of the hands.

These aren't hunter's gloves.

Eventually the thick brush parts and arms follow hands. A leg steps through, and in one final convulsion, the thicket gives birth to the intruder.

Ken lowers the Peacemaker and Arlie shoulders the Remington. Whoever the stranger is, he's not going to cause them a lick of trouble.

"I don't know where you think you're headed," Ken says, tucking his pistol back into its holster, "but I'd say you're way off."

"That's for goddamned sure," Arlie says.

"Trust me gentlemen," the intruder says, brushing leaves and twigs from his arms, "I know exactly where I am, and I am exactly where I wish to be."

"Is that so?" Ken asks. His hand strays back to the butt of his pistol. "Then maybe you've got some explaining to do."

The stranger ignores the challenge, and walks over the lantern, continuing to clean debris from his coat. A cape made of fabric identical to his coat and gloves billows as he passes. His earlier awkwardness vanishes with every stride; he now moves as a violet specter, gliding effortlessly around the clearing.

"A magnificent specimen," the stranger says as he examines Ken and Arlie's kill. "Simply magnificent."

"Hell of a shot too." Arlie smiles. "Dropped him from a hundred yards. Maybe one-fifty."

"Really?" The stranger looks up from under the brim of

his lavender fedora, his eyes crinkling with the knowledge that Arlie is exaggerating the distance. "That is very impressive marksmanship Mr. Garrison; very impressive indeed."

Arlie puffs out his chest, and casts a sly glance at Ken. The stranger may be a purple creampuff, but at least he appreciates good shooting. Ken shakes his head, imagining Arlie's guts decorating the ground alongside the entrails already there.

Ken watches the stranger continue to admire the carcass. Making clucking sounds and appreciative "mmm-hmms" as he circles the kill, the stranger studies it from every angle, even bending down to sniff the carcass at one point. After several circuits, the stranger nods, adjusts his cloak, and walks over to Ken.

"Very good blade work, Mr. Chesterton," the stranger says. "I can't tell you when I've last seen such precision with a knife. Rivals some of my own actually, and I've a fairly steady hand myself."

"Uh-huh," Ken says, his fingertips stroking the Peacemaker's polished grips. "You a knife man then?"

The stranger's head bobs once. "I am, although I tend to favor a longer blade. Better reach, you understand."

"I do." Ken replies and brings the barrel of the Colt up to rest against the stranger's right nostril. "But this here has the best reach I've seen yet, not counting Arlie's Remington there, assuming he's not too dreamy-eyed to use it."

Arlie might not understand everything that's happening, but he's smart enough to back Ken's play. The rifle's back at his shoulder within a second, its muzzle aimed at a spot just below the brim of the stranger's hat.

"What's the deal Ken?" Arlie asks.

"The deal Brainiac is that Mr. Fancy Pants here made two mistakes. First, Mr. Fancy Pants isn't as smart as he thinks he is, are you Mr. Fancy Pants."

"I think I'll reserve judgment on that one, if you don't mind," the stranger says, his voice betraying no fear. "I'm much more interested in hearing what you think my second mistake was."

Ken thumbs back the Colt's hammer and twists the barrel a millimeter into the stranger's nose. "Your second mistake was letting us know how stupid you are so quickly. Arlie and me have never set eyes on you before, cause trust me, we'd remember if we had. But here you are, prancing around in your Sunday best, calling us by name, which you've got no business knowing. How's that for a second mistake?"

The stranger raises an eyebrow. "Very astute Mr. Chesterton. I'm very pleased that your rustic exterior doesn't mask an equally rustic interior. I do so enjoy having associates with intelligence." His eyes risk a glance at Arlie. "Although the other type has their use as well."

With a gloved finger, the stranger brushes the Colt away from his nose. From under his cape, he produces a lavender handkerchief and gently wipes it across his nostrils. He then takes the pistol from Ken's hand and polishes the barrel, removing any trace of himself from the metal.

Ken watches this without comment, as if having his gun taken away is the most natural thing in the world, which it isn't. The Colt's been passed down for three generations, with the admonition it would always stay in Chesterton hands. Ken has always interpreted this literally, even denying Hiram a peek during his Brotherhood initiation. Hiram had smiled at Ken's denial; he understood the demands of family and the burden of honoring an ancestor's wishes.

This stranger is no Chesterton, nor is he the leader of The Brotherhood, but Ken remains unaffected by his handling of Granddaddy's Peacemaker. As the stranger continues cleaning, he locks eyes with Ken, who suddenly realizes there are things worse than a stranger knowing his name.

Arlie also knows the history of the Colt, and the promise that accompanies its passing. He sees it disappear from Ken's hand, only to reappear a second later in the stranger's, and Arlie's palms begin to sweat. He pulls the rifle tighter against his shoulder, ready to join in on whatever retribution Ken decides to unleash. His hands grow slick on the trigger and barrel as he fights to keep the stranger's head atop the red dot on the front sight. "C'mon Ken," he mutters into the stock, arms starting to shake with tension, "make your play."

Ken does nothing, and Arlie experiences a revelation similar to Ken's.

The stranger returns the Colt to Ken's hand, gently hooking the trigger guard around Ken's index finger. He snaps the lavender handkerchief like a chamois and returns it to the inner folds of his cape. Ken wraps his hand around the grips and wills his thumb to pull back the hammer. With the Peacemaker returned, his acceptance vanishes, and all he wants is to erase the stranger's face from his sight, before that superior smile can burrow any deeper into his mind.

Arlie sees the gun vanish from the stranger's care and rematerialize in Ken's hand. He notices the tremor in Ken's thumb and the perspiration beading on Ken's temples. He wipes his trigger hand across his shirt, but once it's dry, he can't get his finger back inside the guard.

The stranger turns to Arlie and smiles. "I see my compatriot has finally arrived."

The brush surrounding them crackles again, but this isn't the tentative sound of the stranger's delicate passage. The foliage erupts with a cacophony of broken limbs and trampled greenery, heralding the arrival of a new player.

"It's important to watch your partner's back, isn't it Mr. Garrison?" the stranger asks, as the noise grows louder. "Here I was, so wrapped up in Mr. Chesterton's firearm maintenance that I almost forgot about you."

The clamor in the woods increases. The stranger sighs.

"I also subscribe to the buddy system," he continues, nonplussed by the rifle aimed at his head, "and it appears that my buddy has demonstrated another example of his flawless timing."

Ken and Arlie close ranks as the thickets at the edge of the clearing begin to undulate. The stranger steps to the side, a lavender midwife to the impending birth.

The brush doesn't part, but evaporates as the stranger's partner appears. Ken and Arlie gasp in unison; their minds, even under the stranger's influence, are unable to process what they are seeing.

The second intruder is half again as tall as the first; his girth roughly that of a mature elm. Massive hands, ending in squared-off fingers, hang from impossibly long arms that descend from shoulders towering two feet above their heads.

"Gentlemen," the stranger extends his arm in greeting, "it's time for introductions. My associate and I have had many names over the years, but I'm sure they would mean less to you than they do to me, and I'm quite a linguist by nature. For now, you may call me Salomé. Mr. Chesterton, Mr. Garrison: Meet The Baptist."

"Oh my sweet Jesus!" Ken exclaims as his eyes roam the figure standing before them. "What is that?"

"That's no way to talk about one of your new masters," Salomé warns, chuckling at Ken's reaction. "Be cautious Mr. Chesterton or you'll offend him."

"How the hell am I going to offend him?" Ken asks. "He doesn't have any fucking ears!"

"Well of course he doesn't," Salomé replies. "A psychic of The Baptist's magnitude has no need for such primitive appendages, and it's not like he needs a place to hang his spectacles."

"He's…he's…" Arlie stutters, craning his neck in awe. "He's got no head!"

Salomé nods. "That puzzled me at first too, but since it doesn't seem to bother him, I decided not to let it bother me. I'd suggest you adopt a similar attitude."

The monstrosity moves into the clearing, each footstep deliberately placed, as if every stride is an effort. Ken imagines a grunt with every footfall, enhancing the illusion of great exertion.

"The Baptist is momentarily taxed," Salomé responds to the motions of the lumbering giant. "It is fortunate we found you when we did; even more fortunate that your evening's hunt was successful. If not for your kill," the stranger shrugs, "other steps might have proved necessary."

The Baptist crosses the clearing and stands before the carcass, its entrails still steaming in the cool, nighttime air. Salomé's lips move silently as he approaches his partner, head nodding along in a conversation only he can hear. Finally, he speaks aloud. "I'm not sure. I can certainly ask."

He turns to Ken. "Mr. Chesterton, this buyer you spoke of earlier. Surely your contract wouldn't suffer too badly if the merchandise was slightly altered."

Ken stares at the twelve-point buck, calculating the bonus offered by the ignorant city boy for an impressive rack. At one hundred bucks a point, his and Arlie's payday has nearly doubled, but only if they stay alive to collect it.

"Depends on what you plan to alter," he manages to say, finding a remnant of his spine in the face of lost dollars.

Salomé winks and draws a long, narrow sword from under his cloak. "Nothing that will be missed, yet something vitally important for the next phase of our endeavor." He grasps the hilt with both hands, faces the deer and with the blade, traces a line along the deer's neck.

"Of course, if you object, there are always alternatives, although I'm not sure how Mr. Garrison will react to the proposition."

Arlie reacts by fainting.

CHAPTER 1

Everything started with Crazy Amy.

Milo Tucker's definition of "crazy" had gone through some revisions, but his unexpected visitor qualified, even under the new guidelines.

"The past has a way of sneaking up and biting you on the ass," Philip Ducalion had said before shaking Milo's hand and boarding his flight. A curious look had washed across the ex-cop's face as they stood at the jet way entrance with hands clasped. At first, Milo had attributed the expression to memories of when Ducalion had served as a backside buffet. From what he had revealed during his stay in the West Virginia capitol, those times were plentiful.

However, as time passed, Milo wondered if his new friend had been more perceptive than his rough exterior and gruff manner suggested. A man intelligent enough to sort through the miasma of Theodore Munsch, Cecil Hawkins and Harold Washington had to be perceptive enough to understand all was not as it appeared. Ducalion had correctly followed the thread that started with Alex Harrison and ended with Milo Tucker, seemingly oblivious to all the Oogie Boogie baggage in between. He successfully connected the dots linking the two Gatherers to the three killers without catching a whiff of the underlying mystical web that bound them.

Or had he?

Twenty-four hours after Ducalion blasted Munsch's mind out of Harold Washington's body, the local authorities had buried the bodies, hosed away the blood and closed their files, satisfied that Harold's past sufficiently explained his final atrocities. By the time Sharon stepped off the plane, hugged her husband and slugged Keith Pridemore, Kanawha County law enforcement had returned to a pre-JoJo state, secure in their belief that all the *really* bad people were tucked into a pauper's grave or wearing a sweater with sleeves that tied in the back.

Ducalion hadn't contradicted any of these assumptions, but Milo doubted he accepted them, especially after spending a week with the Tuckers and their perpetual houseguest Keith. While Sharon had plied the ex-cop with home-cooked meals and estrogen-powered interrogation, Milo wrestled with his new mental tenants, striving to achieve a balance with the six entities he had inherited from Alex Harrison.

During the Tucker food and film marathon, Milo's new "friends" had made several unexpected appearances, usually coinciding with the arrival of a new delicacy or a particularly funny scene. Sharon ignored the intrusions, apologizing for her husband's antics. Ducalion responded with a smile and a wave of his hand, but Milo felt his stare whenever Sharon left the room. It took several scoldings when he tagged along on Keith's frequent outdoor smoke breaks to get the Colony to behave, at least until their company had gone.

Ducalion's parting remark made Milo believe he hadn't scolded the Colony soon or often enough.

Nearly a year later, Milo could chuckle at the confusion generated by seven individuals inhabiting one body, and still go into hysterics at Keith's shock when one of the Colonists appeared without warning. Time and patience had eased Milo's stress and calmed Keith's reactions, but there was still one Colony-related issue left to resolve.

Sharon.

Employing the same logic that allowed the Charleston

Police to explain Harold's sudden leap from thief to homicidal maniac, his wife appeared willing to attribute Milo's occasional use of a Yiddish or Japanese accent to his genetic predisposition for being a goof. Other than the rise in vocal pitch when one of the ladies "took the wheel" there wasn't much to suggest Milo had changed. His initial fear of a parade of rabid Hunters camping on his doorstep diminished as months passed without so much as a slight buzz in his skull. Protests from his passengers aside, Milo refused to accept the rarity of a phenomenon that had placed three similarly affected individuals within spitting distance of a serial killer.

Perhaps Sharon's dismissal of anything otherworldly kept Milo silent. The Tuckers had always presented a united front against Keith's *Tales of the Unbelievable*, and although Milo now counted himself among those *Tales*, he still refused to believe a tenth of the swill Keith tried to feed them.

Sharon refused to consider any of it, which made "Hey honey, I've got six dead folks living in my head now," not only a conversation killer, but a potential request for a permanent room at Ravenswood Asylum.

No thank you.

Convincing a world-class skeptic was a bigger task than Milo was prepared to attempt. His confidence, even bolstered by Trippenstein's guarantees of magical demonstrations, only went so far. If Sharon was willing to play Lois and stare wistfully into the sky as the crowd pointed, shouting *it's a bird, it's a plane*, then Milo was content to play Clark.

At least Clark Kent could fly.

Well, maybe not Clark himself, but his alter ego could shuck the horn-rims, fluff the hair, ditch the Armani and zoom into the stratosphere, and wasn't that great for him. The idol of millions. Admired by men. Desired by women. Sworn to protect a world that hated and feared him…

Oh wait, that was the X-Men.

Milo shook his head to dislodge the persistent superhero analogy and concentrate on his current task: Security camera alignment for Harriford & Sons Department Store. Hardly a job for a champion in red and blue spandex, the weekly camera adjustment required nothing more than Milo's supervision and a two-way radio. Even "supervision" was too strong a word. As Harriford's Security Manager Milo could roam the sales floor in his official capacity without worrying about blowing his cover. If potential thieves didn't already know who he was from the previous year's media coverage, they weren't smart enough to deduce his identity from his Tuesday afternoon walk-through.

As Milo moved from one coverage zone to the next, Senior Detective David McIntyre followed his progress on monitors in the Surveillance Office, running the cameras through their full range of movement and focus. A live target made any necessary adjustments easier and allowed the operator to discover any dead areas between camera positions. During the procedure, David would ask Milo to move in a certain direction or hide behind a fixture. When he did, Milo heard the familiar whine as servomotors tracked his progress and kept the lenses locked on his position.

Another thrilling adventure for Gatherer-Man.

"If this bothers you so much, you should tell Sharon," Kimmy said, appearing next to him. Milo glanced at the camera, momentarily forgetting the electronic eyes wouldn't register his passenger's presence any more than human eyes did.

"Didn't you say Tuesday walk-throughs were boring?" Milo asked, after making sure the microphone on his radio was off.

"They are boring," Kimmy admitted, gliding along as Milo walked to the next camera zone. "Boring, but according to you, necessary."

"Then why are you here?"

"I never pass up a chance to shop," Kimmy smiled. "Besides, we're always here, even when we're not."

"Exactly where do you go when you're not here?"

"Where we always are."

Milo shook his head. "Did you drive all your other hosts this crazy? No wonder Alex let people hear him talking to himself; you made him nuts."

"Alex was a sweet guy," Kimmy said, flooding Milo with her affection for the departed Gatherer, "but he had a bad habit of forgetting where he was; a habit—thankfully—you don't seem to have."

"That's me, Mr. Conscientious."

"Has anyone ever accused you of thinking too much?"

"You've been listening to Sharon again." Milo stopped and waved at the ceiling. David chuckled in his earpiece and started the camera test.

"I listen to your wife whenever you do," Kimmy said, mimicking Sharon's tone and cadence. "The difference is I usually understand what she's saying."

"Jesus!" Milo said, causing several shoppers to turn their heads and stare. Milo grimaced and pretended to speak into his radio.

"Jesus, Kimmy. You've had how many male hosts now? I'd think just the constant proximity to that many testicles would give you some insight. Not all men are Neanderthals; some of us lean toward the introspective side of the emotional spectrum."

"Whatever. Introspect all you'd like, but don't spend so much time looking in that you forget to look out once in a while." Kimmy folded her ethereal arms across her ethereal chest and turned away. His Colony gave him access to knowledge and abilities beyond his own, but pissing off a woman? This Milo could accomplish all by himself.

Before he could formulate a properly penitent response, Kimmy whirled on him, leaning in far enough so that, if she still had a nose, it would touch his.

"And Mr. Milo, since you've been considerate enough to point out my easy access to countless testicles, let me remind you of your easy access to a couple of pairs of ovaries."

Mr. Milo?

Kimmy perched her hands on her hips. "For someone who's spent most of his life bitching about not living up to his potential, you're sure letting it get away from you now."

"You're giving me advice?" Milo asked. "I'm getting a lecture from an eighteen year-old? What's worse, I'm listening to it?"

"I may be eighteen, but I've been eighteen for like twenty years, so that makes me older than you." The epiphany made her smile. "So respect your elder, dammit."

"We are not having this conversation." David radioed an "all clear" and Milo moved on.

"Someone's got a serious case of the Grumps today," Kimmy said, following him into the Menswear Department.

"Trust me Kimmy, you've never seen me with a serious case of the Grumps."

Kimmy's eyebrows rose. "Please. This famous Milo Tucker temper you keep warning us about? Haven't seen it; don't plan on seeing it anytime soon. Admit it Milo; you're a teddy bear with an attitude. Tough and crusty on the outside, sweet creamy goodness on the inside."

"Now I'm a toasted marshmallow?"

"Yeah that works. If you'd just get over all this…"

"You're an evil man."

The indictment didn't come from Kimmy, nor did it come through Milo's earpiece. As Milo and Kimmy began to turn, David yelled for Milo to check his "six."

A woman stood between two clothing racks, her hands tucked into the oversized patch pockets decorating the front of her polyester pantsuit. Dull brown hair spilled over her collar, hiding her upper body and covering most of her face.

Except for her eyes.

Through the matted strands obscuring her features, her irises shone with the intensity of a jacklight penetrating a forest.

Milo smiled at the accusation from the poster child for Salon Selectives. Kimmy gasped, and Milo sensed the shock of recognition coursing through their connection.

And then, Kimmy was gone.

Milo stepped toward the woman. "I'm not an evil man. In fact, I like to think of myself as one of the good guys."

The woman recoiled at his approach. "*Liar!* You're a liar and a thief. You don't deserve what you took from Alex; don't even try to pretend you do."

"What I took from Alex?" Milo asked. He stopped moving and opened his arms wide. Willing his face into its best "take the picture now" expression, he nodded pleasantly at the woman while mentally screaming for his passengers. Handling this psycho didn't require any of their special abilities, but from Kimmy's reaction Milo guessed they knew the nutball's identity, and probably knew why she was so pissed.

Suddenly Milo's surroundings brightened, as if the world was on a rheostat and God had cranked the knob to its maximum setting. His awareness expanded to encompass 360 degrees. Colors intensified and the Menswear department focused into such sharp detail that Milo could almost see the atoms bouncing within the electromagnetic boundaries separating one object from another.

The Colony had arrived.

Fuck me! Trippenstein said, shattering the momentary rush that always accompanied the arrival of Milo's full complement of passengers.

I'm assuming you don't want me to pass that on as an invitation to this refugee from The Breakfast Club, Milo stated, communicating silently as he continued to smile at the woman. *Now, who wants to give me the Hollywood Minute on Ally Sheedy here?*

Be kind Milo, Maria said, gliding across the intervening space to examine the woman. *This is Amy Newcomb, a friend of Alex's — and ours — from the time we lived at Randolph Avenue.*

The halfway house? Milo asked.

Mais oui, Etienne answered, also taking a closer look. *She looked much better then.*

Tajiri joined the observation team. He clasped his hands behind his back and circled Amy, nodding as he looked her up and down.

The years have not blessed this one, the ronin stated. *Etienne's aesthetic observations aside, I must agree that Amy-san seems less capable than when we last met.*

Amy screamed, beating the air around her face and swatting herself on the head and shoulders. "Get them off! Get them off of me!"

Maria, Etienne and Tajiri returned to Milo's side.

Less capable? Kimmy said, frowning. *Yeah, I guess so.*

Ach Milo, Isadore sighed. *It is so very sad. So pretty, but so* farchadat. *Still, she was a good friend to Alex when he needed one, so have some pity for the* gutte neshome.

Milo watched Amy's gyrations slow, then stop. Her hands curled and slid back into her pockets. No panic remained in her demeanor.

Only hatred.

Pity? Milo asked the group. *Let's save the compassion for after we figure out what she's doing here. Anybody have an answer for that?*

C'est facile, Etienne said. *Obviously, she saw the news reports concerning Alex's death and it took her almost a year to find you. J'accuse! J'accuse! This is not difficult to fathom; most of the time it took her six hours to find her socks.*

Milo glanced at the space between the cuffs of Amy's slacks and the tops of her shoes. The Frenchman was right; nothing covered those bony ankles. Still, a lack of foot fashion wasn't enough to dismiss Amy's potential threat.

Let's test that theory, Milo said. *Tajiri, go take another look at her.*

Tajiri bowed his head. His initial forward movement caused Amy to jerk her head and take a step back. As he halved the distance between them, she pulled her hands from her pockets and raised them to her shoulders, as if to protect herself from an attack. Tajiri slipped around her left side and peered back at the others from over her shoulder.

The trembling began in her legs, moving through her pelvis and into her torso. The vibrations from her lower limbs rippled through the rest of her body, culminating in a spasmodic dance of insanity.

Amy Newcomb lost it.

"Stop it! Stop it!" she screamed, whirling in place. Her frenzied pivots toppled racks, scattering chinos and shirts throughout the department. "Make them stop! Please! Make them stop!"

Tajiri observed the seizure from the center of the maelstrom, calmly appraising Amy's convulsions while she spun through his spectral form.

Enough, Milo said, calling Tajiri back. The button in his ear crackled; David reported paramedics were on their way, and he had told them to bring the big butterfly net. Milo waved at the camera. He had forgotten about David's view of the incident.

Tajiri stood at his side. *Your suspicion was correct,* he said, bowing again. *She senses us.*

She's not like Cecil, is she? Milo asked.

Maria shook her head. *Certainly not. This woman is ill, but she is not a Hunter.*

Well thank God for that, Milo said. *I don't know about the rest of y'all, but dealing with a new Hunter every year would just get boring. I like to keep my insanity fresh.*

Looks like you're getting your wish, Kimmy said.

Amy was calmer now. Her shoulders heaved from the force of her breathing. Her hands clenched in time with her inhales. Her eyes burned with madness.

Then she attacked.

Arms extended, fingers splayed out like claws, she jumped, spanning the gap between them in one adrenaline-fueled leap. Milo relinquished control of his body to Tajiri, who possessed the necessary reflexes to dodge the assault and enjoyed an open invitation from Milo to prevent bodily injury without waiting for an invitation, but it wasn't Tajiri who responded.

It was Trippenstein.

The hippie pushed past Tajiri and shuddered into the driver's seat. During the seconds it took Amy to reach them, he spoke some unintelligible gibberish and waved his arms in a circular motion. The air shimmered inside the circle he described, and when Amy's momentum brought her to it, the intersection of motion and magical energy caused a flash of light.

And Amy bounced.

The force of the impact sent Amy flying backward, crashing through racks and landing at the feet of the paramedics David had called. They didn't have a net, but they carried a straightjacket, which they began to buckle around the stunned woman.

What was that? Milo asked as Trippenstein stepped back.

Basic protection spell, Trippenstein said. *Not as flashy as transmutation, but it gets the job done, don't you think?*

Milo surveyed the swath of damage caused by Amy's trajectory. *That was a basic spell? Make sure to warn me before you try anything complicated.*

The paramedics lifted Amy to her feet. She struggled against their efforts to tie off the sleeves. Milo was pleased she hadn't been injured, but Amy's altered flight plan hadn't quelled any of her anger.

"You think I'm the only one who knows?" she yelled, straining at the grip of the men holding her. "You think I'm the only one! You think you'll get away with this, but you're wrong! Liar! Thief!"

One paramedic tightened the straps and the other shrugged at Milo. *Loonies,* the shrug said, *whatcha' gonna do with them?* Milo waved them off. Amy was their problem now.

"Liar! Thief! This isn't over!" Amy screamed. As the medics hustled her out of Harriford's, the words echoed through Milo's brain.

And something nibbled at his ass.

CHAPTER 2

Hiram Fuchs never intended to keep The Brotherhood a secret. As he had explained to Ken Chesterton and Arlie Garrison when they signed on, secrets had a way of attracting the wrong kind of attention. According to Hiram, if people thought you had something buried, they'd line up with shovels. To Ken, shovels seemed appropriate for the horseshit Hiram served up for public consumption.

Lately, Ken wondered if avoiding a second poaching conviction was worth the eighteen months he and Arlie had wasted with The Brotherhood. The game warden who caught them loading that buck into the back of Arlie's pickup might have believed Ken's road kill explanation if Arlie hadn't made the mistake of bragging on his accuracy with the Remington. It wasn't the first time Arlie's big mouth landed them into trouble, but a few minutes later, while John Law had his pinky knuckle-deep in Bambi's entry wound, Arlie dug them back out of the pit with the same set of flapping lips, and that was a first.

Or so Ken thought at the time.

"Goddamn federal faggots telling a man when he can hunt just ain't right," Arlie had muttered as the warden maneuvered his bulk over the side of the truck.

The warden froze, one foot planted on the rear tire and the other swinging over the fender; Ken silently cursed. The Fed with deer blood on his finger probably danced weekends at Boxers & Briefs wearing nothing but his badge and Smokey Bear hat, and didn't appreciate Arlie's characterization of the homosexual contingent in the National Wildlife Department. Ken figured that by the end of the night, he'd be fending off other inmates willing to show him just how nights at Boxers & Briefs usually ended.

No worries there, he'd just offer them Arlie.

Surprisingly, when the warden finished his dismount, he didn't reach for his handcuffs or gun. Instead, he pulled a business card from his shirt pocket and handed it to Ken.

"Lot's of folks feel the same way as your friend," the warden had said, tapping the card. "You boys show up there on Thursday, and we'll forget all about this."

And with a tip of his hat, he had gone.

As the warden's taillights faded down the road, Ken started to rip the card. Arlie stopped him.

"What are you doing?" Arlie had asked.

"I'm tearing this up."

"What the hell you want to go and do that for? You heard what the man said."

"Of course I heard what the man said, but he's gone now."

Arlie snatched the card from Ken's hand. "I don't care if he is gone. He took down my plate number and if we don't show up on Thursday, he'll come looking for us."

"Who gives a shit? This deer'll be jerky by the time we'd ever see him again."

"That don't mean he can't come after *us*."

Ken didn't bother explaining the rules of evidence; Arlie was too busy trying to repair the tear in the warden's calling card. Besides, one Thursday night was a small price to pay to keep Arlie calm and quiet.

A year and a half later, Ken was convinced he should have shot the warden and Arlie both, just for the extra meat. Thanks to Arlie's paranoia, one Thursday meeting had turned into full Brotherhood membership. At first, the association was tolerable, but after moving into the compound, Ken decided getting gang-raped by a cellblock full of convicted felons had to be more enjoyable than living with Hiram Fuchs and his followers.

Under Hiram's leadership, The Brotherhood had bellied up to the Prejudice Buffet and filled their plates with a helping of every hatred on the menu. At last count, the only race, creed, sexual orientation, color or national origin to escape The Brotherhood's loathing was the Canadians, and lately, Ken had noticed Hiram taking notes during hockey games, so the Great White North probably wouldn't be safe for much longer.

Aside from a few mavericks who still had the stones to collect a paycheck (three, according to the most recent statistics), The Brotherhood's membership contained the largest collection of unemployed, uneducated white trash in the state, whose only common goal was to bitch about how everybody had it better than them, and whose only common traits were lack of funds to buy a white sheet and the lack of manual dexterity required to cut eyeholes in it.

The Brotherhood had a long list of things they were against. Every night, the membership, their wives and children herded into the Hall of Truth (which also served as the Hall of Worship on Sundays and the Hall of Fraternal Fellowship on alternate Thursdays) to listen to Hiram deliver his collection of grievances against the world outside their borders. A chorus of "amens" and "uh-huhs" punctuated each complaint, and there was a great wailing and scratching of asses as the recitation continued.

Still, while the comprehensive catalog of what The Brotherhood stood against grew exponentially, no one ever mentioned exactly what The Brotherhood stood for. Ken couldn't recall ever hearing an "amen" or an "uh-huh" in response to a cause or issue they supported. The ass scratching remained a universal constant, so it wasn't an accurate barometer of approval ratings.

The were many groups populating the fringes of legitimate protest organizations, but when The Louisiana Coalition for Tar and Feathering and The Alabama Alliance of Accelerated African Restoration refused the Brotherhood's invitation to a Unity Rally and Rib-a-thon, Ken recognized how far the fringe extended and began to re-evaluate his membership.

This led to the resumption of midnight beer and deer runs, and re-acquaintance with the underground market he and Arlie had supplied for years before The Brotherhood. Ken's continuing disillusionment with Hiram provided fresh meat on his table and folding green in his pocket, a welcome change from the Spam and surplus C-Rations doled out every Tuesday in the Hall of Community Resources, and the worthless chits given to members as payment for services provided.

"Amen" for venison and "uh-huh" for cash. Let the ass-scratchers do the math on that one.

Now, as Arlie navigated the pickup off Big Bottom Road onto the five-mile gravel stretch leading to the compound, Ken contemplated the two passengers riding in the truck bed. Salomé rode perched on the hindquarters of the deer, seemingly unaffected by the wind whipping over the cab, Arlie's ability to hit every chuckhole in the road and the fact he was sitting on a carcass. A few times during the drive, Ken had been tempted to reach out with his foot and tromp the brake pedal, just to send the dandy sprawling. Each time the temptation surfaced, a quick look through the rear window squashed it.

If the rushing air didn't cause a ruffle to flutter or the hat brim to flap, Ken doubted a sudden stop would have any greater effect. His suspicions seemed confirmed with every glance, as Salomé smiled and waved every time Ken turned. That smile erased any thoughts of mutiny.

"This is getting way too weird," Arlie said, slowing to steer around a hump in the gravel.

Ken braced against the dashboard. "I think we passed weird a few exits back."

"That's the God's honest truth." Arlie glanced into the rearview mirror. "How'd we get stuck giving these two jokers a ride?"

"We're gonna end up giving them a whole lot more

than a ride."

"How you figure?"

Ken slapped the back of Arlie's head. "You know, we wouldn't get into half the shit we do if you'd just pay attention once in a while."

"What makes you say that?"

"What makes you think we're just gonna drop these two off somewhere and be done with them? Do you really think they're gonna jump out of the truck, shake hands and say 'Thanks for the ride boys'?"

Arlie chewed at the inside of his cheek. "What do you think's gonna happen?"

Ken stared through the windshield, remembering what happened to the deer's head after Salomé's sword work. Even now, the memory didn't bother him as much as it should. Salomé and The Baptist's method of field dressing should have had him leaving a trail of puke across Kanawha County, but the image of their butchery only caused a mild rumbling in his belly and the faint taste of bile in the back of his throat.

"Arlie, I don't know," he finally said, "but I feel like I'm wading bare-ass through manure, and it's lapping at my short hairs."

"Thanks Ken. That's just the kind of picture I want in my head right now: You swimming buck naked in shit."

"I wouldn't worry too much about me planting things in that empty space between your ears. I'd worry more about the headless bastard in the back, especially now that he's got himself a new battery."

Arlie shuddered and clamped a hand across his mouth, which Ken took as a good sign. Maybe The Baptist's influence wasn't as potent as Salomé claimed. Perhaps The Baptist could only deal with one mind at a time, and Ken, as the bigger threat, was the recipient of all the mojo the headless one could muster.

Or maybe, Arlie wasn't worth The Baptist's trouble. Either way, it was worth thinking about.

A gloved hand tapped the rear window. Ken undid the

catch and slid it open.

"We'll arrive soon," Salomé said. "I think it prudent to review exactly what's expected."

"I expect we'll all be bleeding from about a dozen holes apiece before we even clear the gate," Ken said, turning in his seat. "Hiram's boys may not be the smartest guys in creation, but it don't take much to aim and shoot, and they do have a lot of firepower."

Salomé smiled. "As do we, Mr. Chesterton. As do we."

"Yeah well, you haven't showed me much in that department yet. All your fancy tricks might knock the pins out from under a couple of boys in the woods, but they ain't gonna do shit against fifty men who been itching for an apocalypse."

"An apocalypse?" Salomé said, laughing. "As a veteran of several, I'm sad to report they're never quite as entertaining as you'd like them to be. And while I doubt our impromptu soirée will attain Armageddon stature, I'm sure we'll provide a respite for your compatriots' tedious existence. Of course for some, the respite will be eternal, but omelets and eggs, don't you know."

Salomé cocked his head and held up a finger. Nodding, he continued. "My associate is quite right. I do digress. Instead of revisiting the past, we should forge ahead and create new wonders worthy of our alliance, which brings me to yours and Mr. Garrison's contribution to today's endeavor."

"We're getting you through the main gate, not to mention the twelve-point rack you ruined getting your boy his breakfast." Ken gambled. "Seems to me, Arlie and I have contributed enough to your little telethon."

"Don't be so sure Mr. Chesterton. I'm looking forward to a long and prosperous association with you and your companion. When the time comes, we'll anticipate your complete and unwavering support."

"When the time comes," Ken said, feeling bile rise again in his throat.

Salomé nodded. "When the time comes. Be alert; you'll

know when to act, and what to do."

The truck lurched off the road. Ken reached across the cab and grabbed the wheel, steering them back onto the gravel while Arlie sat there, eyes wide and hands fluttering in his lap.

"Watch where you're going," Ken said. "You flip us over, and I guarantee you the only ones who'll notice it are you and me." Arlie nodded and took the wheel again.

Salomé spoke again. "Assuming we arrive unmolested, I want you and Mr. Garrison to remember one caveat. While a certain amount of bloodshed is expected — nay, necessary given our goals today — we'll want you to utilize your splendid marksmanship and choose your targets wisely."

"What, y'all got some sort of hit list?" Arlie asked, surprising Ken by finding his voice.

"Yeah, that's something I'd like to know myself," Ken said. "God knows there's plenty of Brothers I won't mind putting a bullet in, 'specially if it'll keep me breathing for another day, but if we're going into a firefight, I'd rather not count on mystical horseshit and caveats to let me know if I've got the right bastard in my sights."

Salomé clapped, rocking back and forth on the deer flank. "Isn't the spirit of camaraderie a wonderful thing? Very good questions gentlemen, and just the sort of inquiries I'd expect from fully committed members of our company."

I ought to be committed for listening to this, Ken thought. He noticed Salomé's tendency to look at The Baptist during pauses. Obviously, the psychic's communication drew the dandy's attention, regardless of his immunity to other stimuli. Salomé's apparent distraction made Ken question the pecking order: Were the two equals, or was one master to the other's minion?

And which was which?

"So, in response to your astute observation," Salomé continued, returning his attention to the open window, "we'd like you and Mr. Garrison to shoot everyone you can, as many times as proves necessary to kill them.

"But…" Salomé held up a finger to punctuate his statement. "We don't want anyone injured above the neck. Do as much damage as you will, but leave the heads intact. I trust we need not remind you why."

A rumble issued from Arlie's throat, followed by a stream of vomit that painted Arlie, the steering wheel and half the dashboard in a layer of stomach acid and day-old beer. Ken choked back an answering eruption of his own, fighting both the sudden, intrusive mental image of The Baptist's dietary requirements and the smell of Artie's explosion.

"I'll take that as a yes," Salomé said, leaning away from the window with a final nod.

Arlie moaned as he tried to find a dry surface to clean his dripping hands. Ken rummaged under the seat and found a filthy flannel shirt, which he tossed to Arlie. Immediately, the grimy fabric darkened as it began to absorb the liquid pooling in Arlie's lap, but he wiped both hands across the shirt, and used a sleeve to clear the worst of the coagulating mess from the steering wheel.

"Jesus Christ, that was bad," Arlie said, drying his chin with the remaining sleeve.

"Almost as bad as watching the real thing," Ken replied.

"Almost as bad? I know you've got a stronger stomach than me, but *damn* Ken! I don't see how anything could be worse than that."

Ken saw the peaked roof of the sentry hut rise above the next hill. "Then I hope you're gut's empty, 'cause I think we're about to find out."

Arlie leaned forward and peered through the windshield. "Oh dear God," he whispered.

"I think God's taken the day off," Ken said. He slid the Peacemaker from its holster and laid it against his leg. "God's off, and I'm not thrilled with who He left minding the store." He pulled back the hammer. The double click as the cylinder spun echoed through the truck.

"We're really gonna do this?" Arlie asked, his eyes on the Winchester tucked into the window rack.

Ken wiped a palm across his jeans. "Arlie, most days I'd shoot you if somebody asked politely, so if we've got to do this to keep the freak out of our heads and keep our heads where the Lord intended, I'm not gonna cry about it. How's that sound to you?"

Arlie's forehead crinkled. "That sounds about right to me."

"Well, that's it then. You just get us up to the gate, and I'll take care of things till we get inside the wire."

"I can do that," Arlie said.

Ken grabbed a fistful of Arlie's hair. "But once we're in there, I expect you to handle your share. I'm not wading through the shit alone."

"Nobody's asking you to," Arlie said, tromping the brake pedal as the truck reached the gate. Gravel sprayed and the truck fishtailed, announcing their arrival at The Brotherhood compound.

CHAPTER 3

Sharon Tucker hated shopping with her husband.

When she compared notes with other wives, she realized Milo's willingness to shop made her the envy of all her female friends. She took special notice of the wistful looks in the eyes of her gal pals as she described days spent roaming department stores and specialty shops. At times, tears threatened when she recounted Milo's inclination to spend hours perched on the "husband" chair positioned outside most fitting rooms, and one girlfriend severed their relationship when Sharon made the mistake of mentioning Milo's habit of actually trying clothes on before purchasing them.

Fortunately, Sharon never mentioned Milo's penchant for shoe shopping; she needed to keep some of her friends.

After witnessing the reactions to her husband's proclivities, Sharon always felt guilty. In most cases, she knew the husbands almost as well as she knew the wives, and none of those men seemed particularly Neanderthalic. Regardless of the color of their collar, these men were excellent husbands, fathers and providers, but still their wives got misty at the suggestion that Sharon's husband selected apparel, paid for purchases and carried shopping bags with nary a word of protest. Their jealousy toward Sharon's good fortune caused her to reevaluate her hatred, and see Milo as her friends and acquaintances saw him: The perfect husband.

Of course, this refreshed perspective never lasted beyond the automatic doors of the local Bullseye, the customary first stop on any Tucker shopping excursion. As they passed the bins of sale flyers and the lines of empty shopping carts, Milo's eyes began to twitch. As they traveled past the Service Desk, his neck mimicked his eyes. By the time they reached the clearance racks, his head swiveled back and forth as if mounted on a bearing.

The hunt was on, and Sharon remembered why she hated shopping with her husband. "Off the clock" had no meaning for Milo. Instincts honed from years of patrolling Harriford & Sons Department Store possessed him when they entered any retail establishment, and woe be unto any thieves foolish enough to commit larceny with Milo Tucker in the house.

At least he wasn't trying to arrest serial killers any more.

Today Bullseye had a sale on cotton panties, and Sharon planned to stock up. *Victoria's Secret* and *Frederick's of Hollywood* made beautiful lingerie, but there were certain medical realities they never mentioned in the catalogs. Cotton breathed; silk and satin did not. Milo wasn't a big fan of what he called her "granny panties," but Milo didn't have to worry about candidiasis unless it interrupted his amorous adventures, and after three days of Monistat-induced celibacy, he wouldn't care if she wore burlap bloomers.

Ouch! She chafed at just the thought.

While she contemplated colors and debated styles, Milo stood silently in the aisle, forearms resting on the handle of their cart, eyes glued to the racks beside him. Other shoppers would interpret this posture as the disinterested stance of a husband dragged into the boring world of Haines and Jockey. Sharon's envious friends would see no sign of her supposedly attentive spouse, famous in song and story.

Sharon knew better. She shook her head and dropped

three pairs of lavender panties into the cart.

"You're going to need a new bra to go with those," Milo said without turning his head.

"No I won't," Sharon replied. "I've already got a purple bra."

"Not in the same shade you don't. The one at home is darker."

"It is not."

"I'm pretty sure it is."

"I think I know more about my underwear than you. These'll match just fine."

Milo shrugged. "No biggie. If I'm right, you can always get one next week. It's not like this will be the last time we ever go shopping."

Sharon leaned over the cart and examined the trio of underpants, comparing the color with her memory of the bra in question. Seen against the other panties in the cart, the lavender did look lighter than she had first thought. She retrieved one pair and held them against her arm, trying to remember how the bra looked next to her skin.

"Definitely lighter," Milo said, again without looking. "I don't think it's such a big deal, but I know how you are about everything matching."

Sharon flung the treacherous underpants back into the cart. "How the hell can you tell what color something is without looking at it?"

She sensed a small hesitation before Milo reached out and tapped the rack. The gleaming metal vibrated from his touch. "I saw the reflection in here. Tricks of the trade honey."

"Uh-huh," Sharon muttered, unsatisfied but unwilling to explore the issue further.

For the past year, Milo had explained many unexplainable occurrences with the phrase "tricks of the trade" or with silent winks and cryptic smiles. Milo's attention was absolute, exceeded only by his talent to focus that attention in multiple directions with equal intensity. He could read a book, watch television and hold a conversation without neglecting any of them.

However, what was once impressive had now become unnerving. At times, Milo seemed aware of everything, his perception no longer limited by focus or attention. He would appear in their kitchen just when Sharon needed help dumping trash, when minutes earlier his nose had been in a book. Cups of steaming coffee appeared seconds after she thought about making some, delivered by her attentive husband, who would smile at her puzzled thanks, as if chuckling at the punch line to a joke he hadn't shared.

This was *Ultimate* Milo; free of the self-imposed chains that had always held him back, despite the years she had spent trying to unshackle him. During her five-day absence, her husband had re-created himself, and Sharon knew—*knew* in the deep well of her soul where wives buried the unvoiced resentments accumulated during a marriage—that she begrudged him for accomplishing what she could not.

Sharon tugged at the front of the cart, ready to abandon the lingerie aisle for the Housewares department. The no-stick coating on Milo's favorite skillet had begun to peel, and she was tired of picking Teflon flakes out of her omelets.

"Pick out some more underwear honey," Milo said.

"I've got enough underwear," Sharon replied, tugging on the cart again.

"You can never have enough underwear." Milo moved a pair of panties from a hook in front of his face to a lower hook.

"You're mixing the larges with the smalls," Sharon said.

"I'll put them back," Milo said, adjusting the remaining hangers with the tip of a finger. "They were blocking me."

"Blocking you from what?" she asked.

Milo hooked his fingers into the waistband of a pair hanging at eye level and flipped over the elastic. "Take a close look at the stitching on these."

"Hand them here and I will."

"No, I think you should look at them here."

Sharon raised her eyebrows. Milo winked and rattled the hanger against its hook. Sharon leaned across the cart to examine the stitching. The position placed her ear next to Milo's mouth.

As Milo had intended. He whispered, "Look through the rack at the Jewelry department."

"I thought I was looking at stitching," Sharon groaned as the cart dug into her stomach.

"*Shhh,*" Milo hissed. "Forget the underpants and look through the rack."

Ignoring the embroidered waistband, Sharon leaned in farther and peered through the metal frame. She felt ridiculous with her ass perched in the air and her face buried in panties. Three year-olds played peek-a-boo in clothing aisles, not married women with careers and…

Ooo! A fat woman standing at one of the earring displays removed a hook from the spinner rack and dumped its contents into a shopping bag she held open at her waist. As Sharon watched, the fat woman removed another hook from the display and — *whoosh* — those earrings followed the others into the bag.

"Oh my God!" Sharon squealed as she stood up. "She just stole those earrings."

Milo patted the air with his palm. "I know honey. Keep your voice down or everybody'll know."

"But she's stealing. Somebody ought to do something."

"Somebody is doing something," Milo said. A wicked smile spread across his face. "Pretty cool, isn't it?"

Damn straight it's cool, Sharon thought, blushing as adrenaline sped through her. Shaking with excitement, she lay across the cart and dove into the panties again.

Milo grabbed her by the belt and pulled her back to her feet. "Easy Sherlock, it's just a shoplifter."

"Let me go. I want to watch her steal some more."

"I thought you had enough underwear." Milo moved the cart away from the lingerie rack and began pushing it down the aisle. "C'mon Sharon, let's go get that skillet."

Sharon stepped in front of the cart and stood on the

bottom rail. "Milo Raymond Tucker, if you move one more inch, you can forget about getting laid for the rest of the year."

"Well, Sharon Elizabeth Tucker, that's a very serious threat." Milo's smile didn't falter. "I guess we'd better stay here then."

"Goddamned right we're staying here," Sharon muttered. She climbed down from the cart and searched for another spy hole.

"Sharon, come over here and look through the bottom of the rack. You're jumping around so much you're gonna spook her."

She gave him a look, but ducked in behind him without protesting. Actually, the view from there was just as good, and she was more comfortable without the shopping cart digging into her belly.

"How much has she taken?" Sharon asked. She carelessly rearranged the lowest row of hangers while watching the thief.

"A couple of hooks at least," Milo replied softly. "I stopped counting after the second one."

"What?" Sharon stopped her impromptu merchandising and looked up. "Why would you quit counting?"

"Keep watching," Milo said, twirling a finger to redirect her attention. Sharon stuck her tongue out and continued her surveillance.

"'How much' doesn't matter right now," Milo said, beginning to lecture. "Once something's concealed, the only thing that matters is making sure it stays concealed, and in the possession of the one who concealed it."

"Why would they take it out?" Sharon asked. Another peg of earrings disappeared into the fat woman's bag, causing a shiver to run up Sharon's spine.

"It's a racket like anything else," Milo said. "Sometimes, thieves get nervous and dump stuff on the way to the door. Sometimes they do it just to fake security out. A false arrest lawsuit will earn them more money than a bag of cheap earrings, and they won't get a criminal record."

"People do things like that?"

"Honey, people do everything you could possibly think of, and a few things you'd never imagine."

As Sharon watched the bulbous thief continue to dump earrings into her shopping bag, she became aware of Milo talking again, but not to her. From her position on the floor, she could see his jaw moving, but couldn't hear most of what he said.

"Watch for the bounce. Watch for the bounce."

These words, spoken louder than the rest of his monologue, drifted down to her. She glanced at the thief; if moving, a woman of her size would certainly bounce. She'd bounce, jiggle and shake her way across the store, toppling racks and cracking the foundation. In motion, this woman would bounce like a bowl of gelatin strapped to a Pogo stick; at rest, only her sausage-like fingers moved, and they didn't bounce at all.

"Milo," Sharon asked, "what's the bounce?"

Her husband trembled, as if she had caught him doing something naughty in the bathroom. She saw his chest expand from a deep inhale, and only after he exhaled did he answer her.

"The bounce? It's another trick thieves pull. Bertha isn't alone. The pros usually aren't."

"There's someone else?" She turned her head to scan the rest of the department. "Where's she at?"

"It's a he, not a she." Milo tilted his head to the left. "Check over by the purses."

A tall, thin man stood among the tree-like handbag racks. After shifting a few inches farther down the underwear aisle, Sharon could see he carried a shopping bag identical to the one sagging from its load of stolen earrings. Through the gaps in the purses, she noticed the man's bag lay flat against his thighs.

Nothing blocked her view of the man's head and shoulders, which towered over the tops of the racks. She recognized his furtive motions as a poor imitation of Milo's fluid movements, a clumsy counterpoint to Milo's graceful reconnaissance.

"He's with her?" she asked. "He's what, a lookout?"

Milo nodded. "The matching shopping bags are too obvious."

"So what's the bounce?"

"The guy's more than a lookout. He's a decoy. When Mrs. Sprat is finished filling her bag, she'll switch bags with Jack. Once that's done, she'll get very obvious—I mean, she'll send out every 'I'm a thief' vibe she can muster. She'll pick things up, carry them around, put them down and while security's chasing her, Jack makes a beeline for the exit. I wouldn't be surprised if there's a third one around somewhere else—probably another woman—so they can bounce the shit again."

"So what do we do? Who do we follow?"

"What would I do?" Milo asked, obviously amused with her enthusiasm. "I'd follow the bag, the one with the earrings. I'd also have a different officer follow the blimp, and be completely obvious about it. If they think it's working, Jack won't fart around waiting for a clear shot; he'll haul ass out of here. The second he crosses the threshold, I bust him and have my other guy bust the blimp. Two for the price of one, and both arrests will hold up in court."

"That's amazing," Sharon said.

"That's a typical day at the office," Milo replied.

Sharon grabbed Milo's arm. "Look! She's moving."

Milo restored the underwear to their proper hooks. "That's it then. Show's over."

"So which one do I follow?" Sharon stood, smoothing her slacks.

"The show's over honey," Milo repeated. "Let Bullseye handle their own busts. They seem to have it covered."

"What?" Sharon said.

Milo pointed over his shoulder. "The aisle behind us. At first, I thought he was shadowing us, but once I saw the blimp with the earrings, I figured it out. He's been watching her longer than I've been."

Sharon spun around. Through the bras that hung behind them, she caught a flash of plaid. Looking closer, she noticed an embarrassed face staring at them.

"Jesus Christ," Sharon said. "That kid's security? He doesn't look like security."

Milo chuckled. "In my line of work, that's a good thing."

"Why isn't he following her?" Sharon asked, looking again. The kid hadn't moved. "She's almost out of the Jewelry department."

"Probably because someone's taught him very well," Milo said. "Check out the blimp's bag; they made the switch."

Sharon watched the overweight woman leave the Jewelry department. She now stood in the main aisle, casting surreptitious looks at the ceiling-mounted camera bubbles and moving her hands in and out of her shopping bag. As she moved toward the rear of the store, she removed several small items from random shelves she passed, only to replace them on different shelves farther down the aisle.

Just as Milo had predicted.

Meanwhile, the kid stationed behind them hadn't moved. Milo nodded approvingly.

"Stay with the merchandise," he whispered to Sharon. "Just like I teach them."

"Are you sure she did that 'bounce' thingy?" Sharon asked. "She's still got a shopping bag."

"Absolutely," Milo said. "Watch."

The thin man still stood among the purse racks, but now his gaze focused on one thing: Bertha's progress away from the storefront. When the woman bumped into a floor-stack of microwave popcorn, scattering boxes in a Redenbacher avalanche, the thin man smiled. Every head in the area turned towards the clatter and a herd of emerald-smocked clerks converged on the damaged display.

As Bertha's partner stepped away from the purses,

Sharon waited for the Bullseye security kid to follow him. More people moved toward the popcorn spill, the thin man strolled toward the exits, but the kid never changed his posture or position.

"Honey," Sharon asked, "do you usually give crooks such a big head start?"

"I don't understand," Milo said, frowning at the security officer's delay in pursuing the thief. "What the hell is he waiting for?"

The thin man had reached the corner of the Customer Service desk and loitered at a candy display. Suddenly, Bertha began to bellow, berating the clerks attempting to clear the popcorn boxes out of the aisle. The tone and volume of her verbal attack drew the attention of employees and shoppers at the storefront, causing a slow migration to the accident scene. Even Milo took a second to observe the diversion, while Sharon continued to watch the man with the bulging shopping bag.

The security kid still didn't move.

"Shit," Milo said. He slapped his palms against his legs. Sharon recognized the body language; her husband was riding a wave of frustration on the way to a full-blown hissy fit. She pitied the security kid.

Milo pushed their shopping cart into the panty rack and grabbed Sharon's elbow. "C'mon," he said, pulling her down the underwear aisle.

"We're going?" Sharon asked.

"We're going," Milo said. "You wanted to see a bust didn't you?"

CHAPTER 4

"Christ Almighty!" The cry came from inside the tarpaper shack that guarded The Brotherhood compound's entrance. Lincoln Hackendorf leaned over the half-door and shook his head. "Arlie, I keep tellin' you, you can't come barrel-assing down the road like that. Hiram likes the gravel smooth and besides, one of these days you're gonna tear the tranny out of that beast."

"Just anxious to get home Linc," Arlie said, his eyes focused on the steering wheel.

"Then try to get home in one piece," Lincoln said. "We wouldn't want nothin' happenin' to you boys. There ain't enough fresh meat on the table as it is."

"I don't think that's gonna be a problem any more," Arlie said, casting a glance in the rear-view mirror.

Ken drove the toe of his boot into Arlie's shin. "Fuckin' broadcast it, why don't you," he muttered.

Fortunately, Lincoln missed the comment. His concern for Arlie's undercarriage couldn't compete with the sight of Salomé perched in the truck bed.

Salomé tipped his hat to the gawking sentry. "Good morning to you sir. Fine day for a bit of annihilation, don't you think?"

Ken groaned and Arlie dropped his forehead to the steering wheel, but Lincoln scratched his ear and frowned.

"I appreciate the offer, but foreign food always does

nasty things to my stomach. I'm sure your nilation's tasty as hell, but I think I'd better pass."

"How about you let us through," Ken shouted over the steady *thunk thunk thunk* of Arlie's head bouncing against the wheel.

"Meat and potatoes!" Salomé said, clapping in time to Arlie's cranial conga. "Meat and potatoes. Venison and spuds. Simple fare for a simple man, unencumbered by aspirations and unhampered by the lexis typically possessed by the average ragamuffin. I like you Mr. Hackendorf. I'd imagine your synapses are as pristine as they were the day you were born, and that is a rare commodity indeed."

Lincoln ran to open the gate, still slack-jawed at the sight of the stranger in the truck. Ken knew Lincoln hadn't understood one tenth of Salomé's bullshit, or why the dandy admired Lincoln's under-used brainpan, but Ken was sure a demonstration was coming.

The barrier rose. Lincoln leaned on the short end of the cannibalized telephone pole, his eyes tracking Salomé as the truck passed under the gate. The dandy crooked a finger at Lincoln, who dropped the gate and dashed over.

"I have something to show you Mr. Hackendorf," Salomé said, leaning over the fender. "Something wondrous that will forever end your need for sustenance."

Lincoln stepped onto the bumper, smile beaming at the prospect of an end to Spam and surplus cheese. Ken watched his eyes widen when he saw the deer Salomé sat on.

"My Lord, that's a beautiful buck," Lincoln said. He touched its flank and a bubble of drool formed at the corner of his mouth. "That'll be some fine eating for sure, but there's a lot of hungry mouths here. No way that's gonna feed everyone."

"Be at ease Mr. Hackendorf," Salomé said, sliding his hand under his billowing lavender cape. "A feast is prepared even as we speak, although not the sort you're salivating over."

With his free hand, Salomé grabbed Lincoln by the hair and pulled his head down into the truck bed. His other hand appeared from beneath the cape, holding the long sword. Lincoln pushed against the truck, but Salomé held on, pulling forward to position Lincoln's neck on the edge of the tailgate.

Ken gasped, but Salomé turned and winked. "I'll take care of this one," he said, adjusting his grip on the sword hilt. The blade disappeared in a blur. Ken heard the *clang* of metal striking metal and saw a shower of sparks erupt from the tailgate.

"Alas poor Hackendorf, I knew him not at all," Salomé said. His fingers were still tangled in the sentry's hair, but there was nothing left of Lincoln below his jutting Adams apple.

"Get us into the compound," Salomé commanded.

Ken prodded Arlie, who popped the clutch and floored the gas pedal. Salomé set the head on his lap, held the sword in both hands and laid the blade lightly between Lincoln's unseeing eyes.

"Stare all you'd like Mr. Chesterton," Salomé said as he raised the blade above his head. "Do as I've instructed, and allow me time to make my preparations.

"The Baptist and I will join you shortly."

Their arrival in the compound didn't rattle any of The Brotherhood present. Most members were used to Arlie's driving. Skidding tires and churning clouds of dust were a typical Arlie Garrison parking job. The plumes of disturbed earth surrounding them kept Salomé hidden. Ken heard the wet *slurp* as he pulled the blade from Lincoln's skull.

Before visibility returned, Ken and Arlie jumped out of the truck, guns in hand. As the cloud settled, Ken sighted in on the center of the first body to appear through the diminishing haze. A second later, red spray mingled with the particles of dirt still in the air and a crimson soup rained on the ground.

For every bark of the Peacemaker, an answering explosion sounded from the opposite side of the truck. At least Arlie was keeping up with the shot count. Ken reloaded, choking on the taste of blood filling the air.

As he snapped the cylinder of the Colt back into place, Ken heard a cough on his right. He spun and raised his pistol. Brenda Christner's eyes opened wide at the sight of the Peacemaker.

Ken began to squeezer the trigger, but suddenly he lost the connection between his brain and his gun hand. Grimacing from the effort, he could not make his finger tighten against the metal.

In his mind, he heard Salomé's command: "No."

He switched targets and fired easily, leaving Brenda Christner to faint on the darkening ground.

The sounds of gunfire had brought The Brotherhood running, but the first men to arrive came unarmed, and they dropped with single shots to the chest. The second wave carried an arsenal and stayed clear of the killing zone surrounding Arlie's pickup. Ken heard the whistle of return fire, and fell back to the truck as the first bullets homed in on his position. A moment later, Arlie crawled under the truck to join him.

"I shot Caleb!" Arlie blubbered, jacking fresh shells into the Remington's chamber. "Jesus Christ, I shot Caleb!"

"Better than letting Caleb shoot you," Ken said, wincing as a bullet ricocheted off the front fender. "I got at least ten. How many did you get?"

"About the same, but it don't make no difference now." Three more shots hit the truck, one of them shattering the windshield. "We've got 'em riled Ken. They ain't gonna stop till they get us, and God knows what they'll do to us when that happens."

"I don't plan on being a party favor for Hiram's boys," Ken said. "I'll put a bullet in my brain first."

Salomé's inverted head appeared below the sidewall, the crown of his hat brushing the ground. "Gentlemen, you've made a splendid beginning."

Five more shots hit the truck. The front tires deflated

with a *whuff* and the truck settled on its rims. The descent didn't seem to bother Salomé.

Ken scrambled to the rear of the undercarriage, praying the back tires would stay intact. "Yeah, we got it started, and now it looks like they want to finish it."

"Have faith Mr. Chesterton, and be of good cheer," Salomé said. "Providence has given us Mr. Hackendorf, and Mr. Hackendorf has given us the means to carry the day."

The truck moved again. Ken and Arlie covered their heads, but the rear tires still held, and the frame didn't come any lower. The metal above them groaned as the weight in the bed shifted.

"Crawl out from under there," Salomé said. "Come into the light and witness that which shall illuminate the world."

The dandy's head vanished, almost immediately replaced by a pair of lavender moccasins. Unlike his hat, Salomé's feet made contact with the ground, but as he walked away from the truck, Ken noticed the man left no footprints in the blood staining the compound.

With a shriek, the truck's rusty coils expanded as the undercarriage rose above their heads. The gunfire stopped. Heavy black boots traced Salomé's steps, leaving large depressions in their wake.

Ken closed his eyes and crept out from under the truck. When the shooting failed to resume, he pushed himself off the ground and opened his eyes.

He and Arlie had done some serious damage.

"*Diffusione!*" Salomé said, raising his hands. The accumulated dust and smoke from the gunfire coalesced around him, then rose in a hazy pillar and dispersed above their heads.

The bodies remained where they had fallen.

Brenda Christner wasn't among the corpses, nor were any other women or children. Surrounding the dead stood a circle of the glassy-eyed living—the remaining men of The Brotherhood—with empty hands still cradling the air where their weapons had been. The AR-15s, shotguns and hunting rifles they brought to the party now lay at their feet.

The Baptist walked the circle of men, pausing at each one as if examining him. At every stop in the circuit, the man trembled under the sightless scrutiny.

Ken knew just how they felt.

Salomé strolled over to join Ken and Arlie, clucking his tongue at their disheveled state. "If you two are to help govern an empire, we really need to do something about your appearance. I'd say the first step is to forbid you both from cowering in the dirt."

"What have you done?" Arlie asked, transfixed by The Baptist's inspection. "What happened to those guys?"

Salomé chuckled. "It seems your Mr. Hackendorf was hiding his light beneath a bushel. To classify his mind as underdeveloped would be a gross misapplication of the term. Thanks to this unexpected boon, my associate has informed me that it won't be necessary to inflict nearly the amount of carnage I initially estimated."

"Huh?" Arlie said.

Ken drove his elbow into Arlie's gut. "He means we don't have to kill the rest of 'em."

"Quite so Mr. Chesterton. Quite so." Salomé pulled at his sleeves. "Thanks to an incantation I acquired on the sub-continent, the women and children will go on about their normal affairs without further adjustment, and because of Mr. Hackendorf's contribution, The Baptist will experience no difficulty in holding these fellows in reserve until such time as they are needed.

"After all, fresh is so much better than frozen. Wouldn't you agree?"

The Baptist completed his assessment and with a flick of his finger, the men fell into a line and shuffled toward the largest building on the property: The Hall of Community Resources.

"I concur," Salomé said, nodding at his partner. "They should keep nicely in there. With proper sustenance, they should last..."

"Well, ain't this just been the year for unexpected returns?"

Ken and Arlie turned as one, guns ready and aimed at the source of the interruption: A stranger standing on Hiram's porch, which overlooked the compound.

The stranger wagged a finger. "You boys better point them things in another direction or you're liable to piss me off. I don't take well to threats, as your friend there'll tell you."

The man on the porch wasn't a Brother and Ken didn't recognize him as one of Hiram's infrequent guests, although in his plaid shirt and tattered overalls, he sure looked the part.

Ken centered his sights on the stranger's expansive belly. "Mister, I don't know who you are or what you're doing here, but you picked the worst day in history to come for a visit."

"Nah, I'd say my timing's damn near perfect." The stranger swirled a toothpick around his lips. "This sack of shit you're paling around with deserves a proper welcome, and I'm just the sumbitch to give it to him."

"Salomé," Ken said. "You want Arlie and me to send this guy to hell?"

The dandy waved his hand, still facing away from the interloper. "Do not trouble yourself Mr. Chesterton. Why expend the effort in such an endeavor. He'll be returning there on his own soon enough."

Salomé adjusted the angle of his hat, grabbed the hem of his cape and twirled to face the stranger.

"Hello Garcen."

CHAPTER 5

Sharon felt another rush of adrenaline as she and Milo hurried along the department store's main aisle. "We're really gonna bust the guy with the earrings?"

Milo looked over his shoulder. "Look at that kid. If he's going to piss himself every time somebody steals something, he ought to be working the drive-thru."

"Don't worry about him," Sharon said, tugging Milo down the aisle. "With the Tuckers on the job, Bullseye doesn't need a brat with soggy boxers. We'll get him."

"Wait a second." Milo stopped and grabbed her shoulders.

"Wait for what?" Sharon said.

"I want you to be clear on something." His gaze penetrated her. Sharon closed her eyes to escape his stare, but Milo tightened his grip.

"I don't want you doing anything. Do you understand me? *Anything!* You get to watch. Nothing more."

Sharon tried to squirm free, anger defeating the power of her husband's eyes. "Why? You always told me shoplifters weren't dangerous. What are you so worried about?"

He smiled gently and spoke softly. "They usually aren't, but you never know. Whatever else this guy is, he's a criminal, and you never know what a criminal's going to do."

"Harold," Sharon breathed, remembering the previous year. Milo's cast. Keith's stitches. Ducalion's grim promise.

"Exactly Harold," Milo said. His hands relaxed and he caressed where he had gripped. "Whatever happens, I want you safe."

Sharon flinched. "Bad memories Milo. Don't bring up bad memories." Sharon wiped her hands across her eyes. "Let's go catch us a bad guy."

The Bertha scream-fest and popcorn avalanche continued, as did everyone's pre-occupation with the show. When they reached the Customer Service desk, Milo slipped his Harriford's ID from his pocket and tapped it against the counter until one of the clerks responded. After a flash of the badge and a hurried explanation, the distracted clerk activated the PA system and paged Mr. Johnson to the loading dock for a special delivery. This, Sharon intuited, was a coded message for Store Security.

While they waited for "Mr. Johnson," Sharon noticed two things: First, the tall man with the shopping bag had walked through the main doors and now loitered near the vending machines on the sidewalk. Bertha's volume decreased in response to her partner's absence, and she now allowed the assembled Bullseye personnel to begin reconstructing the Redenbacher display.

Sharon's second observation puzzled her. The kid from Lingerie had now moved out into the main aisle. He still seemed focused on her and Milo, but made no move to approach them or the Service Desk. Milo saw this too; a quick shake of his head confirmed it. When Mr. Johnson arrived, he could expect an earful about his ineffective officer.

With a threatening wag of her sausage-like finger, Bertha walked away from the disaster area and moved toward the storefront. Simultaneously, a man wearing a black corduroy vest over a denim shirt and faded jeans slid in next to Milo.

"You know her bag's empty, don't you?" he asked while

pretending to examine a credit application.

Milo leaned against the counter. "Hers may be, but her partner's isn't. Check your seven o'clock."

Mr. Johnson took a pen from the counter and twirled it between his fingers as he looked around. Sharon didn't see him focus on anyone, but when his eyes returned to the credit application he said, "The tall drink of water by the soda machines?"

"That's the one," Milo said. "Bertha did the filling and he took care of carrying it outside."

Mr. Johnson nodded. "They pulled a switch."

Milo smiled. "We call it a bounce."

"That works too." Mr. Johnson dropped his pen and held out his hand. "I'm Scott Cooper."

"Milo Tucker, from Harriford's," Milo said, giving Cooper's hand a quick shake. "How do you want to handle this?"

"I'll take the grab if you'll supply the details," Cooper said. "What's in the bag?"

"A whole lot of earrings. Probably more than that, but it's what I saw go in."

"Good enough." He raised an eyebrow at Milo. "You sure you're comfortable with me making this?"

"As long as you're comfortable taking my word for it," Milo said. "It's your pond. I'm just swimming through. You want to bring your boy in on this, or can I lend a hand?"

Cooper laughed. "I don't know what boy you're talking about, but I sure wouldn't mind you taking my back. Normally this is a one-man operation."

Sharon checked the main aisle fronting the Lingerie Department. The kid was gone. She shook her head at Milo.

"Huh," Milo grunted. "I thought I spotted one of your guys. My mistake."

"No harm done," Cooper said. "I was eating lunch when they paged. It'll still be there when I get back."

Milo gestured at Sharon. "You don't mind if my wife

tags along, do you? She's been dying to see what I do for a living."

Cooper touched a finger to his temple. "I don't see where it's a problem. You just stay back out of harm's way ma'am. Never can tell what these fools will do when they're cornered."

Sharon gave him a discreet thumbs-up as Bertha approached the counter. "Mr. Cooper, you sound just like my husband. I'll behave, I promise."

"Let's saddle up then." Cooper crumpled the credit application into a ball and dropped it behind the counter. "I'll follow her out and take them both when they hook up."

"Which one do you want if they bolt?" Milo asked, pulling his sleeves up above his elbows.

"If you don't mind, I'll take him. He's the one with the goods, and he looks squirrelly enough to be a handful. If there's a throw-down, I don't want you taking any grief for doing a good deed. Besides, with the missus here, you can corral the big one without anyone yelling harassment."

"That's the plan then," Milo said.

Milo and Cooper fell in behind Bertha and walked through the automatic doors with her. Sharon stayed a few steps behind, watching her husband and his counterpart prepare for the arrest. She recognized the tension in Milo's shoulders and noticed how he walked on the balls of his feet. Heels hovering an inch above the pavement, he looked like a compressed spring. Cooper moved with a lackadaisical ease that matched his speech, just a regular guy out for a stroll.

Once they cleared the doors, Cooper broke left and approached the thin man. Holding a laminated card in his left hand, he reached out with his right and grabbed the shopping bag's handles. A quick twist freed the bag from the thief's grasp.

"Bullseye Security," Cooper said, holding his ID in the man's face. "I'd like you to come back to my office so we can talk about this bag of earrings."

"Earrings? I don't know anything about any earrings," the man stammered.

"That's fine sir." Cooper placed a hand on the man's elbow and began to guide him back into the store. "We can get this squared away back in my office."

The thief nodded, eyes and shoulders dropping in resignation. *Milo was right*, Sharon thought, amazed by the thin man's easy surrender. *These shoplifters don't even put up a fight.*

Milo hadn't approached Bertha yet, and as Cooper and his apprehension passed them, Sharon realized why. Bertha turned in their direction and took a few tentative steps as if to follow. Milo mirrored her movement, but to Sharon it looked as if the woman would follow her partner all the way to the security office without waiting for an invitation. It made for an easy arrest for Cooper, but made Milo merely an interested observer.

And Sharon even less important.

Cooper and the thin man paused at the entrance to allow a shopper in a wheelchair time to navigate through the doors. Cooper tipped his chin at Milo and tossed him a small salute with the hand holding the shopping bag. The thin man caught the gesture and looked in their direction. Milo smiled, waving "bye-bye" to the thief before returning Cooper's salute.

Bertha also witnessed the exchange. She looked from Milo to Cooper, and back again. Her skin flushed as she looked from one to the other, darkening to red as she connected the dots and realized exactly who was responsible for ruining her excursion.

Sharon watched her eyes narrow and the corner of her mouth turn up, showing a hint of yellowed teeth. Milo waved as Cooper disappeared into the store, not seeing Bertha shift her feet and turn toward him. Sharon saw her chubby hands clench into fists and rise to the level of where her waist should have been.

"*Milo, look out!*" Sharon screamed as Bertha began to move.

Milo stiffened in response to her shout, but almost instantly relaxed and squared off against the thundering thief. He rolled his shoulders and slightly bent his knees. He spread his arms and flexed his fingers, adopting a surfer-like stance. Bertha's feet slapped the sidewalk, every step adding momentum to her charge. As she moved closer, she lowered her head and extended her arms.

Just when the collision seemed unavoidable, Milo dropped into a squat and with his hands flat against the ground, spun clockwise, extending his right leg. Bertha passed as he completed his spin, and Milo's leg swept the woman's feet out from under her.

In the time it took Bertha to complete her pratfall, Milo used his momentum to spin again, rising as he turned. He stood over the shoplifter, once again in the surfer's stance, but with his fists held loosely at his sides.

Ultimate Milo strikes again.

Bertha wouldn't be charging again anytime soon. Even with her substantial padding, the impact with the sidewalk had knocked the wind out of her, and she rubbed her head where it had slammed against the concrete. Milo stood ready for another attack, but Sharon could tell one wasn't coming.

Sharon approached him slowly, reaching tentatively to touch his shoulder. As her fingertips brushed his shirt, he jumped aside and turned to face her—one hand held palm-out to hold her back, the other clenched and drawn back, ready to strike.

Deadly intensity burning in steel-gray eyes.

Sharon stepped back. "Milo, it's me."

Sharon knew her husband's eyes. She remembered their first hesitant glances, how his eyes had sparkled with tears when Milo recited his wedding vows. She recalled the thrill she felt when contemplating the promise of brown-eyed babies. Those eyes were her gateway to Milo's soul, and she knew them as well as she knew the sound of his voice or the touch of his hands.

These eyes were not his.

He lowered his hands to his thighs, bent over and took a deep breath. When he straightened again, he smiled and opened his arms.

"Sorry honey. You kind of caught me off guard there."

"More like 'on guard,' wouldn't you say?" Sharon stayed back, examining him top to bottom, refusing to step into his embrace. For the first time, her husband scared her. She knew he never intended to hit her, but his surprised reaction wasn't the source of her fear. Impossible physical prowess and chameleon eyes—those kept her out of her husband's arms.

Milo didn't question her hesitation. That too was damning evidence, but evidence of what? Explanations were necessary, but Sharon knew Milo wasn't going to offer any. Fortunately, she knew exactly where to get the information she needed; information she had avoided seeking for all these months.

Ultimate Milo might resist her interrogations, but she knew someone else who wouldn't.

For now, she mirrored Milo's pose and fell against his chest, wrapping her arms around him. The touch of him weakened her resolve, but this was another distraction her intended snitch wouldn't possess, not if he wanted to keep his hands.

"That was very exciting," Sharon said.

"Just another day at the office," Milo replied, tousling her hair.

"Remind me to visit your office more often." Sharon snuggled in closer.

Bertha moaned from the sidewalk. Sharon released her hold on Milo and delivered a short kick to the shoplifter's flabby hip. "That's for trying to hurt my husband, bitch."

Milo pulled her back. "Honey, don't kick the shoplifter…"

"*Gatherer!*"

The automatic doors stood open, blocked from closing by the arms of the kid Milo had mistaken for store security. Jaded shoppers who had ignored Bertha's clumsy attack and even clumsier fall stopped and stared at the young man.

"*Gatherer!*" he screamed again, this time pointing a finger at Milo, who blanched at the shout.

The kid released his hold on the doors and approached, finger still extended while his other hand rummaged through his pants pocket. Milo stepped in front of Sharon.

When only a few feet separated them, the kid pulled a large, folding knife from his pocket and flipped it open. The serrated blade twinkled with reflected sunlight as he traced invisible circles in the air between them.

"I've been waiting for this," the kid said. He stopped the blade's dance and stared at it, seemingly mesmerized by the shiny surface.

"Waiting for what?" Sharon whispered over Milo's shoulder. "Who the hell is this kid?"

"Be quiet Sharon," Milo said, using his arms to block her in behind him.

"I've wanted this forever," the kid continued, "and you're going to give it to me."

"I'm going to give you something all right," Milo said. He turned, grabbed Sharon by the shoulders and shoved her to his right. As Sharon recovered her balance, Milo took several steps to his left, increasing the distance between them.

"If you don't put that knife away, I'm going to give you the ass-whupping of your life," Milo said as the kid pivoted to follow him.

"You don't understand," the kid said. "Nobody understands. My parents, my friends...even the doctors. Everyone says they understand, but nobody does."

"Then why don't you explain it to me," Milo said, his voice segueing from his "ass-whupping" tone into his "best buds" mode. Hearing this, Sharon moved to rejoin him, but Milo caught the motion and waved her back.

Milo stepped farther away from her. "Explain it to me, and maybe I can help. Lose the knife, and we'll talk."

"No, no, no, no, no," the kid chanted, shaking his head.

              M. Stephen Lukac

"No more talking. No more tests, no more counseling and no more waiting." He looked at Milo. His eyes softened and the corners of his mouth turned up in a small, sad smile. "There's no other way."

Suddenly, Sharon's world contracted to two points. Simultaneously, she saw the resignation on the kid's face, mirrored by the realization on Milo's. Time slowed as Milo ran toward the kid and Sharon ran to Milo. Seconds stretched into infinity as the kid placed the point of the blade against his chest, gripped the hilt with both hands and thrust the knife into his heart. The kid swayed, supported by legs that hadn't yet received the injury report from his wounded heart.

Time resumed its flow. The kid's knees folded. Sharon changed direction, swerving to catch the kid as he collapsed.

Milo stopped, the soles of his shoes scratching the sidewalk.

"Help me Milo!" Sharon said, struggling with the kid's weight.

Milo stood unmoving.

Very little blood came from the chest wound, but it poured from the kid's mouth. Crimson bubbles formed as ragged breath pushed through stained lips. Sharon cradled his head, maternal instincts awakening.

And still Milo didn't move.

"Gatherer..." the kid murmured.

"*Shhh*," Sharon said, wiping her hand across his forehead. "Help's coming. Just hang on."

"Gatherer," he said again, extending his hand to Milo.

Milo stepped back.

"Don't move around," Sharon said.

The kid's breath hitched and he coughed. His eyes opened wide. He reached out again, this time with both arms.

"Harvest me," he pleaded, shaking from the effort it took.

"Please Gatherer...harvest me."

CHAPTER 6

As he juggled keys, two bags of comic books, a bag of burgers and a sweaty chocolate milkshake, Keith Pridemore realized that cellular phones weren't designed for hands-free conversations, unless he wanted to fork over an extra twenty bucks for the micro-mini McDonalds drive-thru headset. He wasn't limber enough to pinch the cigarette-pack-sized phone between his cheek and shoulder, and the constant jiggling wreaked havoc with his reception. That, in combination with balancing the phone and inserting a key into his apartment door without spilling the evening's food and entertainment, ensured he only heard every other word Milo said.

Every other word from Milo was enough to give Keith the story after Sharon's earlier call. "Hysterical" barely began to describe Sharon's state of mind while she recounted the day's events. She gushed with pride describing how Milo handled two earring thieves. She sobbed in horror talking about a teenager dying in her arms.

Her voice quivered with doubt when she admitted feeling as if she didn't know her husband anymore.

Keith had endured these fishing expeditions before; his role of friend and confidant to both Tuckers made it inevitable. In the past, he could get by with thoughtful nodding and silent commiseration; Milo and Sharon never argued for long or over anything serious. Now, with Milo's secret thrust into Sharon's face and bleeding all over her wardrobe, thoughtful and silent weren't cutting it.

Keith didn't know how much longer he could keep his mouth shut. Sharon's tears and boo-boo faces were eroding the legendary Pridemore resolve. Sharon was falling apart and Milo wasn't doing much better.

Tuesday's encounter with Crazy Amy had rattled Milo; today's confrontation with a suicidal teenager had sent Keith's best friend right into Bug Shit Land. At first, Keith had believed Crazy Amy's behavior was probably the result of an innocent convergence of Oogie Boogie bullshit. A psycho's brain operated on different wavelengths, as did Milo's. Place these two bioelectric generators in close proximity, and a certain amount of interference and feedback wasn't surprising. The phenomenon wouldn't make the cover of Scientific America, but it might make an interesting sidebar in The Fortean Times.

The teenager's actions had more serious ramifications.

"I'm not going to find anything," Keith said into the phone, bending over to place the hamburger bag and dripping cup on the floor before attempting the lock again. "I'll check him out for you Milo, but I'm telling you, it's a waste of time."

A chorus of disagreement erupted from the speaker as Milo's passengers weighed in with their opinion of Keith's pessimism. Keith ignored the cacophony and turned his key over, jabbing at the lock repeatedly without success.

"Quiet the kids down and listen to me," he said. Keith pocketed his keys and leaned against the doorjamb. "Who should know about this? Me, you and Garcen. That's it. That should be the entire Gatherer loop. I haven't told anybody—I can't imagine Garcen gossiping like a house frau—and if you've told anybody else on the face of the planet without telling Sharon first, I'm gonna kick your ass."

Milo began his litany of lame-ass reasons for not telling Sharon, but Keith cut him off.

"I don't want to hear it right now Milo. We've had this discussion too many times already, and I'll summarize my position on this issue once again by telling you you're full of shit."

Milo didn't think he was full of shit.

"You are full of shit, but we're not talking about that right now. You want me to dig around for some background on your suicide, so I'll do it, but I'm not going to find anything beyond what the cops already told you. Jared Cavalet, blah blah blah. Terminal illness, blah blah blah. Remission, blah blah blah. Six weeks to live, blah blah blah."

"Blah blah blah," Milo repeated in Keith's ear.

"Precisely. The blah blah blah is tragic, but not important. What's important Batman, is figuring out what to do now that everyone knows you're Bruce Wayne."

Milo preferred the Superman/Clark Kent analogy, which Keith, after a moment's thought, agreed was more apt once he considered the Lois Lane Factor. Keith also believed that—even with the bow ties—Jimmy Olsen was way cooler than Robin as sidekicks went, even though the Dark Knight would always out-rank Big Blue on the badass-o-meter.

"Don't change the subject," Keith said, shelving the fanboy debate. "Something's painted a neon-red target on your back and we need to deal with it."

Milo wondered what the "something" was.

"You know damn well what it was." Keith rapped the cell phone on the wall, a surrogate for the pounding he wanted to lay on Milo's head. "Let me talk to the hippie."

Trippenstein greeted Keith with a sigh.

"It's Christmas, isn't it?" Keith asked.

Trippenstein thought it was possible.

"Possible my ass. What you did at the mall took an awful lot of juice, more than enough to show up on somebody's radar."

Trippenstein didn't dispute the claim.

Milo interrupted by asking Keith if he'd rather be dead.

"No I wouldn't rather be dead," Keith shouted, wincing at the echo of his voice in the corridor. "I didn't want to be dead then, and I'd prefer not to be dead now. Now shut up and let Trippenstein talk."

Trippenstein reiterated his argument from December.

"That's a valid point Tripp, but now we've got to deal with the aftershocks. You guys sent out some ripples and now they're coming back at you."

Trippenstein stated his belief that the teenager was an aberration.

"Aberration? How he hell can seven people be so collectively naïve? I've had my ear to the ground for most of my life, and I didn't get the full skinny on Gatherers until last year. Do you realize how 'out there' a kid would have to be to know what he obviously knew?"

Trippenstein reminded Keith they wouldn't know how normal the kid had been until Keith did the digging Milo requested.

"Fine," Keith said, slumping against the wall. "I'll do the goddamned digging, but believe this Dr. Strange: You, your roommates and your congenial host are standing in the path of a motherfucking shit storm, and I'm not sure there's an umbrella big enough to keep y'all from getting splattered. So the next time Milo's thinking about telling his wife to buy some galoshes, I'd advise you six to exercise whatever influence you have to convince him it's the right thing to do."

Milo thanked him and promised to reconsider talking to Sharon.

"You do that pal," Keith said. "Now let me get to eating before my milkshake gets all melty. And by the way, I picked up your comics since you decided to screw up our Wednesday evening."

Milo thanked him again and asked if Keith had remembered to grab a copy of the *Darkwing* annual for him.

"No, because Slick Rick's order got chopped at the distributor, but we can run down to Mr. Personality's tomorrow night and get it. I'm hanging up now. I'll call you if I find anything earth shattering." He punched the END button and swapped out the phone for his keys.

With his hands free, Keith had little trouble unlocking

his door. He gathered his dinner from the floor and pushed into his apartment, walking carefully to avoid stepping on Emma the Satan Beast in the dark.

He placed dinner and the bags of comics on the divider separating the living room from the kitchen and waited for Emma to tangle herself around his feet. Keith knew the drill; any attempt at movement before his psychotic Burmese welcomed him home would result in a trampled kitty and three nights of feline retribution.

"Do you realize how much your voice carries when you speak?"

The voice and the question came from the couch. Keith turned and stumbled into the living room, thoughts of Emma's safety replaced by the silhouette seated on his sofa. He reached for the light switch, but the silhouette raised a hand and the lamp on his computer desk flickered to life.

The light wasn't enough to illuminate his visitor, but it provided enough light for Keith to navigate his way safely across the room. It also revealed Emma's location: Safely tucked away on the stranger's lap.

"Goddamned traitorous cat," he mumbled, amazed that the unexpected presence in his home wasn't affecting him more. Milo's experiences and Emma's acceptance combined to create an Oogie Boogie Wellbutrin.

It took more to freak him out than it used to.

"I'd tell you to make yourself at home," Keith said as he sat at his desk, "but since you already have, what's the point."

The stranger scratched behind Emma's ears. "Emma told me you'd be home soon and invited me in to wait. Hope you don't mind."

"Mind? Why should I mind? If the Satan Beast wants to have friends over, why should I care? It's her house too."

"She hates it when you call her that."

"I'll make a note of it. Now Dr. Doolittle, was that all or did you two discuss my choices in food and litter while you were waiting?"

"*Shhhhh*," the stranger hissed. "Jesus! You know, you'd

probably get laid occasionally if you'd just turn down the volume. Seriously man, crank it down a couple of notches. I'm trying to stay low-profile here."

Keith leaned forward. The change in angle did nothing to improve the view of his guest's face. "You've been talking to my pussy about pussy? Suddenly I'm not too thrilled with Emma's choice in after-school playmates. Get the hell out of here before I throw your ass out."

"You don't want to do that." Emma yawned as if to validate the stranger's point. She was comfortable with the situation; why should Keith freak out?

"I'm not freaking out," Keith said to Emma. "I'm pissed off. I'm also not gonna get my hands dirty tossing your friend here." He reached for the phone. "Not when there's folks who specialize in this kind of shit."

"Do you really think this is worth troubling Milo over?" the stranger asked.

Keith's hand froze in mid-reach. Ripples and after-shocks. Sitting on his couch. Petting his cat.

"What makes you think I'd call Milo?" Keith asked.

"Actually, I didn't. I just thought the suggestion would be an effective way of getting your attention off of pussy and onto the business at hand."

"Which is Milo?"

"C'mon, it can't surprise you that much. Remember, I heard your conversation in the hall."

"Eavesdropping is incredibly rude y'know."

"So is talking at a decibel level only slightly lower than a Metallica concert, but that doesn't stop you."

"You try having a conversation on one of those Fisher-Price phones mister…mister…What the hell is your name anyway?"

"I'd prefer to keep this anonymous if you don't mind."

Keith smiled. "I do mind. I've always told Emma she can't have boys over unless they introduce themselves properly."

The stranger continued scratching Emma's ears. A sigh came from the shadows. As Emma's back leg began to twitch in response to his ministrations, the stranger finally spoke.

"I am a watcher in deep shadow."

"Save the cryptic shit for the kitty." Keith laughed at a decibel level higher than the volume of a Metallica concert, but stopped once the answer sunk in.

"Really?" Keith said.

"Yup."

"No shit?"

"No shit."

"One of the fifty-five?" Keith asked.

"Not any more, but I used to be. And for the record: I wasn't 'one' of the Fifty-Five; I was First of the Fifty-Five."

Keith whistled. "That's a bold statement."

"Not if it's true. Which it is."

"I'd heard you were gone."

"People hear that all the time. Even when it's true, it's not permanent."

The conversational thread still left the issue of a name unresolved, but at least it had provided Keith with the identity of Emma's guest. He never spoke openly of Trippenstein's former "occupation" either; some names only led to more ripples and aftershocks.

"I know one of your friends," Keith said to break the silence.

"I wouldn't call him a friend. Let's just say we used to work together."

"He's been through a lot."

"Who?" The stranger asked. "Milo or my former subordinate?"

"Both, but I'm assuming you're here to talk about Milo and not Trippenstein."

Another sigh issued from the darkness. Emma's ears and whiskers twitched as she rose from the stranger's lap.

"Can you please not do that," the stranger asked, stroking Emma's back to calm her. "Once I'm out of here, you can say your friend's name as much as you'd like, but till then keep that shit to yourself."

"Fine. We'll call him the hippie; he hates that. Now what do I call you?"

"Why do you have to call me anything?"

"I'm a stickler for details. Besides, when I tell Milo about this—and I assume I'm supposed to tell Milo about this?"

The stranger nodded.

Keith returned the gesture. "When I tell Milo about this, I'd hate to have to keep saying things like 'the stranger said this' and 'the mysterious shadow said that.' I'm going to call you something; I thought you might like some input."

Another pause as the stranger's hand hovered in mid-kitty stroke. Then:

"Call me Stanley."

"Stanley?" Keith closed his eyes and his cheeks puffed to contain the laughter. To hell with it, he wasn't "Stanley's" host. Let Emma make polite apologies. He opened his lips and let the guffaws explode.

"You wanted a name," Stanley said over Keith's braying.

"Yeah, but Stanley?" Keith held a hand in front of his face to catch the spittle. "That's just perfect, oh great and mysterious one."

"It was your idea."

"Sure, sure. Listen to the voice of Stanley and tremble. I can see it now: 'Milo, I bring tidings of great import from he who is called…Stanley.'"

"Are you almost done?"

"Wait, one more," Keith gasped, leaning sideways to relieve the stitch in his side. "It must be done, for the word of Stanley comes forth…from his parents' basement."

Emma arched her neck to watch him roll out of his chair. From the floor, Keith saw Stanley duplicate the cat's motion without dissipating any of the shade surrounding him, but there was something new in the silhouette.

Two burning eyes, cobalt orbs glowing with eldritch fire.

"Call me Stanley." His voice was deeper—aural echoes of an ocular inferno. "Serving one crisis at a time."

Keith's hilarity vanished, evaporating in the cold heat of Stanley's gaze. He scrambled back into his seat. "OK Stanley, I got it. Serving crises. Deep dark Oogie Boogie shit. I've got it."

"I have your attention now?"

"Absolutely."

"My turn to talk?" Stanley's glow faded.

"Go right ahead."

"You sure?"

"The floor is yours."

"How considerate of you."

"Kind of contradicts the whole "low profile" thing though, don't you think?"

"I thought it was my turn."

"It is your turn. I'm just saying…"

"There are shades of power," Stanley said, leaning back on the couch. "Palettes of energy, encompassing the spectrum from visible to invisible. Degrees of control from brute force to subtle leverage. Shouts and whispers."

"Uh-huh."

"Do you see?"

"I'm starting to." Keith considered it. "Coercion versus influence?"

"I'm impressed. It's a lesson the hippie could never learn."

"I was just saying the same thing. Not much for the understated, huh?"

Stanley shook his head. "The mystical equivalent of 'roid rage. All or nothing. Everything big and showy. I never showered with the guy or anything, but I sense some serious size issues there."

"Ew." There was a mental image Keith didn't need.

Stanley shuddered, startling Emma. "Tell me about it."

"So we've established the hippie would probably drive an SUV. Is this an interesting sidebar, or is there a point to this?"

"This is the point. Now that he's 'out' the hippie is calling attention to himself again."

"But he's not 'out.' He's still in Milo."

"Doesn't matter. The power's not in the body; the power resides in the soul, the essence of what the hippie is. When Milo calls him forward, he's as out as he needs to be."

"Like a beacon."

"More like a goddamned lighthouse. It's like the bit with Munsch's bullets. Simple transmutation. Effective, but quiet. Barely a blip on the radar."

"Wait a minute, Munsch's bullets…"

Stanley ignored him. "But the thing at the mall? Man, you called it in the hallway. You nailed it. I told him the same thing. All that force, the power required to accomplish what he did? You don't send up fireworks like that without expecting a few 'ooos' and 'ahhs.'"

"How do you know about…?"

"I mean, you fire the thing off, everybody looks up and next thing you know, the whole crowd's going 'ooo' and 'ahh.'"

"I get it, I get it. 'Ooos' and 'ahhs' are bad?"

"No, global warming is bad. 'Ooos' and 'ahhs' can be fatal. There's a reason the Fifty-Five don't have bubble gum cards."

"So we *are* talking about the hippie?"

Stanley shook his head. "No, we're talking about Milo. You said it yourself: your boy's got a lot of shit coming his way, which is why I'm sitting here petting your cat. The only reason I brought the hippie into it is because you mentioned him first and he's adding to the feces factor."

"Milo's feces factor?"

"Exactly. As it stands, your buddy has a big enough shit burger on his plate. There may not be a ton of Hunters left but they're out there, just dying to find themselves a juicy Gatherer to snack on. With problems like that, your friend doesn't need to be calling any more attention to himself, which is what the hippie is doing."

"The kid today," Keith said.

"Is just the beginning," Stanley completed the sentence. "The hippie brings his own favors to the party, but they're minor compared to the guest list Milo's collecting. A Gatherer with an open slot is rare. It's also a huge commodity to some people, and they're usually not folks you want to hang around with."

"I knew something like this was going to happen."

"As you keep telling me," Stanley murmured.

"What?"

Stanley dismissed the question with a wave. "Just tell Milo to keep his head down for a while and to keep a tighter rein on the hippie. Keeping a low profile isn't just something I practice; I preach it too. Hopefully, if he stays out of the spotlight long enough, the people he needs to worry about will forget about him and move on to something else. It happens. There's always something else to get folks' attention."

"Something to make people forget about a Gatherer with a vacancy?"

He shrugged. "Like I said, it happens. Things happen that you couldn't comprehend, even with what you already know to be true."

Back to the cryptic shit. "Speaking of which," Keith asked, "how do you know about the bullets? And when did you ever talk to Milo?"

Stanley shook his head. "I was kind of hoping you'd let that one go."

"Not bloody likely. Look, the shadows thing, the glowing eyes thing, and the voice of doom thing are very impressive in the Keith-sit-down-and-shut-up department, but they don't do a damn thing to my memory. So answer the question. When did you meet Milo?"

"Never happened," Stanley said.

"Bullshit."

"Bull-truth. Talking to the hippie is in no way dependant on talking to Milo. Yeah, I could pick your boy out of a line-up, but that familiarity doesn't mean I've ever *met* him."

Keith mentally replayed their conversation. In the strictest sense, Stanley hadn't claimed to meet Milo, but he sure as hell had implied such a meeting took place. There was also the disturbing possible interpretation of Stanley's muttered response to a later statement, but Keith decided to focus on one mystery at a time.

He settled for this: "You still haven't answered my question."

Silhouetted shoulders rose and fell, accompanied by a powerful exhale. "I watch from deep shadow," Stanley began, "but where I walk is dimmer still. The dark conceals more than identity. It hides what was and what is yet to be. You walk the path of life, never straying from its course. I live beyond its boundary, traveling when and where I will."

Keith applauded. "You've been saving that one, haven't you?"

Stanley tipped his head. "I've had lots of practice."

"Care to elaborate?"

"I think I've said enough."

"Yeah, that's you. Mr. Information."

"Hey, I'm not here to be Exposition Boy. I just wanted give you a heads-up and hope you'd pass it along."

"I wish I knew exactly what I was supposed to pass along."

"You know," Stanley said with more confidence than Keith felt. "I don't believe in much, but I believe that. Follow your instincts. Follow your heart. Those tend to be the best barometers."

"I think I preferred cryptic to Hallmark."

Stanley lifted Emma from his lap and gently placed her on the sofa. "Then I'll leave you with something from the Penthouse Forum."

"Great. Mystical redneck naughty bits."

"No naughty bits; just a final piece of friendly advice."

"Which is?"

"Tell Milo to invest in some condoms."

CHAPTER 7

"How long are we supposed to wait?" Ken asked, throwing a stone at Hiram's window.

Arlie scooped up another spoonful of beans, using a biscuit to prevent a stray kernel of corn from sneaking onto the spoon. The uneven rocks surrounding The Brotherhood's flagpole didn't provide a steady table and it took all Arlie's concentration to keep his food separated the way Mama had taught.

Brenda Christner's face-breaking smile seemed to reinforce Mama Garrison's lessons in manners. Brenda watched Arlie eat and nodded happily after every bite, standing close enough to serve but not too close. The change was refreshing, different enough from his wife's "slap it on the plate and leave" system to make a simple plate of hot dogs, beans and corn taste like the best Blue Plate special on the planet. No wonder Seth Christner was so damned fat; Brenda Christner had her priorities straight.

Arlie was glad Ken hadn't shot Brenda.

"How long are we supposed to wait?" Ken asked again. A plate of food sat cooling on the rock next to him, delivered by Lincoln Hackendorf's widow, who seemed more concerned with Ken's refusal to eat than with her new marital status. She hopped from one foot to the other, leaning forward every time Ken's hand moved in the direction of his food and dancing back when he picked up another pebble to chuck across the compound.

Rosalyn Hackendorf wasn't enjoying lunchtime half as much as Brenda Christner was.

Ken usually wasn't so insensitive—Arlie had seen him score with women who usually wouldn't give guys like them a second look—but his frustration was throwing a serious wrench into the machinery Salomé had set in motion. Real food, not the microwavable shit or government surplus cast-offs that usually made up The Brotherhood's menu, was only the first benefit. Arlie didn't always understand the man's fancy words, but he appreciated a full belly and an attentive woman keeping it that way, and if this was just the first course, then hoo-fucking-ray for Salomé.

As long as Ken didn't queer the deal.

Arlie looked up from his plate and winked at Brenda, just to see her face brighten. Once again, she didn't disappoint. Arlie dug into his corn, pleased with his newfound way with the ladies.

"Jesus Christ, Arlie," Ken said, reaching past his plate for another stone. "Did you forget you've got a wife and a couple of kids zombie-ing around here someplace?"

"I'm just eating. You ought to try some; it's really good."

"You're getting a hard-on for hot dogs and baked beans. What would you do if she brought you a steak?"

"Would you rather have a steak Ken?" Rosalyn reached for Ken's untouched plate.

"Do you want a steak Arlie?" Brenda asked.

Even with a belly full of franks and beans, a sizzling T-bone sounded pretty damn good. While Arlie's missus would probably frown at the extravagance, Brenda Christner seemed to think a steak to chase down the Oscar Meyers was a fine idea.

Arlie was about to ask for his medium-rare when a stone thumped against the side of his head.

"I don't want a steak," Ken said, selecting a rock larger

than the one he'd just thrown. "Arlie don't want one either."

Arlie rubbed his temple. "Where do you get off saying what I do or don't want?"

"You don't want a steak."

"What if I do want a steak?"

"You do not want a steak." Ken grabbed a rock only a bit smaller than Arlie's head.

That convinced him. "I guess maybe I don't want a steak," Arlie told Brenda, whose lower lip quivered with disappointment.

"Right now," Arlie added quickly. "I don't want a steak right now, but I figure I'll be ready for one later."

That stopped her boo-boo face in mid-boo. "So…," Arlie continued, looking at Ken for guidance.

"So," Ken said, finally getting with the program. "Why don't you girls run along and rustle us up a couple of thick, juicy ones for later. By the time you get them ready for us, we'll be ready for them."

Ken's decision to accept the women's generosity set the ladies to clapping as they ran off to plan their menu.

"Jesus, I thought they'd never leave." Ken discarded the boulder he'd been fixing to throw at Arlie. "I was starting to wish I had shot Brenda after all."

"Maybe somebody ought to shoot you," Arlie said.

Ken's eyebrows climbed his forehead; the tilt of his head showing his surprise at what he had heard. "You feel like repeating that?"

"You heard me." Arlie slapped his empty plate down on Ken's full one, equally surprised by his sudden bravado.

"Maybe I should have eaten some of that," Ken said, resuming his rock hunt. "I don't know what was in it, but anything that grows a set of balls that quick might be worth eating."

"Am I sensing dissension in the ranks gentlemen?" Salomé asked from behind them. Arlie jumped at the question; he hadn't heard the man's approach.

Ken didn't even turn around. "About time you showed

up. I was starting to think you'd taken off."

"No worries on that point Mr. Chesterton," Salomé said. "Why would I abandon such a fruitful enterprise when it's only just started?"

"That ain't what I'm worried about." Ken threw another rock at Hiram's window. "What worries me is your buddy with the poor sense of timing. You remember him, don't you? He's been holed up in there with Hiram since yesterday afternoon."

"Garcen is of no concern." Arlie sensed a trace of annoyance in Salomé's tone. The upward tuck of one corner of Ken's mouth made Arlie think he'd noticed it too, but it didn't keep him from going on.

"Well he concerns the shit out of me. Maybe his timing's not as bad as I thought. The way he talked to you got me thinking he's exactly where he figures he needs to be."

"Mr. Chesterton, you tread into territory best left to those with the knowledge and experience to navigate it. I recommend you follow Mr. Garrison's example and enjoy your new station while trusting The Baptist and I to cope with any minutiae that presents itself."

Ken dropped all but one of the rocks he had gathered and leapt to his feet. "Then by God, you'd best get to coping."

Arlie stood too, backing Ken's play more from habit than any agreement with his partner's grievances. He didn't care what Brenda had put into his lunch; he'd never have the stones to square off with Salomé.

"Me and Arlie didn't have much choice in joining up with you fellas, but I'll be damned if we ain't hitched now. We spilled a lot of blood for you already and I figure you're gonna want more before it's over. So I'm telling you, make with the mojo and get your shit together." Ken heaved his last rock at Hiram's house. "Starting with your asshole buddy."

Even with The Baptist absent, Arlie winced in anticipation of the mind blast sure to come because of Ken's bitching. Distance hadn't hindered the headless freak so far.

Salomé must have noticed the gesture. "Fear not Mr. Garrison. Part of any successful alliance is the open and frank discussion of ideas and opinions. Rising in support of Mr. Chesterton's concerns speaks well of your loyalty, and as you will come to learn, I value loyalty above all else."

He said the last bit with his gaze locked on Ken. *Take the hint*, Arlie silently pleaded.

Tugging at his ruffled shirt cuffs, Salomé walked towards Hiram's house. "Regrettably, The Baptist is temporarily indisposed, having nearly exhausted Mr. Hackendorf's unintended—though thoroughly appreciated—contribution to our cause."

Arlie shuddered again, knowing exactly what that meant.

"For the moment, he's perusing what commodities remain. I doubt he'll be fortunate enough to uncover another hidden jewel amongst the detritus, but one can hope. Besides, providence has provided where planning has failed, but that is an issue best addressed after alleviating Mr. Chesterton's anxieties regarding our uninvited caller."

Arlie flashed a "What the hell?" eyebrow wiggle at Ken, but Ken only smiled—the patented Chesterton "I won this round" baring of teeth. Arlie wasn't too sure; calling this a "win" seemed like bragging. As they followed Salomé to the base of Hiram's porch, Arlie let Ken get a couple of steps ahead.

If Ken suddenly exploded, Arlie didn't want to get any shit on his shirt.

"Garcen, show yourself," Salomé called. "You've trespassed long enough."

Hiram's door remained closed.

Salomé cleared his throat and adjusted his cape. "Garcen! You stretch the limits of patience and hospitality. Quit cowering in there and come out. I would have words with you."

A slight breeze pushed dirt across the compound. A tree swallow warbled. Ken picked at the grips of the Peacemaker. Arlie scratched his ass.

Hiram's door remained closed.

"Maybe he ain't there," Arlie said.

"He's there," Salomé replied.

"Maybe he snuck out last night."

"Garcen does not possess the subtlety to sneak."

"Maybe somebody took him a hot dog," Ken said. "There's a lot of that going around."

"Maybe somebody wouldn't be so cranky if he ate once in a while," Arlie countered.

"Maybe somebody ought to learn how to use a can opener and boil water so he didn't have to be waited on hand and foot."

"Maybe somebody ought to shut up."

"Maybe somebody ought to make me."

Salomé sighed. "Perhaps there's a reason no one ever attempts a coup in this misbegotten place."

That put a stop to the flying maybes. Arlie flipped Ken the bird behind Salomé's back. Ken responded with a double-fisted salute of his own. Salomé turned his attention back to Hiram's porch.

"Garcen, by all that's holy, I command you to come forth. Do not delay the inevitable."

"Fuck this," Ken said and marched to the flagpole. He grabbed the rock that had made Arlie forget about a steak. On the way back, he smiled at Salomé. "Here's how we get someone's attention in this misbegotten place."

Arlie didn't think a human arm could launch a rock that big, but Ken reared back and sent the stone sailing. It flew up and over the railing and crashed through Hiram's window, which exploded in a shower of glass and wood trim.

"Try yelling for him again," Ken said, brushing dirt from his hands. "I got a feeling he'll answer you now."

Garcen's response came immediately, accompanied by

a larger crash and shower of glass and wood trim. When Arlie regained his balance after jumping away from the debris, he saw the intruder's answer lying in the courtyard.

Hiram Fuchs wouldn't be joining his brethren in the Hall of Community Resources, at least not under his own power.

Arlie and Ken traded another look behind Salomé's back. Salomé walked to where Hiram had landed and examined the corpse. Hiram's head pointed ninety degrees away from his body; beyond that, he appeared uninjured.

"I didn't hear no snap," Arlie said. "He must've been dead before he fell. Right Ken? He must've been."

"Do I look like Quincy?" Ken replied. "The how or when don't make no difference. Dead before, dead after. Dead is dead and who gives a shit how."

Arlie figured Hiram probably gave a shit.

"Where's the rock-throwing sumbitch?" Once again, Garcen had the drop on them. Hiram's unexpected arrival had distracted them enough for the old coot to sneak out of the house.

"Which one of you two peckerwoods been chucking the boulders?" Garcen asked, leaning over Hiram's railing.

"That'd be me," Ken said. "Daddy always said I had a hell of an arm."

"Your daddy was right," Garcen said. "Although I expect he's spinning in the dirt right now from seeing you hooked up with this purple piece of shit."

"He might at that," Ken said. His right hand dropped to the butt of the Colt, but he didn't draw. "But that'd be between me and him and none of your goddamned business."

"Fair enough," Garcen said. "Let's just stick to current events then."

Salomé coughed, pulling Garcen's attention away from Ken. "If you've finished attempting to intimidate my associate, perhaps we can get to the meat of things."

"The meat of things? That's a funny way of putting it, considering what your boy's doing over there in the barn."

"Garcen, you of all creatures should know that one only does as one must. We do not choose our nature; we embrace it."

"Well, given what you've chosen to embrace over the years, I think it might be time to raise your standards a bit. Maybe one of them computer dating services or a 900 number."

Salomé's shoulders shook in silent laughter. "How is it that no one has killed you yet? How do you continually fritter away the tactical advantage of your remarkable stealth without someone exploiting your fondness for frivolous banter to end your miserable existence?"

"I don't know. Why don't you ask your asshole friend the one-armed bandit?" Garcen snapped his fingers. "That's right; you can't because I frivolously bantered his sorry ass into oblivion."

"I thought we were limiting our discussion to current events," Salomé said.

"Fine." Garcen pointed at Hiram's corpse. "That current enough for you?"

"By my way of thinking, the demise of this congregation's former leader was an unavoidable casualty. His removal, in both the literal and metaphorical sense, was assured the moment I encountered these two fine fellows. He shan't be missed; I doubt he possessed any unique skills."

"That's just one more thing you're wrong about," Garcen said. "He was very skilled at pissing me off."

"Don't most people have a similar effect on you?"

"No, most folks just annoy the hell out of me. If I threw everyone that annoyed me through a window, there wouldn't be a solid pane of glass anywhere in the state."

"Then I'll consider this unfortunate's proficiency in angering you a happy coincidence and move on to other matters, namely, your immediate departure."

"Have a care frilly-boy. I'm sure I could find another window that ain't been broke yet."

"Oh please." Salomé flicked his hand at the air. "Your

presence here irritates me, but you pose no threat. You may spend the rest of your days hurling bothersome buffoons through windows if it suits you, but other than some noise and a further decline in this compound's already deplorable aesthetics, you will have absolutely no effect on my campaign whatsoever."

"Then why are you in such a hurry to get me gone? Why don't you walk up here, whip out that fancy pig-sticker of yours and show me a little what-for?"

"Because to do so elevates you from an easily forgotten, momentary annoyance to an issue worthy of my attention, which you are not."

"That answers my second question but not the first. If I ain't worth paying attention to, why are we still talking?"

Salomé gestured to Ken and Arlie. "My subordinates feel ignoring you is somehow a dereliction of my duties. Rather than attempting to convince them of your utter incompetence, I've decided to take a proactive stance in hopes of mollifying their concerns."

"Geez, you sure do talk pretty now. Getting out on your own has done you some good. Makes me kinda glad I gutted that boyfriend of yours."

"Don't exaggerate your importance; there's no one here you need impress. Your participation in those events was largely observational. We both know who truly carried the day and I'm well aware of your disdain for dirtying your hands."

Garcen's eyes narrowed. "Well if your memory's that good and you're not worried about me, why ain't you worrying about those boys paying you a visit?"

"Why should I be concerned? Those 'boys' of yours? The Fifty-Five could not organize an afternoon tea in their present state, let alone hope to oppose me. They are in total disarray, most lost in petty bickering while the rest jockey to fill the vacuum left by your favorite. The watchers in deep shadow couldn't find their way out of the dark with a map and a flashlight, so don't threaten us with shades of their former glory."

Arlie watched that one sink in, but he didn't think it hit as hard as Salomé intended. The old man's face smoothed out and the hint of a smile pulled up the corners of his mouth.

"So much for current events," Garcen said, grinning. Arlie didn't care for the smile that went along with the statement. Salomé was too cocky to notice and Ken didn't care, but Arlie had survived a lifetime of grief by reading people, and Garcen was telling them more than his words revealed.

A quick glance confirmed Arlie's suspicions. Salomé and Ken were nodding to each other, each seemingly satisfied with the confrontation, ignorant of the danger Arlie smelled. He looked up to see if Garcen would say anything else.

"Shit," Arlie said.

The porch was empty.

"There," Salomé declared, directing Ken's attention to Hiram's house. "Does that alleviate your anxiety? Can we move past this crisis of faith and get on with matters of import?"

"I'm happy," Ken said. "What about you Arlie?"

Where had the geezer gone? Who were the Fifty-Five? What did Garcen know that Salomé didn't? Where the hell was Brenda with his steak?

"Yeah, I'm happy," Arlie said, swallowing the questions crowded behind his teeth.

"Outstanding." Salomé clapped. "I applaud your happiness gentlemen, for in truth it's all I require. Now, I would advise you to partake in whatever meager distractions present themselves, for I will soon require your services."

"Who we killing this time?" Ken asked.

Salomé laughed. "Nothing so bloody Mr. Chesterton, simply an errand. A vital errand, to be sure, but nothing more. I will have the details for you shortly, but until then, I do believe I sense the aroma of steak on the air. Enjoy gentlemen. Don't allow the ladies' hard work to go to waste."

A scream encompassed the compound, echoing from the Hall of Community Resources.

"How fortuitous," Salomé said. "It appears it is mealtime for everyone."

CHAPTER 8

The Colony's warnings sounded in Milo's head. One alley led into another darker and dingier passage. Sounds of footsteps echoed off the cinderblock walls as their pursuers matched their pace.

Still, Keith wouldn't stop talking about rubbers.

Their conversation hadn't started with prophylactics. The first topic for discussion after Keith picked him up for the drive to Huntington in search of Milo's missing *Darkwing* annual had been the results of Keith's Googling for suicidal teenagers.

"Your boy had a blog," Keith had said as Milo clicked his seat belt.

"I thought he had leukemia."

"He did."

"You just said he had a blog."

"He had one of those too, but it didn't kill him. Technically, the leukemia didn't kill him either, but that's not a mystery, is it."

"No, the mystery is what a blog is and why you think it's so important."

Keith grimaced. "How can you remain so technologically retarded in this modern age?"

"The six-pack didn't come with a geek." Milo tapped his forehead. "Ask me about Feudal Japan and I'll blow your socks off."

"We'll get to them in a minute."

"That sounds sufficiently ominous."

"Babe, we haven't even gotten to the ominous part yet."

Keith's definition of a blog triggered Milo's internal alarms, especially when Kimmy recalled her experiences with online journaling.

"Why would you write about personal shit on the internet?" Milo asked.

"That wasn't for me, was it?" Keith said.

"No, he's asking me," Kimmy explained.

"You Blogged?"

"It didn't have a fancy name back then, but a lot of kids kept an online diary."

"Wait a minute," Milo interrupted. "You just told me the other day you've been eighteen for twenty years. Now, I might be technologically retarded—"

"Which you are," Keith said.

"—but I know damned well there wasn't an Internet twenty years ago, so how the hell can you know so much about this blog thing."

Kimmy said, "I already said we didn't call it that."

Keith said, "Technically there was an internet twenty years ago, but there wasn't a World Wide Web, which gets a lot of people confused."

Milo exploded, causing Keith to swerve in and out of the passing lane.

"I swear to God I'm signing everyone up for an etiquette course. It's bad enough having six people fighting for a chance to speak; I don't need a seventh from the driver's seat."

"Funny you should mention a seventh," Keith said.

"Hold that thought," Milo said, waving a finger. "Kimmy, explanation please."

"Alex wrote a lot," she said. "Even before the accident. Fiction mostly, along with some poetry. After we got out of Ravenswood, he tried to start again, but he just didn't have it in him. He couldn't stop writing, but the stories wouldn't come."

"A real *klezmer* that one," Isadore said. "Ach, the *poezie* in his head. Given enough time, I think it would have made it out again, but…"

"But," Kimmy continued, "he didn't stop writing. He kept a journal."

"Online?" Milo still couldn't wrap his mind around the concept.

"People find diaries when you shove them under a mattress; ask any girl with a younger brother," Kimmy said. "For a while we had a social worker to worry about. Online was safer."

"How can something with worldwide access be safer?" Milo asked.

"Think strategically Milo," Tajiri weighed into the discussion. "Placing his journal on the web was anonymous. One grain of sand on a beach of billions. Hiding order beneath the cloak of disorder. Even if someone was to find it, there was nothing to connect it to Alex."

"Or us," Kimmy said.

"Let me guess," Milo said. "Sometimes you let Alex's fingers do the walking."

"While we did the talking? Yeah, every once in a while, but not all of us. Me and Mickey mostly."

"I prefer the *messages instantanée*," Etienne said. "I do so love chatting with *femmes crépues*."

"So let me boil this down," Milo said. "Alex blogged, Kimmy blogged, Mickey blogged and Etienne did God knows what. It's all out there for anyone to see, but it doesn't matter if anyone sees it because even if they do, no one will know who it belongs to."

"Unless they know what they're looking for," Keith said, a freshly lit cigarette clamped between his teeth.

"Oh Jesus, how did I know that was coming?" Milo muttered.

"Jared Cavalet had a blog," Keith said again, this time without interruption. "He'd been at it for a couple of years, mostly bitching about movies or pining after the cheerleader *du jour*. Then he got leukemia and the real bitching began. Not to speak ill of the dearly departed, but this kid whined like a pro, and really really really really didn't want to go gently into that good night."

"Who does?" Milo said.

"No one in my intimate circle of friends," Keith said, "but did you catch the fact that I said 'really' like a thousand times? I'm not much for dramatic hyperbole, but I'm telling you, this kid was determined."

"He found the blog?" Milo asked.

Keith nodded. "I think he found Alex's."

"Damn. I guess he was one hell of a beachcomber, huh Tajiri?"

Maria, not Tajiri, answered. "Things happen Milo. I know you don't believe it—"

"Don't say it Maria."

"—but things happen for a reason."

"Bullshit," Milo said. "Save it. What did he find Keith?"

Keith only stared, navigating with peripheral vision while fixing Milo with a stupefied look.

"What?"

"I don't know," Keith said, shaking his head and putting his eyes back on the road. "It still freaks me out when you get into a full-bore conversation with them. I don't even notice the shift anymore; if I'm not watching you, it sounds like the whole group's in the room with us. It's when I watch that I get freaked."

Milo sighed in agreement; he too paid little attention to the transitions. Whether silently or aloud, his communication with the Colony had grown almost too comfortable. When they spoke, he saw them. There was body language and facial expression to put with their words, even though their bodies were translucent and the words came from his own mouth.

But what surprised him most was how quickly he and Keith had accepted the situation.

"What did he find?" Milo asked again.

"I'm assuming he found Alex's journal," Keith said.

"There was a link embedded in Jared's blog, but it's dead now. From the references he made, I can't imagine it being anyone else's."

"But you can't be sure. You said the link's dead."

"Yeah, it's four-oh-four, but it's definitely your island Gilligan, down to the Professor and Mary Ann. Jared mentions Alex, Etienne and Tajiri by name and talks about something he calls the Silent Death, which suspiciously sounds like the Hippie."

"Totenstill," Trippenstein said. "It's actually German for 'dead silent,' but I like the sound of Silent Death."

"Tripp didn't come out much back then," Milo explained.

"Well, according to the Satan Beast's new boyfriend, he ought to consider staying in more often." Keith didn't speak again until they arrived in Huntington. Milo spent the remainder of the drive silently moderating the Colony's discussion about Jared Cavalet and Alex's journal.

They said nothing more about Emma, how Keith's cat had acquired a boyfriend or why it mattered.

The first hints of spring had brought the Marshall University students out of their housing and downtown Huntington bustled with cars and pedestrians. Keith made four circuits around the block, searching for a parking space close to The Comix Zone, their last resort for hard to find issues.

"Why don't we head over to Purple Earth," Milo asked as Keith began another trip up Twelfth Avenue. "He should have what we're looking for."

"Too close to Commerce Avenue," Keith said.

"And what's wrong with Commerce Avenue?"

"Ask the hippie."

Milo didn't get the chance. Trippenstein pushed past him, and as he did, Milo caught a flash of what the hippie was thinking.

Flashes of an alley. Dark. Dirty. Crowded with burned-out cars and abandoned shopping carts. Debris and waste lining a path to an improbably ornate red door set into a featureless wall shrouded in shadow.

"Exactly who is Emma paling around with these days?" Trippenstein asked, ignoring the scene at the forefront of his thoughts.

"I was wondering how long it would take for one of you to ask."

"We're asking now."

"No, *you're* asking, which makes sense given who came to visit me last night."

Milo shoved Trippenstein back with the rest of his passengers. "What kind of shit are you two getting me into now?"

"Let me get us parked first." Keith executed an illegal U-turn and slipped into the wake of a Minivan vacating a space with a full hour left on the meter.

Milo repeated his question to Trippenstein.

Let it go for right now, Trippenstein cautioned.

What's with the alley? Milo asked.

Let it go Milo.

Does Keith sound like he's going to let it go? He's been pissed about something since he picked us up.

The boy's been broiges *for a lot longer than that,* Isadore said. *He feels caught between you and your* froi.

"Sharon?" Milo said aloud. "What the hell does any of this have to do with Sharon?"

"We're going to talk about that," Keith said, wrestling with the steering wheel to align his car with the curb. "You bet your ass, we're gonna talk about that this evening."

I told you, Isadore said. *You don't live this long without learning things about people.*

"Fine," Milo said, ignoring Isadore's knowing smile. "Let's talk about it now."

Keith set the parking brake, switched off the car and climbed out.

"I thought you wanted to talk." Milo took his time getting out, not wanting to scuff the door on the asphalt.

"I do, and we will," Keith said, watching Milo's progress from the sidewalk. "I just want to make sure you don't screw up my car."

Milo pulled free of the Mazda and closed the door without a trace of sidewalk scrape. "So talk."

"Jared found Alex's blog," Keith said as they started the four-block walk to Comix Zone. "He didn't give a lot of details about what he found there, but he was very chatty about what he did with the information."

"Which was?"

"For one, you can consider the mystery of Crazy Amy solved."

Maria gasped. "Jared went to see her?"

"He visited the halfway house with a bullshit story about volunteering for a senior project and went straight for the girl with the shampoo deficiency."

"Why would he sic her on me?" Milo asked.

"I'm not sure he did," Keith said. "From what he wrote, I don't think Jared knew you existed when he saw Amy. He didn't get to you until after the JoJo anniversary."

"PageSmart," Milo said.

"Yup. Never underestimate the media's desire to milk a tragedy during sweeps. Munsch at PageSmart. Harold at Harriford's. And footage of you from both. Actually, it was a sweet piece of deduction."

"That's a bold statement."

"Hey, I'm just giving the kid his props. It took some smarts to add what he must've found on Alex's blog to some eleven o'clock highlights and come up with your sorry ass."

They crossed the intersection of Twelfth Avenue and Fifth Street, turning north to head toward Lincoln Place. A group of pierced and tattooed delinquents blocked the sidewalk fronting a bar, forcing Milo to step off the curb to get around them. Keith bulled his way through the crowd, earning several nasty looks and a few muttered threats.

As Milo hopped back onto the sidewalk, Keith stopped and turned to face the more vocal members of the clique. "Assholes," he said, tucking a cigarette into the corner of his mouth.

The posse's alpha stepped forward, smiling at the opportunity to elevate his position in the pack. Keith locked eyes with the hoodlum, slipped his Zippo out of his pocket, opened the lid and ignited the wick in one motion. Without blinking, he lit his smoke with one hand and flipped the kid off with the other.

The punk stopped, then back-stepped into the safety of his friends.

Message received.

"Way to go Constantine," Milo said as Keith returned the lighter to his pocket with a gunslinger's flourish.

"I pity anyone who fucks with me today," Keith said.

Milo laughed, stopping to watch the Colony slip through the subdued revelers. Even at a distance, Milo felt their wonder at the lengths people went to, to mutilate themselves in the name of expression. It was the ultimate choice of style over substance, Milo told them silently. Highlight the outside while the inside withers and dies.

Unfortunately, not everyone had Milo's perspective on the differences between interior and exterior.

Isadore paused to gawk at the intricate patterns of ink and metal adorning one delinquent's face. With a shake of his head, he tuned to rejoin the others, but was temporarily blocked by one of the pack Milo hadn't noticed before, one favoring layers of black over the minimal, gaudy coverage of his fellow drinkers.

His ghostly form passed through the man easily enough, but once free of the obstruction, Milo could feel the drain of Isadore's passage as easily as he saw it on the old man's face.

Keith was ready to move on. "If I could just find Alex's blog this would be a lot easier."

"Why can't you find it?" Milo asked, continuing to watch the man in black's reaction to Isadore. His head turned, neck cocking to the right as if he heard something he wasn't expecting. He rubbed his hands together, then down the sleeves of his leather jacket.

That was fremd, Isadore said, mimicking the man's

movements as he approached Milo.

I noticed, Milo said. *What happened?*

"I can't find the blog because it's gone," Keith continued. "No such user, no such page."

It's all farchadat. Isadore waved his hands in frustration. *For goodness sake, I walk through brick walls with less menie. This one* — he pointed behind him — *it's like walking through soup.*

The soup man caught Milo staring and his look of puzzlement transformed into one of recognition. This was enough to get Milo's feet moving again.

"You don't understand," Keith said, hurrying to catch up. "The internet's like an infinite landfill. Sure some stuff might disappear if you don't pay the bill, but this is free shit we're talking about."

"Maybe it's because Alex has been dead for over a year," Milo said. He risked a backwards glance and saw the soupy man in black speaking into a cell phone. *Shit,* he thought, a sentiment the Colony echoed.

"What, you think everybody in the world reads the Charleston obituaries? Uh-uh, no way. That shit's gone for a reason and the reason's not giving me a case of the warm tinglies."

Milo increased his pace and turned right when they reached Eighth Avenue. Once out of sight of Isadore's playmate, he stopped to lean against a building.

"What's with the turn?" Keith asked. "You've practically got us heading back the way we came."

"Isadore had a run-in with one of the guys outside the bar."

"A run-in?" Keith strolled back to peer around the corner. "How the hell does Isadore have a run-in with anyone?"

"That's what I'd like to know," Isadore said while Milo concentrated on catching his breath.

"Are we talking about the guy wearing more black than I own?" Keith asked.

Milo nodded. "Isadore said he felt something when he

walked through him."

"Felt what?"

"We're not sure," Milo said. "I felt it too. Kind of like having the wind knocked out of you."

"That can't be good."

"Trust me, it wasn't. What's he doing now?"

"He's yakking to somebody on the phone. I'm assuming that's not good either."

"Especially when you consider the fact he looked like he knew me from somewhere."

"Yeah, I'm gonna put that in the 'sucks' column," Keith said. "Who is this guy? Some jealous husband?"

"What did you just ask me?"

"Which word didn't you get?"

"I got all the words just fine, but that's not what you're asking me."

"So what am I asking you?"

"You know goddamned well what you're asking," Milo pushed off the wall, adrenaline counteracting the aftereffects of Isadore's encounter. "Where do you get off?"

"Where I'm getting off isn't the issue." Keith continued his corner surveillance, ignoring Milo's aggressive posture.

"I'm about three seconds away from having Tajiri kick your ass."

Keith looked at him long enough to raise his eyebrows and shrug. "Bring that chop-socky shit on," he said. "Your kung-fu is no match for my redneck-do and the roll of quarters in my pocket. No offense Tajiri."

"None taken Keith-san," Tajiri said.

"Well, I'm offended," Milo said, puzzled by Tajiri's lack of resentment. As a group, the Colony had no response to Keith's accusation, when they should have proclaimed his innocence.

Obviously, they understood something he didn't, which was nothing new.

"How could you think something like that?" Milo asked.

Keith turned, his eyes conveying a depth of emotion

Milo wouldn't think possible from The Hammer of Justice.

"Because the Milo I know wouldn't keep anything from his wife," he said.

"Which makes me an adulterer?"

"It makes you different."

"Duh."

"I'm just saying, if you're keeping the Colony secret…"

Milo finished his thought. "What else haven't I told her?"

"Exactly."

Milo chewed on that while Keith finally told him about Emma's new boyfriend. The story confused more than enlightened, but Trippenstein's frequent—and silent—exclamations of "shit" hinted at future explanations.

However, Stanley's final admonition didn't make sense to anyone, beyond Keith's interpretation, which the Colony finally corrected.

"Took you long enough guys," Milo muttered, smiling at the relief in Keith's expression.

"Then why was Stanley so concerned about your dick?"

"Maybe it gets lonely in his parents' basement."

Keith chuckled. "That's what I told him."

"As for the rest, Tripp?"

Trippenstein came forward. "You're sure it was him?"

"Given the fact that I'm still not one hundred percent on exactly who 'him' is?" Keith said. "Yeah, I'm pretty sure."

"Shit," Trippenstein said.

Keith stepped away from the corner, grabbing Milo's arm as he ran past. "Explain while we run guys."

"What happened?" Milo pushed Trippenstein back as they sprinted down Eighth Avenue.

Tires squealed, heralding the convergence of three black sedans at the intersection of Eighth and Davis. Twelve car doors opened in unison, disgorging a dozen ebony-clad men. Together, they started pounding the pavement toward Keith and Milo.

"That's what happened," Keith said, swerving left to cross the avenue. As they reached the opposite sidewalk,

Milo saw a dark corridor between the buildings and called "Alley!" Keith spotted the opening and dashed in.

"I've got it," Trippenstein said as Milo entered the passageway. The hippie spun Milo around and flicked two fingers at the way in. A shadow slid across the entrance, enveloping the alley in darkness seconds before the twelve reached it. Stumbling, Milo regained control and followed Keith.

"What happened to the light?" Keith asked, doubled over and gasping.

"Trippenstein threw a whammy at it," Milo said, for once happy about the Colony's prohibition against smoking. "Looks like it's blocked for the moment."

Keith slapped the back of Milo's head.

"What the hell-?" Milo cupped his wounded skull.

"That's the one thing Stanley said I totally understood. No more whammies. Whammies make noise, and in case you've forgotten, we need to make with the quiet right now."

"Make with the quiet?"

"Don't you think?"

"Dude, when did you start talking like Buffy?"

Keith grimaced. "About the same time all the agents showed up Neo."

That was fair. Hugging a wall, Keith led them through the alley, the occasional *bang* of shoe leather against trash can punctuating their passage.

"So much for quiet," Trippenstein said.

"Shut up," Milo and Keith said.

"I'm just saying I could shed a little light here and save your toes."

"My toes are fine," Keith said, just before another bang echoed. "Christ, Stanley was right about you."

"When did I become the major topic for discussion?" Trippenstein asked while Milo picked his way across a pile of debris. "I thought you guys talked about Milo's dick."

"Hello," Kimmy said. "Ladies present."

"What, you didn't know Milo had a dick? Do you and

Maria go on vacation every time Milo takes a leak?"

Milo climbed off a pile of broken pallets and crushed boxes and collided with Keith.

"Do they?" Keith asked.

"Do they what?" Milo said, using the wall for balance to step around Keith.

"You know, do they…leave the room?"

"Is this what you think about?"

"Not every day, but sometimes."

Whammy noise aside, Milo appreciated the darkness for hiding the blush he felt rise on his face. "We have so got to get you laid."

"Thanks for broadcasting it," Keith said, pushing past Milo to retake point.

As they approached the entrance to Seventh Avenue, the effects of Trippenstein's spell dissipated, allowing the fading sunlight to light the mouth of the alley. Keith motioned Milo to stay back, and risked a peek up and down the street.

"West is a no-go," he said, wiping his palms across his jeans. "There's a sedan at the end of the block. East looks better; we've got a two block cushion."

"Why not double back?" Milo asked, to Tajiri's immediate approval. "It's only a couple of blocks. We grab the car and—*whoosh*—we're gone."

Keith agreed, but before they could turn, Milo doubled over and a crash sounded from the direction of Eighth Avenue.

"They broke through," Trippenstein said, forcing the words through Milo's clenched teeth.

"That's why no more whammies," Keith said. "Looks like we're heading east."

Trippenstein's distress faded faster than Isadore's, letting Milo follow Keith across Seventh Avenue and down to Davis Street. A quick glance south decided their route; the trio of cars had become a single sentinel parked at the curb. The only open course was north to the river.

"So if you're not getting any strange," Keith said as they

reached the sidewalk on Davis, "why was Stanley so concerned about your johnson?"

"Maybe you heard him wrong."

"It's possible, but I doubt it. I tend to be very attentive to anything dick-related."

"Even when it's not your dick?"

"Empathy my friend, empathy." Keith checked left and right as they crossed Sixth Avenue. Their pursuers apparently had exhausted their supply of black sedans, but not personnel. Sentries in black loitered on the corners in both directions.

"Was Emma's boyfriend really that concerned about my works?" Milo asked.

"Unless you've started wearing rubbers someplace else, I'd say yes."

"Not to get too personal, but I haven't worn them anywhere for years. One of the benefits of marriage my brother."

"What about…the other thing?"

"Sharon's on the pill."

"Better living through chemistry. I can dig it."

The view at the next two intersections mirrored the previous crossings. They could move north on Davis unobstructed, but the other routes were blocked.

They're herding us, Tajiri said as they walked toward Third Avenue.

"Screw this shit," Milo said, stopping midway down the block.

"Damn straight." Keith dug in the pocket of his trench coat and pulled out the roll of quarters. "Let's party."

"Two on twelve? Are you out of your mind?"

"Who's calling who crazy?"

"I'm not talking about a fight. I say we pull a Houdini."

Keith rolled the quarters between his palms, bit his upper lip and nodded. "These were for laundry anyway. What's the plan?"

"The plan is we pull a Houdini. I supply the plan; you supply the details. It's your town."

"All right. Let me think."

Keith sidewalk danced for a full minute, sweeping his arm in an arc like an epileptic second hand. His finger settled on the dark space separating two buildings, he slapped Milo's arm and sprinted into the murk.

Milo followed.

"Maybe it was a stock tip," Keith said as they ran.

"Maybe what was a stock tip?"

"Stanley's thing at the end. Maybe he wasn't talking about your dick."

Tires squealed on Davis Avenue. Keith sidestepped left, leading them into a tighter passage.

"Somebody broke into your apartment just to give me financial advice? Doesn't seem too likely."

"And this does? Who knows; maybe Trojan stock is on the upswing."

Another gap appeared on the right. Keith disappeared through the opening. Milo slowed to take the corner, but Trippenstein screamed in his head.

Turn around!

Milo ignored the warning, even when the rest of the Colony joined in for the chorus. Whatever ground they had gained from the Houdini was dwindling with every step, but they still had a lead and Milo didn't want to squander it by stopping.

He followed Keith into the gap.

Every turn so far had led to a narrower space, one alley funneling into another, but now they stood in a large cul-de-sac, littered with trash and debris too wide to have passed through any of the routes leading in. It was a B-movie, post apocalypse set piece complete with burn barrels, rusted hulks of automotive corpses and the occasional flutter of paper.

And an improbably ornate red door set into a featureless wall shrouded in shadow, with one addition from Milo's vision.

"Is this Commerce Street?" Milo said, the question echoing throughout the chamber despite his whisper.

"Not without some Einsteinian nonsense," said Keith. "We didn't run *that* far."

"So there's more than one of these doors in Huntington?"

"I'm guessing so."

Trippenstein pushed forward. "There's only one of these doors anywhere, but it's not set at any one location."

"There you go," Keith said. "Einsteinian nonsense."

"What about him?" Milo asked, pointing to the only element missing from Trippenstein's memory.

One suggestion, Trippenstein cautioned. *Don't piss him off.*

A guard stood next to the door, the top of his head exactly as tall as the edge of the top rail. From where Milo stood, there didn't appear to be a millimeter of difference in height. The sentry wore a black tuxedo, complimenting the elaborate design of the door to his right. A matched set.

"Gentlemen," the doorman said, the cultured voice matching his couture but not his visage. He placed his palm on the door, which opened without a click and swung in without a creek. "Your party has already arrived and is waiting inside.

"Welcome to Club Scythe."

CHAPTER 9

Her husband was gone.

Sharon shook, chills traveling from the soles of her feet to the top of her head, independent of any temperature change or errant breeze. The knowledge of Milo's absence shook her like an explosion, so powerful she looked around to see if anyone else had noticed the force of the blast.

All was calm.

Her hour at the Information Desk had passed like the hours preceding it: quietly. Thursday nights typically did. A buffer between the frenzy of a new week and the celebration of the weekend, Thursdays offered little excitement beyond the appearance of the Special Order shipment and the ensuing commotion that accompanied its arrival.

Sharon folded slips as the printer spat them out, shoving each into their corresponding books. Customers familiar with PageSmarts' delivery schedule hovered around the desk like Koi waiting for a second-grader to twist another quarter in the food dispenser. It was a familiar dance, a comfortable component of most Thursday nights.

Right up until the time Milo disappeared.

She knew they shared a connection. Her husband's presence was constant, even when he wasn't close. Milo's aura—God knows she'd never use *that* word around Keith, but there was no other way to describe it—constantly enveloped her regardless of his physical location, just as it had from the moment they exchanged "I do's." The feeling was continuous, unvarying and like her eyeglasses, which over the years had progressed from an occasional convenience to an everyday necessity, she didn't notice her utter dependence on it until it was gone.

However, her reaction to its absence was more violent than the frustrated sound she made when she forgot her glasses in the morning.

To quell the spasm, Sharon dug her nails into her palms, chiding herself for momentarily crossing the mental Oogie Boogie Maginot line. A comics run to Huntington couldn't be termed a high-risk endeavor, even with Keith as a tour guide.

The printer had gone silent. A stack of order slips waited in the paper tray and Jimmy Capella, her Information Desk partner, stood staring at her.

"Are you all right?" he asked, hands frozen over the computer keyboard.

"I'm fine." She ignored the hole in her heart and mustered the biggest smile she could manage. Her low-wattage grin did nothing to alter Jimmy's look of concern.

"You don't look fine."

"But I am fine," she said, employing the maternal tone provided by her pair of X chromosomes. "Must've caught a chill, that's all."

Jimmy glanced at the entrance, watching patrons come and go through the double doors. "It's seventy-two degrees outside. How you gonna catch a chill?"

It's simple, Sharon thought. *Picture half of everything that makes you who you are vanishing off the face of the planet — no — vanishing from every realm of existence. Imagine something ripping you in two. Visualize the sun disappearing from the sky and tell me how you'd stay warm in the ultimate darkness.*

"Maybe the air conditioning kicked on," she said, pulling the sheaf of papers from the printer.

Jimmy grimaced, but went back to processing orders. The printer hummed in anticipation of more slips.

        M. Stephen Lukac

Sharon thought about Milo.

And a black hole in Huntington.

She'd read the accounts. People knew their loved ones had died before the phone rang. Twins experienced phantom pains that corresponded to siblings' injuries. Ghostly visitations in the middle of the night, the recently departed delivering messages from the great beyond.

Bullshit.

Her disbelief in things unseen wasn't in question. Her faith in faithlessness wasn't the issue. She couldn't divine Milo's status—either alive in this world or dead in the oblivion waiting beyond—but what bothered her more was the feeling that he had never existed at all.

She wedged a slip into the pages of an oversized art book and began to admire the cover: a mosaic of different paintings arranged to form the title and painter's name. The effect was subtle and required concentration...

Milo!

The chill threatened again.

She dropped the book on the counter, shamed by her distraction. Her husband was gone and she was critiquing dust jackets?

Husband?

There was a blast from the past. She hadn't thought about Roger in years, and although they had never married, he had wanted them to. Sharon shook her head, trying to dislodge the memory from her mind. Roger might have convinced her if he hadn't been such an ass about...

Goddammit!

Milo was her husband. Roger was a one-hit wonder from an early eighties retrospective; Milo was her husband. She pinched her earlobes, Milo's favorite trick to stay awake behind the wheel. She was never much of a co-pilot on long trips, falling asleep as soon as she buckled the seatbelt.

The pain pulled her back for a second, but she still teetered on the edge of the water, fighting the tide of forgetfulness. Sharon began to pray for strength, but stopped before invoking the Bastard's name.

There would be no help from Him. Other memories from the Roger era cascaded through her mind, reminding her why she'd never petition Him for assistance. He had His chance and He blew it. Fifteen years was long enough for her to accept she would never know the joy of a life cradled within her or the feel of a tiny hand wrapped around her finger. Time had taught her she was destined to grow old surrounded by casual friends and loyal co-workers, but remain alone within that circle.

But she wasn't alone. She had made a life for herself, with friends, co-workers and…and…

Milo!

It was as if the Bastard's hand had descended, wielding a swab of cosmic Wite-Out and eradicating Milo from the pages of her life. As seconds ticked into minutes and the coating dried, only a faint shadow of him showed through the whitewash. Sharon repeated his name, slurring one syllable into the next until the whispered mantra lost all meaning.

Milo. Milo. MiloMiloMilomilomilomilomilomilomiLomiLomiLomi.

"You say something boss?" Jimmy asked.

Sharon had to wet her lips before she could speak. "Something is the word for it. What were we talking about?"

"I dunno. You did some kind of shake and fade and then you started chanting about Chinese noodles."

"Chinese noodles?" She laughed. "What the hell was that about?"

"Maybe you're jonesing for some Lo Mien."

Lo Mien? No, that's not right. Not quite…

"Stop trying to make me hungry Jimmy. The last thing I need is more carbs."

"Carbohydrates never hurt anyone."

"Says the eighteen-year-old," Sharon said, feeling her tummy push ever-so-slightly against her waistband. "Dr. Atkins and the boys from South Beach would probably disagree with you."

Bullshit, Jimmy mouthed silently, exaggerating the word so Sharon could read his lips. "We've sold so many of those books that there shouldn't be one fat person left in Kanawha County, but they still keep coming."

Sharon wiggled her fingers at the teenager. "Keep typing Mr. Sensitive."

Jimmy turned back to the keyboard and muttered, "Now I'm hungry for Chinese food."

The pile of unprocessed orders completed its migration into three neat stacks of books just as Sharon's relief returned from his dinner break. She instructed Jimmy and Russ to start the notification calls and escaped the Information Desk to begin her nightly rounds of the sales floor.

Some customers welcomed her greetings and offers of help; others frowned at her salutations, as if she were condemning their marathon browsing sessions. Sharon let the dirty looks pass without comment, knowing the most offended would probably end up spending the most money.

She wound her way through the stacks, occasionally returning a stray book to its proper place. In the Relationships section, she *ahemed* at two ten-year-old boys eyeing the sex manuals on the top shelf. *Keep dreaming guys,* she thought as they scurried off. Sex wasn't a big deal once you were allowed to have it, assuming you could find someone to have it with.

Maybe she should have asked the boys if they had an older brother.

No amount of bumping and grinding could take the place of a solid career and a comfortable life. Sharon glanced at the top shelf as she passed. Why dedicate an entire shelf to something so pointless? She had heard her staff talking in the break room, trading stories of sweaty nights and bed-shaking climaxes, and wanted to scream at the waste of time and energy.

She had nothing against men in general, and, unlike

many of her female counterparts in the PageSmart organization, had no inclination to explore the alternative joys of Sapphic bliss. Everyone was excessively concerned with what happened below the beltline and no one she knew had an answer as to why. Sex was nothing but a distraction. Period.

Sex would only break her heart. Again. Exclamation point.

So, why did she find herself perusing cucumbers in the produce section with more than salad on her mind?

Question mark.

Sharon's wandering brought her to the front of the store. To her left, customers queued between stanchions waiting for their turn to check out. A quick calculation of number of items multiplied by average cost made her smile. Her monthly manager's bonus was assured.

To her right, the café was just as busy as the registers. Some couples drank frothy mochas and traded meaningful looks, but most patrons sat alone, flipping pages in between sips of coffee and bites of croissant sandwiches. Sharon felt her stomach rumble, from hunger, not from a yearning for companionship.

Deciding a latte might hold her over until the end of her shift, Sharon turned to enter the café, but stopped when she noticed the bulletin board hanging beside the entrance. A pin had fallen out and an announcement for an upcoming autographing hung askew, blocking part of the oversized sign welcoming shoppers to PageSmart.

Sharon hated that sign. She had hated posing for the official portrait almost as much as she hated the finished product. Posting her full name, phone number and email address next to her picture did nothing to further customer relations as the company intended, but instead acted as an invitation to every lonely Charleston male with a hard-on and limited dating prospects. Her voice-mail and inbox filled with tentative approaches and downright lewd propositions rather than legitimate complaints or—God forbid—praise for services well rendered. She had warned her District Manager that when they found her corpse floating in the Kanawha River, somehow that sign would be to blame.

He had laughed at the idea, and the poster remained.

"Excuse me ma'am," somebody behind her spoke as she reset the signing on the corkboard.

Sharon whirled around to find two good ole boys standing at parade rest.

"Didn't mean to startle you ma'am," the taller of the two said. He then tipped the bill of his John Deere cap, a touch of civility in stark contrast to his rough appearance.

The shorter man elbowed his gallant companion. "Cut that shit out Arlie," he said.

Arlie swiped at the other man's arm. "Just being friendly."

Sharon stifled a laugh. "Welcome to PageSmart. What can I help you gentlemen with tonight?"

Arlie straightened his posture at the word "gentlemen," returning the elbow as if to say, *See, it worked.*

"Ma'am," Arlie said. "Me and my associate here have come to inquire from y'all the details concerning the…the…" He looked at his friend, panic creeping into his eyes.

"Autographing," his friend prompted.

Arlie smiled. "Autographing! That's it. Me and Ken were coming to get the details of your autographing—" He looked at Ken for confirmation. Ken nodded. "—Autographing with that psychic fella on Saturday night."

"Jack Theodore? Certainly. What would you like to know?"

"What would we like to know?" Arlie repeated.

"Yes. What details did you gentlemen need?"

"What details did us gentlemen need?" Arlie parroted again, this time to Ken, not to Sharon.

"Asshole," Ken said. He gave Sharon an exasperated look. "We were just wondering if we needed to buy tickets or make reservations to see him."

"It's only a signing," Sharon said, pointing over her shoulder at the sign. "Mr. Theodore won't be doing any readings here. He's saving that for his seminar at the Civic Center Sunday night."

"He's signing books here and reading them there?" Arlie asked.

"I'm sorry," Sharon said, chuckling at Arlie's confusion. "He's not reading from his book. That's what it's called when he talks—" Sharon made quotation fingers in the air "—to dead people."

"He talks to dead people?" Ken asked.

"That's what he says," Sharon said. "Apparently a lot of folks believe him."

The men's reaction surprised her. Rather than the cry of bullshit she expected, the two nodded at each other as if Jack Theodore's claims of otherworldly communication made all the sense in the world. There was also an undercurrent of something else in the gesture.

"I'd advise you boys to get here early on Saturday," she said, wanting the pair gone. "We're going to have a big crowd."

"We'll be on time," Arlie said.

"We wouldn't want to miss anything," Ken added, which sent Arlie into giggle fits, and that earned him another elbow.

"You'll have to excuse my friend ma'am," Ken said. "He gets excited about…meeting celebrities."

"Yeah, excited." Arlie sniggered harder, rubbing the spot on his gut where Ken had struck him.

"I know what you mean," Sharon said. "Last year we had Gary Fox here for a signing and he…"

Gary pushes his chair back when the body hits the table. Alex jumps out of his chair and confronts the killer, but something from the right distracts them.

Not something. Someone.

He's a big man, with a look in his eyes that frightens and soothes her at the same time. The intensity in his glare pierces her skin and wraps around her spine, holding her up while every nerve in her body wants to send her to the floor in a dead faint.

The big man charges, until the killer downs him with a wave of his hand and she feels her heart break…

"He did what ma'am?" Ken asked, genuine concern in his voice.

That was a good question. Gary Fox's autographing had been a huge success, the biggest event PageSmart had ever hosted. The money had rolled in, thanks to not only Gary's mystery fans but also an unexpected influx of comic book readers recruited by…

…by…

It was there. The memory dangled at the back of Sharon's mind, daring her to snatch it at the apex of its pendulum swing. The night of Gary Fox's appearance wasn't something she'd ever forget. The author. The killer. Alex.

The confrontation that made no sense. Alex and Cecil Hawkins, squaring off and spouting nonsensical challenges in a multitude of cheesy accents. Cecil's escape and Alex's pursuit.

Alex's death.

But in between, after the face-off and before the chase, Alex had knelt beside her; left something in her care.

Something important.

"Ma'am, are you all right?" Arlie said.

"She don't look all right," Ken said, the concern gone.

Sharon's vision blurred. The good ole boys were fuzzier, and not because their beards had grown. Breathing was difficult. Someone had laid an opaque sheet over her face, dampening light, sound and oxygen. She wiped her hands across her face, trying to clear her senses.

"Maybe we ought to ask somebody else," Ken said.

Arlie shook his head. "Maybe we ought to get her some help."

The haze began to dissipate, allowing Sharon to understand their words, but not enough for her to respond.

"I don't think we have time for that," Ken tapped his wrist.

"We've got until Saturday night."

"No," Ken said, cocking his elbow. "We don't have time to get tied up with a lot of questions."

Arlie's head tilted, his ear almost touching his shoulder. Then, realization flooded his face.

The shakes hit Sharon again, with as much potency as they had at the information desk. She almost laughed as the fog lifted; she was having a seizure and Daryl and Daryl were discussing schedules.

"Maybe we ought to ask him." Arlie pointed past Sharon's shoulder at the bulletin board.

Was her picture that bad? Sure, her hair was longer than it had been, but *him*? Him? Why worry about sleeping alone when men couldn't tell she was a woman from a life-sized photograph?

So much for posting a profile at lonelyhearts.com.

Sharon turned to look at her manly portrait. She moved slowly, the spasms sapping any grace and speed she normally possessed. The Welcome sign she saw hanging sent a flood of adrenaline coursing through her veins, counteracting the shakes and dispelling the last wisps of miasma.

And she remembered everything.

CHAPTER 10

The door to Club Scythe closed behind them with a solid thud. Keith pirouetted in the narrow foyer, looking everywhere but down the stairway opposite the entrance.

Milo gambled on a look down the stairs and came up empty. The descent was too steep and long to allow any view into the chamber below. Except for three rows of polished black tile and a scattering of furniture legs, Milo couldn't tell what awaited them at the bottom of the steps.

The sentry—who Trippenstein had identified as Stone—wouldn't tell them.

After his greeting and invitation, Stone had stood as silently as his namesake, one arm holding the door and the other motioning for them to enter. Keith had tried every verbal gambit in his repertoire to no avail. Milo attempted to appeal to whatever sense of chivalry the tuxedoed guardian might possess with similar results.

One arm stayed on the door; the other invited them in.

Stone sniffed at them as they finally passed—the air passing through his wide, flattened nostrils at hurricane speeds—and laughed. Milo heard the low rhythmic thrum in Stone's throat as he crossed the threshold. Keith buried his nose in his armpits as the door swung shut, inhaling a dose of dried Right Guard.

Milo didn't bother to check his hygiene.

While Keith finished his inspection, Milo crouched.

Even with his head pressed to the floor, the architecture denied him a better view of whatever lay beyond the lowest step.

"We are never buying comics in Huntington again," Keith said. He leaned over the edge of the staircase. "It looks like a bar."

"Lot of trouble for someone just to buy us a drink," Milo said, rising.

"I don't think it's 'us' someone's interested in." Keith blew out a gust of breath and placed a foot on the first riser. "I'm betting you're the guest of honor and I'm back to playing wacky chauffer sidekick."

"It's a good character." Milo joined him on the stair.

"Always gets the best lines."

"But never the girl. Why do you think that is?"

Keith shrugged. "Probably because the wacky chauffer sidekick spends all his time covering the guest of honor's ass."

"Yeah, I'm the reason you never get laid."

"I find rationalizing my own deficiencies by laying blame at the feet of others a viable method of maintaining my fragile sense of self-worth."

"OK, now I'm really hoping this is a bar, because after that soliloquy I need a drink."

"Let's see who's buying."

As their descent revealed more of the chamber below, Milo experienced a rapid-fire series of déjà vu. Trippenstein's memories overlapped with his increasing view, allowing him a momentary preview of what the next step would reveal. By the time they reached the bottom of the stairs, Milo knew exactly where he was, but the knowledge didn't help him process the information.

"It's big," Milo said.

"No," Keith said. "The Astrodome is big. The national debt is big. My sister's ass is big."

"I didn't know you had a sister."

"I do and she's got a big ass. Not 'Jennifer Lopez back that booty up' big but 'Oh my God call Greenpeace cause

Shamu made another break for the beach' big."

"That's a big ass."

"That's one of the reasons I don't take her around making introductions. I like being The Hammer of Justice. I don't want people calling me 'the guy with the sister with the big ass.'"

"You really think people will call you that?"

"*I* call people that. Why should everyone else be any different?"

An answer didn't exist that wouldn't provoke a debate lasting until universal expansion reversed and existence collapsed, so Milo ignored the rhetoric. Trippenstein chuckled at Milo's metaphor; it was apt considering their surroundings.

The entrance to Club Scythe's main floor was an almost imperceptible arc, the apex of the open doorway protruding slightly farther into the lower foyer than the jambs. Dredging his memory for long-forgotten geometric theorems, Milo estimated the center of the club to be farther than they could walk in several lifetimes.

From the finite boundaries of the vestibule, Milo saw an ocean of black tile stretching to the limits of his peripheral vision. Large round tables created islands in the ebony sea, their lacquered finish reflecting light from no visible source and reaching to both horizons. No sign of the inner wall was visible, the interior too vast to allow examination from outside the circle.

Club Scythe: A claustrophobic's wet dream.

In tacit agreement, he and Keith stepped through the doorway simultaneously, and the neighborhood got a lot smaller, as if a reality drain plug in the center of the floor had opened and the universe contracted by several million light years.

Cavernous became cozy as infinity redefined itself in the space of a footstep.

A wooden podium stood just inside the entrance, manned by another tuxedoed employee. Lacking the imposing physicality of Stone the Doorman, the maitre d' compensated by projecting an aura of attitude that hit them with almost as much force as the realigned dimensions of Club Scythe.

Antonio—according to the polished gold nameplate affixed to his lapel—also seemed to have a nasal condition.

"*Dove siete stati? Nessuno mantiene l'attesa del signore Eleazar. Sapete costoso deve riservare l'uso riservato del randello?*" Antonio followed his sarcastic greeting with another deep sniff; whatever he smelled caused his face to collapse inward.

"*Bastardo!*" Etienne shouted. "*Non siamo cani da fischiare per né bambini per resistere al comportamento difficile di un lackey senza valore. Se i signore Eleazar sceglie aspettare il nostro arrivo, forse dovreste prendere che come segno della nostra importanza e vi comportate di conseguenza.*"

"What he said." Keith said, mirroring Milo's look of surprise at the torrent of Italian unleashed by the Frenchman.

Antonio effortlessly downshifted from combative to haughty. "*Benissimo, benissimo. Lascilo mostrarvi i signori alla vostra tabella allora.*"

"We'll find our own way," Milo said, precisely following Etienne's silent prompting, down to the finger snap under the maitre d's nose and the offended stomp into the body of the club.

"Rock on Frenchy," Keith muttered as they left Antonio in their dust.

"Forgive the intrusion," Etienne said, more to Milo than to Keith. "I simply cannot abide boorish behavior."

"From anyone but you?" Milo asked.

"*Exactement.*"

Keith laughed. "I didn't realize you spoke Italian."

Etienne exerted enough control to wink Milo's eye. "The bohemian is not the only one with hidden talents. Thankfully mine are more suited to polite company and do not make with the—how you say—bang so much."

"This kind of bang we can live with." Milo scanned the club for their host.

Heads up, Trippenstein directed Milo's eyes to the left. *I think we've found Eleazar.*

The stations constituting Club Scythe's perimeter sat atop rounded daises, low tables half-circled by a high-backed, padded bench. Two brass rails separated these booths from the tables on the main floor, keeping Mr. Eleazar safe from the common patrons, although Milo couldn't imagine anyone *common* frequenting Club Scythe.

Eleazar sat alone, a grey slash bisecting the bench. Thinner and paler than seemed healthy, their host barely covered the gap in the upholstery. Eleazar craned his neck to watch them cross the floor and raised a skeletal hand in greeting. Two sentries with fashion sense similar to the chase team on the streets stood at the ends of the bench, and at a lower table on the opposite side of the rails, two men and two women spoke quietly while passing sheaves of paper between them. Milo and Keith bypassed the support personnel and approached Eleazar's table directly.

"Milo!" Eleazar called as they stepped onto the dais. "Have a seat, have a seat. You've brought company. Fine, fine. Good, good."

Eleazar kept his place in the center of the bench, forcing Milo and Keith to sit on either side, uncomfortably close to Eleazar's bodyguards.

"A drink, a drink," Eleazar said, and the paper chase at the lower table paused as one of the men tripped over his feet racing to the bar. "We'll have you fixed up in no time, no time."

"That's not really necessary," Milo said.

"Nonsense, nonsense. What are we, barbarians? Negotiations are easier with some lubrication."

"So is cornholing," Keith said, nodding at the guard standing at his left shoulder.

Milo cringed, but Eleazar clapped. "A good one, a good one. Now I see why you associate yourself with him." He swung a bony finger at Keith like a metronome. "Funny man, funny man."

Eleazar's finger stopped in mid-wag and his nose

crinkled. He leaned to his left. Keith duplicated the movement, but the bodyguard at the end of the bench blocked him. Eleazar stretched, nearly burying his face in Keith's sleeve, and sniffed.

"Not good. Not good," Eleazar said, returning to an upright position and shifting a bit towards Milo.

"What is with you people?" Keith asked. He turned to Milo. "Do I need to change deodorants?"

"Not that I've noticed," Milo said.

"It isn't your odor I find offensive," Eleazar stated. "It's the stench of the company you keep."

Milo pressed his palms on the table and tensed. Eleazar might not like the way Keith smelled, but the jibe seemed aimed directly at him, and he wanted to be ready to bolt. Trippenstein told him to calm down; he knew what was coming.

"You've had a visitor," Eleazar said, ignoring Milo for the moment.

"I have lots of visitors," Keith replied. "I'm a sociable kind of guy."

"You need to exercise more discretion in who you allow across your threshold."

The penny dropped. Keith flicked his gaze away from Eleazar and looked at Milo, who finally took the hippie's advice and relaxed.

Slightly.

"The Watcher walks where he will, leaving the deep shadow to intrude where he is not welcome. Am I right, am I right? He bullies his way in and involves himself in things that are not his concern." Eleazar tapped on the table. "This is how things used to work, but not any more."

Their drinks arrived. Milo dipped his upper lip into the glass, letting the clear liquid moisten his suddenly dry mouth. Keith snatched his glass without looking and downed the drink in one gulp, slamming the empty tumbler down in front of Eleazar.

The Hammer of Justice was in the house.

"Listen Buckwheat. If you've got a nasal problem, get

some spray. Buy a case and share the cure or don't invite us back. If you've got a problem with who parks it on my couch, talk to my cat. She's the one who let the son of a bitch in, in the first place."

Silence hung between the three; the bodyguards and pencil pushers ignored the outburst. Somebody deposited another drink in front of Keith, who sipped this one, waiting for their host to respond.

Eleazar pivoted to face Milo. "You choose your friends well."

"It wasn't a big catalog," Milo said, dodging the kick Keith fired under the table.

"Very good, very good." Eleazar folded his hands in his lap. "You must understand, I know of this man, and his arrival never brings glad tidings."

Ain't that the truth, Trippenstein told Milo.

"I've never dealt with him directly," Eleazar continued, "but a man in my line of work hears things."

It was apparent that Keith's visitor wasn't the main topic of this meeting, but since Eleazar had broached the subject, Milo figured a little probing couldn't hurt.

"While we're on the subject of Stanley, maybe you could clear something up for us."

"Stanley? I know no Stanley."

Keith tugged at his shirt and snuffled loudly. "Stanley?"

It took Eleazar a second to make the connection, but once he did, he laughed louder than Milo thought possible for someone so thin. The bodyguards and pencil pushers joined in; the apparent humor in the name overcoming any sense of discretion.

"Oh, how far the mighty have fallen," Eleazar said, wiping tears from the corners of his eyes. "Tell me Milo, why would you concern yourself with such a has-been?"

Milo deferred to Keith, who surprised him by recounting the details of Stanley's visit without adding any sarcastic editorial comment. When he repeated Stanley's cryptic warning, Eleazar sat up and turned to Milo.

"This puzzles you?" he asked.

"It puzzles the hell out of me."

"Understandable. Understandable, given your lack of experience in these matters.

"You'd be amazed by the level of experience I have at my disposal," Milo said, winking at Keith.

"Not at all Gatherer," Eleazar said, studying Milo's expression as he dropped his information bomb. "Your scent may be different, but I recognize it as well."

Milo pressed his lips together, hoping his face didn't betray the volume of the variations of "holy shit's" bouncing through his brain at the revelation.

Unfortunately, Keith didn't possess the same restraint.

"Holy shit! Put it on a billboard, why don't you."

"Keith…"

"No, I'm serious. Rent yourself a big one out on I-64 and tell the world. The way things are going, pretty soon Sharon'll be the only person left in West Virginia *not* to know about the Colony."

"Can we please save this discussion for another time?" Milo asked. "I don't think this is a good place to be airing family laundry."

Eleazar—who had followed the exchange like a Wimbledon spectator—looked at Keith, who held up his hands in resignation.

"Fine. Whatever." He shook his head and went back to his drink. "I'm sorry to have interrupted."

"Not at all. Not at all," Eleazar said, beaming. "This is quite entertaining, if a bit off-topic. Please feel free to continue if you'd like."

"I think we've finished for now. Isn't that right Keith?"

Keith planted an elbow on the table and slowly extended his middle finger.

Eleazar applauded.

"Excellent. Excellent. Such a show. I salute you, gentlemen. You've taken what could have been a tedious negotiation and turned it into quite the party. Let me repay your generosity by clearing up your confusion concerning this

Stanley's remarks.

"I'm surprised you fail to see the warning here, but not overly so. By virtue of your recent immersion into all things arcane, you've attempted to ascribe obscure meaning to a relatively straightforward message. Sometimes, my friends, a hot dog is merely a hot dog and a donut nothing more than a donut. Don't let the opening of your eyes to all things wild and wondrous blind you to mundane — but still important — truths."

Milo mulled this over, especially the hot dog/donut analogy. Relieved of its Oogie Boogie context, the equation wasn't difficult to solve.

"Sharon and I are going to have a baby?" Saying it aloud propelled the concept from the hypothetical to the real, causing Milo's throat to close and choke off his air supply.

"Mazeltov!" Eleazar toasted Milo's deduction. Isadore silently echoed the blessing, followed by the rest of the Colony. Keith mirrored Milo's reaction: mouth hanging open and eyes wide from oxygen deprivation.

"Another surprise," Eleazar said, chuckling. "And more entertainment, to be sure, but close your mouths boys. Mrs. Tucker's gestational status isn't anything to be concerned with at present, at least not because of your visitor's intrusive recommendation."

A pinpoint opened in Milo's esophagus, allowing the most rudimentary vocalization. "Sharon. Baby. Father? Me?"

"But perhaps not for years," Eleazar cautioned. "This Watcher — this *Stanley* — is more problematic than the rest of his meddling crew. Timewalkers always are. Spend enough time darting between seconds and you're bound to spread some confusion where it's not warranted."

Timewalker? Trippenstein sighed in his skull, but the word made sudden sense to Milo. Fears of unexpected fatherhood melted away as he suddenly understood something Keith had told him earlier.

Stanley had claimed to know him, or — more specifically—to know what he looked like. Milo couldn't remember meeting anyone clothed in shadow who favored neon contact lenses, but that didn't mean he wouldn't meet him one day. Trippenstein tried again to warn him off the subject, but confirmed the validity of his hypothesis.

His meeting with Stanley hadn't happened yet.

"You understand," Eleazar said, correctly interpreting Milo's expression. "I also see that comprehension doesn't bring you the comfort you believed it would."

"It's a little hard to accept," Milo said. "But it makes sense."

Eleazar nodded. "The truth usually does." He laid his hand on Milo's forearm. "The truth is hard, it's never fair and no matter how badly we say we want it, we rarely appreciate it once we possess it."

Milo pulled his arm away, scratching the skin Eleazar had touched. "You're just Mr. Sunshine, aren't you?"

"Not for many years now."

Another look—this one bristling with concern—passed between him and Keith. As Milo's nails raked the flesh of his arm, he noticed Keith scoot farther down the bench, less worried about the bodyguards than his proximity to Eleazar. Milo scraped harder, wanting the feel of Eleazar's hand obliterated from his memory.

Their host noticed the reaction and laughed. "Relax gentlemen, relax. There is nothing preventing me from enjoying the light of day. I simply prefer to conduct my business under cover of night."

Keith didn't look convinced, but Milo stopped gouging his arm. If a double carotid cappuccino was Eleazar's goal, he wouldn't have wasted so much time on small talk. Besides, given the opulence he'd seen, Milo felt certain there were at least a couple of pints of O Negative in the Club Scythe wine cellar. Whatever Eleazar was, he didn't appear to be one of *those*—assuming *those* even existed.

It was time to get off the list of "nots" and start filling in the "am" blanks.

"I appreciate the information," Milo said, "but why

 M. Stephen Lukac

don't we get to why we're here."

"I agree. I agree. We'll have plenty of time for meta-physical discussion and 'getting to know you' later. Let's get to the meat of the matter. Let's—as they say—talk turkey, as long as you don't think the phrase means I consider myself a Thanksgiving feast."

Eleazar directed the last at Keith, who began to extend his middle finger until Milo waved him off.

"Milo," Eleazar said, "I am a wealthy man. I've accu-mulated more money than I can ever hope to spend and gathered—pardon the pun—enough power to enforce my will anywhere I choose. Money and power: the two most valuable commodities. They feed off each other. You'd think one would shrink as the other grew, but that's not the way it happens. After so long, the two lose any semblance of separation and become nearly interchangeable. What money can't buy, power provides, and vice versa."

He shook his head. "Forgive the lecture, but I want you to understand that I have no reason to hide anything from you, as you'll soon see.

"'Alexander looked out upon his empire and wept, for there were no more worlds to conquer.' I understand how he must have felt. Here we sit, at the center of worlds, our destinations limited by only our imagination. The whole of existence lies just beyond that threshold, and it's still not enough."

Milo watched Keith turn to stare at Club Scythe's foyer, and smiled at the wide-eyed wonder painted across his friend's face. One benefit of Milo's yearlong tumble down the Oogie Boogie rabbit hole had been the expansion of the Pridemore Panorama, opening doors the conspiracy buff had never known existed.

Dark clouds and silver linings.

"Think about it," Eleazar continued. "I have everything I'll ever want, except the time in which to enjoy it. I can walk any street I choose and be just as secure there as I am in my own home. No one would be foolish enough to harass me and even if he did, he'd not live long enough to regret his action. I have annoyances, not enemies. Save one."

"You can't take it with you," Milo said, beginning to suspect the purpose of this audience.

Eleazar nodded. "Even my resources have limits, and believe me, I have exhausted them all. I don't accept defeat—a man in my position dare not—but I had begun to consider the reaper's touch an unavoidable conclusion to all I had achieved."

"Until?"

"This bookstore. This PageSmart. Out of nowhere, this shop becomes a nexus of pain and suffering, bodies dropping as if from the sky."

"Two bodies don't constitute a nexus," Keith mumbled.

Eleazar waved the protest away. "The constant media attention to this book store reminded me of a truly horrid book I once read. I can't recall the title, but it concerned a wealthy man who, forced to confront his impending demise, wagered on the validity of reincarnation and placed all his assets into a trust payable only to his reborn self, as proved by a series of seemingly insurmountable tests. The story reeked of machination and contrivance, but I couldn't help sympathizing with the protagonist's dilemma."

"Hell of a lottery to play," Keith said. "What if he came back as a cockroach?"

"Exactly. Exactly. However, once my memory of the book resurfaced, I couldn't rid myself of it. What if the hypothesis had merit? What if I could guarantee myself another lifetime to enjoy the fruits of this one?"

"I don't see you as a man who puts much faith in 'what if,'" Milo said.

"I don't," Eleazar said. "Fortunately, another option presented itself, thanks again to the incidents at PageSmart. I discovered you."

"And that helps you how?" Keith asked.

Milo already knew the answer.

"It's simple Mr. Pridemore. I want Milo harvest me."

CHAPTER 11

Keith didn't want to witness a Tucker fight-a-palooza, and he was reasonably sure Milo didn't want an audience for his verbal ass kicking, but Sharon made it very clear that any attempt on his part to escape the apartment would result in an ass kicking of his own.

As Milo should have known, a Sharon Tucker ass kicking — verbal or physical — was something to avoid.

As he cowered in the kitchen, safely removed from the escalating crossfire, the adage "be careful what you wish for" flashed through his mind like a cliché ticker. There was no way for Milo to avoid looping Sharon into the Gatherer information stream now that she had finally — *finally* — confronted him about the constant flow of weirdness invading their lives, but Keith wasn't feeling any better about the impending disclosure.

After hearing Eleazar's plan, Keith wasn't feeling good about anything. The kid with leukemia, a buck knife and a jones for eternal life had been creepy, but West Virginia's answer to Al Capone had driven the sinister pointer right off the goddamned scale, and that wasn't an admission Keith liked to make to anyone.

Milo hadn't reacted at all to Don Cornholio's proposal. As Eleazar laid it out chapter and verse, Milo sat still, unaffected by the list of preparations and compensation. When one of the suited bean counters joined them at the table,

Milo glanced at the contracts placed before him, but made no comment.

Eleazar and his goons had taken Milo's silence as acquiescence, but Keith knew better. He believed Milo's only concern was getting them out of there with their skins—and souls—intact, something Milo confirmed once they were back on the road to Charleston.

More than that, he wouldn't say.

Keith didn't mind the silence. They'd already resolved the important issues of the evening, and while the Eleazar situation would bear further discussion, there was time. The old man had looked…well *old*, but it wasn't as if he was going to die tomorrow. The Eleazar Colony application could be backburnered until a later date, and as long as Milo didn't drop any hints about a future rejection, Eleazar's assumption of acceptance would keep most of the major immortality-seekers off Milo's back. Any serious players with designs on the open slot would catch a whiff of Eleazar and opt for the Ponce de Leon route. It wouldn't stop everyone—assuming there were more industrious or crazy kids out there with a terminal diagnosis and formidable Google skills—but Milo and the gang could handle anything short of a major Oogie Boogie offensive.

What he couldn't handle, even with the assistance of the Colony, was the unleashed wrath of Sharon Tucker.

"What the hell have the two of you gotten into now?" Sharon had screamed as they entered the apartment. She was good; she'd waited until they were both inside with the door closed behind them.

"Hi honey," Milo said, attempting to defuse the bomb by ignoring its existence.

Good plan, Keith had thought, *but it's never gonna work.*

"Hi honey my ass," Sharon yelled, cranking the volume way past ten. "I want some answers, and nobody in this room's gonna have any peace in their lives until I get them."

Milo walked into the storm, but Keith had reached back and turned the doorknob, hoping to slip out before the tsunami washed over him.

That didn't work either. "Keith, if you don't let go of that door, switching hands in mid-stroke will no longer be an available option."

The vulgarity of the threat scared him more than the threat itself; Keith was a confirmed righty. If Sharon was willing to break out the genital arsenal, there was no escaping her onslaught. Better to settle in and ride out the storm.

The kitchen made an acceptable shelter.

"Jesus, Sharon, what's wrong?"

"Where were you?"

"We went to Huntington. You knew we were going to Huntington."

"For comics?"

"Yes, for comics. Why else would we go to Huntington?"

Bad move Milo, bad move. Keith couldn't see Sharon's face, but he knew she'd be looking at Milo's hands. She probably reached out, took both his hands in her own, gently turned them over and back again before slamming them down with enough force to dislocate Milo's shoulders.

"Ouch!"

"Where are your comics Milo?"

Busted.

"The comics?"

"Yes. The comics. Oh wait, I'm sorry. They're not comic books any more, are they. You have to call them funny books now. Keith calls them funny books, so you have to call them funny books too, because God knows you wouldn't want to anything Keith didn't approve of."

Keith frowned. "You two know I can hear you, right?"

"Keith Pridemore, the last thing you want right now is my complete, undivided attention."

"I'm just saying," he muttered, occupying himself by reprogramming the clock on the Tuckers' coffee maker.

"The comics are in Keith's car," Milo said, too triumphantly for Keith's taste.

"Keith," Sharon called, poisoned honey dripping from every word. "Be a dear and go get Milo's comics out of your car."

"I'm not allowed to leave the apartment."

"I'm making an exception."

"I'm fixing the clock on your Mr. Coffee."

"Keith..."

"I've temporarily lost the feeling in my legs."

"Keith!"

"I'm fully exploring the potential of my other hand."

"You get any spooge on my counter and I'll kill you."

"No spooge, I promise."

How had Milo kept the BIG secret for a year when he couldn't lie his way out of a comics' run with no comics to show for it? Now, he felt bad for his earlier suspicions. Not because of the hurt in Milo's eyes at the accusation, but because of his stupidity in believing Milo had any real skills in the deception department.

"Keith doesn't seem willing to go get your comics."

"Well, if he's really doing what he says he's doing, I'm kind of happy about that. Aren't you?"

"Then I'll go get the comics. Keith, switch hands for a second and toss me your keys."

"Sharon, would you please tell me what's wrong. *Please*. I can't fix it if I don't know what's broken."

Keith nodded, pleased with the tactic. Mr. Sensitivity beat Mr. Denial every time.

"You want to know what's wrong?"

"I really do."

"Fine. Tell me where you were."

"We were in Huntington. I already told you that."

"While you were in Huntington, did you suddenly fall off the face of the planet?"

Keith stopped punching the "set minutes" button, chilled by Sharon's question.

Einsteinian nonsense.

Milo laughed. "Not that I know of."

"Would you have noticed it if you did?"

"I think so."

"You do?"

"I really do."

"Then you're wrong."

"How am I wrong?"

"We don't have enough time to cover the first page of that list, so let's limit ourselves to discussing the error in your belief that you'd notice if you fell off the face of the planet."

"Sharon, what the hell are you talking about?"

Keith heard a sniffle, followed by the sound of hands hitting clothing. Sharon's next words were slightly muffled.

"I called your mother. At eleven o'clock at night, when I know your mom never stays up past ten. But she was awake tonight. She was drinking tea and smoking. She didn't tell me about the smoking, but I could hear her through the phone."

"Mom started smoking again?"

Keith heard another slap.

"Would you just listen to me? Your mom was up because she had a dream."

"A bad dream?"

"A nightmare. She dreamed one of her sons drowned in the pool."

"What? Which one?"

Another sniffle. "Paul. He fell off the diving board, hit his head and drowned."

"I remember when that happened, but I pulled him right out of the pool. He swallowed a little water, but he wasn't dead. Not even close. Paul isn't dead. I mean, he isn't, is he? Jesus, Sharon, if you're trying to tell me that something happened to Paul..."

"Paul's fine. Your mom got off the phone with him just before I called."

"Thank God for that."

Mr. Coffee's clock blinked its displeasure at Keith's inattention, but he was busy tracing timelines in his head.

He knew the story about Paul Tucker and the diving board. Everyone knew the story. There wasn't an entry in the Tucker history he didn't know. Everyone who knew a Tucker knew everything about the Tuckers, a family of natural storytellers. The diving board anecdote usually served as an explanation for some mindless idiocy perpetrated by the youngest Tucker sibling and Paul gave the family plenty of reasons to revisit the moment. Keith ignored his memories of possible head injuries and brain damage to consider the what-ifs.

"OK, now we know why my mother was upset, but you still haven't told me what's wrong with you."

"I called Keith's mom too."

"You did what?" Keith said, rushing out of the kitchen. Milo and Sharon were on the couch, their earlier, aggressive postures abandoned in the face of maternal nightmares.

"I called your mom too," Sharon said, wiping her eyes.

"Is she all right?"

"She's fine. A little shook up, but fine."

"Let me guess: she had a dream too."

"She said she did. She said she dreamed about taking her daughter on a picnic." She leaned forward far enough to punch Keith's arm. "You never told me you had a sister."

Milo pulled her back. "It's a big ass thing honey. He doesn't like to talk about it."

"So my mom dreamed about a picnic. What, were there mutant ants or something?"

"Nope, just her, her husband and her daughter. One happy family, eating Colonel Sanders and chasing butter-flies."

"What's so upsetting about that?" Milo asked.

"I wasn't there," Keith said.

"So? You must have missed a couple of picnics here and there."

"That's not what I mean." He knelt in front of Sharon. "It was after, wasn't it?"

Sharon nodded. "When she woke up, she was crying,

and at first she didn't understand why. Then she realized it was because she dreamed you never were born, and she didn't even miss you. She said it felt so real, more real than any dream she'd ever had. It was as if someone plucked you out of her brain and put you back again."

More Einsteinian nonsense.

Keith stood and walked to the sliding patio door. He needed a cigarette, and ever since Milo had been riding the wagon, he'd taken to blowing smoke out the open door. An empty gesture, but at least he was making an effort.

Milo was smart enough to connect the dots, and even if he couldn't work the crayon, the hippie could.

"Milo, your mom said the same thing." Sharon was crying again. "She said Paul died in the pool, but she still had George, and that was some comfort. You never saved Paul because there never was a you. But then she woke up, and everything was back the way it belonged."

"She wasn't sleeping," Keith said, watching smoke drift through the screen. "Neither was my mom."

"I know," Sharon said.

He heard Milo shift on the sofa. "How do you know?"

"I know because I wasn't sleeping either." The couch springs creaked as Sharon bounced out of her seat and paced through the living room. "I know because I'm in love with my idiot husband and am somewhat fond of his equally idiotic best friend. I know because something ripped both of you out of my soul and then put you back without even a 'pardon me.' Now you're here and everything's all right, but I still remember what it felt like without you and I can't fool myself into believing it was all just a fucking dream."

"Honey—"

"Don't 'honey' me Milo. Either you tell me what happened to you tonight or I swear to God I'm walking out that door."

"Sharon!"

"We were at a bar," Keith said. He regretted usurping Milo's chance to do the right thing, but he'd regret hearing the door slam more. Milo heard her threat with a husband's ears, years of intimacy cushioning the force with which she spoke. Keith, as the recipient of many ultimatums, heard the conviction behind it. Hearing the warning during its empty, half-hearted, build-up phases added to his understanding. Sharon had reached the critical mass he'd warned Milo about, and was seconds away from a marital thermonuclear meltdown.

"We were at a bar," he repeated, staring at his reflection in the sliding door. "It wasn't a titty bar, and we never meant to go there, but that's where we were."

"Don't try to confess his way out of this Keith. You can't cover for him anymore."

"*Shut up!* One time Sharon. Shut up and listen." A dangerous gambit away from PageSmart, but he hoped the harshness would shock her into giving him enough time to explain.

"We went for comics, but got sidetracked. There's a man in Huntington that wants something from Milo and he wasn't letting us leave town until he told us what it was. He corralled us into a place I had heard rumors about, but I guess the rumors were true."

Keith turned in time to see the light bulb flicker to life above Milo's head.

"That's why it looked so big from the outside..." Milo began.

"And not so big once we were in," Keith finished the revelation. He stepped in front of Sharon. "I think maybe we did fall off the face of the earth, or maybe stepped off is closer to the truth, and when we did, reality *whooshed* in to fill the gaps. Eleazar called Club Scythe a nexus. All of a sudden, I don't think he was being poetic."

Sharon raised both hands, shoving her open palms in Keith's face. "I don't want to hear any of this Oogie Boogie nonsense."

"Sharon, you just had a close encounter with this Oogie Boogie nonsense," Keith said, grabbing her hands and pulling them to his sides. He half-expected Milo to jump him for laying hands on his missus, but he pressed on. "I know you think I'm full of shit and I'll admit, most of the time I usually am, but this isn't one of those times."

Anger wrestled with heartache for control of her eyes; the tears streaming down Sharon's face came from both combatants. Keith swallowed his discomfort at witnessing the battle. He'd seen Sharon cry before; they'd been friends for a long time.

He'd never been the cause of her tears.

"Tell her!" he yelled over his shoulder, realizing Milo would never have an opportunity like this again. As much as she was fighting it, their temporary disappearance had opened Sharon's mind, plowing her mental field sufficiently to allow the idea of the Colony to take root. After a night's sleep and time to rationalize the experience, the window would close and explaining Milo's condition would be ten times harder.

"Not now," Milo said. His husband hat was firmly in place. His shuffling feet telegraphed his desire to swoop in and embrace his wife. Explanations could wait.

Except they couldn't, and Keith wasn't the only one who knew it.

"My name is Maria." The voice was high, crisp and clear. It startled Keith, accustomed as he was to hearing the Colony speak in whispers.

Milo's fidgeting had stopped; now he stood still, hands clasped at his waist. There was no anxiety in his appearance; even his features were softer, a glimpse of what a Tucker sister might have looked like.

And the eyes…the eyes were enough to melt a man's heart—a disquieting discovery for a man to make about his best friend.

"I was born in 1670," Maria continued, "the fourth daughter of Edward and Sarah Goodspeed. We lived in Salem Massachusetts. In 1692, the Court of Oyer and Terminer condemned me for consorting with Satan and sentenced me to death when I would not confess and repent. Only the kindness of an itinerant friar saved my soul from being consumed along with my flesh, and he nearly paid for his generosity with his own life."

"What the hell…?" Sharon muttered, transfixed by her husband's "performance."

"*Shhhh*," Keith hissed. "Let her finish."

Maria smiled at his intervention, a hint of Milo evident in the gesture. "Over the years I spent with Friar Adsel, I learned the size of his heart was only surpassed by the size of his mind. The Lord had blessed him with the ability to gather departing souls unto himself, prolonging their chances to accomplish what circumstance had denied them. Friar Adsel was a Gatherer, Sharon, as is your husband."

"My God Keith," Sharon said as Milo's body shuddered from Maria's departure.

"I know," Keith said.

"Holy shit!"

"I know."

Sharon whirled to face him again. "Milo's lost his fucking mind."

"No, he hasn't."

"He hasn't?"

Keith shook his head. "It's whacked out, I know, but it's for real."

"Honey?" Milo's voice cracked, a sure sign of a Colonist coming fully forward.

Sharon crossed the room. "Milo, what's going on?"

"I always meant to tell you, but a part of me never wanted you to know."

"Know what?"

"This." He slapped his chest. "What's happened to me."

"What *has* happened to you?"

"Oh, for chrissakes, quit your bitchin' already."

Milo's stance shifted as the words passed through his lips, the unmistakable voice of Trippenstein taking its turn at the microphone. Sharon jumped back, startled by the exclamation.

"Hi Sharon, I'm Trippenstein. Mystical protector,

watcher in deep shadow, yadda yadda yadda. Sorry to butt in like this, but your hubby's pissing me off, and discretion's never been my strong suit."

"Ain't that the truth," Keith said.

"Quiet you; I'm talking to your partner here."

"Must you make everything a spectacle?" Tajiri interrupted. "Is this how we wished to be introduced to Mrs. Tucker?"

"*Oy vey*, such *geruder* in front of the *froi*," the Hebrew contingent weighed in.

"I think I liked it better when he was hiding," Kimmy said.

Etienne completed the chorus. "I'm surprised he stayed hidden for so long. *Egads, quel moi.*"

Sharon clamped her hands over her ears, but the Colonists argued on, oblivious to the nervous breakdown happening in front of them. Keith saw her knees begin to buckle. He caught her just as her legs gave out. He lowered her to the floor, preparing to unleash a shit-storm of his own.

Milo beat him to it.

"Enough!" Milo's voice sliced through the disagreement as he reestablished control over his passengers. Kneeling next to Sharon, he looked at Keith, who saw a rainbow parade pass across his irises. The Colony had stepped back, but not by much.

"Don't," Milo told him, fanning air on Sharon's face.

"I was just—"

"I said 'don't.'"

"Don't you think—"

"It was my decision," Milo said, his jaw clenched with the effort to keep the volume down. "My decision. Not yours, not theirs. Mine."

"Looks like it got made for you," Keith said.

"I know." Milo's shoulders sagged. Whether because of resignation or exhaustion, his aggressiveness vanished in the space of a sigh.

As he ran his fingers through Sharon's hair, his face

showed Keith something he hadn't seen since Alex Harrison's death: Milo was afraid.

A single tear rolled down his cheek. "Now, the decision's hers."

CHAPTER 12

While he enjoyed the advantages of a partner as psychically powerful as The Baptist, Salomé never failed to remember that today's benefit could quickly turn into tomorrow's detriment.

Heaven help him should he ever forget.

The full moon shone through the window of his appropriated bedchamber. The unfiltered glare annoyed him; the previous occupant had failed to accent the room with even the most basic treatments. The lunar sentinel bathed him in a palette of ivory radiance, mottling his flesh with the dappled projections of the imperfections in the glass. He felt a phantom burning where the light touched his skin, as if the pale reflection of hydrogen fire could sear him from 93 million miles away.

A brilliant reminder of the dangers of distance.

Salomé dressed, ignoring the rustles coming from the other side of the bed as his latest conquest did the same. She finished quickly; it took little time to wriggle into a simple housedress and plastic sandals. As he buttoned his shirt and fastened his cuffs, Salomé smiled. Plain wrappers often hid the most delicious treasures.

Such was the unexpected delight of this backwards community.

Alas, none of the other males had possessed the latent talent of Lincoln Hackendorf, but one had to anticipate bumps on an unknown road. The brethren were plenty and time was short, so conservation wasn't an issue. If The Baptist chose to consume all the chattel at hand, their impending delivery would render any argument against excess moot.

Once fueled by a suitable source, his companion might occasionally venture forth on his own, restoring a portion of Salomé's privacy, sorely absent since the beginning of their association. It wasn't that Salomé didn't enjoy the companionship—like-minded colleagues with similar objectives were rare—but The Baptist's constant mental and physical presence tired him more than he had anticipated.

Moreover, a ten-foot voyeur stationed in the corner did little to enhance his amorous mood.

Give me what I need and you'll be shut of me.

The words trickled into Salomé's mind, borrowing his tone and tenor to deliver The Baptist's demand. This was the true power of the behemoth's gift: recipients of his attention "heard" him in their own voice, colored with their perception and delivered in a manner consistent with whatever internal narrator naturally resided in their subconscious.

The Apostles' gift to an infinite degree.

The plea was tiring as well. The Baptist's gift of mimicry didn't extend to an equal proficiency in comprehension. The filters ran in only one direction, which led to numerous misunderstandings and Salomé's heightened sense of caution with his own thoughts.

"If I wanted shut of you, be assured I'd have taken steps long before this." Salomé preferred to speak aloud when communicating with The Baptist; it helped keep his mind focused, and when dealing with someone powerful enough to split the planet in two, confusion wouldn't do at all.

You seek solitude. You wish me gone.

"Dear boy, my desire for an occasional moment alone shouldn't be taken as an attempt to sever our partnership."

The creak of bedsprings pulled Salomé's attention to the opposite side of the mattress as Annabeth Garrison's housedress slid down her exquisite form, covering the tender morsels he had spent the afternoon devouring. The loose-fitting shift concealed her swollen bosom and rounded hips, completing her transformation from wanton slave to dour housewife.

The dress also covered the bites, bruises and scratches.

If Annabeth noticed his one-sided conversation, it didn't seem to bother her. Perhaps her apathy stemmed from the aftershocks of her climaxes, a series of orgasms powerful enough to soak the sheets of their stolen rendezvous. Annabeth's unexpected enthusiasm had fueled his ardor, which in turn sent her into higher states of physical ecstasy. Eventually, their assignation had moved beyond simple copulation, cascading into a battle where each spasm from one triggered an answering paroxysm from the other, building until they both lay spent in a pool of their mingled fluids.

If such was the influence of his gargantuan associate, Salomé would never allow the affiliation to end. Perhaps he should purchase a leash.

The female pleased you?

Salomé laughed. "Pleased me? The female carried me to the precipice of Nirvana and threw me over the edge. The female drained me to the point of such utter dehydration that I feel the need to consume an ocean merely to replenish myself. Yes my friend, the female pleased me."

Annabeth remained immune to his praise, standing still and silent beside the bed.

"Now, send her away."

Where shall I send her?

"Wait!" Salomé held up a hand to forestall The Baptist's action, the vagueness of his request guaranteeing an ignominious end to the evening's diversion. After surrendering her body with such abandon, she didn't deserve a destination determined by a casual lack of specificity coupled with The Baptist's questionable interpretation.

"Let her rejoin her flock of cackling hens. I'm sure there are victuals to prepare, clothes to mend or some such menial labor. She's performed well today; let's not consign her to some remote corner of Hell as a reward."

As you wish.

Plastic footwear scuffed the bare floor as Annabeth shuffled out of the room. Salomé waved goodbye as the door closed behind her, his memory of their congruence fading to a pleasant trace of musk as her footsteps echoed down the stairs.

"Now, on to business." He stood, tugged at his cuffs and walked to the window to survey the activity in the compound below. Other than Mr. Chesterton and Mr. Garrison, the visible population skewed to the feminine demographic, interspersed with youth of both genders. The men remained sequestered, vertical cordwood awaiting their turn to fuel the psychic fire of The Baptist's belly.

While the children threw balls and chased each other in pointless pursuit, the women meandered about the dooryard in groups of two and three, circling Chesterton and Garrison in orbits of potential servitude. Mr. Chesterton busied himself with the maintenance and polishing of his father's firearm, shooing away the occasional offers of food and companionship like a horse swatting at flies. He had yet to sample the benefits of his ascension to Salomé's lieutenant.

Nevertheless, he would.

Mr. Garrison was more predictable in the satiation of his appetites. Gastronomic gratification overshadowed his forays into physical pleasure, but Salomé had seen him—on several occasions—scamper off with a woman for a discreet taste of forbidden fruit, only to return and attack his food with renewed gusto.

Foolish man, Salomé thought, to covet your neighbor's bounty while ignoring the feast on your own table. A vision of Annabeth writhing beneath him caused a stirring in his loins. He forced the memory away.

"Mr. Garrison seems to be enjoying his new station," Salomé mused, turning from the window.

The other worries me. His mind is resistant. His will, formidable.

"He's a cunning one; that much is certain."

He may yet challenge you.

"I think not. That which concerns you is precisely what ensures his loyalty. He's seen the price of treachery and washed his hands in the rebellion of others. His will to survive will counteract any thoughts of revolution. Trust me; Mr. Chesterton is ours for as long as we require him."

And after that?

"After that, we shan't require anyone but ourselves. Once we've dealt with this bothersome issue of your constant feeding, the masses will fall over themselves in their desire to serve."

My needs are a bother?

"Only in the strategic sense. Don't be offended, but it's nearly impossible to develop any long-term tactics when your need for sustenance remains so unpredictable. It wouldn't do at all to mount a major offensive only to have you puttering out at a decisive moment."

I don't putter.

"It's not a criticism, only a statement of fact, a situation I've gone to great lengths to rectify."

A great bother. . .

Was that an attempt at humor? In all their months together, never had The Baptist shown even the slightest glimmer of wit. Perhaps their connection wasn't as unidirectional as he believed.

"Have a care my friend. You're beginning to develop a personality."

Perhaps my lack of charm is merely a reflection of your banality.

Sarcasm as well? How delightful. Moreover, his vocabulary had increased. Here was an unforeseen improvement.

The flooring groaned as The Baptist moved from his corner and lumbered toward the door.

"Where are you off to? Shall I accompany you?"

That won't be necessary. I require more…sustenance.

"Then let us be off. I've had my eye on a donor who should prove quite helpful."

I will choose my own food.

The Baptist's arm rose from his side and blocked Salomé's path to the door. Somehow, this display of independence didn't satisfy him to the degree he had anticipated; it began a wave of trepidation sufficient to burn away the remnants of his earlier pleasure with Annabeth.

"I will leave you to it then."

Salomé reached under his arm, pushed the door open and stepped aside. The Baptist squeezed through the opening and began the slow walk along the hall and down the stairs. Salomé walked back to the window, troubled by the exchange. Ignoring the view of the compound, he focused instead on his faint reflection in the glass.

The image failed to comfort.

The lavender and lace he once thought resplendent appeared ridiculous projected against the distant trees visible through the window. Could this be how others saw him? Could the corporeal version of this spectral apparition inspire anything but derision? How would he project strength if he couldn't stomach his reflection in the palest mirror?

Salomé turned away, then back far enough to glimpse himself in the farthest reach of his peripheral vision. The altered perspective changed nothing. Laughter bubbled in the back of his throat, restrained only by his rapidly dwindling ego.

Garcen's words crawled through his mind, elbowing his fading confidence aside as he sank lower into despair. Confronted now with the old man's point of view, his dismissal grew teeth and bit deep. Errand boy? Sycophant? Here was the proof. Staring him in the face. Confronting him eye to eye.

Garcen had been right.

There was still time. Time to discard the foppery. Time enough to escape the confines of The Brotherhood compound and disown this pathetic endeavor. Time enough to jettison this futile attempt at dominance and avoid the fate of his former master.

Wait.

Was that all this was? His memories were vague, but the accompanying dread still resonated. Had his one-armed mentor's defeat scarred him so much that megalomaniacal ambitions were his only avenue toward healing? Was he so anxious to evade obscurity that he'd risk everything on an ill-conceived play for ultimate power?

Had his effort to escape the destiny he'd witnessed caused him to duplicate it instead?

Salomé dashed away from the window, covering the room in hurried steps. He bounced from bed to bureau, from closet to door. No destination drove his pace, only motion mattered. Stopping would allow the baggage trailing him to slam into his back, burying him under the accumulated weight of so many failures.

Purpose could wait.

As his frenzied motion throughout Hiram's bedchamber mocked the chaos in his mind, a separate chord began to resonate in his skull. At first soft, the discordant note throbbed in time with his hurried steps. It grew louder as his speed increased, overwhelming cognitive function and then, as the beat reached its zenith, usurping even the autonomous flight response that had set his feet in motion.

Laughter.

The syncopated chortle filled his mind. It ricocheted along his spine, freezing his limbs with an abrupt spasm. There was no defense against the hilarity. His bones vibrated from the echo of it.

Then, it stopped.

Salomé's muscles collapsed as the paralysis dissipated. He sank to the floor, lowered by unseen hands as gentle as the unseen voice had been harsh. Lying prone on the unfinished floor, Salome shook as his body shed its accumulated tension.

I have found suitable food.

The Baptist's voice flooded Salomé, revealing the source of his doubt and panic.

Now you understand the strength of bothersome needs. Now you see the power of proper sustenance.

He struggled to his knees; the force of The Baptist's intrusion prevented him from rising fully.

Your fears are well founded, but misplaced.

He crawled back to the window and pulled himself up to the sill.

Do not fear repeating the mistakes of your former master. Fear repeating your mistakes as a servant.

In the compound below, his minions moved as they had before.

My minions. My followers. The first of many. The first of all.

Salomé tried to focus his will, his unsteady hands beginning to trace sigils in the air.

No parlor tricks will change your station.

His elbows slid off the windowsill. No, not slid—they were pushed. His chin caught the edge of the frame as he fell.

The floor is where you belong.

"Let me up!" Salomé screamed, wincing from both the pressure on his back and his whiny tone.

You will be my voice. My face. You will be my herald and deliver my bothersome demands to the masses. Anything else you achieve will be through my good graces.

"No." He pushed against the floor, straining to rise. He would not play the lackey again, subverting his own desires for the accomplishments of another.

You will.

The invisible weight slammed between his shoulder blades again. He spread his arms out to alleviate the strain. Unwillingly prostrate, he thought about nascent priests receiving Holy Orders.

An apt metaphor.

Holy Orders…Yes, this is fitting. Lie still, and receive my communion.

The weight on Salomé receded slightly, concentrating itself at the small of his back. As he raised his head to refill his starving lungs, the force burrowed into him and raced up his spinal column, exploding in his mind like a thousand claymores.

Psychic shrapnel pierced every neuron of his brain, flooding him with the agonies of every victim The Baptist had ever claimed. Colliding visions of violent death arched his back in empathetic pain as he relived the ends of scores of lives and the unexpected horror of continued existence in the gullet of their executioner. The gastric torture of slow digestion merged with psychic violation, extending the trauma of dissolution until the absorbed entity fractured in a shower of damnation.

There *were* things worse than death.

You will serve me, The Baptist commanded as the tide of atrocity slowed. *You will serve me, by choice or by fiat, but you will be of service.*

I leave it to you to decide the manner of your fidelity.

CHAPTER 13

Famous authors almost never came to Charleston.

They might pass through the city, speeding along the Interstate as they traveled to warmer climes and bigger gigs, but they never stopped for a visit. Regardless of how many dollars publishers might collect from the sales of their books, the creators didn't find it necessary to pause long enough to press the flesh and scrawl their names.

For years, West Virginia was absent from publicity itineraries. All that changed when Gary Fox came to town.

Fox didn't have an annual spot reserved at the top of the New York Times Bestseller list, but he had a recognizable name, an impressive backlist of solid work and—most importantly—a small but rapidly growing group of enthusiastic fans, thanks in part to his work in comics. Prose readers didn't seek out Fox-penned funny books on the strength of his name, but comic's fans bum-rushed the Mystery shelves once Fox established his bona fides as a writer possessing what Keith termed "chops."

Milo had discovered Gary Fox with his first novel, a mid-list offering with a minuscule print run buried in PageSmart's Mystery section. Because of her husband's enthusiastic praise, Sharon had convinced Keith to order additional copies of *Losers*, and hand selling had accomplished the rest. When *Weepers* came out the following year, Charleston had an audience primed for a new Gary

Fox release, this time bolstered with more copies and better promotion. Even Keith joined the Fox Fanatics, but only after the author "made his bones" during a multi-issue, mega-crossover *Darkwing* event.

The men in her life were such boys.

Sharon wasn't so naive to credit Milo with jump-starting Fox's career, but she used the story when she asked his publisher to include Charleston on the *Vital Statistics* tour. Maybe the anecdote persuaded the folks in New York; maybe it didn't, but shortly after the publisher announced the list of cities, she received an email from Fox saying he couldn't wait to meet her husband.

Of course, the Tuckers hadn't heard from the author since Cecil Hawkins dropped a dead midget on the auto-graphing table and asked Fox to sign him.

That fiasco had given authors another reason to avoid wild, wonderful West Virginia, and they stayed away en masse, until Jack Theodore, Psychic Extraordinaire.

Keith directed an army of booksellers around the signing table, trying to meet the specifications demanded by Theodore's advance team. Sharon watched the activity from inside PageSmart's Feature Room, Milo's traditional post during an autographing. Milo fidgeted beside her. She didn't know whether his nervousness came from her invasion of his space, or was a remnant of the previous night's revelation, but she didn't care either way.

She wasn't letting him out of her sight until she under-stood everything about this "condition" of his.

"Keith needs to leave those guys alone," Milo said.

"Yeah, that's going to happen." Sharon reached over and grabbed Milo's hand. "Stop picking."

"Huh?" Milo shook free of her grip and looked at his fingers. The skin around his nails was raw and bleeding in a few places. "I didn't realize I was doing it."

"You always do it," Sharon said. "*Pick, pick, pick.* It's all I hear."

"Nervous habit."

"A messy one too."

"They're not bleeding that bad."

"I'm not talking about the blood. Look at your pants."

Milo looked down and brushed flakes of dead skin from his slacks. "Yikes."

"That's what I'm talking about."

"Is it always this bad?"

"Do you know how many pounds of dead skin I've vacuumed out of your chair over the years?"

"That would be a yes then?" The *pick, pick, pick* started again, even as he denied it.

Sharon slapped his hands apart. "Stop it."

"Sorry." He slipped his hands into his pockets, which at least muffled the sound of the tic.

Sharon sighed, tired of dancing around the elephant in the room.

"This is where it happened?" she asked.

"Which 'it' are you referring to?"

"You know damn well what I mean."

"I'm just trying to narrow it down."

"Milo..."

He turned to face her and leaned against the window. "This is the window where that woman died."

"That's not what I—"

"And isn't that the same table Cecil dropped the body on?"

"I think so, but that's not what—"

"So you'll admit more than one 'it' happened here."

"I swear to God Milo, you'd better stop cross-examining me."

"I'm not cross-examining you; I just want to understand the question."

"Fine." If he thought he was going to avoid the discussion by starting a fight in public, Mrs. Tucker's oldest son hadn't been paying attention for the past decade. "Isn't this where Alex dumped a head full of dead people into your skull before running off to get killed?"

Sharon winced at the volume of her voice, magnified by the inevitable timing of yelling just when all other noise had stopped. Keith raised his eyebrows, silently pleading for them to hold the drama until after the signing. She nodded and he went back to bullying the staff.

"Theodore's people have him all worked up," Sharon said. "I should be helping."

"Then go help." Milo crossed his arms. "I'm fine."

"I would, but this is more important than some puffed up celebrity with a ghost-written bestseller and besides, you don't really want me to go."

"I do so want you to go." He glanced at her without moving his head. "That is, if you really think you should."

"Ah-ha," she exclaimed, shaking a finger at him. "You don't want me to go."

"I didn't say that."

"But that's what you meant." She mirrored Milo's pose. "Take it from someone who's pulled that trick more times than she can count."

"Am I really being that pathetic?"

"I wouldn't call it pathetic. I'd call it finally learning something. Maybe next week we'll work on color-coordination."

"All right, but if five guys in a Denali pull up to our apartment, I'm making a break for it."

She wrapped her arm around his waist and rested her head on his shoulder. He pulled her close and kissed the top of her head. She breathed him in, letting his familiar scent wash away the apprehension she'd felt since meeting his new crew.

No, that wasn't right. He called them a Colony.

"So how does this work?"

Sharon felt him tense and tightened her hold. The physical contact soothed her; she hoped it would have the same effect on him.

It did.

He murmured in her hair. He talked about Alex, told her about the seven souls he had carried in his mind and how six of them now resided within him. She watched Keith as Milo spoke about Cecil, who he called a Hunter, and how his gift was similar to, but less than, Alex's own. Keith stopped haranguing the staff and watched her as she listened to Milo recall the day in Harrifords when Tajiri defeated Cecil, who wasn't really Cecil, but Harold Washington trapped in Cecil's body.

The confusion she felt must have registered on her face, because Keith nodded sympathetically, shrugging his shoulders in classic Pridemore style.

Her mind created faces to go along with each passenger Milo described, bodies to house the skills each entity possessed. Sharon felt her eyes fill as Milo talked, realizing she would never look at her husband the same way again, never see him without seeing the other six her imagination had created.

What did that mean for them?

There was more. What had happened at the mall the previous Christmas; the nagging gaps from Bullseye; why Jared Cavalet killed himself and what he was begging for as he died, and finally, Eleazar's proposal.

It was too much to process. After spending a year worrying about the changes in Milo, finally having the answers did nothing to ease her mind. Aside from the metaphysical nonsense—which she still hoped could be explained by some kind of chemical imbalance—there were simpler, yet more troubling, issues to work through.

Her insecure husband had never kept secrets; the confident Milo had a trunk full of them. His general dissatisfaction made their marriage the one successful aspect of his life; the content Milo had six strangers—six dead strangers—to thank for his new, positive outlook.

How could one wife compete with the intimacy provided by six, two of whom were women? One woman wasn't enough; Milo had to have two, and from the sounds of it, one was barely out of her teens?

Sharon gasped, pulling away from Milo as she connected the sexual dots.

"That's how you got so good in bed?" Another verbal explosion at exactly the wrong time. This time, everyone working the autographing table turned, wry smiles decorating their faces.

"Honey, *shhh!*" Milo reached for her, but she shrugged him off.

"*Shhh* my ass. What exactly have those two bimbos been teaching you?"

"Excuse me Mrs. Thing, but I am not a bimbo." The feminine voice coming from Milo's mouth, accompanied by a change in his eye color, destroyed any thoughts of a drug-induced return to normalcy.

As did Sharon's response. "I'm not talking to you, you little tramp. I'm talking to my husband." *Oh God*, Sharon thought. *Now I'm talking to them.*

"Kimmy, please." Milo's voice sounded normal, and his eyes were brown again.

Only for a second. "I'm sorry Milo, but that's so not fair. I'm a virgin, remember?" Milo's head twisted to face her and his eyebrows raised. "Or at least I used to be before Mrs. Happy Pants here."

The corners of her husband's mouth curled and Sharon reared back to slap the smirk of his face. Her face. Dammit, men didn't have *that* look in their repertoire. This was a woman's look, a prelude to an estrogen-fueled battle royal.

She hoped the passengers felt pain.

Her hand never moved. Keith had grabbed her from behind and pinned her arms to her sides. This was a picture she wanted for the Christmas cards: Keith preventing her from smacking Milo, who stood waiting for it, fists planted on cocked hips. *White Trash Seasons Greetings from the Tuckers.*

The eight of us.

She shook Keith off her back and Milo grimaced, obviously forcing the *child* back onto whatever mental street corner she worked.

"This isn't over bitch," she whispered, staring through Milo's eyes to address the competition.

Milo blinked and looked over her shoulder at Keith. "Still think it was a good idea to tell her?"

Sharon turned to her boss. "Yeah Brainiac. I'm not done with you either."

Keith raised his hands and backed off. "Easy. I don't want a piece of this."

"You've already got a big piece of this." Sharon and Milo said in unison.

Keith smiled. "At least you're still working on the same wavelength." He slipped between them and threw his arms over their shoulders. "Group hugs people. We've got company."

"Group hugs are the least of my worries," Sharon said through clenched teeth.

"Sharon, it's not like that." Milo leaned in front of Keith, but Keith pulled him back.

"Save it for later kids. Our celebrity has arrived."

The clapping began in the back of the store and moved toward the front as Jack Theodore and his entourage walked through the stacks. By the time the group reached the signing table, the applause sounded like thunder.

"He looks like he's twelve," Sharon said when the author slipped behind the table.

"Probably writes like it too," Keith said, frowning as Theodore climbed onto a chair to wave at the crowd. "What a poseur."

"Good evening Charleston!" Theodore yelled over the din, which rose in response to the greeting.

"Gary Fox didn't act like this," Milo said.

"Gary Fox was too busy hiding under the table," Keith replied.

"He had reason to."

"I'm not fronting the brother," Keith said. "I'm just saying."

The cheers died down as Theodore continued to gesture. When they faded to a few hoots, he cleared his throat.

"I'm very happy to see so many of you out here tonight. Before we start signing, I just wanted to tell you how much I appreciate all your support and just what it means to all of us on *Crossing the Threshold*. Thanks to you, our show's one of the highest rated independent productions in syndication history and we'll be expanding into twenty new markets before the end of the year."

"I can't believe people actually watch this shit," Sharon muttered.

"Be nice Sharon," Keith chided. "That asshole's making us our bonus for the month."

"Oh great. We're taking money from stupid people. How can anyone believe Dennis the Menace really talks to dead people?"

"It's hard to say what people will believe," Milo said, not directing the comment to anyone. "People tend to believe exactly what they want to believe."

"Bullshit," Keith countered, keeping the happy manager's smile firmly in place. "He's an Oogie Boogie wannabe, raking in millions from his bullshit television show and his bullshit book."

"That's a lot of bullshit," Sharon said, watching Milo's expression change in rapid succession. She guessed at the cause. "What do the experts say?"

Milo gave her a look, but at least it was one she recognized. "Trippenstein tends to agree with Keith, which is surprising on one level, but not so much on another. He says it doesn't take much to fool people looking to get fooled, whatever that means. The others are just enjoying the show."

"I'll bet they do that a lot," Sharon said.

"Shhh!" Keith warned. "His highness is talking."

Theodore waved the crowd to silence again. "Don't worry about how far back in the line you are. We're staying until everybody gets what they came for. Just remember, no readings tonight. There are folks here who'll give you a request form if you want one, and I promise to review every single one of them when we get back to the office."

"There you go." Keith gestured at Theodore. "No readings tonight folks. Can't do my shtick without a net."

"One last thing," Theodore said over the chorus of disappointment. "I want to thank our hosts for tonight. Where are Kevin and Sheryl?"

Keith rolled his eyes. "He's a real prince, isn't he Sheryl?"

Sharon huffed. "He sure is Kevin. What an ass."

They untangled themselves from Milo and stepped forward, raising their hands to a smattering of appreciation from the crowd. Theodore turned on his perch and waved at them, seemingly surprised at how many people stood behind him. He scanned the group in the feature room, spreading fake smiles and half-hearted waves among everyone, until he looked at Milo.

Theodore's manager and publicist managed to catch him as he fell off his chair.

"That was good," Keith moaned, motioning for his booksellers to start the line. "Not dead midget on the table good, but pretty damn close."

"What happened?" Sharon asked.

"I'm not sure," Keith said. "Maybe someone with an ego that big shouldn't try to balance himself on a wobbly chair. I'm just glad he didn't break his neck."

"Yeah Kevin. That would be a real tragedy."

"Shut up Sheryl."

Sharon expected Milo to double over laughing at Theodore's impromptu pratfall, but he hadn't moved. He stared at the table, eyes locked on the clumsy psychic.

She followed his gaze and saw Theodore staring back. His handlers continued to set open books in front of him, which he signed with three distracted slashes, all his attention focused on Milo.

"What the hell?" Keith asked. "He's gonna piss these people off if he doesn't turn his ass around."

"Why's he watching Milo?"

"I don't know."

"I think I do," Milo said.

Keith executed a series of double takes, watching the two men glare at each other. "Oh no. You don't mean…?"

"Maybe your boy's not such a wannabe after all."

Sharon's confusion only lasted long enough for the puzzle to drain through her recently installed Colony filter. She then mimicked Keith's head bounce, finally staring in shock at Milo.

"Milo, what does he see?"

"Give me a minute." He mumbled something else, but Sharon didn't hear it.

Someone obviously did. She looked back at Theodore, whose face had gone white. He raised his hand and offered a hesitant wave. A second later, his complexion paled even further.

"Who's he waving to?" Sharon asked.

"Maria, I think." Milo smiled weakly. He tilted his head. "Yeah, definitely Maria."

"For Christ's sake, tell her to stop," Keith said. He started to walk toward Theodore, but stopped and blocked Milo's view of the author.

As Sharon watched, Theodore's face scrunched up, pinpoints of color blooming on his cheeks. After a quick glance at the queue, he dropped one hand below the level of the table and extended his middle finger.

"Oh, that was a mistake," Milo said. "Somebody ought to tell him Trippenstein was flipping off Keith, not Theodore."

"The hippie gave me the finger?" Keith asked.

"You're blocking my view."

"But apparently I'm not blocking *their* view."

"Um…you could say that." Milo was talking to Keith, but watching a point just left of Theodore's chair. "Oh Isadore, don't do that."

Lacking Milo's view of events, Sharon could only imagine what was happening, but Theodore's reactions made the visualization easy.

Theodore leaned back in his seat, eyes widening as they tracked something come closer. His lips moved in silence, even as his handlers tried to redirect his attention to the front of the table. The waiting fans—their patience originally fed by the level of celebrity at the end of the line—

started to grumble. Waiting for hours to get only a look at somebody's back?

Sharon could sympathize, but the current view of his front wasn't any better and potentially more career damaging than ignoring hundred of fans.

Theodore had relaxed his posture and now sat hunched forward in his seat, engaged in animated conversation with the empty air.

"Oh Jesus," Sharon said, more from a final, independent confirmation of Milo's claims than from Theodore's new imaginary playmate.

Not so imaginary anymore.

Keith couldn't decide which way to turn. "That's it! I swear to God, no more book signings for you."

"If he goes I go," Sharon threatened. Then, turning to Milo: "Can't you call them off or make them heel or something?"

Milo squinted as he considered it. "I don't know Sharon. I've never tried to make them do anything."

Here was an idea no one had thought of yet. She couldn't believe they waited a year to tell her.

"It would help if we knew what they were talking about..." Sharon mused.

Milo tightened his lips and raised an eyebrow.

"Oh, yeah. Right." So what if she wasn't up on her Colony etiquette yet. "What *are* they talking about?"

"There seems to be a European Star of David or two in Theodore's family tree. I think he's doing some research with Isadore."

Keith slapped his hips. "Well, isn't that just fucking peachy? Will you please call off your dogs so I can sell some books?"

Sharon prepared to suggest the same thing. If Theodore wanted to fill in some familial blanks, there'd be plenty of time at the post-signing reception, right after she got some seven-on-one time with her husband and his crew.

She didn't have the chance to speak.

Two overlapping shotgun blasts sounded from the

main sales floor. Shredded ceiling tiles showered the crowd as they scattered away from the assailants, their annoyance with Theodore's distraction vanishing in a hail of double-ought pellets.

CHAPTER 14

Milo was moving before the noise from the panicking crowd drowned out the sound of the shots.

He hooked his arm around Sharon's waist and flung her behind a bookcase, trusting the heavy shelves to protect her from any rounds not aimed at the ceiling. Keith's dumfounded stare tracked him as he dashed past the autographing table. Milo screamed for him to find cover; there wasn't time to toss him to safety with Sharon.

Isadore gave Theodore a similar warning, but Milo was only dimly aware of the continuing conversation with the author. He heard the rack of slides, recognized the sound of spent shells ejecting as fresh ones slid home.

Thank you Mickey, he thought, realizing who was responsible for the memory. This was a new twist; note to self for future reference.

As Milo pushed through the waves of fleeing shoppers, another pair of shots thundered. He veered right, tracking the sound. Two shotgun barrels appeared over the swarm of people moving against him; he braced for another blast.

Trippenstein's presence crept forward, trickling into Milo's hands and fingers. He didn't force the hippie back, only reminded him about making any loud "booms."

Milo felt the corners of his mouth turn up as Trippenstein pulled a golden oldie from his bag of tricks. He emerged from the crowd to find himself confronted with the business ends of two shotguns and barely had time to flinch before hearing the hammers fall with dry *clicks*. Wisps of smoke curled from the ends of both barrels; the scent of smoldering marijuana drifted past him, pulled along in the wake of screaming patrons.

The good old boys holding the malfunctioning scatterguns traded puzzled looks, the taller of the two reversing his weapon to peer down the barrel. The shorter man moved aside, wincing at his partner's stupidity. Milo considered having Trippenstein reverse the spell—assuming his familiarity with molecular structures encompassed gunpowder as well as pot—but nixed the idea before it fully formed.

They'd never get the stains out of PageSmart's carpet.

Next! Trippenstein called as he stepped back and Tajiri prepared to take point.

Milo grabbed the barrel of Shorty's shotgun and pulled, but there was no resistance from the assailant, who released the useless lump of metal and wood without a struggle. Then, Milo saw the pistol strapped to the man's leg and understood why.

Tajiri's first instinct was to interrupt Shorty's draw, but Milo vetoed that plan and reached for Stupid instead, who cooperated by maintaining his grip on his shotgun while Milo grasped the stock and pulled.

The motion yanked Stupid off-balance. He stumbled, and Milo used the momentum to spin him 180 degrees and clamp an arm around his neck. They continued the pivot in unison, turning to face Shorty just as he cleared his holster and brought the pistol to bear.

Milo lacked the advantage in firepower, but thought the human shield factor might even things out.

Not so much.

Shorty didn't seem affected by the barrier. His eyes narrowed and as he raised the pistol to the level of Milo's head, a smile slid across his lips.

"I know what you're thinking," he said, sighting down the barrel, "but me and Arlie aren't that close. You two can dance all you'd like, but it ain't gonna stop me from gettin' what we came for."

Milo adjusted his hold on Arlie's neck. "Maybe, but Eleazar won't be happy if you bring the merchandise back damaged."

Shorty laughed. "Well, there's damaged and then there's damaged, and if you'd seen what I've seen, you'd know my boss ain't too picky when it comes to scratches and dents."

"I'm no expert, but I'd say that thing makes more than a scratch."

"You'd be right," Shorty said, cocking the hammer. "But since I'm not aiming at the merchandise, who gives a shit?"

"Not...? What?"

"And who the hell's Eleazar? Sounds like you got more trouble than Arlie and me crashing your shindig."

Arlie, who had quietly struggled until now finally spoke up. "Not to be selfish or anything, but maybe we could pay some attention to *this* problem, if y'all aren't too busy chin wagging."

"Simmer down Arlie; this ain't a problem at all. Seems like this boy's the only one here with a set of balls, so while you keep him occupied, I'll just go collect what we need." With that, Shorty circled around Milo and his dance partner, keeping the pistol trained on their heads.

Milo rotated to follow his progress, torn between maintaining control of Arlie and taking Shorty out of the equation. The Colony had now gathered around him, their opinions equally split between the two options. The additional input didn't help. Sharing ability, memory and intellect made many things easier, but it didn't aid a bit in multitasking.

"I'm open to suggestions here," Milo said, watching Shorty disappear into the stacks.

"Why don't you butt out while you can," Arlie said. "Let me and Ken get on with our business, and you tend to your own."

Milo smacked the top of Arlie's head. "Thanks for the

submission, but I wasn't asking you. Anyone else want to weigh in?"

Tajiri—the leader of the Stop-Shorty contingent—said, *It is apparent who the obvious threat is. We should incapacitate this one and pursue his compatriot.*

Sans compter que le fait que l'autre a un pistolet, Etienne added. *Unless* le magicien *intends to restore the bullets in this gun, I recommend we stay here.*

Maria shook her head. *Need I remind you that Sharon and Keith are still in the store? Do we want this Ken person to find them?*

Milo growled. "If Ken lays a hand on Sharon there won't be enough of him left to scrape off the carpet."

"Ken don't want anything to do with nobody named Sharon." Arlie cried, bucking against Milo's chest. "Look mister, just let me go and we'll get out of your hair as soon as we round up that psychic feller."

"Isadore!" Milo yelled. "Where is he?"

I talk to him for five minutes and now I'm his nanny?

"Not Isadore," Arlie interjected. "Theodore."

That earned Arlie another *whap* on the head. He had to remember it wasn't necessary to speak to communicate with the Colony. Still, it was nice to have a reason to abuse the gunman.

Just find him, Milo pleaded. *And if someone could get me a location on my wife, I'd appreciate it.*

Tajiri made sense though. Arlie was annoying, but not very dangerous, especially with his only ammunition filled with Hawaiian Sensimilla instead of gunpowder. A third conk on the head—with the butt of the shotgun instead of an open hand—would downgrade him from a second-class pain in the ass to an unconscious epilogue, leaving Milo and Company free to neutralize Ken.

Milo paused long enough to marvel at how easily he decided to rush into harm's way. All it took was a Gatherer/ Wife in Jeopardy combo platter.

The stock of Arlie's shotgun proved more resilient than his head, and after tucking the unconscious man under a shelving unit, Milo followed Ken into the main body of the store.

He moved silently down the aisles, crouching slightly as he took deliberate, measured paces. He wasn't concerned with Ken seeing him—the gunman was too short to see over the tops of the gondolas—but his lowered stance allowed him to peer through the units themselves. He felt surprisingly comfortable stalking Ken; except for all the books, it wasn't much different than shadowing a shoplifter at Harrifords.

Although Harriford's criminals usually weren't armed.

At several junctures, he found customers huddled against the end caps. The calmer patrons pointed him farther along Ken's path; the more frantic ones could only manage a sigh of relief when they saw he wasn't armed. Milo directed both types to the storefront, telling all to stay low and move quickly.

Tajiri walked abreast of Milo, matching him step for step. Milo sensed the others combing the store for Sharon while Isadore searched for Theodore. For a moment, he considered sending Tajiri to help his oldest passenger, but immediately realized it didn't matter which entity did the looking. He still associated their abilities with their spectral appearance, sometimes forgetting that the only physical prowess any of them possessed manifested through him.

He was glad Tajiri had decided to ride along.

What do they want with Theodore? Milo thought as he crossed into the children's section. Lately, he had been the target for every crazy in Kanawha County; it was difficult to imagine anyone else in the crosshairs.

Now you understand the karma of every Gatherer, Tajiri said. *Now, you truly understand the need for secrecy.*

Yeah, this crew's all about the understated, Milo mused. *That's why you all lined up to work the receiving line with Sharon last night.*

That is different Milo-san.

Different? Different how?

You dedicated your life to hers long ago, long before the rev-

elation of your true nature. We understand family. We under-stand commitment. You may not have chosen to accept us — choice is often a casualty of circumstance — but now you have. We honor you for that, but would also have you honor those that came before us, and there is no honor in deception.

Milo stopped in the center of the aisle. *No honor in deception,* he thought, and the light bulb switched on. Understanding engulfed him as neurons connected, recon-ciling twelve months of doubt and indecision in a nanosec-ond of comprehension.

"Wow!" he said, almost gasping. "That was an experi-ence."

Wisdom always is, Tajiri said, presenting him with a deep bow. He returned the gesture, and heard a bullet whine over his head at the same instant he heard Ken's pistol fire.

Good timing, Milo said, crab walking to his left.

Indeed, Tajiri agreed. *Providence provides in the most inter-esting manner.*

"I got an experience for you," Ken shouted from several aisles away. "Stick your head up again and I'll show you."

I think we're gonna skip that, Milo told Tajiri. Then, to the rest of the Colony: *How we coming gang?*

Kimmy and Maria reported finding Sharon behind the information counter, directing customers and employees through the main entrance to safety. Isadore and Etienne had Theodore cornered in the Feature Room, as far away from Ken as they could manage without leaving the store.

Keep him there, Milo instructed, dashing across the inter-section of the fiction and mystery sections. *We don't know if there's anyone waiting outside. Does he have any idea what these assholes want with him?*

Etienne answered. *At this point le clairvoyant is having difficulty doing anything that does not involve shaking and squealing like a little girl. Our grande-pere seems to have upset him more than the ruffian with the pistol.*

Milo knew how he felt. He paused behind a cardboard display of paperbacks. From his two o'clock position, he heard a boot scrape the carpet. Not the panicked footsteps of someone trying to escape, this was the sound of attempted stealth. He turned to Tajiri and wiggled two fingers in front of his eyes, then pointed ahead and to the right.

I will reconnoiter in that direction if you'd like, Tajiri said. He smiled as he set off, amused at Milo's tactical communication. Milo felt his face flush.

When would he remember the resources at his disposal?

There's still plenty of time for that, Trippenstein said from beside him. Milo jumped at his sudden appearance, rattling the books in the cardboard dump. Ken fired again. A hole appeared in the cover art adorning the top of the display.

Hell of an editorial statement, Trippenstein commented as bits of pulverized paper floated through his ethereal form. *I thought everyone liked Stephen King.*

"It would be nice if you'd give me some warning before you do that," Milo whispered.

At least you heard me, Trippenstein said. *Keith has been talking to the air for the past ten minutes, hoping one of us would hear him.*

Where is Keith?

Hunkered down behind the registers. Trippenstein gestured toward the front of the store. *He's really close to Sharon, and they're getting almost everyone out.*

Is the stupid guy still unconscious up there?

He was the last time I checked.

Milo nodded. "That's something at least."

Don't plan the celebration yet. That TV guy's getting antsy and if he decides to bolt, Isadore's not gonna be able to stop him.

Another shot boomed and Milo heard this bullet bury itself in the shelves above his head.

"I'm not as worried about Theodore as I am the nut with the overactive trigger finger. If we take him out, we can all go for a beer."

Trippenstein peered around the corner of the aisle. *Depending on how big of a boom you're willing to tolerate, I can*

          M. Stephen Lukac

finish this right now.

Milo was about to suggest anything short of a thermonuclear detonation when Keith rendered the question moot.

"Have some of this you fucking bastard!" Keith screamed from behind Ken's position, a hail of hardcovers sailed over the tops of the gondolas.

"Now *that*," Milo told Trippenstein, "is an editorial comment."

He heard Ken scrambling to avoid the incoming fire launched out of the Political section. He caught a glimpse of the dust jackets as the mortars fell: A glamorous photograph of a well known, well-built, right-wing pundit known best for her intolerance of everything. Milo had noticed a stack of her latest book piled against a pillar leading into the aisle; Keith had plenty of ammo.

Determined not to waste the distraction, Milo broke cover and ran to where the books were falling. Luckily, Ken's attention was on Keith's barrage, not his unprotected back.

As Milo ran faster, he felt Tajiri push into him, assuming control of his limbs. He launched Milo's body into the air, right foot extended forward like a battering ram. Ken must have heard their approach, because he turned just as the kick landed, trading the broken spine Tajiri had intended for what would undoubtedly be a badly bruised hip.

The impact still pushed the gunman into the shelves, and as they landed and Tajiri relinquished control, Milo heard Ken's skull connect with the side of the gondola. A shower of dislodged books covered Ken like a patchwork quilt as he collapsed on the floor, eyes fluttering into unconsciousness. Keith walked up as Milo recovered from the kick.

"Me or you?" Keith asked, pointing at the floor.

"Oh, definitely you," Milo said. "Those books did a load of damage."

"Don't get pissy," Keith said, kicking the remnants of his airborne assault out of the way. "It's the first time these books were actually good for something."

"Besides all the money you make selling them?"

"There is that, but I always feel bad exploiting the exclusionary tendencies of others."

"I'll remember that when the Nobel nominations roll around."

"At least I won't have to worry about Peace Prize competition from you."

Trippenstein hijacked Milo's voice. "As much as we enjoy listening to you two go at it, do you think it's safe to call 'olly oxen free'? Your celebrity guest is ready to burst an aneurism."

"Thank God," Keith said. "I was afraid somebody shot him."

"Isadore kept an eye on him," Milo replied.

"So to speak."

"Exactly." Milo jumped over the horizon of the shelves, trying to get a peek at the information desk. "Did you see Sharon?"

"She's up there." Keith shook his head. "But let me tell you again before she comes back here: No more autographings for you."

"Me?"

"You."

"What, you're blaming me for this?"

"After the week you've had? Two rednecks show up armed to the teeth, start shooting the place up and you're asking me if I blame you? You'll be lucky if I let you through the doors after this."

"I had nothing to do with this."

"Bullshit."

"Bull-truth. They both said they were here for Theodore. I don't think either of them would know a Gatherer if he bit them on the ass."

Keith bent over as if to inspect Ken's hindquarters for dental impressions. "Etienne didn't bite him, did he?"

"Nobody bit anyone," Milo confirmed. He jumped again, still looking for Sharon. "Where the hell is my wife?"

"Where the hell are the cops?" Keith asked. "I don't even hear the sirens yet."

Milo felt a small amount of pressure in his mind, confirming the Colony had returned. He checked over his shoulder; his passengers stood bunched in the aisle behind him, forming a ring around Jack Theodore.

"Hail hail, the gang's all here," Milo told Keith.

Theodore stepped around Milo and stared at the mound of books covering the gunman. He shook his head, *tsked* and then walked up to Keith.

"Is this how you treat all your guests?"

Obviously, there was no empathic element to Theodore's psychic abilities or he'd have sensed the danger in whining to Keith. Milo tensed, silently imploring his friend to control his temper.

The prayer wasn't effective.

Keith thrust his finger into the psychic's face. "Be happy you only had to hide under a table for a couple of minutes. The last guy that came for a signing got a dead midget dumped in his lap."

Milo stepped between them. "Calm down ladies. Mr. Theodore, do you have any idea what these men might want with you?"

No answer came. Theodore turned away from Keith's rudeness and focused on the crowd behind him. Kimmy waved, and once again, Theodore returned the gesture.

He looked at Milo. "How is any of this possible?"

"That's a longer conversation than we have time for."

"Who are all these people?"

Theodore's reaction was puzzling. Compared to the rest of the paranormal smorgasbord, Milo knew his little collective had to be a bit of a surprise entrée, but the psychic behaved as if he'd never seen a disembodied spirit before. Keith had called him a poseur, but the man had to possess some skills; the wave-fest proved that.

Why was Jack Theodore, medium to the masses, acting like a teenaged boy peeking at his first centerfold?

More questions for the post-arrest, pre-recrimination,

book-signing clusterfuck wrap-up show.

"We can talk about that later," Milo said. "Right now we need to find the nearest exit."

"I think perhaps we should wait for the authorities," Theodore responded. He ran his hand through his hair, prepping for the cameras that would accompany the police. "Has anyone seen my agent?"

"I seen him," answered a new voice. "I left him bleeding all over your fancy carpet."

Milo hadn't hit Stupid Arlie hard enough.

He'd sneaked into the aisle behind Keith. Arlie had one arm hooked across Keith's elbows and the other wrapped around Keith's neck, nearly duplicating Milo's earlier hold on him.

"Mama always told me I had a hard head," he said.

"You'd better appreciate it while you still have it," Milo snarled. He looked down, trying to spot Ken's pistol among the scattered books. No luck.

Arlie followed Milo's look. "If he's dead, so's this one. Salomé be damned; if he's dead, I'm taking this fool's head."

"Ease up Arlie," came a raspy reply from the bottom of the pile. "I appreciate it, but ain't nobody dead yet."

Arlie smiled as Ken pulled himself to his feet. Milo found the missing pistol, still wrapped in Ken's fist.

Ken looked at his hand, as if surprised to find his gun there. He smiled too. Arlie stepped aside to give his partner room to move in the aisle. Keith coughed, choking from Arlie's rough handling.

"Straight-up trade," Ken offered. "This guy for that one."

Theodore blanched. "That's not going to happen. The police are on their way. Nobody's going anywhere."

"We're not taking any chances," Milo said, reaching back to grab Theodore's arm. He pulled and pivoted, forcing Theodore toward the assailants.

The refrain of surprise he heard in his head mirrored the look on Theodore's face. One didn't treat celebrities like commodities; this was the unwritten agreement between the glitterati and those who basked in their glow.

Milo hadn't signed the treaty.

The Colony shouted in his mind, berating him with clichés, platitudes and biblical references. They bombarded him in five-part harmony, their overriding message one of shock, dismay and — most troubling — betrayal.

Only Tajiri remained silent, but when the others paused to catch what passed for "breath," Milo heard the ronin's voice.

He who is moral can be shamed.

"He who is fond of the people can be worried," Milo said, drawing the next line of Sun Tzu from Tajiri's memory.

"You'd better worry you son of a bitch." Theodore tried to sound threatening, but the gun barrel pressed against his temple took the menace out of his voice.

"I don't think it's going to matter too much," Milo explained, to both Theodore and the Colony. "I don't think these boys came to invite you to a barbeque." He motioned to Arlie. "Now make with your end."

Arlie released Keith, who staggered across the same space Theodore had crossed. He shot Milo a grateful look as he joined him — gratitude tinged with hesitation.

Milo winked.

The gesture mollified Keith and finally quieted the Colony.

"A deal's a deal guys," Milo said. "You've got your man. Hit the road."

Arlie seemed to like the sound of that, but Ken didn't appear as anxious to make for the exit. His brow furrowed; Milo could almost hear the gears grinding, and they ground until Ken experienced a light-bulb moment of his own.

Ken shook his head, favoring Milo with a predatory grin. "Almost. You almost had me believing you were hard core."

"What makes you think any different now?" He tried to summon the iron that would reinforce the attitude, but he was pretty sure Ken had his number.

He passed Theodore off to Arlie, and took a step forward, twirling the pistol on his index finger. "I remembered." He used his other hand to tap his temple. "I remembered talking about the merchandise. I remembered telling you I didn't want and scratches and dents."

He moved another step closer. "And then I realized what would happen if we walked out of here with Mr. Happy Brain and nothing else. I suspect you thought about that too; that's why you traded so quickly."

Milo attempted a casual shrug. "Keith's my best friend and I don't know that guy from Adam. How else am I gonna choose?"

"You're gonna choose to get your best friend out of here when the shootin' starts. You're gonna choose to get that gal I heard you asking about out of harm's way. You're gonna choose to save your ass and the asses of anyone close to you rather than standing up to the big bad men with the guns.

"Fuck everybody else; I'm watchin' after me and mine. That's hardcore. Taking Arlie all the way out so he can't come back and bite you in the ass. That's hardcore. You ain't hardcore."

"Then what am I?"

"That shouldn't be too hard to figure out." Ken closed the remaining distance. In one motion, he stopped spinning the pistol and pressed the cold barrel into the flesh between Milo's eyes.

"You're a hero. At least you're gonna be once you lead us out of here."

"I'm not leading you anywhere unless it's into a cell."

Ken grinned—gave him an *aw shucks* mouthful of teeth—before reversing his grip on his gun and bringing the wooden stocks down on Milo's head.

Milo stayed on his feet for a moment, as the pain of the blow encircled his head before making its way down his body. His knees gave out seconds before his vision darkened, and falling, he heard Ken say:

"Nobody said you had to be awake to be a hero…"

INTERMISSION

When the call comes in, Todd Liefeld grabs a cameraman and a field producer, herds them into Mobile Three and makes a beeline for PageSmart.

The scanner keeps them appraised on the fifteen-minute drive, but most of the information consists of ETA's and calls for more backup. The other chatter focuses on Jack Theodore's abduction, but Liefeld isn't interested in the whereabouts of some television psychic flavor of the month.

Liefeld is chasing Milo Tucker.

Starting at the MacCorkle Avenue subway station, running through PageSmart, Harriford & Sons' Department Store, and the Pocatalico Exit of I-77 and culminating with the destruction of the London Heights Mall, Milo Tucker has walked a line connecting every catastrophe occurring in Kanawha County for over a year. Liefeld can recite every instance with eidetic precision; for whatever stories he didn't report live, he's studied the tapes like a conspiracy nut with fresh footage from Dealey Plaza.

After Christmas, things settled down on the Tucker front, almost enough that Liefeld had thought about abandoning his pursuit of the security guard and continuing his hunt for Point Pleasant survivors and Mothman witnesses. There are circumstances begging for explanation, but without new incidents, Liefeld has little hope of breaking the story.

Multiple 911 calls from PageSmart might reinvigorate the investigation.

Several reports mention another hostage besides Theodore. Two perpetrators, two hostages. The ratio makes sense. Probability works in favor of the second hostage being Milo Tucker.

The man is a trouble magnet.

Liefeld briefs his team as they go. The cameraman rolls his eyes at the field producer. They thought the reporter's obsession had faded. They've wasted hundred of hours on this quixotic quest already. Like Liefeld, they thought the chase was over.

Liefeld has a different plan.

*   *   *

Keith blames himself for being out of the store when the events started that led to Alex Harrison's death and Milo's acquisition of the Colony. Without the additional business from Gary Fox's appearance, the interim bank deposit wouldn't have been necessary and without the extra bank run, he'd have been front and center when the shit hit the fan, and with the Captain on the bridge, things may have worked out differently.

He'll never blame himself again.

He watches the gunmen drag Milo down the main aisle, his unconscious form propped between them as Jack Theodore walks three steps ahead. The psychic pauses and turns his head at every intersection as if to dash off, but a growl from the shorter attacker keeps him moving forward.

Keith brings up the rear, not from coercion but from the inability to do anything else. The Hammer of Justice is nothing more than a plastic mallet, whacking away at a brick wall without raising even a little dust. He studies their backs as they shuffle toward the exit; maybe he can remember enough detail to identify them later.

Yeah, because so many convictions come from a thorough description of the perpetrator's ass.

They reach the vestibule, captors and captives pausing at the double doors, Keith veering left and vaulting the cash wrap. He almost lands on Sharon, who greets him with an exhale that's half annoyance at his clumsiness and half relief at his identity. She shifts to give him room to hunker down but keeps her eyes on the counter's edge.

Keith knows why.

He offers her a hand and pulls her to her feet just as the quartet pushes through the doors, but a glimpse is all she needs. Silently, she searches Keith's face and finds the confirmation she doesn't want to see.

Her expression emasculates him in ways five years of celibacy never did.

*   *   *

As soon as they clear the doors, Ken realizes his fear of capture is unfounded, the dead weight suspended between he and Arlie unnecessary.

The sidewalk fronting PageSmart is crowded, but only with displaced patrons who care nothing for the details of the fracas inside. Once out of immediate harm's way, self-preservation gives way to curiosity and escape isn't as important as information.

Pedestrian rubberneckers all hoping for a ringside seat to the carnage.

For a second, he considers feeding their need for mayhem, but no. Theodore's moving exactly as he's been instructed and the hero's not giving them any trouble. Arlie questions him with a tilt of his head; Ken shakes the inquiry off.

They've got a clear path to the truck. Why complicate things?

The crowd is so intent on the limited view through PageSmart's windows they allow the four to pass by without action or comment. Ken watches Theodore's reaction to the disinterested parting of the human sea surrounding them and chuckles. A few minutes earlier, the mob would have done somersaults just for the chance to shake his hand. Now, they move out his way without a second look. Recognition fades in the face of an event that might get their faces on the Eleven O'clock News.

They'll be kicking themselves when they realize they may have been the last people to see him alive.

Ken's done the math, not that there were a lot of digits to add. He's seen The Baptist's appetite in action; no surprise he might be hankering for a taste of what Theodore was packing between his ears.

Dead man walkin', Ken thinks all the way to the truck.

They dump the hero in the passenger foot well while Theodore climbs into the truck bed. Arlie exchanges the dud double-ought shells for fresh and climbs in the back with him. Ken rips several lengths from a roll of duct tape he finds under the seat and trusses up the hero, just in case he wakes up during the drive.

He's not sure if The Baptist will want dessert with his take-out, but if he doesn't, Ken won't let the hero go to waste.

There's always target practice.

*   *   *

Barbara Zuliekowski doesn't wait for anything.

Bad enough that PageSmart didn't have the book she wanted in stock; worse, they made her wait a week while they ordered it. How was she supposed to make her selection for the Sterling Park reading group if the store didn't keep her choice on the shelves?

She could have gone to the mall, but that meant more waiting. Waiting for the mongoloid garage attendant to process her lifetime parking pass. Waiting for the teenaged hooligans to clear off the escalators so she could ride to the second floor in peace. Waiting for inconsiderate salesclerks to finish babbling to their slacker friends while *real* customers with real money to spend cooled their heels. After all that, they probably wouldn't have her book either.

Her late husband Emile Zuliekowski—God rest his soul—didn't like waiting either. Every night after Dan Rather and Wheel of Fortune, when she strips off her housecoat, support hose and Depends, she sees the remnants of his disdain for delay. The lessons Barbara learned as a new bride stayed with her long after Emile went on to Glory.

Just as they should.

She feels the blood rise in her cheeks, hears her pulse pounding in her ears. After seven days—*seven days, Lord have mercy*—the incompetents finally have her book in stock, and now she can't get through the crowd to buy it.

A harlot wearing a black t-shirt decorated with a devil circle tells Barbara there's something wrong inside, something going on with the author they had signing books. The whore in the evil clothes says something about guns and fighting, but Barbara doesn't want to hear it.

She wants her book. She wants her copy of *Heartland Heartbreak* so she can show Mary Backlewurts what good literature is all about. Barbara doesn't care about guns, authors or strumpets with godless symbols plastered to their bosoms.

Barbara. Wants. Her. Book.

Now.

Barbara pushes the hooker aside and bullies her way toward the entrance. There she sees two of the clerks: the attractive blonde with the perky figure (but Lord, Emile, doesn't she have a potty mouth, with all the S-words, D-words and—mother of God—the occasional F-word) and her boss, the scary bohemian with the ponytail and—of all things—an earring.

By God, they'd get her book for her or she'd know the reason why.

*　　*　　*

Trippenstein's meadow is very crowded.

He doesn't have anything against company, but he also

doesn't want to open up his refuge to every Etienne, Maria and Isadore who needs a weekend getaway. There's usually plenty of room in Milo's head for everyone to have their own space, but when Ken's gun strikes skull, Trippenstein has the feeling it's time to dive deep, and he pulls everyone down with him.

Hell of a time to develop a conscience.

There's no time to show everyone around; things are happening fast topside. Milo might be nighty-night, but the mikes are still open and the screens are working fine, so he needs to pay attention.

Convincing the others isn't so easy.

Kimmy lays in the grass, flapping her arms and legs, making lawn angels. She's worried about Milo—they all are—but the temptation's too hard to resist. Maria sits next to her, legs drawn up under her skirt, enjoying the gentle breeze that always blows across the meadow.

Etienne does pirouettes across the plain. Spin, spin, pivot, plié, and back again. Isadore applauds the port de bras, almost childlike in his enjoyment of the setting.

Tajiri seems unaffected by Trippenstein's sanctuary, which annoys the hippie on one level, but encourages him on another. The ronin stands next to him, silently watching events unfold as Milo is bundled into the pickup truck and carried away.

At least someone else is taking the situation seriously.

Tajiri comments on Milo's nobility, his willingness to sacrifice for the benefit of others. Trippenstein disagrees. Better to retreat and fight another day.

What about honor? Tajiri asks.

Honor thyself, Trippenstein replies.

Tajiri lets the response hang there, suspended in the thick atmosphere of the meadow. He focuses on Milo's predicament, choosing to ignore the hippie's selfish nature.

Words aren't necessary to convey Tajiri's disappointment. It radiates along the link they all share. None of the others feel the need to mask their thoughts and emotions. Trippenstein knows differently. He spent years alone in the meadow, only surfacing when circumstance — or curiosity — got the better of him.

Although much has changed, Trippenstein still guards his secrets well, and in the hidden heart of what remains of his individuality, he begins to plan for the worst.

*   *   *

Jack Theodore is too confused to be scared.

The author/psychic/celebrity bounces around in the truck's cargo bed as his captors drive away from PageSmart. They careen along the streets of downtown Charleston, narrowly avoiding the arrival of police and emergency units.

Fortune favors the foolish.

He'd known the West Virginia appearance was a mistake, but hadn't imagined the enormity of the error. He'd allowed his handlers to overwhelm him with earning projections and demographic studies, ultimately deciding to follow the lure of dollar signs rather than the warning in his gut.

He'll never make that mistake again.

He thinks about jumping out when the truck slows down to take a corner, but the driver trades speed for safety, and never decelerates. Every turn is an adventure in physics, one two-wheeled carom after another.

Soon, Theodore is too queasy to consider a high-speed leap.

At least his guard is receiving similar treatment, worse because he's only using one hand to steady himself. With his other hand, he holds the shotgun more or less on Theodore, though at such close range, accuracy is a given.

He cranes his neck to look into the cab. Only the driver is visible through the window; of his would-be rescuer, he can only get occasional glimpses of the top of his head. No one else is in the truck, which puzzles him.

The old man had called him Milo, and according to him, where Milo went, the rest followed. It's a dubious claim.

He knows of spirits with strong attachments to the living; every studio audience he faces has at least a dozen. The dead have issues. Sometimes after departing, issues are all they have left. That's what Theodore does; that is his mission.

Helping the dead achieve resolution and closure.

But six? Six spirits attaching themselves to some poor, West Virginia schmuck? What had the old guy called him? A Grouper? No, that was a fish. Collector? Recruiter? No, none of these either.

A Gatherer.

Bullshit.

The dead have issues, but they also have a wicked sense of humor, a morbid propensity for playing pranks on the living. Most times, they settle for throwing dishes across the room or making things go bump in the night.

Maybe Appalachian spooks prefer satire to slapstick.

*   *   *

Sharon is one second away from a total stimuli overload.

If one more thing happens, she's giving up. She's got a section of sidewalk all picked out, and if anything else tries to pry its way into her brain, she's sitting down and shutting off. So long, farewell, *auf wiedersehen, adieu.*

Enter Barbara Zuliekowski.

On good days, Mrs. Zuliekowski is enough of an annoyance to send booksellers running in fear from the sales floor to the stock room. When the sun shines, the birds sing and sociopathic hillbillies don't kidnap loving husbands at gunpoint, Mrs. Zuliekowski is merely a poorly dressed, ridiculously made-up, walking, talking, jiggling mass of superior attitude coupled with serious cash and obnoxious body odor. When everything is going right, Sharon only has to lock Keith in his office for an hour to prevent him from separating Mrs. Zuliekowski's head from her shoulders.

The sun's gone down, the birds are quiet, sociopathic hillbillies have absconded with her husband and getting Keith into his office is impossible because the Charleston police have decorated every square inch of PageSmart in fluorescent yellow crime scene tape.

Definitely not a good day.

Forget it. She doesn't care. Keith can kill her. Why not spread the horror around?

With her hearing focused on another round of pointless questions from clueless cops, Sharon watches Hurricane Zuliekowski make landfall on the shores of Keith. She almost interrupts the officer's interrogation to suggest he call for another ambulance, but stops herself. If it doesn't bring Milo back, she's not interested. From this point forward, she vows to ignore anything that doesn't further this one goal.

The rest of the world can go to hell.

Mrs. Zuliekowski starts the confrontation with an open-handed shove to Keith's shoulder. To his credit, Keith ignores the imposition and continues to berate the police officers surrounding him. However, Mrs. Zuliekowski refuses to be ignored.

She unleashes another slap, this one forceful enough to knock Keith off-balance. Sharon sees his eyes narrow as he steadies himself.

Her boss's expression allows her a small measure of hope; a hint of warmth courses through her, the first heat she's felt since watching Milo be carried away.

However bad her situation, it could be worse. She could be Barbara Zuliekowski.

Keith opens the discourse with a summary of recent events, informing Mrs. Zuliekowski of the trivial nature of her problem when compared to the larger issues at hand. With sweeping gestures, he calls her attention to the sea of uniformed personnel and asks her to consider her request in terms of the present situation.

Mrs. Zuliekowski rises on her toes and leans in, countering Keith's explanation with a declaration of indifference. Her needs have no connection to current events, except for the continued inconvenience caused by them.

Keith smiles. Mrs. Zuliekowski settles back on her swollen heels and folds her arms, misinterpreting the smirk as capitulation, unprepared for the torrent Sharon knows is coming.

Towering above the woman, Keith invites her to violate herself with a variety of items, most of which were never designed for insertion in a human body. Mrs. Zuliekowski reels back, shocked at the prospect of intimacy with farm equipment, kitchen utensils and barnyard animals. She gathers her wits and steps up to deliver a suitable rejoinder, but Keith holds her off with a raised middle finger.

He's just getting started.

Next, he describes his vision of the Zuliekowski family tree, making genealogical connections between siblings and cousins that, in addition to being inadvisable from a genetic standpoint, violate the laws of both God and man. He suggests her deplorable physical condition might be the result of chromosomal irregularities inherent in incestuous relationships.

Then he gets nasty.

The haranguing deteriorates into Keith's Greatest Hits, and because Sharon can sing the choruses from memory, she tunes it out. Everything else fades into background noise and blurred images, leaving her one focal point.

Milo.

A voice insinuates itself, breaking through the barrier of isolation she's set. She whips her head around to identify the source, but realizes quickly it comes from within. It's a memory, a promise of aid if the worst happens.

She walks away from the cop and finds an area relatively free of activity. There, she unclips the cell phone from her waistline and pulls up the electronic directory.

Keith sees her move. He stops his verbal attack on Mrs. Zuliekowski, who's been reduced to an incoherent, blubbering shell. Further escalation on Keith's part is unnecessary; the old woman's moved beyond the threshold of constructive abuse.

Keith mouths a silent question. Sharon holds up the phone. Keith's forehead scrunches in thought, and after a moment mouths another word. A name.

Sharon nods.

His brow furrows again, followed by a quick, but somewhat reluctant, nod.

Sharon dials the phone.

*　　*　　*

Andrew Bennett is shaking and Philip Ducalion loves it.

There are two possible causes for Bennett's tremors: fear or anger. Regardless of which option proves true, Ducalion considers the reaction a win. If the electronics magnate is angry, it means Ducalion still has the touch for pissing off the rich and famous, an ability he hones and refines at every opportunity. Actually, he really doesn't care how wealthy or well known his target is; he considers himself an equal opportunity agitator.

The rich just make it more fun.

If Andrew Bennett, founder and CEO of Benelec and majority stockholder in The Meadows Resort, is quaking in fear, it means Ducalion's investigation is on the right track. That's fine too.

He'll have plenty of time to piss him off later.

The phone rings twenty minutes into their interview, causing Bennett to smile. Ducalion seethes at the interruption; it throws off his timing and disrupts the slow build of insult and innuendo that has Bennett's blood pressure climbing. Bennett allows the phone to ring several times before answering it, his smile widening with every electronic chirp. Ducalion understands the tactic; he's used it himself.

While Ducalion wrestles with the temptation to snatch the phone from Bennett's desk and throw it across the room, he notices Bennett's expression darken. His smile vanishes. His eyes narrow. His knuckles turn white as he tightens his grip on the handset.

"It's for you," Bennett says, telling Ducalion what he already knows.

He silently counts to ten, savoring Bennett's discomfort before moving to take the phone from his hand.

The voice he hears almost stops his heart. "Emergency call," the *Whodunit* operator says. "Codes confirmed. Connecting you now."

Ducalion wills his pulse to resume, closing his eyes in anticipation as circuits connect. Life or death. Redemption or damnation. Heaven or hell.

There are only two possibilities.

A series of clicks sounds in his ear, followed by the voice of his caller, and he realizes there's a third option. He exhales slowly, simultaneously thankful for his reprieve and angered by the lack of resolution. He gives himself a moment to embrace both emotions, then shakes himself free of the feelings as information from Charleston fills his ear. There aren't many details, but there are enough to remind him of another promise made.

He says the only thing he can, the only thing his caller expects to hear.

"I'm on my way."

CHAPTER 15

The soothing hum of the engine and the motion of the truck kept pulling Milo back from the edge of consciousness. The throbbing in his skull counteracted the sound and sway, but the pain also drove him back into the comfortable darkness.

A confluence of the three stimuli settled the issue. The noise of the engine changed as the truck briefly left the ground. The landing rattled the frame, rocked the suspension and threw Milo headfirst into the front of the foot well, which aggravated his headache beyond his ability to ignore.

Opening his eyes did little to increase his view. The dashboard cast enough light to illuminate the driver, but nothing else within the passenger compartment. In the intermittent moonlight, Milo could see the back of someone's head through the rear window, but couldn't identify him.

Not that there were many possibilities.

He tried to pull himself off the floor, but his arms and legs wouldn't respond. From the tingling in his limbs, he first thought his awkward position had cut off the circulation, but eventually realized he was bound at the ankles and wrists.

When a passing semi flooded the cab with light, he saw the silver flash of duct tape above the tops of his shoes, and stopped struggling. Milo's dad had always said you could fix just about anything with a roll of duct tape; some things were true everywhere.

Disregarding the burning sensation as his extremities woke, he searched the cab for the Colony. Normally, it was a rare thing to wake and not find at least a few of his passengers loitering around; he found it difficult to believe they wouldn't be waiting for him in a situation like this.

Their absence only surprised him for a moment. Why should anything about this night be normal?

"Hang on Arlie," Ken shouted as he twisted the steering wheel. "We're about ready to hit more of those chuckholes and I don't want our boy getting tossed out."

Milo braced as well as he could, grateful for the warning and the information. Ken's "boy" had to be Theodore, which meant no one else from PageSmart was making this trip.

As long as they hadn't left anyone seriously injured behind, Milo could stop worrying about Keith and Sharon and concentrate on extricating himself from this mess.

"I was wondering when you'd wake up," Ken said without taking his eyes off the road. "I didn't think I hit you that hard."

"Doesn't have to be hard if you hit the right place," Milo said. His first plan had been to feign unconsciousness for as long as possible, but the response slipped out before he could stop it. "I don't know why you bothered anyway. Seems like you got what you came for."

"Huh?" Ken said, the surprise in his tone telling Milo he hadn't really expected an answer. He'd probably repeated the same question several times during their drive, on the off chance Milo was playing possum.

That was twice the redneck had outsmarted him. Milo decided to punish himself later, if he lived long enough. Time to start looking for another hole in the fence.

"You pays your money, you takes your chances," Ken continued. "That'll teach you to stick your ass out where it don't belong." He chuckled. "Not that I think you're gonna get much of a chance to remember the lesson."

"Maybe I'll have the opportunity to return the favor," Milo said, choosing spunk over subtlety. "You might be surprised at what I could teach you."

Ken clucked his tongue. "Maybe I would be, may be I would. But you ain't gonna bully me into finding out, so I'd save your breath."

Another dip in the road bounced the front tires off the ground and launched Milo into the dashboard. He took most of the impact on his shoulders, but the jolt had enough force to reboot the throbbing in his skull, which had finally dialed down to one.

"What's the point of all this anyway?" Milo asked through gritted teeth. "What's Theodore to you?"

"Not a blessed thing. I got nothing against the man; ain't got nothing for him either. Somebody placed an order, and me and Arlie's Federal Express."

"Psychics pretty popular in the boonies, are they?"

"You'd be amazed."

"Then why not just get an appointment? Make a phone call or send an email."

Apparently, the suggestion struck Ken as incredibly funny. His braying filled the cab and he pounded his open hand against the steering wheel. The extent of his amusement caused his partner to knock on the rear window.

"Everything all right in there Ken?"

Ken choked on his laughter, coughing just as loudly while continuing to beat on the wheel. Between coughs and snorts, Ken repeated Milo's questions. Arlie reacted the same way, but his amusement had a hysterical quality Milo hadn't heard in Ken's voice.

All of a sudden, Milo was less anxious to reach their destination.

As quickly as the thought formed, inertia snapped him against the seat. Milo felt the truck shift as Arlie hopped out of the back and heard a metallic creaking a few seconds later. Ken goosed the accelerator, moving them slightly forward. The tinny noise repeated, followed by another small vibration as Arlie climbed back onboard.

The presence of a gate didn't make Milo feel any better.

Beyond the barrier, the ride was smoother. Ken's driving improved as well. More light spilled into the cab; high wattage halogens appeared above the top of the doors at regular intervals.

They were entering a compound.

With the road noise reduced to little more than a constant *whoosh*, Milo heard a woman whisper his name. He almost panicked, fearing Ken had snatched Sharon on the way out of PageSmart. His throat constricted as he pulled at the strips binding his wrists. If anything happened to…

Milo, the voice repeated, *Sharon's fine. Now be still.*

Maria.

He scanned the truck again. Nothing.

We're here, Maria said. *Trippenstein said to tell you we're in the meadow.*

Milo remembered the sanctuary, and the hippie's reaction to company. If he'd pulled everyone down that deep, things were worse than Milo thought.

And things looked bad enough already.

It's just a precaution, Maria said.

Against what? Milo asked. *What do y'all know that I don't?*

Maria sighed. *I'm not sure any of us knows anything. All I can say is Trippenstein was quite adamant.*

Which didn't prove a damned thing. The hippie's instincts were usually reliable, but Milo had to consider the years he spent hiding in Alex Harrison's subconscious, masquerading as Totenstill. Remembering Garcen's reaction from the previous spring, Milo wasn't prepared to call Trippenstein's caution anything more than a desire to save his own ass.

Trippenstein asks you to recall that the well-being of his — do I have to say that? Maria paused, presumably waiting for permission to paraphrase.

Very well. She finally continued. *Trippenstein says saving his ass depends entirely on saving your ass.*

Yeah, that much was true. Unless there was another Gatherer around to take a hand-off, if Milo bought it, the rest of them died too. Milo's head was killing him, but the pain wasn't the telltale ache associated with a Gatherer in the area.

Or a Hunter.

Milo didn't completely trust Trippenstein's altruism. He still didn't know everything about his Colonists, but that was a matter of time, not access. With the others, he could browse their memories like an infinite library, the details of their existence only a thought away.

Not so with Trippenstein.

The hippie had walls and barriers that even Milo couldn't breach. Supposedly, there were reasons—secrets too terrible to reveal—but again, the history of Trippenstein's deceptions made that difficult to believe.

Unfortunately, the current situation didn't give them time for a round of Truth or Dare.

Ken brought the truck to an abrupt halt, rocking the frame on its tires. He climbed out of the cab without saying a word to Milo; getting Theodore out of the back was the more urgent task. He heard the tailgate rattle and felt the vehicle shimmy as they pulled the psychic out, none too gently by the way the truck bounced on its springs. Theodore cried out seconds before Milo heard him thump to the ground and suddenly his little patch of floorboard didn't seem all that inhospitable.

Deciding to press his luck, Milo rocked on his ass until the force of his movement allowed him to press his chest against the bench seat. Pushing with his feet, he wriggled and turned his way into a prone position, stretched out across the width of the cab. The cold vinyl felt good against the length of his body, but he didn't have time to enjoy the sensation; he didn't know how long he'd have to survey his surroundings.

Rolling slightly, he elevated his head to the top of the seat, just high enough to peek through the rear window. The cargo bed was empty except for a spare tire and some suspicious rust stains. They looked old enough to be of little concern. Theodore's continuing screams of pain and protest confirmed Milo's cursory examination; no one who had lost that much blood could yell that loud.

Ken and Arlie were only visible from the waist up, but from their jerky motions and the way their arms swung, Milo could tell they were stomping a mud hole in Theodore's ass. At first, it struck him as strange—why risk a public kidnapping just to beat him down.

Unless whatever they wanted from the psychic didn't depend on his survival.

This realization narrowed the possibilities. Sure, they could probably collect a ransom without a breathing victim, but it seemed too soon to burn that bridge. Payers tended to require proof of life before agreeing to payees' demands, and while it was relatively easy to prop a corpse up for a photo-op with a current newspaper, it would be infinitely more difficult to fake a phone call.

Not that Milo thought the absurdity of the concept would deter his redneck captors.

As he thought this through, Milo expected the Colony to weigh in with its normal plethora of opinions, but nothing came. Even Maria was silent, although he could feel her revulsion at Ken and Arlie's treatment of Theodore.

Some wounds never faded.

The tenor of the beat-down changed, the men getting in what seemed to be a final whap as their attention shifted to the small house at the far end of the compound. Milo couldn't see the source of their distraction, but Trippenstein broke his silence with a "shout."

You need to get us out of here! he screamed. *Now, now, NOW!*

"You want us gone? You'd better make with the mojo then," Milo muttered. The grey tape resisted all his efforts to loosen it.

"No mojo," Trippenstein answered, surprising Milo by speaking aloud. "I wouldn't cast a whammy within twenty miles of this place; not for all the money in the world."

Milo shrugged as much as his bonds allowed. "Kind of an either or situation here Tripp, unless we're carrying a knife I don't know about. Maybe Tajiri could do something."

"There's no time; no time," Trippenstein chanted, a taste of panic seeping into Milo's mind with the words. He felt the hippie recede from his consciousness, pulling Maria back with him.

I'm battening down the hatches, Trippenstein told him, *but I don't know if it'll be enough.*

Enough for what? Milo asked, watching the bumpkins' stance transform from aggressive dominance to passive submission. *What the hell is going on out there?*

Believe me, you don't want to know. Trippenstein's "voice" faded, dwindling to little more than a murmur. *You wouldn't happen to be close to passing out by any chance, would you?*

No.

Then I'm apologizing in advance.

The fading stopped. Trippenstein's presence roared up from the depths of Milo's mind, like a mental bullet fired from the bottom of a deep well. Before he could react, the hippie slammed forward and took control of Milo's body.

He had no time to protest. Trippenstein turned his head, ignoring the pain the abrupt movement caused, and focused on the dashboard. With another mumbled *sorry* he arched Milo's back and drove his already-injured head into the padded metal.

Darkness followed.

CHAPTER 16

To an untrained eye, the situation at PageSmart looked normal. Enter. Select. Pay. Exit.

Lather. Rinse. Repeat.

Customers moved throughout the store, marching like soldier ants, looking for tasty nuggets to take back to the nest. As Ducalion stood watching from the main entrance, the insect analogy seemed apt, except for a small—but important—difference.

Ants were much smarter and more discriminating.

Men in blue overalls stood on ladders, their heads and shoulders swallowed by openings formed by missing ceiling tiles. Wires hung like overcooked pasta, twirling around workers too experienced to heed warnings about not standing above a certain level, or disconnecting power before performing maintenance. Along the perimeter, other craftsmen wielded spackle and paint like rebel artists, indifferent to the complaints of their audience.

Ducalion doubted the level of dissatisfaction had anything to do with the wounded condition of the store.

He strolled across the sales floor, making diagonal passes from one wall to the other. While, the repair crew fussed with the most visible destruction, he noted the smaller defects, calculating the odds that the forensic techs had missed them. The damage was subtle enough to ensure their irrelevance.

Almost.

He lost count of stray buckshot holes after two circuits. Whoever these yahoos were, they weren't shy with their ammunition. More surprising, there weren't any blood-stains on the walls or the floor.

Trigger-happy and injury conscious. Strange combination. The Tuckers had a saying for this kind of weird shit. Poopy Oopie? Boogie Woogie? Something like that.

On his third trip from left to right, Ducalion had to dodge a tribe of public assistance urchins. A second later, their trail-boss shouldered past him, unrestrained flesh undulating under a thin cover of tie-dyed cotton. It figured; the women he wished would shrug off the chains of Victoria's Secret never did.

After the parade passed, Ducalion wandered toward the circular counter that dominated the center of the store. He stopped short of a grand entrance when he heard Keith's familiar bellowing.

"I don't give a shit," the manager announced to everyone, pacing behind the counter. "I don't care about orders, deliveries or customers at this point. In fact, I'm not thrilled with the idea of listing the things I don't give a shit about. What I want is somebody with a badge and a gun— right the fuck now! —to tell me they've found my road dog."

The sentiment was understandable but the delivery lacked tact, a shortcoming guaranteed to annoy anyone in PageSmart upper management. The customers clustered around the desk seemed divided in their reaction to the tirade. Every outburst pushed the crowd a collective step back; the cadence and invective kept them all within earshot.

The public loved a good performance.

Ducalion raised his hands in preparation to applaud, but somebody interrupted the show. The killjoy had dark, shiny hair, slicked back and plastered to his skull. A thin line of hair decorated his upper lip, and he wore a tan suit that Ducalion was sure had a checkered pair of matching pants hanging in the closet at home.

As he turned, the lanyard bouncing against his tie confirmed what the coiffure and couture had suggested: a corporate asshole unimpressed by Keith's emotional rendition of "Where the hell's my friend."

"Pridemore, I believe that's enough," the suit said, trying to throw some bass in his voice. "There's no need to exacerbate the situation with a public display of unprofessionalism."

Keith wasn't buying the bass. Maybe it was the current crisis, but Ducalion suspected there wasn't a big market for the suit's bullshit under any circumstances.

Keith proved him right. He slapped the counter and leaned over to address the suit. "Shane, you're not on my list right now either, but I'd be willing to make an exception."

Shane the Suit huffed, failing to hear the warning that was obvious to Ducalion. If he were scoring the threat, he'd give Keith a seven for originality but only a four for delivery. For a higher rating, the suit's mustache should have at least twitched.

However, the round wasn't over yet.

"I'd like to discuss this in your office," Shane suggested. "The sales floor really isn't the place for it."

"I told you I'm not moving," Keith snarled. Then, to the onlookers: "Didn't I just finish telling everyone I wasn't moving from this spot until I got some goddamned answers?"

The crowd murmured in agreement, some of them going as far as to repeat the statement to Shane the Suit. Apparently, he didn't need reminding.

"Think of Mrs. Tucker," Shane said. "Surely she needs our consideration at a time like this."

Ducalion smiled. While he could appreciate the tactic, he predicted the approach would fail. Where Sharon was concerned, the sympathy card was no better than a deuce.

Keith knew it better than he did.

"Sharon wants the same thing I do," Keith said in a

measured tone, accompanying every word with a rap on the polished wood. "Sharon wants even less than I do. I want those bastards' balls on a platter. I want dickheads to stop barging in every time we have a guest.

"All Sharon wants is her husband back."

Shane nodded. "We all want that. Actually, we seem to have a great many common interests. Home office feels the same way, which is why I think we should continue this discussion in your office."

"Let me tell you about home office." Keith slammed the swinging gate open and stomped across to the suit. "Home office doesn't care about anything but money. Last year they were screaming about lost revenue while we were washing a woman's blood off the front windows. They bitched up a storm when I ordered a new table to replace the one that nutball dropped a body on. Do you have any idea how hard it is to get dead midget off of walnut veneer?"

"Nearly impossible, from the sound of it."

"Damn right it is."

"However, I think it might be best to address your concerns privately. If you'd like, we could include Mrs. Tucker in the conversation. After all, this concerns her as well."

Ducalion heard a metaphorical thump—the sound of one shoe dropping. The scene sharpened before him; the verbal thrusts and parries made sudden sense. Shane the Suit hadn't grown a conscience. Empathy wasn't standard equipment in the middle management model; it couldn't be special ordered either.

However, he could probably fake it.

He'd seen the charade before. Hell, he'd worked the con himself. All cops had the song in their repertoire, but they never sang it to their brothers and sisters. You saved that shit for company.

Or someone on their way out the door.

If things had truly been normal, Keith would have caught it. From the tilt of his head, Ducalion figured the bullshit alarms were already starting to ring. It was taking longer than it should, but Keith had to feel the beginnings of the sandpaper hand job.

Best to step in before the suit got into full stroke mode.

Ducalion stepped through the spectators and positioned himself between Keith and his soon-to-be ex-boss.

"Thank God!" Keith said, throwing his arms around Ducalion's shoulders. "I know you don't have a badge anymore, but at least you're armed."

"Good to see you too Keith." He locked eyes with the suit. "I'm not interrupting anything, am I?"

Shane coughed. "No, no, not at all. I was just telling Keith I thought we should speak somewhere else." He seemed to shrink under Ducalion's gaze. "If you're a friend of the family, you're certainly welcome to wait until we've finished."

"What's the matter Shane?" Ducalion asked. "Don't you have the balls to fire him in front of witnesses?"

"What?" Keith and Shane exclaimed simultaneously.

Ducalion slipped out of Keith's embrace but kept a hold on his arm. "He's cutting you loose brother. Sharon too, if I'm reading it right."

The loss of color in Shane's face was the only answer they needed.

"You son of a bitch," Keith said, trying to shake free of Ducalion's grip.

"Down boy," Ducalion said. "Right now, you're probably gonna walk with most of your benefits intact and a fat check to boot. And if he has one for you, he's got one for Sharon too. Don't screw that up just to get some payback."

"You son of a bitch," Keith said again, still struggling to get past Ducalion.

"I...I...I don't know what—"

"Save it, Shane-O," Ducalion warned, letting his hold on Keith slip just enough to send Shane scrambling back. "I know the song. 'Sorry to inform you, blah, blah, blah. A regrettable decision but blah, blah, blah. Best for all concerned, blah, blah, blah.' It's pitiful, but from what Keith tells me, consistent."

"Now, wait one minute," Shane said, calling on the bluster that had sent many an eighteen-year-old bookseller running for a handcart. "I *am* sorry, it *is* regrettable, and while I agree with corporate that it is best for all concerned, I don't think I should bear the brunt of your anger over a situation I had no hand in creating."

Ducalion pivoted and pushed Keith into the crowd, where a set of hands circled his waist and prevented him from advancing on Shane. The time had come to demonstrate the proper way to set a mustache twitching.

"You got a check?" Ducalion asked, taking a step.

Shane patted the breast pocket of his jacket. "Right here."

"You got two?"

Shane nodded. "As a matter of fact, I do. Very generous, I might add."

"That's fine." Another step. "But here's your dilemma Shane. You've got two checks tucked in there, but there are three people here with an overwhelming desire to stomp a mud hole in your ass the size of the Mississippi Delta. Now, I'm not a mathematician, but I'd say that puts the odds squarely in our favor. How do things add up from where you're standing?"

Shane had obviously received high marks in arithmetic. Beads of sweat formed in a line above his eyebrows—and wait—the hairs on his upper lip began to dance.

"If you think I can be intimidated into reversing home office's decision—"

Ducalion stepped closer. "If you do any reversing here, I'm afraid you're gonna get bent over and experience a kind of cornholing made famous in song and story. And don't think I wouldn't love to hear you squeal—cause you know I would—but I'm sorry to say you're not my type."

Another step.

"As for intimidating you? Well hell Shane-O, I could stand here all day and make you dance, but *regrettably* I've got more important demands on my time." Ducalion extended his hand and snapped his fingers. "Show me the money."

"There are papers to sign," Shane said. "Waivers and releases. I can't hand over these checks without written assurances—"

Ducalion left his open palm hanging in the space between them and turned to face the audience. "Anybody here have any homoerotic fantasies they'd like to explore? Domination? Bi-curious? I got a prime piece of ass here begging to be violated."

God bless them, a few men from the back actually moved forward, and that's when Ducalion knew they'd be walking out of the store with a couple of fat PageSmart checks in hand. He paused to glance at Keith, and saw he had stopped struggling and was now laughing with the rest of the crowd.

However, Ducalion couldn't tell if his sudden jocularity was a result of the verbal smack down he'd witnessed or the person who'd caught him after Ducalion's toss. From the swell of cleavage spilling out over the woman's neckline, Ducalion guessed it was the latter.

A check and a chick. Maybe Keith's day wouldn't be a total wash.

CHAPTER 17

"Wakey wakey, gentlemen. It's time to feed the bulldog."

Consciousness beckoned, spurred on by the whiny, effeminate tenor delivering the words, but Milo couldn't break the surface. Caught on the threshold of awareness, he could hear everything happening around him, but something prevented him from opening his eyes and putting pictures with the noise.

From the sound of it, there was something to see.

At least he wasn't pretzel-bent any more. He could feel the uneven surface of a dirt floor beneath him, even if he couldn't muster enough motor control to move. The speaker's annoying voice echoed slightly, suggesting a large room, but without visuals, there was no way to be sure.

"How badly did you injure them Mr. Chesterton?" the whiner asked.

"We barely left put a mark on the one you sent us after," came the response. Milo recognized Ken's gruff tone. "The other one's probably playing possum. He's a sneaky bastard, that one is."

"Let him play all he wants. His condition is unimportant, and with our acquisition of Mr. Theodore, utterly superfluous."

"Yeah…well…he should have thought of that before he

stuck his ass in where it didn't belong."

"His inclusion exposes us to unnecessary risk."

"Risk? We had to yank this guy out of a store in front of —I don't know—a million people, and you think bringing Deputy Dawg along is a risk?"

This speaker was Arlie, the tall stupid one. With the exception of Theodore, everyone was accounted for.

Almost everyone.

Now completely awake, Milo tried again to shift. He didn't want to call attention to himself, but the paralysis was maddening. If he had to be numb, at least it could extend to the throbbing in his now twice-injured skull. There should have been at least one upside to this insane situation.

In considering the insanity delegation, Milo remembered he had a few things to settle with Trippenstein. Bad enough he had to worry about getting stabbed, chased, threatened, shot, clubbed and kidnapped; now he had to worry about his own crew lining up to take a shot? Lying prone on the floor, Milo couldn't think of one reasonable explanation for the hippie to bounce his host's skull off the dashboard, and it wasn't as if he had anything else to occupy his time.

The conversation continued.

"So where is he?" Ken asked.

"He'll be joining us shortly," the whiner replied. "Until he finishes…processing…his last donor, Mr. Theodore—for all his abilities—does him no good."

Milo heard the ellipses surrounding the word "processing," and whatever he meant by it, it didn't sound good. "Processing" didn't seem like a fun date. The whiner's delivery of the word didn't make it sound like a sport Milo wanted to play, but if they chose Theodore for a pick-up game, too bad, so sad.

He felt a twang at the thought of abandoning the psychic to his fate, but his short stint as the author's protector hadn't worked out so far, and lacking the ability even to twitch a finger, Milo didn't see the situation changing.

Better to focus his attention on preserving his own ass.

"What makes this guy so important?" Ken asked. "What's the matter Salomé; your buddy getting tired of the menu?"

Salomé? Why did that ring a bell?

Milo's effort to place the name frustrated him, and the man's laugh was equally annoying. "Not in the least. The Baptist has been scavenging too long to be bored so quickly. No, our reluctant guest serves a higher purpose than simple variety."

Milo filled the dark silence by imagining what "processing" had to do with a "menu."

"Think of it this way," Salomé said. "Compared to the fuel offered by your former brethren, Mr. Theodore is a large pink rabbit. You know, the one that rolls along beating the large bass drum."

"And keeps going and going," Arlie finished the description.

"Exactly so," Salomé said, accompanied by the sound of fingers snapping. "I'm impressed Mr. Garrison. You're catching on quickly."

Don't bet on it, Milo thought, remembering how easy it had been to disarm Arlie back in PageSmart.

He heard the swish of fabric moving and then Salomé continued.

"For the next phase of our endeavor, we'll require the additional fortitude provided by Master Theodore. If his public persona is a true indicator of his personal power, he'll serve us well indeed."

Everybody ought to be thrilled then. If his voice was working, Milo could have told them all about Theodore's abilities. Nobody talked to the Colony without some serious…

Uh-oh.

Salomé had compared Theodore to an Energizer. Milo wasn't sure where the bunny ranked on the Oogie Boogie power meter, but from everything he'd learned a Gatherer was the royal flush of psychic poker. If the attention he'd experienced recently had demonstrated anything, it had made his position on the enchanted food chain abundantly clear.

Maybe "food chain" wasn't the proper metaphor to use under the circumstances.

Another realization quickly followed: Perhaps his current role as motionless lump had its advantages as well.

Now you've got it, Trippenstein told him, his presence little more than a shadow flitting across Milo's mind.

Son of a bitch! Milo screamed with the only voice available to him. *If we get out of this, I'm digging up your corpse just so I can have something to beat on.*

There's just no subtle with you, is there? The question came so softly that for a moment Milo thought he had imagined it.

Trippenstein? he called. *Tripp?*

I'm here, the hippie answered. *We're all still here.*

What's happening? Why can't I move? Am I still tied up?

No. More silence. Then: *I kind of disconnected your nervous system.*

You did what to my what?

Shhhhhhhh! It's only temporary. Trust me, it's for the best.

How the hell does turning me into an omniplegic lump classify as for the best?

Would you rather be lunch?

So much for subtle, although there was a certain satisfaction in having his suspicions confirmed.

Not even in the metaphorical sense, Milo said.

A loud, metallic creak drowned out whatever response Trippenstein might have made. After the screech, Milo heard a series of slow, muffled thumps, followed by puffs of dust that clogged his nostrils.

A new player had entered the building.

"So happy you've decided to join us," Salomé said, but Milo detected the sarcasm in his voice. Maybe the new arrival caught the note too; he didn't respond to the greeting.

"We got who you wanted," Arlie said.

"We?" Ken asked.

"I seem to remember you getting your ass buried by a pile of books."

"Was that before or after the other guy clocked you upside your head?"

That shut the debate down. Milo had a third opinion, but no one was asking him.

Salomé finally broke the silence. "I agree with The Baptist. This success should be shared by all."

All right, Milo thought. *I need to pay attention. Somebody skipped a couple of lines of dialog.*

"As long as that isn't the only thing we'll be sharing," Ken said.

"Mr. Chesterton, you wound me." Salomé sounded genuinely hurt. "Haven't you gentlemen already reaped the benefits of our short association? Have I not showered you with more opportunities than you've enjoyed your entire life?"

"That's for damn sure," Arlie rose to Salomé's defense, which couldn't have made Ken very happy.

Good.

The conversation paused again, and Milo started to wonder if Trippenstein's whammy had begun to affect his hearing.

"Huh?" from Ken.

"What the hell does that mean?" Arlie chimed in.

"Distractions my friends. These are nothing but distractions. On to the business at hand."

Lost in his immobile shadow, Milo heard the panic in Salomé's tone. His words came too fast, overpowering the other speakers in the conversation. Whatever direction the discussion had taken—and thanks to this Baptist's unwillingness to speak up, Milo wasn't sure what that direction was—Salomé was building roadblocks as quickly as he could.

"What does Annabeth have to do with this?" Arlie asked. "Did something happen while we were gone?"

"Happen? Happen?" Salomé's voice rose several

octaves in the space of four syllables. "What could have happened? Why would you worry?"

"He brought her up," Ken said, suspicious accusation dripping from the statement.

The *whisk* of steel scraping steel brought the subject of Annabeth to a close. Milo heard scrambling footsteps on both sides, the sounds of flight.

In stereo.

"Enough," Salomé said, the harshness of the word failing to conceal the fear in his tone. "We waste precious time."

"Whoa buddy. Go easy with the pig sticker," Ken said from Milo's left.

"Yeah, yeah," Arlie said from Milo's right. "If you're in a hurry, let's just get this done."

Neither man sounded convinced. Without body language to put the words into context, Milo's interpretation was limited, but he didn't believe the capitulation was genuine. It might be time for a new episode, but there was a big fat "To Be Continued" at the end of this one.

"Get him up," Salomé commanded, and Milo wondered if he'd feel the hands when they grabbed him. His mind tensed, but failed to transmit the instruction to his body. He heard footsteps again and smelled the dust they raised.

However, he didn't move.

Someone moaned near his head. The footsteps concentrated in the same area and soon grunting accompanied the movement. The moaning grew louder and segued into incoherent words, phrases and sentences as Ken and Arlie dragged Jack Theodore into consciousness.

"Wait! Wait!" the psychic screamed. "What are you doing? What is this?"

"You've been chosen for a great honor," Salomé said, his voice circling the room. "You should understand that your selection is a tribute, not a condemnation."

"Tribute? Honor? What do you think you're doing with that?"

Apparently, visuals didn't add much in the way of clarity. Theodore sounded as confused as Milo felt. He also sounded scared.

There was more than enough of that to go around.

"Hold him," Salomé said. "Hold him you two."

More scuffling ensued. A *whoosh* carried over the sound of the fracas. Then another. Then two more in quick succession. Milo recognized the sound, although he'd always figured it for a sound effect manufactured for kung-fu movies.

Salomé was making the pig-sticker sing.

Theodore's pleas deteriorated into guttural sobs. Ken and Arlie traded quiet instructions, unintelligible beneath the psychic's cries. Milo strained to twitch or speak or move, but nothing happened. His ears roared from the pressure of his concentration, but he couldn't even raise his eyelids enough to let in a sliver of light.

His status as a spectator remained.

"Cease Mr. Theodore, and be still. Embrace your fate, as we send you to a world far better than this."

The sobs grew louder.

"Mr. Garrison, take a handful of his hair. Mr. Chesterton, pull his arms back. The two of you working in concert should stretch him sufficiently."

"You be goddamned careful with that thing," Ken said, his exertions adding a layer of strain to his voice. "I don't want to lose anything important 'cause he's jerking around."

"Have no fear Mr. Chesterton. My cause is just; my aim will be true."

"Just remember, you cut something off of me and you'll be processing it too, only I don't think you'll be celebrating nearly as much."

"I'll keep that in mind," Salomé said, another—faster— double *whoosh* accompanying the pronouncement.

With the sword singing harmony, Theodore's cries reached a crescendo, ending in an aria of pain as Ken and Arlie coordinated a final pull. Milo breathed a silent prayer, hoping Salomé's aim matched his boasts and that the end came quickly.

Salomé hummed softly. Suddenly, the loudest *whoosh* by far rang out, followed by the wet sound of contact and the clang of steel on bone.

An echoing thump finished the song.

Milo's pulse pounded up the back of his neck and across his skull—the only physical reaction possible in the wake of Theodore's apparent murder. He entertained a small hope that what he had heard had been merely a drama acted out for his benefit—and if so, Oscars for everyone—but the ensuing silence made it unlikely.

He's dead Jim. Trippenstein returned, this time communicating more forcefully.

Great timing Tripp, Milo scolded. *Where were you a minute ago? We might have been able to do something.*

Nothing but getting ourselves killed too.

Milo felt pins in his hands and needles in his feet. His arms and legs warmed as his circulation resumed. His first instinct as feeling returned was to move, but Trippenstein shouted him back to paralysis.

Not yet! he screamed. *If you never trust me again, you've got to trust me now!*

I need to move, Milo said, wincing slightly from the tingling in his limbs. *They're distracted. Maybe we can get away.*

It's not going to happen, Trippenstein replied. Something lurked behind the knowledge, an unspoken "but" the hippie wouldn't reveal. Milo hadn't divined all Trippenstein's secrets yet, but at least he could spot them.

They're not done yet, the hippie continued, *but they're getting close. You're going to move, but it has to be when I say, not a second before.*

Done with what? Milo risked opening his eyes a bit, but the slivers of light pierced his brain and he squeezed them shut again. *Theodore's dead. What do they have to be done with? Planning the wake?* A possible answer occurred to him. *Or you talking about done with me?*

They haven't even started looking at you, which was kind of the point of the exercise, but that's going to change pretty quickly. We've bought ourselves a few seconds, that's all.

Another realization popped into Milo's mind. Apparently, the paralysis hadn't been limited to his body.

What exactly do you know? he asked. *You seem to have a lot of information for someone who's been hiding for the past few hours.*

Only rumors, Tripp said. *Just preparing for the worst-case scenario.*

Which is?

There wasn't time for an answer. The slow, plodding footsteps returned, heading for the area where Ken and Arlie had held Theodore.

"Nicely done," Salomé said. "Come closer my friend, and let me present you with the fruits of our labors."

Just as Milo considered trying to look again, Trippenstein interrupted.

You ready?

Ready for what? To look? The curiosity was killing him. His ears could only tell him so much, and the hippie was being his reticent self.

When I tell you to go, I need you to make a ruckus. If you can get a couple of shots in, that's fine, but I need you to make skin to skin contact with someone for at least a five count.

What was the point if it wasn't going to get them out of there?

Have you got a particular target in mind? Milo asked.

They simultaneously arrived at the same answer: The stupid one. Arlie.

What happens then? Milo said.

Then, Trippenstein said, *we call in the cavalry.*

The plan made sense, but the lack of details bothered him. Maybe it was the constant diet of deception and manipulation he'd experienced lately, but Milo was fed up with being kept in the dark.

So, screw Trippenstein and his half-assed strategizing. Screw the rednecks, screw the fancy guy with the pig sticker and definitely screw the quiet guy with the heavy feet.

Milo opened his eyes and immediately wished he hadn't.

Ken and Arlie stood over Theodore's corpse, Ken's hands clamped firmly over the ears of the psychic's severed head.

A wisp of a man clothed all in purple faced them, holding a long sword in a two-handed grip. Salomé. He raised the blade above his head and snapped it down, bisecting Theodore's skull along the bridge of his nose.

Ken exchanged the partially split head for the sword. Salomé turned and walked the mangled skull several paces away, stopping at two support columns oddly placed in the center of the room.

Support columns wearing shoes.

Milo traced the impossibly long line of the legs, looking past the massive waist, along the broad expanse of chest and across the wide span of the giant's shoulders. The figure—The Baptist? —towered so high above the floor, his head was lost in the shadow of the ceiling. As his gaze traveled to the apex of the roof, Milo realized the shadows hadn't claimed anything.

The Baptist had no head.

Salomé extended his arms, presenting Theodore's head to his partner. As The Baptist took the offering and lifted it to the empty space between his shoulders, Milo watched the large hands move apart and heard a crack accompany the motion. His mind flashed on a baker adding eggs to a recipe, and the image would have been enough to turn his stomach, if Trippenstein hadn't hijacked him again.

There wasn't a dashboard handy for skull bouncing, so, as Theodore's brain slid out of the halves of his skull, the hippie pulled him off the floor and sent him careening into the redneck flunkies. They tumbled to the floor in a tangle of limbs, Milo wrestling with Trippenstein for control of his body.

While the gelatinous mass oozed down into The

Baptist's torso, Salomé drew his sword, faced Milo and lined up for another killing stroke. Ken and Arlie easily pinned Milo to the floor. Trippenstein didn't make much of an effort to escape, but used the opportunity to wrap Milo's hand around Arlie's bare forearm.

Milo heard the hippie counting down from five, feeling his presence withdraw with each number, but flowing out, not in. When Trippenstein reached "one," Milo shook as if a current had run through him. He had his body back, but there was no sense of the hippie settling back into his sub-conscious.

There was no sense of Trippenstein at all.

CHAPTER 18

God damn, son of a bitch.

God damn, son of a bitch.

The targets changed but the song remained the same.

Keith bounced around his soon to be former office, tossing belongings into two open boxes resting on his soon to be former desk. In addition to the personal items, he also appropriated the manager's desk blotter, the manager's stapler, the manager's leather-trimmed portfolio and the manager's pewter letter opener, which he slipped into his pocket instead of a box, in case he wanted to stab someone on the way out the door.

They fired him for someone else's murderous activities; why not cause a little mayhem himself?

Of course, Shane wouldn't cop to the *real* reason, but it wasn't too hard to interpret the innuendo. The official explanation was Keith's treatment of the Zuliekowski bitch. *Riiiiiight.* Verbally abusing a mobile corpse should have earned him a parade and the keys to the city, not his walking papers. Even if there was a valid case against him — an eventuality he refused to consider — his transgression had been a solo effort. Sharon had nothing to do with it.

She'd accepted the termination with more grace than Keith had shown, if a zombie could be considered graceful. While Keith had overturned most of the furniture and

Shane had cowered outside the door, Ducalion pulled her away from the cops holding court in the employee lounge and led her back to the office. The police hadn't protested the interruption. If the look on Ducalion's face wasn't sufficient incentive to take five, most of the detectives still remembered who was responsible for causing the violent evacuation of Harold Washington's grey matter on I-77 (even though it hadn't really been Harold's brains decorating the windshield of that clunker, but that was an entirely different conversation).

You didn't say "no" to someone with that kind of talent on the trigger.

Ducalion walked her through the door, sat her down in one of the chairs facing Keith's desk and took up a protective stance behind her. Shane peeked around the jamb, but waited to enter until Keith agreed to stay behind the desk for the duration of the proceedings.

Another look from Ducalion convinced Keith to make — and keep — the promise.

The interview didn't last long. Keith already knew what he needed to know, and Sharon was in no shape to contest the decision. They signed their respective waivers, traded them for their severance checks and waved bye-bye as Shane made a dash for the exit.

Technically, only Ducalion waved. Sharon continued to stare at her feet and Keith fired off a one-fingered salute.

In Shane's wake, Ducalion accompanied Sharon to help with the emptying of her desk, leaving Keith alone to strip his presence off the room he'd considered a second home for many years. It didn't take as long as he'd expected.

A sweep of his arm brushed the action figures and statuettes from the perimeter of the desk and into one box. He ignored the various performance and sales awards hanging from the walls, preferring to let the next sucker see what he or she was competing against. The remaining items didn't even half fill the second box.

It was a crappy legacy for a ten-year career.

His packing completed, Keith plopped into the familiar

leather cradle of the manager's chair and rested his heels on the corner of the desk. He steepled his fingers under his nose and closed his eyes. The Alpha state came almost immediately; he still had the Zen working for him.

His thoughts raced along the dual tracks of reflection and retribution. On one hand, he felt liberated, freed from the corporate insanity of the retail rat race. He had the sense, the sheepskin and the skills to reinvent his professional self. He was young enough to start over and old enough to make it work. The only variable was who would be lucky enough to add him to the payroll.

The retribution track looked less sunny.

Last year, he'd chided Ducalion for his dourness; now he'd begun to understand it. There was a bill to be paid, a debt of pain due on demand, and the demand was growing exponentially, threatening to overshadow every other consideration. The name on the invoice didn't matter; anyone with a pulse was fair game for collection.

If he felt this way after less than a day, he wondered how Ducalion continued to exist after all these years.

Keith weighed the possible responses to the questions he knew were coming. Not that they mattered; Ducalion's reaction would be to shoot someone. It was the one constant in a world gone mad. Gunfire was an acceptable answer to everything, even the question "Do you want fries with that?"

This was why Keith would never make a drive-thru run with the man again.

Keith could give him a list of targets without risking any fast food employees. Crazy Amy. Eleazar. Anyone with a computer, an internet connection and a terminal illness. And if none of those people worked out, Milo's files at Harrifords would give them plenty of folks to terrorize without raising any Oogie Boogie issues. Shoplifters might not be violent by nature, but that didn't mean one of them hadn't grown a set of balls without the brains to use them correctly.

Something didn't compute. Sure, Milo had made more

enemies than the average retail employee, and the law of averages dictated that eventually one would come after him, but Milo hadn't been the objective, had he? Theodore was the one with the bull's-eye on his back; Milo was just an unfortunate bystander.

So who should Keith tell Ducalion to shoot?

"You look pretty relaxed for a guy that just got his ass handed to him."

Keith's heels fell from the edge of his desk, his meditative state disturbed by the interruption.

The speaker stood framed in the doorway, partially hidden in the shadow created by the intersection of office darkness and hallway light. Only a silhouette was visible, but God, what a silhouette it was.

Keith sat up and slid his legs into the kneehole, thankful for the cover his desk provided. Five years was a long time, long enough for an impressive profile to instigate an unexpected round of pup tent pants.

"It's been a long time since *anyone* handed me my ass," he said, nonchalantly reaching down to pull his trousers away from his groin. "However, somebody did hand me a big, fat severance check, which has done wonders for my relaxation quotient. That, and the unemployment, will keep me rolling in coleslaw for a long time. What's your excuse?"

The shadow shifted and brought his unexpected visitor farther into the office. Well, her chest had made it across the threshold; the rest of her was still loitering outside.

"We didn't have a chance to talk earlier," she said. "Your buddy made with the body slam but kind of left it at that."

Keith remembered the firm cushions pressed into his back while Ducalion went off on Shane. He owed that man a beer.

"I usually like to introduce myself to men before I get physical with them, but in this case I didn't mind making an exception." She crossed the space separating Keith's desk from the door, a simple act that caused the oxygen in the room to vanish along with his blood supply above the equator. Now that he had a good look at her, he realized five years had nothing to do with the pup tent equation.

He'd feel the same after five minutes.

She laid the fingers of her left hand on the outer edge of his desk and extended her right. "I'm Andi Johnson. It's very nice to meet you."

Andi Johnson. Andi Johnson. The name played over and over in his head as he took her hand. Andi Johnson.

Andi Johnson, Andi Pridemore. Andi Pridemore, these are my parents. Yes please, reservations for two. Mr. and Mrs. Pridemore. Keith and Andi, the Pridemores.

"I'm probably gonna need that hand back at some point," Andi said, smiling. Keith immediately released his grip, already missing the touch of her skin.

"Keith Pridemore, and I'm very happy to meet you too," Keith said. He started to stand, then remembered the seismic eruptions happening down south and turned the motion into a half-assed bow.

Andi's smile widened, and Keith knew that *she* knew exactly what was happening. A woman didn't go through life looking like Andi Johnson without fully understanding her effect on the opposite sex.

Damn it.

"Now that we've been properly introduced, what can I do for you?" Keith groaned inwardly at his pitiful attempt at suave and debonair.

"I think you have the question backwards." Andi pivoted slightly and, without breaking eye contact, hiked a perfect buttock onto the desktop. Keith stared open-mouthed at the point of contact, hating the furniture for its good fortune. He also wondered if the desk would fit into one of his cardboard boxes.

Andi gently lifted his chin. "I'm up here. I need you to focus sport."

"Uh-huh," Keith mumbled, electricity coursing along his jaw line. He tried to shake off the intoxicating effects of Andi's touch, but the woman had a serious mojo working.

And again, she smiled with the knowledge of her effect on the XY chromosome, which pulled Keith off his cloud long enough to remember what he was dealing with.

This was the Beast, the Anti-Christ. She clothed herself in different forms, but all were one and one was deadly. This was the Destroyer of Worlds and the Devourer of Bank Accounts. She fed on hearts and snacked on souls, leaving empty shells drained of their testosterone and self-respect.

This was Woman, and to forget that—even for a second—was to damn oneself to everlasting perdition.

Perched on the edge of his desk, her black, ribbed sweater tucked into faded jeans, a corduroy vest straining against its fasteners, Andi Johnson represented everything wrong and horrific and despicable and good and true and light and wonderful.

Dammit! Focus.

"Backwards how?" he finally asked, knowing that by responding, he had taken the first steps down the road to damnation.

A twinkle in her eye sealed his fate. "I'm actually here to help you. Well, not you as much as your friends."

"Milo?" This was beginning to sound like a sales pitch. "And how do you plan on helping Milo?"

Andi leaned forward and reached under her vest, causing the material to stretch further. Before Keith's aneurism could fully materialize, she withdrew her hand and smacked him on the bridge of the nose with a business card.

"Ouch!" Keith said, and snatched the card from her hand. He flipped the crème-toned vellum over and read the single line of text.

ADRIANNE JOHNSON—PRIVATE INVESTIGATOR

"I don't think 'Andi' is a valid diminutive for Adrianne," Keith said, rubbing his fingertips over the embossed lettering.

"Somebody should have probably told my father that

before he filled out my birth certificate." Andi resumed her languid pose, but Keith's pulse continued to climb.

Keith tossed the card into his box o' crap, hoping his casual act was more convincing than his sophisticated schtick. "So what's a private dick going to do for me that the cops can't?"

"A private what?"

"Dick. Dick. A private dick. You're unfamiliar with the term?"

"I'm very familiar with the term," Andi said, and the smallest hint of a blush rose in her cheeks. Then she muttered, "Not lately though."

"What was that?" Keith pantomimed a deaf ear. "What did you say?"

"You heard me."

"What?"

"I said 'You heard me!'"

Keith jiggled fingers in both of his ears. "People out on the street heard you that time."

They shared a laugh, which died off into an uncomfortable silence.

Eventually, Keith found his voice again. "So, what are you going to do for us that I can't get downtown?"

Andi—thankfully—let the entendré pass without comment. "What I'm going to do, my fine, faithful friend, is work twenty-four hours a day, seven days a week, fifty-two weeks a year until we get your buddy back into his wife's loving arms."

The seductive sales pitch had returned. "And what is this full-service sleuthing going to cost me?"

"Not a dime," Andi said. "Same as downtown." And with that, she slid off the desk, and Keith thought the sound of her denim gliding across the polished wood was the most beautiful sound he had ever heard.

A thought occurred to him. "And what will you do for me that my over-zealous friend with the piss-poor attitude and oversized hand cannon can't?"

Andi strolled away, her display of posterior physics

making Keith want to endorse his fat severance check over to Johnson Investigations. When she reached the door, she turned back and tossed her auburn hair over her shoulder.

"When we find him," she said, pulling another smile from her repertoire, "—and we *will* find him you know. When we find him, you and I are going to have a celebration better than anything that gruff-looking son of a bitch could show you."

CHAPTER 19

Milo closed his eyes as Salomé raised his sword. Cursing Trippenstein, he kicked his feet in the dirt, scrambling to escape the rednecks' hold before the killing stroke fell.

Futile, wasted effort.

He swallowed hard, letting it come. He breathed deeply, praying for the peace of acceptance. He relaxed his muscles, falling slack in the grasp of his captors.

The air above him parted with a whistle, and he clenched his teeth in anticipation. He hoped the poets were right in their assertions that death wouldn't hurt and if they were wrong, that the pain wouldn't follow him across the border.

The whistling stopped, a scream exploded in his head and Milo marveled at the wisdom of the bards. The end *was* painless. In fact, the difference between life and death seemed negligible. He still felt the fullness of his lungs, swollen with his final breath. He still felt Ken and Arlie's hands on his arms, holding him down.

And the Colony had returned from their Trippenstein-induced exile.

Death seemed a lot like life and after a second of rumination, Milo realized something had stayed Salomé's hand, probably something to do with the scream in his head.

"I don't believe it," Salomé said, and Milo opened his

eyes to see the dandy standing over him, his sword still poised to split his head in two.

"Believe it," Milo whispered. "Believe it, believe it, believe it." Anything to keep that razor-sharp edge away from him.

"He isn't," Salomé declared. He lowered the blade, but still fixed Milo with a murderous glare. "It's impossible to find a diamond in such a rough place."

Milo heard a murmur. Pitched too low to discern the words, the voice reminded him of the muffled clamor he sometimes sensed when the Colony held court amongst themselves.

Salomé nodded in cadence with the low sound. He stopped bobbing along at the same time the murmur ceased. "Amazing." He leaned forward to address Milo. "Simply amazing. Do you know how remarkable you are?"

"Too remarkable to kill?" It sounded like a good answer to him.

"Not at all."

Damn.

"Too remarkable to waste." Salomé held up a finger. "Your death is inevitable." He cocked his head and the subliminal muttering briefly resumed.

"Inevitable, but delayed," he said when the unintelligible voice went quiet. Annoyance crept into his tone. "Your concealment was successful, but ultimately pointless. Consider that while you await the hour of your offering."

"Offering?"

Salomé waggled the sword before slipping it back into its scabbard. "A glorious opportunity to contribute to a higher cause. If your participation is less than voluntary, so much the better, especially for Mr. Chesterton here. He seems quite anxious to assist you in the shuffling off of your mortal coil." With a mock salute and a swirl of lavender, Salomé strode out of the room. Ken and Arlie scurried after and eventually, The Baptist lumbered away, leaving Milo alone.

As alone as Milo ever managed.

"*Cher Seigneur,*" Etienne exclaimed once the room was clear. "I will only say this Milo: Life with you is never boring."

"It's the only promise I've ever kept," Milo replied, standing to brush the dirt from his pants. "Of course, I made that promise to Sharon, but why shouldn't everyone benefit."

"Grumble later Milo," Maria said. "Right now, we have other things to worry about."

"What's to worry about? We're going to die."

"Been there, done that," Kimmy said. "Not so anxious to do the deed again."

"We're not going to die," Maria scolded. "At least not today."

"I'll agree with you on that one," Milo said. "I don't know how long it'll be till the next feeding time, but I doubt it'll be today."

"That's a comforting thought," Isadore said. "Please Milo, cheer us up some more, could you?"

Milo walked away from the center of the room and began to pace the perimeter. "Sorry Isadore, I'm not in the mood to shake my pom poms. You'll have to amuse yourselves."

Tajiri joined him at the wall. "We seem to be in some sort of outbuilding."

Milo ran his hands along a seam formed by two warped boards. Sunlight trickled through the imperfect joint. "Out where?"

"It doesn't matter. It doesn't matter what lies beyond this wall. What matters is that we break through to the other side."

"You're making Jim Morrison references?" Milo had to chuckle. "Now I know we're doomed."

"Only if you allow us to be Milo-san," Tajiri said. "Only if you allow us to be."

"Then let's all hold hands and sing Kumbaya," Milo exploded. "Oh wait, none of you have hands any more."

"Milo," Maria said.

"Let's do a couple of choruses and then we'll huff and puff and blow our way out of here."

"Milo," Kimmy said, moving to stand next to Maria.

"Better yet, let's have Tajiri take center stage and kung-fu his way through the wall. He can do anything, can't he? All righty then. C'mon Tajiri, show me some of those moves."

Etienne joined the ladies. "Milo," he said.

"What part of this don't you understand? That man is going to cut my head off and feed it to that monster. Don't you get it? Head? Off. Brain? Gone. End of story. Roll credits."

Tajiri and Isadore flanked the other three. The Colony formed a phalanx, a protective semi-circle while he ranted.

Milo didn't care.

"Sharon was right," he said. "She always said I'd wind up doing something stupid at work and get myself killed. Turns out, I did the stupid thing at *her* work, but here we are."

"Such a defeatist posture doesn't flatter you," Tajiri said.

"Neither will decapitation."

"So we just give up?" Isadore asked. "When they come back, you'll just bend over and let them have their way."

Milo frowned at the image that invoked. Isadore quickly added, "You know exactly what I mean.

"What are my alternatives? Seriously Isadore, what's Plan B?"

Maria answered for him. "We've squeaked through tighter spots. We made it through Munsch. We made it out of the mall, or have you forgotten so quickly."

"I'm not the one with the memory problems," Milo said. "We didn't do a damn thing to Munsch except piss him off. If it hadn't been for Ducalion, we'd be dead. As for the mall, that was Trippenstein, not any of us. And in case you haven't noticed, our hippie friend's nowhere to be found."

"We kind of figured that out when we all got booted

from his meadow," Kimmy said. "I can't believe he bailed like that."

"Don't be too harsh on the bohemian," Etienne said. "I'm sure he had his reasons."

"You're defending Trippenstein?" Milo scoffed.

Etienne shook his head. "Merely holding out hope. Our absent friend may yet carry the day."

"Hooray for that," Milo muttered. "Someone else saves our ass again."

"Milo Raymond Tucker!" Maria yelled, channeling Sharon and Milo's mother to perfection. "Don't you dare. Don't you dare complain about Trippenstein while not thirty seconds ago you gave us all up for dead. At least he's trying."

"Do you really believe that?" Milo asked. "Do you honest-to-God think he's out there rounding up some help?"

"I don't know what he's doing, but at least he's doing something!"

"Don't you think I know that?" Milo fell back against the wall. Like a balloon with an open valve, he slid down the boards and sat in the dirt, legs splayed in front of him.

"I know I'm supposed to do something, but I don't know what it is. I keep thinking I'm better than this, but for the life of me, I don't know what I'm supposed to do."

The Colony vanished from the center of the room, instantaneously reappearing on the ground before him.

"This should be it," he told them, looking at each in turn. "All my life, I kept waiting for the chance to do something important, and now that I have it, it turns out I can't do a damn thing. I never imagined I could be anything as powerful as a Gatherer; hell, I never even knew Gatherers existed. All my life I've been telling myself I could do something if only…if only…"

"If only what?" Kimmy asked.

Milo traced his fingers in the dirt, creating swirls and patterns as he spoke.

"This isn't the life I imagined. When I was a kid,

everyone told me that one day I'd grow up and do great things, and after hearing it year after year, I started to believe it. I think that's what screwed me up. It was a done deal; everybody said so. As I got older, I quit working toward it and just waited for it to happen.

"But things got harder. It's like I had a head start on everyone my age, but eventually the years caught up with me, and suddenly I wasn't so special anymore. I kept ahead of the curve through high school, but there were people passing me left and right. By the time I got to college, I was just another dipshit cutting classes and partying too much.

"I quit school when the money ran out, so now I was just another nobody without a degree trying to get a job that didn't involve nametags and paper hats. I took a test for the state police, and for a while I thought I had the magic back. It was like I was a kid again, everyone telling me how great I was—and even better—how great I was going to be. My scores were in the stratosphere and I had recruiters calling every day.

"But you can't be a cop if you can't run. You can't be a cop if you can't do a chin-up. If you've got arthritis in your shoulders and cartilage missing from your knees, you can't keep up with the bad guys and if you can't keep up with the bad guys, there's hardly any point in pinning on a badge. So sorry; better luck next time."

The monologue shocked him. He'd thought about this every day, and while it had to be old news for the Colony, Milo had never articulated this line of frustration aloud. Impending death had a way of loosening the tongue.

"Then I met Sharon." He smiled, and the warmth he felt at the mention of her name brought tears to his eyes. "She didn't care that I didn't have a degree. She didn't care that I wasn't a cop. Hell, she's never been happy with my job at Harrifords; she thinks it's too dangerous. Go figure.

"I thought being a good husband would be enough, but it wasn't. I thought doing a good job every day would be enough, but it's not. I kept hearing all those voices from the past, telling me I should be doing more and doing it better, and damn it I listened. I made myself miserable for not living up to somebody else's definition of my potential, because deep down inside, I agreed with them."

"*Ach*, Milo," Isadore said. "You're way too hard on yourself *boychik*."

"Isadore's right," Kimmy said. "We've been around. We know about these things."

"And look where it's gotten you," Milo said. "Y'all have got how many centuries between you? Now it's over, and I did it in less than a year. Jared Cavelet's dead. Theodore's dead. Trippenstein's God knows where."

"And whom shall we blame for that?" Tajiri said. "Shall we lay responsibility for all the woes of the world at your feet? People die every minute of every day Milo. Let us sit upon the ground and sing sad songs for all those lost. Never mind the countless lives saved by your confrontations with Munsch. Forget about the sacrifices that placed us in your care, and you in ours. Disregard Alex and Mickey, because — according to you — their failure rendered their deaths meaningless."

"I never said that." Milo shook his head. "I never said that at all."

"Your every action screams it," Tajiri countered. "Your capitulation dishonors not only your spirit, but the spirit of everyone who's come before you. Your ancestors wail at the gates of paradise, so heavy is the burden of your shame."

Keith would have called those fighting words, but Milo couldn't muster the strength to be angry. If Tajiri wanted to humiliate him into action, he'd only been half-successful. His despair overwhelmed him, submerging his love for Sharon under tides of disgrace and ignominy. He was glad she'd never see this side of him.

Death was preferable.

Suddenly, a memory surfaced, blocking out Milo's surroundings and immersing him in the past. He stood in a dark alley, hidden by shadow as he watched the street beyond, his fingers curled around the grip of a pistol. The weight in his hand felt foreign, but simultaneously comforting. There was power in the talisman of the gun, power enough to calm the remembered pounding of his heart, even though he had never held a firearm before.

As he pondered the strange duality of the familiar and alien, phantom tires screeched up the street, shattering the stillness of the recollection. Milo felt himself lean forward, trapped by the inevitability of the past. Elongated ovals of light flashed in the intersection to his left, flattening as the sound of a racing engine grew closer. He flexed the hand holding the pistol.

He needed to be ready.

Milo prepared to leap out, knowing he would assume a standard combat stance and fire five shots into the oncoming car. The first would destroy the front tire on the passenger side, sending the vehicle into a clockwise slide. The next four bullets would stitch a line down the driver's side, shredding the engine, the driver, a rear-seat passenger and the gasoline tank. After the car exploded, he'd continue to squeeze the trigger on spent chambers until stopped by a paramedic.

This had never happened to him, but it had.

"This doesn't belong to you," a stranger's voice told him. "At least, not in the classic sense."

As the speeding car entered the intersection, everything began to happen exactly as Milo remembered it, or perhaps *predicted* was the more appropriate word, since it was impossible to remember that which had never happened.

At least, it used to be.

A body leapt into the street, but Milo stayed where he was, an unarmed observer to the carnage about to occur. He—who until a second ago had been *him*—raised the gun and fired at the car. As the bullet left the barrel, fire erupted from the pistol and stopped in a scarlet plume. The vehicle halted as well, poised on a tire as it began its pirouette. All motion in the tableau ceased, except Milo could now move, suddenly freed from the inevitability of the past.

"Sometimes, you just have to stand your ground," the stranger spoke again, obviously sharing Milo's ability to act within the frozen diorama. Milo turned toward the sound of the voice to see the double of the cop in the street.

It was Mickey, Milo realized, unsure of how he knew, but certain of the identification.

Mickey walked past him, following his shade into the street. He circled his doppelganger, leaning in and leaning back as he observed this moment from his past.

"Shit lingers," he said. "There are echoes and ripples that never totally go away. Some things you take with you and some things you leave behind." He shrugged. "It happens."

"Where are we?" Milo asked. "Are we still in that building?"

"Of course you're still in that building," Mickey snapped. "What do you think this is? Beam me up Scotty? Where the hell else would you be?"

"I only thought—"

"You're not thinking at all. We're not standing here, y'know. This is nothing more than the ghost of a memory, something caught in the tide when Alex pushed the others out. Most of me is gone, but as long as the others survive, a part of me will too." He pointed at the almost crystalline flame suspended from the end of the pistol barrel. "And as memories go, you couldn't ask for a better one, could you."

"I don't understand."

"Trust me kid, I'm getting to that."

Mickey buried his hands into the deep pockets of his overcoat and approached the alley.

"When a car's bearing down on you, I figure you've got three choices. One: you can get the hell out of the way; two: you can let it run over your ass; or three: you can blast the shit out of it until it stops. The key word here is 'choice.' Whatever winds up happening, you can bet the outcome depends on one thing and one thing only.

"You."

Milo shook his head. "It's not that simple."

"It *is* that simple. Everything's that simple. Don't talk to me about repercussions and consequences. I'm here to tell you, it *all* comes down to you. All of it. Everything. What you have to decide is whether you're gonna get your ass run down or start blasting."

"I can't control that. I can't control anything any more."

"Bullshit! The actions of others? Nope, not a damn thing you can do about it. The trick is how you react—how you respond. That's what determines your reality, and if anybody tells you different, you tell them to stick it up their ass."

"And when it's not enough…?"

"Then it's not enough." Mickey shrugged. "Nobody's keeping score pal. There isn't a trophy for the guy with the most wins. Death isn't the end of everything, y'know. Look at me; I've been dead for years."

Mickey raised a hand and snapped his fingers. The borrowed memory behind him blurred into motion, tires screeching as Milo's view began to fade.

"The car's coming," Mickey's voice trailed into nothingness along with the landscape. "Are you gonna get your ass run over or are you gonna start blasting?"

Milo opened his eyes, once more trapped in the rednecks' prison and surrounded by his Colony. If they hadn't shared his encounter with the ghost of Colonists' Past, they knew about it now, and stared expectantly, waiting for his reaction.

Milo stood, brushed the dust from his pants and faced his passengers.

"Somebody think of something," he said. "We're busting out of here."

CHAPTER 20

Arlie couldn't understand why everyone was so upset.

The Baptist had what he wanted. According to Salomé, the psychic's brain would keep him ticking for a good, long time and with enough juice to get done whatever it was they wanted to get done. The bonus here was it also meant there wouldn't be any more head chopping until the needle hit E, and that was just fine with Arlie.

And since Salomé seemed to want whatever The Baptist wanted, he ought to have felt pretty spiffy, but he marched around Hiram's living room like a big purple ball of mad. It was hard to figure out the problem from listening to only Salomé's half of the conversation, but the gist seemed to be Jack Theodore's brain not fitting the specs as well as it should have.

That, and something to do with the extra guy they'd brought back.

Ken wasn't happy either, but Ken rarely was, so that wasn't any surprise. Salomé emptied his bladder in Ken's direction just as quickly as The Baptist refilled it, and Ken didn't look like he appreciated the shower. He hadn't made a move to retaliate—not yet—but as he let the piss roll down his back, his eyes moved across Hiram's walls and kept stopping on the Japanese ninja sword hanging above the mantel. Arlie wasn't sure how much shit his friend planned to take, but he knew Ken had to be reaching maximum capacity.

The Baptist wasn't the only one with a full tank.

Arlie just wanted a cheeseburger.

A simple want, and one easily filled with plenty of fresh meat in The Brotherhood freezers and no shortage of Brotherhood wives willing to slap beef for him. While the others continued to wave their dicks around, he rolled the picture of a fresh half-pounder around his mind, and it did absolutely nothing to quench his craving. He added cheese to the image, slapped some thick slabs of bacon across the top and doused the whole thing with ketchup and mustard.

Nothing.

"We brought you what you wanted," Ken repeated for the fourteenth time, interrupting Arlie's mental cooking. "Don't take it out on us 'cause all of a sudden you decided you wanted something else."

"No one could have anticipated this development," Salomé said, and Arlie couldn't tell if the statement was for Ken or The Baptist. "I think we should consider ourselves fortunate to have the additional power at our disposal."

Definitely meant for Ken but directed at The Baptist.

"Damn right you're lucky," Ken said. "Y'all wouldn't have squat if it weren't for me and Arlie."

Onions. Long strands of fried onions coiled atop juicy Black Angus, cradled in a fresh bun — so fresh your fingers left dents no matter how gently you handled it. He heard Ken say his name, but the vision of the burger pushed all other concerns aside.

Silence dominated the room. Everyone had quieted down, except for Salomé, who tapped his foot in an uneven rhythm. Flashes of disappointment and violence assaulted the periphery of Arlie's thoughts, but the power of beef kept them at bay.

Salomé and Ken didn't appear to share the protection, as both men raised cupped hands to cover their ears, not that the gesture gave them any defense against The Baptist's intrusion.

"Enough!" Salome shouted, wincing at his own outburst. "I beg of you, cease this incessant complaining."

Ken squeezed his temples hard enough to turn his knuckles white. He pulled his hands away and like a swimmer, swirled a finger through each ear. When his digits came out stained with blood, Ken lost it.

"I'm fuckin' bleeding!" he screamed. "You headless freak, what the hell have you done to me?"

"Caution Mr. Chesterton," Salomé warned. "This is not the time to antagonize him."

Ken held out his hands. "Like I give a damn right now. He's turning my brains to goddamned mush."

Maybe a tomato. Maybe some lettuce. Lettuce was good. A couple of crispy lettuce leaves might do the trick. Arlie could hear the crunch of greens in his mouth, feel the surprising coolness counteract the heat of the sirloin.

God, he wanted a cheeseburger.

"Do you see what you're doing?" Salomé said to his partner with a sweeping wave towards Ken. "How much power do you require, when you can already accomplish this? Will you sacrifice us all just to satisfy your thirst for this Gatherer?"

"Is anybody else hungry?" Arlie asked, wiping drool from his lips.

"What?" Ken wiped his fingers across his jeans. "What the hell are you babbling about?"

"All of the sudden, I could really go for a cheeseburger," Arlie said. "I don't know about the rest of you, but I'm starving."

"You broke him!" Ken yelled. "Bad enough you're trashing my head, but now you've gone and broken Arlie."

"I'm fine Ken," Arlie said. "Just kind of hungry."

"I've sprung a leak and he's thinking about food. Now tell me he's not broken."

"It is passing strange," Salomé said, eyes narrowing in Arlie's direction.

"Nothing strange about it," Arlie said. "I don't see what all the fuss is about. We got that psychic fella y'all wanted and something extra besides. You said it yourself, that big brain ain't gonna last forever. Now you've got

             M. Stephen Lukac

something for when it peters out. Everybody wins; let's eat!"

Once more, the room fell silent. Again, Salomé interrupted the quiet, but this time with a tentative chuckle. As the preliminary huffs escaped the dandy's lips, Ken caught the bug and was soon shaking with laughter. Arlie joined in too, the hilarity dampening his hunger. Then, with the three caught in the throes of a full-blown giggle fit, a discordant note entered Arlie's mind. Deep and rhythmic, it sounded like someone had attacked a Wookie with a feather, and as it got louder and stronger, Arlie realized it was the sound of The Baptist laughing. Gasping, he looked at Ken and Salomé to see if they heard it too. Their hitched breathing and puzzled expressions were all the answer he needed and the shared revelation set them all off again.

"Mr. Garrison," Salomé said between wheezes, red-faced and teary-eyed, "this is why I will always treasure you. While we bandy about recriminations, you dive directly into the quagmire and emerge holding the pearl our intellectual proclivities prevent us from discovering. I salute you sir. Truly, there is wisdom in inanity."

"Way to go Arlie," Ken said, leaning over to punch his friend's shoulder.

Arlie beamed. Ken's congratulations didn't sound as pretty as Salomé's, but somehow it meant more to him. It'd be a while before anyone had the sack to call him stupid again.

But he still wanted that cheeseburger. And some fries. Real fries, not those skinny shoestrings they served at the drive-thru.

"Now that that's out of the way," Ken said, "what's so special about this other guy."

"This other guy?" Salomé sat on the hearth, still fighting to regain his composure. "Such a banal description for such a powerful man."

"Powerful?" Ken asked. "He didn't seem all that powerful to me."

"One shouldn't restrict one's perceptions to only the

visible, as our good friend Mr. Garrison has aptly demonstrated." Salomé nodded to Arlie, who nodded right back.

"This 'guy'—as you call him—is a Gatherer, a repository for discorporated spirits, and as such, a man of nearly infinite mental acuity."

"A what for a who?" Arlie asked.

Salomé sighed. "He collects souls. Simply put, his mind houses the spiritual essences of those who have passed on. Rather than crossing over into heaven, hell, Nirvana or any of the other mythological afterlives, these five"—he raised an eyebrow in The Baptist's direction—"yes five entities now reside within him. Can either of you comprehend the capacity required for such a feat?"

Arlie scratched his head. "Um, a lot?"

Salomé nodded. "More than could possibly be measured. As such, his mind eclipses Mr. Theodore's in the same way Mr. Theodore's eclipses Mr. Garrison's."

"So, 'a lot' really covers it then," Arlie said, pleased to hear someone else was next on The Baptist's bill of fare.

"Indubitably," Salomé said. "Indubitably."

"So what's the big hoo-hah?" Ken asked. "Let's crack that sumbitch open and put him to work." He cracked his knuckles. "I'll be happy to split his noggin if you'd like."

"When the time comes Mr. Chesterton, but not a moment before." Salomé raised his hands in a "hold on" gesture. "This, of course, is the source of our friend's momentary displeasure. In order to utilize the Gatherer's mind, we must first exhaust Mr. Theodore's, and Mr. Theodore has quite a bit of potential to tap. It might be days—even weeks—before we'll be ready to reap the benefits of your unexpected acquisition."

"So we keep the hero on ice till you're ready for him."

"Exactly so. However, incapacitating a Gatherer for such an extended period of time may prove problematic."

"How's that gonna be a problem?" Arlie asked, having moved from the French fry question on to the choice of drinks.

"The problem is there'll be folks looking for him," Ken

said.

"There's folks looking for Theodore too," Arlie countered. "Don't mean they're gonna find him."

"Yeah, but if they're looking for Theodore and find this guy, we're still screwed."

Arlie hadn't considered that.

"Gentlemen, gentlemen, let us not disperse the convivial atmosphere by falling back into acrimonious recriminations. While I share your concerns regarding our captives, I'm not overly troubled by the possibility of discovery. According to the Fourth Estate, your egress was relatively unnoticed and all reports seem to mention 'numerous leads' which tends to be synonymous with a decided lack of concrete information."

"So nobody knows shit," Ken translated.

"I am confident that is the extent of their knowledge vis-á-vis our little enterprise."

Arlie clapped his hands. "That's it then." He rose from his seat and patted his pockets until he felt his keys press against his palms.

"Where do you think you're going?" Ken asked.

"I already told you," Arlie said. "I'm hungry and I'm going out for a cheeseburger. Y'all want me to bring you something back?"

CHAPTER 21

Whatever could be said about The Brotherhood, and Milo had uttered just about every obscenity in the English language, they knew how to construct a solid building. With the Colony trailing behind as an ethereal demolition crew, he'd paced the perimeter of the structure without finding one loose board or even an exposed nail head.

The absence of exploitable weaknesses was having a deleterious effect on his newfound bravado.

"Not even a window to break," he muttered, standing in the center of the room. "I could break a window."

"That's probably why there aren't any," Kimmy said.

"It's not easy to hang a window," Isadore said. "Everybody thinks *ach*, I'll just cut a hole in the wall, but it's not that simple. Do you know what happens if you just cut a hole in the wall?"

Nobody cared what happened, but that didn't stop him.

"I'll tell you what happens. *Klap!* The wall falls down, that's what happens."

"Great," Milo said. "We'll just cut a hole in the wall and watch it fall. That'll fix everything."

"If we had some tools, it wouldn't be a bad idea," Etienne offered.

"If we had some tools, I'd just take the door off its hinges."

"Rather than reviewing what we lack," Tajiri said, "perhaps we should catalog what we possess."

"That's a good idea," Milo said. "We can get that done in—I don't know—a minute and a half. Then I can get back to bitching."

"Who would expect a barn to be so hard to get out of?" Maria asked.

Milo looked around again. "Is that what this is?"

"I believe so." With outstretched arms, she twirled in place. "It's a big, empty building out in the middle of nowhere. What else could it be?"

"Yeah, it's a barn," Kimmy said. "I saw it when they brought us in." She winked at Milo. "Thank God it doesn't smell like one."

Milo inhaled deeply. "You're right. It doesn't smell at all."

"Only *le sang* of the late *Monsieur* Theodore," Etienne said, motioning toward the stained area of the earthen floor.

Now that Etienne said it, Milo caught the tang of copper in the air, and noticed a small knot of flies hovering over the still-damp ground. His stomach clenched in response.

"The never-ending circle," Tajiri observed. "Life ever feeds at the trough of death."

"Looks like the trough is drawing a crowd," Milo said. "If we don't get out of here soon, we're gonna be hip deep in bugs."

"There's a pleasant thought," Kimmy said, shuddering.

"Still…" Milo mused, looking up at the high ceiling. Something about the flies had triggered a thought, a hazy recollection that dangled just out reach of his conscious mind.

He walked over to the bloodstain and watched the insects swarm above it. In groups of two and three, flies broke formation and dove into the soup, pausing long enough to gorge themselves and then returning to the holding pattern. As Milo stood there, some of the flies climbed away from the group, only to be replaced by twice as many new arrivals.

"Shoo fly, shoo fly, fly away home," Milo whispered, tracking the departures as they ascended. His blurry memory began to coalesce as he traced the flight paths into the eaves.

"Barns get pretty hot, don't they?" he asked Maria.

"Like an oven," she replied. "At midsummer, my family's barn was as hot as a kettle set over a fire."

"Not a good thing to have, is it? A hot barn filled with hay, or straw, or manure, or whatever it is you keep in a barn."

"Not a good thing at all," Maria agreed. "But then again, we rarely kept it closed up like this."

"Yeah, but you had to shut the doors sometimes." A smile spread across Milo's face as he spied what he wanted to see. "That's why you have those."

He pointed up at the trusses, where the apex of the roof met the wall. Set into the triangular junction, metal slats twinkled with reflected sunlight.

A vent.

"Just enough ventilation to keep the place from going up in flames," Milo said. "I can't believe it's in there too solidly."

"Probably just a few nails or screws holding it in place," Isadore said. "After all, who worries about a vent?"

"Who needs to?" Etienne asked. "Who would bother to climb so high?"

"I shall do it," Tajiri said, already studying the wall.

Kimmy looked up. "How are we going to get all the way up there?"

"Providence has smiled upon us after all," Tajiri said. "These beams protrude sufficiently to provide a path to the top."

Milo measured the span between the supports. With his arms fully extended, he could place his palms flat against the two by sixes.

Barely.

"I know it was my idea Tajiri, but are you sure about this?" Milo's shoulders began to ache, even without exerting any pressure. "I know you're Superfly and all that, but remember whose car you'll be driving."

Like wings unfolding, a flood of warmth spread across Milo's back and the pain vanished. Tajiri's presence felt closer—not completely forward, but not in the background like the rest of the Colony. There was a strange duality to the sensation, different from his earlier experience with Mickey's echo.

"Way to go with the psychic Ben-Gay," Milo said, "but this is gonna hurt like hell when you're finished."

"I will do my best to minimize your discomfort," Tajiri assured him.

Milo closed his eyes and inhaled deeply, calming his mind to allow Tajiri to come fully forward. When he opened them again, he stood with the rest of his passengers and watched his body climb the wall.

It wasn't the most difficult ascent Tajiri had ever attempted, but he was years out of practice. Milo's lack of conditioning increased the challenge, but Tajiri quickly began to suspect that his host's physical shortcomings were due more to unrealized potential rather than medical ailments. Once freed from their current predicament, Tajiri planned to explore the full extent of Milo's alleged infirmities.

On the ground, Milo caught snatches of Tajiri's thoughts. He sensed flashes of insight and snippets of interior monologue, but that was all. The rest of the Colony were open books as they observed and commented on Tajiri's prowess, but Tajiri himself existed only as an occasional flutter on the screen of his consciousness.

Was this how they perceived him, or had his current position somehow changed the communication equation?

At the top of the wall, Tajiri braced his feet against the support beams and attacked the metal vent. The rivets holding it gave easily. Several seconds after reaching the summit, Tajiri had an opening barely wide enough to squeeze into, but with some effort and a few deep breaths, he passed through the wall...

...To find himself dangling twenty-five feet up.

Adjusting his grip on the vent hole, he pulled his knees

to his chest and planted both feet against the wall. The maneuver shifted some of the weight from his shoulders and gave him a better view of the ground. Fortunately, there wasn't anything blocking his potential landing zone, but neither was there anything to cushion his descent.

A fall from this height wouldn't be fatal—even in Milo's body, he had enough confidence in his skills to believe that—but an injury would negate any advantage gained by their escape. Further study seemed pointless; nothing about the outer wall or the terrain below was likely to change in the next few minutes.

However, as Tajiri prepared to re-enter the barn, he noticed the slope of the roof, and its proximity to the vent hole digging into his fingers. Once again, providence had supplied them with the solution to an apparently insurmountable dilemma.

If going down wasn't possible, going up was the only option.

He repositioned his feet slightly and pushed off, transferring his grip from the vent to the edge of the roof in one motion. Gravity threatened to pull him down, but the force of his kick-off provided enough momentum to pendulum his legs above the level of the roof. With a heave and a twist, he rolled over and onto the gentle slope of the roof.

The shingles gave Tajiri enough traction to navigate the southern side of the roof. He shuffled to the edge and peered down, pleased with what he saw. Another roof jutted out from the side of the building, only a dozen or so feet below where he stood. That roof sloped as well, so that the drop from its edge to the ground was only slightly taller than an average man's height.

Movement to his right reminded Tajiri how exposed he was, and he dropped to a squat, hoping the sudden move didn't attract anyone's attention. He duck-walked to the apex of the roof for a better view of their surroundings.

Their prison sat at the bottom of a small depression, with woods spread out to the south and west and several buildings grouped on the hill to the north. With the afternoon sun at his back, Tajiri wasn't overly concerned that the people he saw moving around the compound would notice him, but as he watched, he realized it wasn't likely they would react if he were to run screaming in their midst.

They walked between the buildings like robots, their steps the automatic, measured paces of those with no direction or destination. Tracking their courses throughout the compound, he confirmed his hypothesis; this was motion for motion's sake. Whoever these people were, their actions spoke of control, not self-determination.

Curious, he thought as he returned to the southern edge of the roof and hopped down. By the time Tajiri stood in the weeds beside the barn, he hadn't answered any of his questions.

The others joined him, Milo favoring him with a bow. Tajiri smiled and returned it.

"Shall I rejoin the others?" Tajiri asked.

Milo nodded. "For now. I think I can get us where we need to go."

Kimmy moved to the west, pointing at the far corner of the building. "If I remember right, we should head this way."

Etienne confirmed it. "*C'est vrai.* Follow *le jeune fille,* she seems to know the way."

Milo moved, but in the opposite direction.

At the east corner, he dropped to his knees and peeked around the wall. Parallel red clay tracks led away from the building and curved away to the right up a small hill. To the left, tall grass separated the road from a copse of trees; to the right, the strip of grass was wider, partially hiding the rusted husks of farming equipment.

"Milo," Isadore whispered, "are you praying?"

"Why would I be praying?"

Isadore shrugged. "Everything's still attached. We're out here instead of in there. God is great. Pick one."

"Let's worry about Thanksgiving later." Milo chuckled. "We've still got unfinished business here."

The declaration generated confusion among everyone

but Tajiri; so much for instantaneous understanding. The route up the hill appeared to be clear, but it wouldn't hurt to watch and wait for a moment.

"We can't bail out," Milo explained. "I guarantee you if we come up missing, these guys'll be in the wind so fast no one will ever find them."

"But couldn't we alert the authorities?" Maria asked.

"Hear, hear," Etienne chimed in. "Let us leave these barbarians to the *gendarmes*."

Milo snuck another peek around the corner, happy to have waited. "It's not that simple guys."

"It is not simple at all," Tajiri said.

"Look up there," Milo said, knowing the Colony already saw what he did. At the top of hill, a lone figure moved left to right across the horizon. When he reached what Milo assumed was the other side of the unpaved road, the man turned and shuffled back in the opposite direction. Obviously a sentry, the man didn't seem like a willing soldier in Salomé's army.

"Think about that guy," Milo said. "What do you think will happen to him if Salomé and his pet monster pull up stakes? I don't know how many others there are like him, but I'd bet lunch money a lot of them didn't drink the Kool-Aid."

"So now you're Moses?" Isadore said. "What, we're going to lead them all to the Promised Land?"

"Not quite," Milo said.

"We're going after Pharaoh."

CHAPTER 22

It didn't matter that in the past seventy-two hours Arlie Garrison had committed at least thirteen felonies and been an accessory to at least three others. He didn't care that he might be one of West Virginia's most wanted criminals. He hadn't even bothered to change his clothes, ignoring the spatter on the cuffs of his pants and the toes of his boots. Let somebody ask about the blood on his knuckles and under his nails; he didn't give a shit. He'd ask for a Wetnap and some take-out and tell the nosy Ned to stay out of his business.

He needed a goddamned cheeseburger.

He'd already passed three sets of golden arches, two cowboy hats and a host of other oversized, trademarked corporate logos, but for some reason, Arlie had kept the pickup tooling on down the highway. As the fourth McSign dwindled in the rearview mirror, he thought about turning around, but his inner beast of hunger reasserted itself and the search continued.

He wasn't sure what he was hunting for, but he trusted his rumbling gut to know when he found it.

It turned out to be a roadside diner; an unpainted cinderblock cube set barely a car length back from the berm. A bright yellow sign with lighted arrows on top directed traffic into the mud pit of a parking lot. "Good Food" was the advertisement, with what looked like inverted plastic nines used in place of the letter "d." Questionable ambiance aside, the fleet of eighteen wheelers and West Virginia State Police cruisers surrounding the place was testimony to the quality of the menu.

The gut never lied, and Arlie fishtailed off the road to sample the fare at Good Food.

A silver bell taped above the ill-fitting screen door announced his arrival, and twelve pairs of eyes swiveled in their sockets to watch him walk in. Arlie nodded at the diners, prompting a wave of bobbing Orange County Chopper ball caps and Smokey Bear hats. Seemingly cleared by the clientele, Arlie made his way to the counter and the tent pole named Jill-Beth, according to the doily pinned to her chest.

"Whatcha' have?" Jill-Beth asked, plucking the nub of a pencil from her hair, which was the same shade of pink as her uniform. All that pink coupled with her non-existent figure made her look like the leftovers on a paper cone of cotton candy.

I want the biggest cheeseburger you've got, Arlie thought, swallowing saliva so he didn't drench the woman when he spoke.

"I need to be arrested," is what he said, loud enough to drown out every conversation in the dining area.

Pinky's pencil stopped in mid-scribble. "Say that again honey."

I want a cheeseburger, Arlie heard the words in his mind. *A cheeseburger, a cheeseburger, a goddamned cheeseburger!* Properly rehearsed, he tried again.

"I want to be arrested," he screamed. "Arrested, arrested, goddamned arrested!"

Maybe Ken was right. Maybe The Baptist had broken him.

"Is there a problem here?" One of the state troopers had interrupted his meal long enough to come to Peppermint Patti's aid. The nameplate tacked to his pocket read BEVINS, and Trooper Bevins obviously had a thing for cotton candy.

"I think he's on something Duwayne," the waitress

said. "Is that it honey? Are you on something?"

"I want someone to arrest me!" Arlie nearly sobbed. How many times did he have to ask? "Why is it so hard to get arrested here? What the hell's wrong with you people?"

And why wouldn't his mouth work right?

Trooper Bevins jammed his thumbs behind his Sam Browne belt and rocked back on his heels. Arlie's mouth might be on the fritz, but his eyes were 20/20 like always, and he had no trouble reading the look on the Statie's face.

Officer Duwayne was getting ready to show off for Jill-Beth.

"I think you might be right," Bevins said. He smiled, showing more gum than teeth, the perfect compliment to Jill-Beth's pink motif. "I think this boy's been smokin' stuff he probably shouldn't."

That actually made sense to Arlie; he usually had the killer munchies after a couple of bowls of the good stuff, but his post-bong tastes tended to run in the Frito-Lay vein rather than dead cow, and besides, he hadn't taken a toke in months.

He turned to explain this to the officer, but once again, his mouth wasn't accepting requests from his brain. "You should arrest me right now officer," he said. "I'm one of the guys who kidnapped that psychic from that bookstore." Slightly different than his planned request for condiment suggestions, but Trooper Duwayne seemed just as interested in this.

"Well, how about that Jill-Beth?" Bevins said, sliding his hands around his waist to rest on his handcuff pouch. "This fellers not a doper; he's a stone cold kidnapper."

This was getting out of hand. Time to forget about his cheeseburger (and oh, the heartache that decision caused) and concentrate on getting out of Good Food without an armed escort. Duwayne seemed like a decent, if slow, guy. Maybe he'd buy an excuse of extreme hunger.

"Don't forget murder," Arlie explained. He tried to bite the inside of his cheek to keep the words in, but they just slid right out over his tongue. "Theodore's deader than dog shit, even though it wasn't me that did the killing. I killed Caleb though, so that ought to count."

Damn, damn, damn. How did a cheeseburger run turn into such a balls-up? Arlie clamped both hands over his mouth before he confessed anything else, not that there was much left to confess.

Jill-Beth the Cotton Candy waitress was dialing the phone and Trooper Duwayne had his cuffs out, dangling them off the end of one finger. "You gonna give me a problem son?"

Looking over Bevins' shoulder, Arlie saw the trooper's lunch buddies waiting for an answer. Forks and spoons hit the table as hands reached back to rest on pistols and batons. No way was he going to give this bunch an excuse to pound his ass into the ground. No trouble coming from him. No sir.

He opened his hands to tell them just that. "Y'all can kiss my redneck ass!" That didn't come out right. One more time.

"Why don't you pussies just come on and getcha some. I got a whole can of whup ass just waiting for you."

That wasn't it either.

Regardless of Arlie's original intent, the assembled officers of the Kanawha County barracks were happy to oblige his request and proceeded to administer an ass-whupping of their own. Arlie tried to explain, but when his intended protests came out as racial slurs and maternal innuendo, he decided to shut up and take it. They'd have to get tired eventually.

At some point after the pistol whipping but before the boot-stomping, Arlie felt a pair of meaty paws clamp down on his wrists and heard the jingle of metal. It seemed like too little too late, especially since he wasn't resisting, but he was in too much pain to care.

Arlie's body tingled and for a moment, he worried that they might have used a stun gun on him. The sensation moved over him like a breeze, finally pooling in his lower arms. Amidst the thuds and thumps dispensed by the troopers and their trucker friends, Arlie thought he heard someone whisper in his ear, warning him not to drop the soap anytime soon.

And then, the voice was gone. The tingling stopped as well, and Arlie's overwhelming need for a cheeseburger vanished with it. All that remained was the pounding, with Trooper Duwayne providing color commentary.

"You know what I've been thinking?" he said as his fists continued to play cadence on Arlie's skull. "I've been thinking I don't read enough. All of a sudden, I'm dying to get my hands on some Hemmingway."

CHAPTER 23

The people in the compound moved like the living dead. They shuffled. They lumbered. They passed each other with jerky adjustments, avoiding collisions by the barest of distances. Like a bad amalgamation of *Night of the Living Dead* and *Invasion of the Body Snatchers*, the silent movement was unsettling, but didn't impede Milo's reconnaissance.

He mimicked their behavior just to make sure.

The Colony was under no such restriction. They flittered around, peered into faces, and peeked around corners, flooding Milo with constant information, none of it worth a damn. Even doing his zombie impression, he could see everything they did, and unless the congregation decided to break into a chorus of *Thriller*, there wasn't much to see.

The temptation to simply leave was strong. The gate was close, unguarded and wide open. Etienne and Kimmy voted "Aye" every time Milo considered it, but Tajiri, Maria and Isadore were just as quick to agree with his decision to stay.

The road from the barn led them to a circular driveway, with three other trails branching off the oval. In addition to the route to the main gate, one of the roads curved away to the southeast. Rows of one-story buildings flanked this path, extending for as far as Milo could see. These would have to be living quarters. Most of the foot traffic seemed to originate from this direction, looping once or twice around the circle before returning.

The other road headed due east. Along its length, the visible structures were larger, more industrial, less homey. This road led to the working area of the community: Storage, production, and whatever else paid the bills. Milo didn't see any traffic going or coming from this direction. No surprise there; the citizenry seemed barely functional, let alone industrious.

One building dominated the main compound, over-looking the circular turnaround. More elaborate than the houses to the south and less institutional than the buildings to the east, this structure had to be Brotherhood Central, the group's headquarters and home of the head asshole in charge. If they wanted a shot at the architects of this insanity, this was where Milo would find them.

Milo veered away from the shuffling automatons and slowly climbed the steps leading to the porch. He worried that the long ascent left him too exposed, inviting interfer-ence from the circling minions. He needn't have worried. No one paid any more attention to his approach than they had to his intrusion in their wanderings. These sad folks weren't body snatchers, waiting to pounce on the uniniti-ated; they were the Borg, ignoring everything but an obvious attack.

He planned to accommodate them, but not in front of witnesses that could become cannon fodder at a headless bastard's whim.

"God, I miss Trippenstein," he muttered, maintaining a steady pace up the stairs. "A *kaboom* or two would come in pretty handy right now."

Trippenstein may yet be our salvation, Tajiri mused, mir-roring Milo's steps. *Nevertheless, I would not place all our hopes on his narrow shoulders.*

When they reached the top stair, Milo paused before stepping onto the porch. The boards looked solid, but weathered enough to creak if he took a wrong step. *Walk on the sides,* he realized. *Heel to toe in a rolling motion, his weight balanced on the outer edges of both feet.* That should minimize the chance of a betraying noise.

Milo felt Tajiri's surprise at his strategy. He'd anticipated Tajiri's suggestion before the ronin could offer to act in his stead. As Milo silently crossed the space to the front door, he knew his movements were identical to those his passenger had planned.

OK, that was weird, he thought. The Colony murmured its assent.

You've become quite the adept, Tajiri told him. *Quite surprising, considering the short time we've been together.*

Gratifying yes, but don't get overconfident, Isadore warned. *Your success would be an unsuitable epitaph.*

Duly noted. Milo wrapped his hand around the screen door handle and tugged. The door moved freely; nothing was keeping them outside.

Here goes nothing, he said, opening the door and slipping in.

Once across the threshold, he paused and listened. No one outside raised an alarm; no heavy footsteps clunked up the porch stairs in pursuit. Inside, all seemed quiet except for a faint, rhythmic squeaking coming from somewhere on the second floor.

He stood in a great room, combining office space, a small sitting area and dining area. On the back wall to his left, he saw a swinging door. The kitchen, he assumed. There was another door to his right, this one sporting a knob and a small window covered by a cheap, pull-down blind. A back entrance? Probably. Milo crossed the room—heel to toe, heel to toe—and peeked under the plastic coated shade. The view was typical rural West Virginia landscaping: discarded appliances and moldy furniture cluttering a wide, unfinished deck, but it was outside, so that was a win for the visitors. He disengaged the deadbolt before returning to the entrance. Locks and adrenaline didn't mix well.

A flight of stairs bisected the main floor, placed just

inside the front door. It was at the foot of the stairs that Milo could hear the squeaking the loudest.

You know what that sounds like? he mused, fighting the mental pictures that tried to accompany the thought.

I know what I think that sounds like, Etienne said, his ethereal form leaning over the steps and leering up. *It appears that even among these philistines, l'amour has raised its ugly head.*

Milo and Isadore groaned. The women remained silent, but feelings of revulsion coursed along the link Milo shared with Maria and Kimmy. Etienne laughed. *Come ladies,* he said, enjoying their discomfort, *everyone does it, even the villains. At least one thing about this backwater community is normal.*

If it had been possible to slap a spirit, the Frenchman would have had two handprints on his cheeks. As it was, Maria settled for a maternal scowl and Kimmy stuck out her tongue.

Tajiri's reaction surprised Milo most. He also looked up the stairs, but when he turned back to look at Milo, his expression wasn't one of lust or disgust, but of grim satisfaction.

The Gods smile down on us, he said to Milo. *If you are correct — and in this and this alone, I trust Etienne's judgment — we hold the tactical advantage. If your enemy is distracted, attack.*

The tempo of the squeaks increased, building to a constant squeal before resuming their normal pattern.

"Don't get much more distracted than that," Milo breathed, looking up.

Tajiri nodded. *Indeed.*

You mean we're gonna have to go up there and see that? Kimmy cried. *Oh please. Can't we just go back to the barn and wait for them to kill us?*

The complaint answered one of Milo's questions, but raised another concern. His first instinct had been to send the Colony upstairs for a quick look-see. Having someone to work point was always a sound strategy; five points would be five times as sound. But if his forward scouts were too grossed out — or in Etienne's case, too engrossed — to function, the benefit could quickly become a liability. Better to keep everyone close.

Beyond that, there was the issue of what to do once they reached the second floor. Surprise was on their side; that wasn't in doubt. What to do with it was. Under Tajiri's control, he understood what his hands were capable of, but attacking empty-handed seemed inadvisable.

He looked around the room, taking in the propaganda that passed for decoration. There was more hate per square inch than a Klan rally. Posters with racial epithets and crude cartoons with exaggerated stereotypical features adorned every wall. The Brotherhood seemed opposed to everyone: Blacks, homosexuals, Jews, and Asians. If these numb nuts ever found a rainbow, they'd piss on it instead of looking for the pot of gold. Confronted with unmistakable evidence of their captors' prejudices, Milo wondered if they deserved the help he was risking his life to provide.

You can't condemn a group for the beliefs of a few, Isadore said.

Who says it's a few, Milo asked. *Sure, they're zombies now, but who's to say what they were before? Are you looking at this shit? Even if they didn't sign up for Salomé's program, they weren't angels before. Who the hell are we saving here?*

Milo, there are children here. Have they sinned so badly to damn them forever? They feed at their mother's breast. Should we punish them for not knowing the milk is sour? Do we leave them to their fate in the name of justice or act to save the righteous among them? Only the Lord knows what flowers hide among these weeds.

How could he argue with that?

Still, unless the Lord had an arsenal waiting at the top of the stairs, Milo couldn't imagine going up armed with nothing but a pure heart and good intentions. This was a hate group; where were the crates of automatic rifles? Where were the lockers filled with surplus camouflage and grenade bandoliers? What weapons did these ignoramuses have in their ideological arsenal: Harsh language and crayons?

Terrorism on a budget.

Frustration set his feet in motion. Milo paced in a small circle, marching to the cadence of the bedspring boogie. He searched the walls. Nothing. He scanned the desk and bookcases. Nothing. The office space was empty. The dining table was bare. The sitting room held nothing but threadbare furniture and logs stacked next to a cold fireplace.

But the mantel…

This was a Godsend, simultaneously confirming Isadore's faith in things unseen and Milo's growing certainty that they had been captured by geeks. This was the centerpiece of every "weapons" dealer who manned a booth at comic shows and fantasy conventions. Regardless of the displays of medieval broadswords, exotic knives and ceremonial daggers, one item always dominated the inventory, usually labeled "Not for Sale" as a beard for the basement-dwelling patrons. This was the ultimate knick-knack for the warrior wannabe, who'd probably never remove it from its stand.

The Samurai Katana.

Milo crossed the room, where Tajiri was already staring at the long sword. "We can't be this lucky," Milo said. "This has to be a toy."

I thought perhaps a replica, Tajiri said. *But now I believe we may indeed be "that lucky."*

Milo reached up with both hands and lifted the sword from its cradle. With his right hand grasping the hilt and his left hand holding the scabbard, Milo brought the weapon down to eye level, feeling Tajiri's anticipation grow.

This daito *is a* tachi, *not a* katana. *It is too long to be anything else,* Tajiri explained. *Also, the* saya *appears to be authentic for such a weapon. There are signs of wear here and here –* Tajiri moved Milo's fingers to a spot slightly below the crosspiece and then to another area closer to the end of the scabbard—*from where the sword hung from a belt. This is not the ware of a vendor hoping to profit from an ignorant buyer.*

"Because it's a *tachi*, not a *katana*," Milo repeated. He had no idea what he was saying, but at the same time was aware of the information's accuracy.

These dealers you remember, they buy mass produced katana *and sell them to those who aspire to what they do not understand. It is as you say, a toy, but a realistic toy. Something for posing and swinging, shouting all the while.* He waved his hands in disgust. *Draw the sword Milo, and see if I am correct.*

The sword felt heavy in his hands, as if Tajiri's reverence had added weight to the blade. He reversed his grip on the scabbard and slid his left hand down to the crosspiece. He pulled his hands apart, hearing the steel sing as he freed it from its sheath.

Tajiri's pleasure almost overwhelmed him as the length of the blade became visible. He pointed out the *hamon*, the temper line where the sharp edge faded into the normal steel of the blade, and explained the grooves in the steel etched for lightening and added flexibility. These were details a replica maker wouldn't bother adding; these were the marks of a true master.

The Lord had provided after all.

CHAPTER 24

West Virginia State Trooper Duwayne Bevins couldn't believe what he'd been missing. As he wove through I-64 traffic, lights blaring and siren wailing, the extent of his intellectual deficit moved him to tears. At one point, this sadness exploded into full-blown sobbing, forcing him to pull off the road before becoming a danger to those he had sworn to protect and serve.

There was no excuse for it, no excuse at all. His status as a peace officer required knowledge, not ignorance. How could he call himself a public servant while proudly proclaiming his choice to eschew reading? How many years had he wasted on trivial entertainment when the wisdom of the universe beckoned from every mall in the state?

Of course, there was a sliver of awareness in Duwayne's mind that questioned not only the source of this new preoccupation with the printed word, but also the sudden expansion of his vocabulary, but he quickly dismissed these concerns as unfortunate remnants of his mental darkness, trying to reassert themselves before dying under the brilliance of his new enlightenment.

Yep, that made sense.

To celebrate this spiritual awakening, Duwayne had left Arlie Garrison in the custody of his brother officers, barreled past the TV news crews congregating in the Good Food parking lot, jumped into his cruiser and hauled ass out of Marmet. He could have purchased a book somewhere in southern Kanawha County, but like a starving man unexpectedly reacquainted with the concept of food, Duwayne required a sumptuous buffet, not a single dish.

Such a smorgasbord could only be found in Charleston.

PageSmart, Duwayne repeated under his breath. The two syllables, pounded into his brain. One destination, keeping his foot pressed to the floor. The road opened before him as motorists vacated the middle lane, pushed to the sides by the wedge of intellectual need heralding his passage.

The radio mounted under his dashboard squawked with reports of a dangerous driver tearing up Interstate 64 North. He heard frantic requests for information, assistance and eventually, air support. The forces of ignorance were strong; loathe to release him from their cage of illiteracy. He smiled at their futile efforts, flexing his calf muscles to goose a little more horsepower from the already-roaring engine.

Huh?

He almost lost control on the Greenbrier Street exit ramp, but the tires held and he shot through the intersection. Two Charleston City units fell into formation as he rocketed toward Lee Street. Their drivers hadn't seen the subject of the pursuit, but eagerly joined the chase. Duwayne let out a whoop when he noticed the escort in his rear view mirror.

Duwayne cranked the steering wheel hard right and skidded into Virginia Street. There, shining like a beacon in the twilight, were the lights of PageSmart. The V8 chewed through the remaining blocks and howled in protest when Duwayne slid to a stop in front of the bookstore. He jumped out of the car, drew his weapon and charged the entrance. Behind him, the Charleston cops could only sigh and shake their heads.

PageSmart again.

"I need a book," Duwayne screamed as he burst through the doors, holding his gun above his head. "I need a book now!"

To his surprise, the customers and staff didn't panic at his dramatic entrance. In fact, their reactions mirrored those of the police bunched in the vestibule.

Not again.

Duwayne fired a round into the ceiling in frustration, but the gunfire had no effect. A few people ducked, but most went on with their business as if he weren't there. Where was the fanfare? Where was the celebration? Where were his fellow bibliophiles, ready to welcome him into their ranks?

A young man wearing jeans and a T-shirt approached him, staring at the hole in the plaster above them. Here was his guide, his mentor, his conduit into the world he had denied himself for so long. Jimmy, according to the tag hung from his neck.

"I really wish you hadn't done that," Jimmy said.

"I need a book," Duwayne replied, nearly breathless at the prospect of realizing his goal.

"Yeah, no shit dude." Jimmy opened his arms. "So does everyone here. You don't see them busting caps just to get my attention, do you?"

"I need a book." Why didn't Jimmy understand? Why didn't he bring him what he needed? Duwayne lowered his arm and holstered his pistol. Tears welled in his eyes. Why was this so hard?

Jimmy's face scrunched and he stepped back. "Yo man, no need to get all depressed and shit. Freeze on the boo-boo face and I promise I'll get you hooked up."

Duwayne gasped, understanding why things weren't progressing as they should. "I need Sharon," he exclaimed, thrilled by the sudden clarity of his thoughts. "You can't help me. I need Sharon."

Jimmy moved forward, motioning for Duwayne to lean in. "Not for nothing, but that's probably not a name you want to go shouting right now."

"Get Sharon for me." Duwayne searched the crowd, looking for the face of his salvation. "Sharon!" he shouted. "Sharon! Somebody please get Sharon for me!"

"She's not here." Jimmy grabbed Duwayne's shoulders and gave him a shake.

"Sharon! Sharon!"

"Dude, I'm telling you she's not here."

"But I need her. I need to see Sharon."

Jimmy shook his head. "Then you're going to have to go somewhere else. Sharon doesn't work here any more." He pulled Duwayne down and whispered, "The bastards fired her this afternoon. Keith too. They're both gone."

Gone? Sharon was gone? Who would get him his book? Who would tell him what to read? Who would rescue Milo now?

What?

Jimmy. It has to be Jimmy. Duwayne heard the rip of Velcro behind him, heard the sound of metal sliding against leather. It's Jimmy or nobody.

He grabbed Jimmy's wrists and pulled his hands from his shoulders. The young man was stronger than he looked, but Duwayne held fast. His body tingled. Sweat rose on his palms. A wave of heat collected in his spine and rushed down his arms, pooling in his hands. As his fellow officers pulled him back, Duwayne shuddered and all thoughts of literature vanished from his mind. Duwayne couldn't understand where he was, or what was happening to him.

Jimmy Capella watched the arrest, rubbing his wrists where the cop grabbed them. He didn't understand what had happened either, but he knew he had to tell someone, someone who'd appreciate the incident.

Sharon. He had to tell Sharon. Sharon would get a huge kick out of this one.

CHAPTER 25

Milo stood at the base of the stairs, his right toes testing the bottom riser like a hesitant swimmer on the shore of a lake. The squeaking from upstairs had slowed, then stopped, then resumed with a different rhythm. The tempo shift conjured up even more disturbing mental images, so Milo concentrated on his footing.

And the sword.

The *tachi* wasn't heavy, but it felt awkward in his hand, even with Tajiri's running instruction on the proper way to carry it. Milo favored a two-handed grip on the hilt, emulating a poor man's Bruce Willis/Pulp Fiction stance on the way to save Ving Rhames from the Sodomites. The scabbard seemed extraneous, dead weight good for nothing but toting and distraction. Tajiri was aghast at the suggestion. He insisted Milo keep the sword sheathed while they ascended to the second floor, quoting some arcane sensei's technique regarding the power of what he called "Iaido".

It sounded very pretty and like something Milo might applaud if he saw it in a movie, but for now he was happy with "big sharp thingy." Ancient Japanese tactics and fighting methods sounded fine for future training sessions, but if he could poke some holes and separate some limbs, that'd be just fine.

They settled on keeping the sword in the scabbard.

Milo gauged each step before placing his foot, not trusting the stairs' silence. As the upper hallway came into view, he maintained his pace, resisting the urge to rush. Closer to the source of the squeaking, he heard labored breathing intermixed with soft moans. Hypothesis confirmed.

Yuck.

Still, naked meant vulnerable, and vulnerable was an advantage Milo didn't plan on wasting. What to do with that advantage remained the greater issue.

Unilateral judge, jury and executioner? Maybe immobilization and capture was the better option. Let the system do what it was designed to do or take preemptive action? Faith or assurance.

Or maybe he'd be dead within the hour and spend eternity arguing woulda, coulda shoulda with the Almighty.

The upstairs hallway was short: A seven-foot corridor split sixty/forty from the top of the stairs. Two closed doors stood on Milo's left; another pair faced each other on his right. The bedroom noises pulled his attention right, and then drew him to the door on his left. From the moaning and groaning, he knew which door hid the lady.

Time to find out which tiger was keeping her company.

The sword, the sword, the sword, he thought, reaching across his body for the hilt. *I'll keep the scabbard,* he promised Tajiri.

Tajiri ignored the plea. *One hand on the* tachi, *the other on the doorknob,* he suggested instead. Hard to open the door with his hands full of sword.

D'oh!

One step at a time. He placed his hand on the doorknob, paused and listened. No change in the sound on the other side of the door. Pulling back, he turned the knob slowly, feeling the latch slip free of its socket. Listening again.

No change.

The hallway felt crowded. The Colony bunched around him. Questions, doubts and fear poured into his mind; five times the anxiety feeding his own. Nerves jangling, Milo inhaled deeply and asked his passengers, *Anybody want to stick their head in and give me an idea about what we're walking into?*

Nobody did.

It's probably better this way, Tajiri said. *If The Baptist's in there, we might be tipping our hand.*

On the disturbing mental image hit parade, the picture of The Baptist getting busy was enough to make Milo reconsider his role as an avenging angel. Talk about a guy needing some head…

Enough. He centered himself, listening as the squeaks, moans and heavy breathing reached a crescendo. *Now or never,* he thought, and burst through the door, immediately understanding why amateurs should never attempt homemade pornography.

The room was small, but even if it had been a palatial suite, the activity on the bed would have demanded all of his attention. A man and woman lay on the bed, his narrow white ass bouncing with all the rhythm and grace of a straight, white man on the Soul Train dance floor while she writhed beneath him, face contorting in a parody of passion that turned her features into a taffy pull.

Milo registered this in the space of a heartbeat, all the time it took the man to register his intrusion and untangle himself from his lover. He rolled off and jumped to his feet on the far side of the mattress.

Bad decision. Not only were his clothes piled on the side closest to Milo, but a large, weathered pistol sat on a nightstand stationed on the same side of the bed.

"Hi Ken," Milo said, trying to maintain eye contact with the naked killer. "Did I interrupt something?"

Ken didn't answer. He didn't try to cover his groin (something Milo really, really wanted him to do), nor did he attempt to move away from the bed. It was a frozen moment, devoid of any motion except for the twitching baton between Ken's legs and the gyrations of the woman tangled in the sheets, who hadn't seemed to notice Ken's absence yet.

"Oooo baby, you're doing me so good," she moaned. She smoothed her hands down the sides of her body, taking time to explore all points of interest from north to south. "That's so nice baby," she cooed as her fingers twirled through the hair on her mons. "So nice."

Here was a situation never covered in any of the manuals: Reluctant hero armed with a seven hundred year-old Japanese long sword squaring off against a nude, murdering white supremacist over the writhing form of a naked nymphomaniac on autopilot. Yeah, something like that deserved at least a chapter in the Gatherer's Book of Hoyle.

Ken's anonymous playmate was enjoying herself way too much given the presence of an audience and the absence of a partner. Milo pulled his attention away from her autoerotic performance just in time to see Ken raise his knee onto the edge of the mattress, his gaze glued to the weapon just out of his reach. Milo appreciated the change in posture; Ken's leg blocked his view of the dreaded Appalachian trouser snake.

"Uh, uh, uh," Milo said, grasping the hilt of the *tachi*. "Why don't we leave Mr. Gun right where he is."

"I'm not gonna need that Colt to take care of you," Ken said, raising his hands and settling back on his feet. "I don't care how bad Salomé and his freak want you; they're gonna have to find his next meal someplace else."

"I don't think you're gonna do much shooting at all without that pistol. Looks like your other gun's back in its holster." Milo cringed as he said it. It was junior high gym class all over again. He looked down for a second; the show was still going strong.

"If it's any consolation," Milo added, "you seem to have a lasting effect on the ladies. Normally, I'd have to be at least in the same zip code to get a reaction like this."

"Take a good long look," Ken said, his eyes and voice equally cold. "It's a close as you'll ever be to pussy again."

"You'd be amazed at how inaccurate that statement is," Milo muttered, prompting dual groans in his head.

Good to know you're still there, he told Maria and Kimmy. He was surprised the guys had been silent for so long.

Especially Etienne.

Ken had obviously misinterpreted Milo's declaration as a challenge. He took two steps to his right, reaching the lower corner of the bed. "Bring it on then asshole. Bring it on."

Sword time, Milo thought, sensei mumbo-jumbo be damned. He yanked the sword free, but misjudged the arc of his draw. The blade wound up where he expected—cocked and ready on his right, parallel to his body, its tip pointed at the ceiling—but he lost his grip on the scabbard and it went sailing behind him.

Thank God, he still had the sharp part.

"You ain't got the stones," Ken said. "Putting a blade in someone, that's real killing. It's dirty. It's messy. It's like carving into breathing Jell-O." He smiled, mouth stretching into a feral grin that told Milo he didn't need a blade or a gun to bring the pain; his teeth would do just fine.

Milo turned to his left to keep the bed between him and Ken and barked his shins on the box springs. He bit on his lower lip to keep the "OW!" inside. Ken's bedmate gasped, riding the unexpected shimmy like a wave.

"Slam it baby," she groaned. Her hips rose from the bed as her hands slid beneath her buttocks to support her. "Oh Arlie, you never been like this before. You just keep gettin' better and better."

Arlie?

Ken's expression immediately shifted from raging wildebeest to Pooh caught with his paw in the honey pot. Milo switched the sword from right hand to left and brandished it at him like the world's longest *shame shame shame* finger.

"This is Mrs. Arlie?" he asked.

Ken said nothing. Nothing needed saying.

"You don't do that," Milo screamed. Kidnapping and murder was one thing, but boning your best friend's wife? He looked down at the bed. Arlie's missus was still feeling the flow, even without a hand on the spigot.

At least, no hand he could see.

The Baptist.

"A gang bang? You're gang banging his wife? That's what this is about? You guys went to all this trouble just so you could cop a piece of strange tail?"

"This ain't all about pussy," Ken said. "This is just a bonus. This is just the beginning. There's a whole world out there been cornholing guys like me forever. Now's my time for gettin' some back."

"So you start by stabbing your boy in the back?" Milo flashed on the odds of Keith ever trying to get Sharon in the sack. He didn't need a calculator; it would never happen.

"You think Arlie's gonna mind?" Ken asked. His tone had changed. Softened. Any sense of confrontation was gone; Ken was selling something. "Since we hooked up with Salomé, that boy hasn't wasted a second thinking about her. Or his kids. He's been too busy filling his gullet, but it's just a matter of time before he starts filling other things. Man, that's the beauty of it. Anything we want, just waiting for us to take it."

Milo wasn't buying. Shine it up, decorate it with fancy paper and wrap it with a shiny bow; a gift-wrapped dog turd was still a piece of shit.

Ken must have sensed Milo's incredulity; he changed tactics again.

"You're wearing a ring," he said, pointing at Milo's left hand. "You know what I'm talking about. It's a chain, isn't it? A big old ball and chain, dragging you down, holding you back." He shook his head. "Not any more. After I take care of you, I think we'll all go pay *your* missus a visit, give her a taste of what she's been missing."

Milo closed his eyes, breath hitching at the insanity. "You sad, pathetic pile of dogshit. You want to conquer the world? Be my guest. You want to chop some more heads? Line 'em up dickwad. But me and mine? You just made this a whole lot easier."

Milo tightened his grip on the sword's hilt. The tension

in his hand turned his fist to stone, the stratification traveling through his arm, across his shoulders, up his neck and
settling behind his eyes. It was as if Ken could see the
change. His skin whitened. His eyes went wide. He shuddered at the transformation before him.

With his free hand, Milo reached behind him and slid
Ken's pistol off the table. The polished grips felt smooth to
the touch, but the gun had no weight—no gravitas—to
match the feel of the *tachi*. The pistol was only a tool, a
device, an empty threat. Now, he understood Tajiri's reverence.

The long sword was an extension of his arm. An imple-
ment of the soul, not of the body.

In one motion, Milo swung the pistol underhand and
lobbed it onto the bed. It bounced once on the bunched
linens and landed with the barrel pointed at Ken. Another
change washed across Ken's face. His previous bravado
tried to reassert itself, but as his hand twitched against his
naked thigh, anxious to reach for his weapon, Milo saw
realization dawn in the his eyes.

The gun was a die; the bed, a craps table. Milo understood the consequence of his action; he knew what circumstance his offering would entail. His indecision was gone,
buried under the enormity of Ken's betrayal. The way Milo
saw it—and the Colony shared his diagnosis—Ken had
pissed away any chance of salvation, and his only opportunity for redemption lay in the choice he was about to make.

Some lines needed crossing, and Milo stood at the
border, waiting for Ken to invite him across.

It happened as if scripted.

As Ken reached out for the gun, Tajiri came forward and
Milo felt the familiar prickle as the ronin started to take
control of his motor functions. This time, rather than
stepping back with the other passengers as he usually did,
Milo dug in, unwilling to limit his participation to detached
observation. If he was going to get blood on his hands, he
damned well wanted to be wearing them when it
happened.

Simultaneously, Ken's hand reached the gun and the sword began its arc, translating from the vertical to a horizontal plane. As Ken wrapped his fingers around the grips, Tajiri shifted Milo's shoulders and hips, channeling every ounce of Milo's two hundred and twenty pounds into the swing.

Ken lifted the pistol from the bed and thumbed back the hammer.

Milo yelled, an explosive *kiyee* that added to the power of their strike.

Ken's hand twitched once more, firing a round that embedded itself in the wall above the headboard.

The force of the blow spun Milo in a perfect circle, pivoting on his left foot, coming to rest just as a fountain of blood splashed him and the bed.

Ken's head rolled across the floor before his body realized it should fall as well.

The unexpected shower roused Mrs. Arlie from her erotic stupor; the amount of blood an unwelcome dessert to her booty buffet.

Her screams cut deeper than Milo's *tachi*.

So much for sneaking around, Milo thought, cringing while the window glass vibrated from the pitch and volume coming from Mrs. Arlie's lungs. *Unless anyone in earshot thinks Ken found a new spot in the erogenous zones.*

He waited for the groans from inside, but all was quiet. Maybe he needed some new material, or perhaps the humor seemed innocuous compared to all the gore.

Or maybe…

"Bravo my good man. Bravo." Applause came from the open doorway. Milo turned, nearly tripping over his feet and impaling himself on the long sword. The *tachi* suddenly felt foreign in his hand, too long and heavy for graceful handling.

Salomé stood under the lintel, framed by the massive bulk of The Baptist behind him. He clapped slowly, methodically, his expression contradicting the hollow bang of his hands.

Salomé raised his hand and flicked a finger in the direction of the bed. Before the second flick, Mrs. Arlie stopped in mid-shriek, her eyes rolled back in her head and she flopped back on the mattress.

"Such a handy talent," Salomé said. He looked down, first at Ken's head and then at the still-leaking body. He clucked his tongue.

"What a waste. It took quite a while to determine the proper price to ensure Mr. Chesterton's devotion, and now you've gone and dispatched him in mid-payment. No matter. I'm certain I'll have no difficulty procuring a suitable replacement."

Milo tried to reestablish a threatening stance, but he couldn't position his body in the proper posture. Like the feel of the sword, every movement felt wrong, almost out of focus. He couldn't set his feet a comfortable distance apart, his center of gravity alternated between his chest and his knees, and his arms—well, his arms felt like putty with lead weights dangling from the ends.

And still, the Colony was silent.

"I suppose you're feeling a bit out of sorts," Salomé said. "I would imagine you've become quite accustomed to the endless prattling of your, shall we say, more subtle companions; so accustomed that their absence must seem somewhat unnatural. I sympathize, I do, but it can't be helped. You see, I wouldn't want anyone interfering in our little tête-à-tête, and from what I've seen, those tenants of yours have a nasty habit of popping out at the most inopportune moments, as Mr. Chesterton has discovered."

Milo clenched his teeth and "screamed" for the Colony, calling role in the continued silence of his mind.

"You're not the only one hiding his light under a bushel," Salomé said. "Thanks to Mr. Theodore's reluctant contribution, my associate here has divined a quite effective method of quieting the chatter in your brain. I hope you appreciate the effort he's expending just to provide you with some peace of mind. It's really very taxing."

Salomé pushed his cloak from his shoulders and drew

his sword, still stained with Theodore's blood. The blade was so thin it almost disappeared as Salome turned his hand.

"Again, no matter," he said, snapping his wrist. The rapier whistled through the air. "I don't believe he's going to have to keep it up for very long."

CHAPTER 26

Useless.

Everything was useless. Everyone was a waste of flesh; sucking down oxygen they had no right to breathe. The cops. The reporters. All the friends calling to offer support while fishing for gossip to pass around the water cooler.

Useless.

Sharon poured another cup of coffee, hating herself for giving in to even this small indulgence. She wouldn't allow herself anything Milo might not have, but without the caffeine, she'd have passed out a long time ago. It was a small cheat, but not the only unavoidable one.

She couldn't stop breathing either.

She took in a mouthful of the scalding brew, letting the pain burn away those fatalistic thoughts. Not only was it counterproductive, the possibility of a world without her husband in it threatened to destroy whatever shreds of sanity she still possessed.

As difficult as the momentary deletion of Milo and Keith from her reality had been, the current situation made her long for that oblivion. The memories would be too much to bear.

So, she punished herself with the burnt, acrid coffee, looking through the pass-thru to where Keith and Andi had set up shop, covering the dining room table with maps, police reports and Internet printouts. Keith shuffled through the paper and made an occasional note in the margins. Sharon couldn't tell if he was making any progress, but trusted she'd know if a "eureka" moment occurred.

Andi, the pushy private detective with the Victoria's Secret figure, didn't seem nearly as concerned with crunching data as she was with crushing her breasts into Keith's back. Sure, every once in a while she'd reach over his shoulder to point at a photograph or grab the pen from his hand to scribble something, but this was the first time Sharon had seen research conducted as a full-contact sport. Keith didn't seem distracted by all the touchy-feely, a sure sign of how bad things actually were.

She thought she'd be happy when Keith finally found a woman (no matter how recent Andi's arrival, there was no doubt she was going to be Keith's woman; the boy only had so much resistance), but Sharon found herself resenting the detective's presence. Could she be so shallow that she'd begrudge Keith some companionship after all these years alone? Had she grown so accustomed to his undivided attention to Clan Tucker that she'd become territorial in the presence of another female? Milo wouldn't feel that way, she was sure of that. He'd be proud at his friend's good fortune and an absolute pest in his quest for intimate details.

Sharon laughed in spite of her mood; Keith deserved a little payback to go along with his romantic success. In time, she was sure she could bond with Andi. She'd have to, unless she wanted to lose him too.

No, no, no. She couldn't think like that. Milo was missing, nothing more. "Lost" was a classification she wasn't prepared to consider.

Where the hell was Ducalion? As a white knight, he wasn't living up to expectations, which were high, but understandable given the man's overpowering attitude. When she had seen him swagger into PageSmart's offices, she almost expected to see Milo walk in behind him. That was the confidence the man projected: the surety that no

                    M. Stephen Lukac

problem was beyond his ability to fix, no wrong so absolute he couldn't make it right.

Sharon was still waiting.

Phil had been a huge help; there was no denying that. He'd blown through all the PageSmart red tape, and procured her a bigger severance payment than her former employer had intended. He'd done the same with the Charleston police, wading through their procedures and questions like the busy work they were. Ducalion had answered their questions before the queries were out of their mouths, and from his tone, Sharon knew the interrogation was the same as everything else.

Nothing but a waste of time.

Sharon wanted him to shoot someone; she really didn't care whom. If that didn't work, then they'd pick someone else. Eventually, they'd find someone whose perforation could help. Until then, Sharon would be satisfied with spreading as much pain as possible.

Why shouldn't everyone hurt this much?

She carried her coffee into the living room, purposely avoiding Keith, Andi and their useless piles of paper. Keith looked up and nodded to her as she stepped out of the kitchen. He didn't have to say it. He was getting nowhere.

Useless.

The door to the apartment banged open. Ducalion, carrying a box of doughnuts, strolled in, flipping the door shut with a cocked foot as he passed through. The sight of him — a weathered man carrying a box of pastry — kindled a flicker of hope in her chest. It was stereotypical, sure, but oddly comforting.

"Whatcha got there Phil?" Keith asked, leaning back into Andi's cushions.

"I got news and I got doughnuts," he replied, dropping the box on top of Keith's homework. "Let me know what order you want them in."

"News!" Sharon said. She crossed the room. "They found Milo? Where is he?"

Ducalion reached out and cupped Sharon's chin. "No

darlin', we haven't found him yet, but I think we're closer than we were." Movement caught his eye and he turned to watch Keith open the Krispy Kreme box. "Be careful with those. They're hot."

"So?" Keith asked.

"So, how the hell should I know? They had a big red sign in the window that said 'hot doughnuts.' I don't know if that's good or bad, but it's true. I've got the burns on my palm to prove it."

"Phil!" Sharon cried.

"All right, all right," he said, pulling out a dinette chair to straddle. "Here's what they've got."

Ducalion held up one finger. "The staties have arrested some clodhopper named Arlie Garrison at a diner outside of Marmet. Seems he walked in and started confessing to everything but the Kennedy assassination."

"Which Kennedy?" Keith asked. Andi boxed his ears and motioned for Phil to continue.

"Garrison copped to snatching Jack Theodore, but then things turned into a rugby scrum and by the time they climbed off, Garrison clammed up and started yelling for an attorney. He never mentioned Milo's name."

"But he knows where Milo is," Sharon said. "He has to."

Ducalion nodded. "That's everyone's guess, but he's not talking. If I'd have been there before he lawyered up, I might have had a chance of convincing him to reconsider the Marcel Marceau strategy, but..." He shrugged.

Sharon felt the tracks on her cheeks as the brief hope she'd had trickled down her face.

Keith shoved the stacks of paper away and opened his laptop computer. After a few preliminary keystrokes, he asked, "How do you spell Garrison?"

"G, A, double R, who gives a damn," Ducalion said over his shoulder. "Don't waste your time. The geniuses downtown have already tried that one and come up empty. This guy's been invisible for almost two years, and it looks like his family still is. They found a marriage license and a couple of birth certificates, but that's it. No current address on file." He turned back to face Sharon. "But I've got a couple of ideas."

Sharon fell to her knees in front of Ducalion's chair. Not in supplication, but like a child waiting for a favorite story. Phil played right along, favoring her with a father's smile, something she hadn't seen in too many years.

"Things got goofy after they nailed Garrison," Ducalion said. "Bevins, the cop who actually made the arrest? Right after he cuffed him, he decided to indulge in a little NASCAR fantasy and go barrel-assing up I-64. Had half the cops in the county on his tail thinking he was 10-88, right up until he pulled into your old joint."

"PageSmart?" Keith and Sharon asked together. Keith was grabbing for his cell phone before the reality of their new employment situation kicked in and he turned the reach into a half-hearted stretch. Andi patted his shoulders. Sharon felt a lump grow in her throat.

She had to keep reminding herself she wasn't the only one with a loss here.

"What happened at PageSmart?" she asked.

"More goddamned goofiness." Ducalion pulled a notebook from his pocket, flipped several pages and began reading. "Shots fired. Lots of screaming. Blah, blah, blah. Sounds like our boy had a taste for the classics. Kept yelling about wanting some Hemmingway until he grabbed one of the clerks."

"Who'd he grab?" Keith asked.

Sharon held her breath.

Ducalion read further. "Some kid named Jimmy. James Capella. I don't have anything else on him, and neither do the police. After they took the cop down, I guess he freaked out, made like a bunny and got his fluffy tale out of there. They're looking for him right now."

"You folks really know how to throw a party down here," Andi said.

"Yeah, well, somebody needs to keep better track of the guests," Ducalion said. He closed the notebook and tossed it on the table. "At first I thought this cop with the Dukes of Hazard fetish might have heard something interesting from Garrison; it's the only explanation that fits, but right now I'd say Bevins and Garrison are about even on the bug fuck-o-meter."

"I don't see how any of this helps," Sharon said.

"We just don't have enough pieces to fill in the puzzle yet," Ducalion explained. "I'll guarantee you there's a connection there.   Garrison and Bevins, they're fishing buddies, third cousins, secret lovers or something like that. Once we're able to draw the line between the two, it'll give us enough leverage to crack one of them."

"How long?" Sharon asked. "How long's that going to take? How long do you think Milo has?"

"It's not going to take long at all," Ducalion said. "Bevins isn't going to be able to keep up that bullshit possession story for more than a couple of hours. Right now it sounds convincing, but he's going to slip up soon enough and that'll be the ball game."

"Possession?" Keith asked. "The cop's saying he's possessed?"

Ducalion laughed. "Yeah, but just for a little while. I guess there's a demon out there that just needed a lift to Charleston. You've got to respect an evil spirit with a sense of economy."

Keith hopped out of his seat. Sharon jumped at the sudden move, but recognized the look in her former boss's eyes.

"Let me guess; Garrison says he was possessed too?" Keith got right in Phil's face, another good sign from where Sharon sat.

Ducalion leaned back and blew a puff of air across his lips. "Something like that, but he doesn't have as impressive a vocabulary as the trooper, and that isn't saying much. I don't remember exactly how he phrased it, but apparently the only reason he's in custody now is because of a cheeseburger."

"A cheeseburger?"

"A cheeseburger."

"The sandwich?"

"One and the same. That's why Garrison says he went to the diner. He wanted a cheeseburger. Now you tell me, how crazy is that?"

"Pretty goddamned crazy," Keith muttered. He walked away from the dining table and started to pace the living room. Sharon turned to follow his progress.

"The redneck wants a cheeseburger, but confesses instead," he said. "Then, the cop decides he's gotta get a copy of *For Whom the Bell Tolls* and goes ballistic on I-64."

It was obvious that Keith had a destination in mind, but couldn't find the right road to take him there. As she watched him wear a path in her carpet, Sharon began to feel something similar. It had started with Ducalion's notes, but with Keith repeating it over and over, the tickle had turned into an itch.

She had heard something like this before.

Keith expanded the chant. "Garrison to Bevins. Bevins to PageSmart. PageSmart. Why PageSmart?"

"All this dancing's giving me a headache," Ducalion said.

"*Shhhh!*" Keith hissed. "I almost got it. It's right in front of me but I can't get a handle on it."

Sharon rose to her feet as well. There was something there, scratching at the front of her brain. A memory. Something important. Something vital.

Keith crisscrossed the living room, gesticulating wildly, his arms moving as quickly as his legs. The faster he paced, the quieter he spoke, until the sound of his voice dropped to a whisper, repeating the same three words like a prayer.

Garrison. Bevins. PageSmart.

Garrison. Bevins. PageSmart.

Garrison. Bevins. PageSmart.

And then he stopped.

He stared at the wall. His lips moved soundlessly, his eyes focused on an invisible spot. Sharon clasped her hands between her breasts. Tensed. Waited.

Ducalion broke the silence. "About time," he exclaimed. "You're driving me nuts."

Keith extended his arm, palm up.

Stop!

Sharon wanted to scream.

"Give me a break already," Ducalion said. "Have a seat. Cut back on the caffeine. Jesus Christ. All this bouncing around isn't helping a goddamned bit."

The light shone.

The angels sang.

The dam in Sharon's head broke and she remembered Jack Sprat the earring thief and his moose of a wife. She remembered Milo's instruction at Bullseye.

Watch for the bounce.

She ran to Keith, who was smiling. Understanding danced in his eyes. Sharon threw her arms around his neck; her renewed sense of hope required human contact. Keith grabbed her by the waist and swung her in a circle. His rebel yell threatened to fracture her eardrums.

They turned to Ducalion and Andi, who looked like they were ready to order matching straightjackets for the celebrating pair. Ducalion opened his mouth to ask the obvious question, but the words never made it out.

The front door burst open. Jimmy Capella stood in the doorway; one hand braced against the jamb, the other gripping the knob. He bent over, chest heaving as he tried to catch his breath. When he finally straightened up, he looked at each of them.

Jimmy's face registered puzzlement when he saw Andi, but he smiled and nodded at the sight of Ducalion. He looked at Keith and his smile grew wider. He winked, and then he noticed Sharon.

He dashed over, pulled her from Keith's arms and into an embrace of his own. Sharon returned the hug, feeling heat where Jimmy's hands pressed against the back of her neck. Sharon closed her eyes as the warmth spread throughout her entire body.

She heard two metallic clicks, and then Keith was

yelling, telling Ducalion and Andi to "put them away for God's sake!" Sharon didn't care.

Jimmy's posture changed. He pulled his hands down, seemingly uncomfortable with his proximity to his former supervisor. He stepped back and surveyed the room again. There was no recognition in his expression this time, only embarrassment and fear.

Sharon looked around as well. The familiar surroundings seemed new, like coming home after a long vacation. She shrugged the nostalgia away with a grateful look for Jimmy and a punch in the shoulder for Keith.

Sharon approached Ducalion, feeling a difference in her stride. Everything was different now. Purpose had replaced despair. She was determined now. She didn't question the emotional one-eighty. She welcomed it.

Ducalion stood dumbfounded, more so when Sharon reached under his jacket and yanked his pistol from its holster.

"Phil," she said, understanding exactly what they had to do now. "How many guns do you have?"

CHAPTER 27

The bedroom love nest turned abattoir was too small for a duel, but Salomé and The Baptist seemed satisfied with the arena. Salomé slashed a figure eight in the air with his sword, a predatory grin twisting his face. The Baptist gave no indication of his intentions or preferences; blocking the only exit appeared to be enough.

After the psychic lobotomy he'd given Milo, it probably was.

His options seemed limited. Even if it were possible to slip past the headless behemoth, he'd need to get around Salomé first. He considered the long sword in his right hand, comparing its ungainly length to the invisible blur in the dandy's hand. Nope. Nope, nope, nope. That's exactly what they wanted Milo to do, the gambit they were expecting. He'd be better off committing hara-kiri, assuming he could work up the nerve to attempt it.

But Milo was afraid of two things: pain and heights.

His odynophobia was broad enough to encompass everything from hypodermic needles to broken bones to total dismemberment. Whenever he encountered a situation with a high "owie" probability, Milo usually moved in the opposite direction.

Quickly.

His acrophobia was more focused, a binary condition expressed by a simple equation. Low was good; high was bad. Confinement helped. His tolerance of altitude was in direct proportion to his level of enclosure. That's why he had enjoyed the view from the top of the Sears Tower, yet experienced dizziness on the third rung of a stepladder. The dichotomy wasn't lost on him; he simply chose not to examine it.

High places, bad. Low places, good.

The speed with which Milo determined his course of action surprised him. He was moving before calculating the ramifications of his strategy or weighing the probability of success against the terror generated by his decision.

He retrieved the scabbard from the floor and wasted seconds inserting the sword. His clumsiness reinforced his assessment; without Tajiri's assistance, Salomé was going to carve him like kosher salami. With the *tachi* properly seated, Milo held the long sword in front of him like a jousting lance and ran toward the window.

The rounded end shattered the glass in the lower pane. A few jagged shards remained lodged in the frame, but the opening looked sufficient. Milo shielded his head behind crossed arms and leapt at the hole, remembering at the last instant to tuck the sword against his body to prevent the scabbard from catching the sides of the frame.

He felt a sting in his left calf as he passed through. The pain was nothing compared to the simultaneous euphoria and horror of being airborne. Milo watched the patchwork of shingles rush beneath him as he traveled toward the edge of the roof he hadn't known was there. He tried to arrest his horizontal velocity, but couldn't muster the coordination to change his trajectory. He was a mortar, not a missile, and he could only scream as physics and gravity conspired to carry him over the rim and down to the ground.

At the top of his arc, he dropped his head to see if Salomé had followed him through the window. The inverted view revealed no pursuit, but as a bonus, the movement pulled him into a roll, and Milo saw sky as he fell the last few feet. Landing on his back wasn't the most pleasant thing he'd ever experienced, but it had to be better than hitting headfirst.

Still, *ouch.*

He lay on the ground for a moment, experimentally flexing his muscles. Fingers wiggled, arms moved and legs bent. He tried inhaling. Functional, but not firing on all cylinders. It would come back.

Hopefully, so would the Colony.

Milo had hoped The Baptist's muzzle might have a range limit, but if it did, he hadn't reached it yet. Granted, the distance between the second floor bedroom and the front yard wasn't astronomical, but he thought his willingness to fly might score him a karmic break.

No such luck.

Using his elbows, Milo raised his torso off the grass. The attitude adjustment soothed his aching sternum and helped get some extra oxygen into his lungs. It also gave him a better view of the compound and the ability to see if his unexpected landing had caused a stir in the population roaming the grounds.

The mindless meandering continued, but Milo noticed a subtle difference in their gait. Before, their movements had seemed purposeful, almost choreographed. There were no collisions or hesitations; everyone just wandered about on their individual orbit.

Now, these parabolas seemed misaligned. The zombie dance seemed to stutter and pause. Intersections occurred more frequently and took longer, the people waiting while someone decided their course.

Perhaps The Baptist's limitation wasn't distance, but number. As egotistical as the thought was, Milo had to assume the quarantining of the Colony required more effort than the pacification of the locals.

"You fell down."

Milo involuntary twisted toward the voice, straining his back and startling the youngsters who'd snuck up on his right. He stifled a groan and clenched his teeth, trying to transform the grimace into a smile. The boy and girl joined hands and stepped back.

"You fell down," the girl repeated, knitting her barely-existent brow. As the spokesperson of the pair, she must have felt it was important to receive confirmation of her observation. The boy made a show of rubbing his cheek with the ball of his thumb, obviously fighting the urge to pop it in his mouth. Milo was impressed with the pre-schooler's self-control.

"I fell from up there," he said, indicating the second floor window with a chin nod.

The girl looked up at the shattered glass. She had to crane her neck to see it. Milo figured the elevation seemed more impressive from the height of a four-year-old, and followed her gaze.

"Wow," the girl said. "That's a long ways to fall."

Milo had to agree, his perspective from the ground matching hers. "It is, isn't it?"

"Uh-huh." She dropped her head to look at his face again. "Mr. Hiram's gonna be honked that you broke his window."

"Who's Mr. Hiram?"

The girl pointed at the house. Yeah, that explained everything.

"Mr. Hiram's just going to have to be honked then," he said. He turned to the little boy. "What about you? You think Mr. Hiram's gonna be honked?"

The boy nodded. The corner of his mouth stretched toward the point of his thumb, his muscles attempting to circumvent his mental discipline.

"Have you seen our mommy?" the boy asked.

Milo thought about the only woman he'd seen since his capture, now sautéing in a roux of Ken's bodily fluids. Fate wouldn't be that cruel.

"What are your names?" he asked.

"I'm Luvenia," the girl replied. "And he's Donnell."

"Donny," Donnell corrected.

"Mama calls you Donnell, so I call you Donnell." Luvenia had her matriarchal tone down pat.

"Daddy calls me Donny," the boy protested weakly, wilting before the superior firepower of the double X chromosome.

Welcome to the club kid, Milo thought.

Angry noises sounded from inside the house. High pitched shouting and creaking boards. The kids cowered and moved to put Milo between them and the structure. It was time for more decisions, and he had no time to think about it.

He grabbed their free arms and pulled them close. The fear evident on their faces mirrored what he felt inside, and the realization finally hit him. These kids weren't under anyone's control. Whatever hands still made the other puppets dance; these youngsters' strings had been cut.

"We're going to play a little game," Milo told Luvenia and Donnell. "You two need to hide, but I don't want you hiding alone. There are other kids here, right?"

Both little heads nodded.

"I want you to find as many as you can and take them with you. Some of them might act a little strange—like they're asleep or something—but I don't think it'll take much to wake them up. If you can wake some grown-ups too, that'd be great, but I want you to concentrate on the kids." Rousing the adults would probably tax The Baptist's resources more, but Milo remembered where he was and the local demographics. He didn't need an army of Kens joining the party.

The sounds from the house got louder as Milo's pursuers made it to the first floor. He felt an itch inside his head, and his pulse quickened with possibility. Was this it? Had the Colony made it back?

I will devour you. A strange voice pulsated throughout his skull. *I will swallow everything you are and make it my own. I will feed upon your gift and it shall nourish me for years to come.*

The kids showed no sign of hearing the voice. The message was for Milo alone, and alone was what he was.

So be it.

Milo raised his eyebrows in a silent question, and the kids responded with conspiratorial nods. He shooed them away with a swat on their fannies and watched as they ran toward the other houses, collecting peers along the way. *Hide well*, he thought as they disappeared among the ramshackle buildings.

There is no place to hide, the voice of The Baptist spoke. *I am everywhere. I am everyone. I am Legion.*

Legion? *Legion?* Milo laughed as he picked himself off the ground and scooped up the long sword. The freak factor was high enough without the Sleepy Hollow refugee throwing around Exorcist references. Still chuckling, Milo headed off in the direction of the vacant barn.

When he was halfway down the hill, Milo stopped because he heard the front door crash open, followed by Salomé's voice. Milo couldn't understand his words, but the tone was unmistakable: The Baptist needed to haul ass. Evidently, the lumbering wasn't part of the act.

A surprised shout made its way down the hill. Too deep to come from Salomé, the exclamation meant someone out of puberty had seen something shocking. *Take that*, he thought, not caring if The Baptist "heard" him or not. Another doggie had escaped from the psychic corral; a sure sign the headless freak's control was slipping. It was tempting to keep chipping away at The Baptist's resources, but Milo suspected he'd set the entire compound free before he'd release his hold on the Colony, and once again Milo decided that two-on-one odds were better than the alternative.

One on one sounded even better.

"Hey asshole," Milo shouted, sprinting a few more yards down the hill. "Why don't you bring that pussy-ass sword down here and show me what you've got." He scanned the brush on either side of the road. Decent cover, but he knew he wouldn't need much. He chose the edge farthest away from the barn, predicting Salomé's attention would focus on the building. The barn made a better target.

As he ducked into the weeds, he heard Salomé jogging

down the trail, purple booties slapping the dust. Christ, even his footsteps sounded prissy. Milo laid down the sword and felt around the ground, rummaging through the saw grass and stickers. Bingo! He wrapped his hand around a softball-sized rock and pulled it free of the damp earth.

Salomé accommodated him by passing his blind before stopping. Even better, his sword was back in its scabbard. Mama must have taught him not to run with sharp things in his hand.

God bless Mrs. Salomé.

"You're making this harder than it needs to be," Salomé called. He walked toward the barn. "Your fate is inevitable. Embrace it."

Milo switched the rock from his left hand to his right. He stood up slowly, wanting Salomé to try another taunt. His big mouth would drown out any sound made by the moving brush.

He hoped.

"Let us be civilized about this," Salomé said. "Come out now and I shall make your passage painless. I assure you, there are worse ways to meet your end."

Mouth clamped shut to keep the smartass comeback in, Milo jumped out of the brush and after a three-step wind-up, hurled the rock at Salomé's head.

Thunk!

Salomé staggered, and dropped to one knee. The brim of his purple pimp-hat darkened. The blood poured between the fingers he had pressed to the wound.

"Embrace that, bitch." Milo said, immediately pursuing his main objective. Ignoring the spatter as Salomé tried to turn away, Milo reached under his purple cloak, grabbed the narrow scabbard with both hands and pulled with all his strength.

The leather loop holding the sword in place would not break. Salomé bucked and twisted, but Milo kept his grip, yanking in every direction he could manage. Finally, Milo heard seams rip and fabric tear and stumbled back, holding

Salomé's sword.

And his pants.

Milo tossed everything over his shoulder, cringing as the lavender fabric fluttered across his cheek on its way into the weeds. Wiping his cheek, Milo squared off with the bleeding man, never happier for the invention of leggings.

"I think you lost something," Milo said.

"I have more trousers," Salomé replied, seeming more concerned with his head than the loss of his pants. "You however, will never regain the advantage you've squandered."

Milo flexed his fingers and moved in closer. "I'm not the one fighting in his long johns. How's that for advantage?"

"Pitiful." Salomé lowered his hand and rubbed his fingers together, watching the blood smear across his palm. "This is the only blood that will stain my hands today."

"Got that right," Milo said. He missed Tajiri's talents, but relished the thought of whooping this ass on his own.

Salomé widened the distance separating them. He spread his feet apart and brought his palms together. "I don't need my blade to deal with you." His mouth moved and sound passed through his lips, but Milo couldn't understand the words. However, the song sounded familiar.

A breeze blew across Milo's body, pulling the loose dirt of the road off the ground. It swirled around Milo's ankles, climbing his legs as Salomé raised his hands above his head. Now Milo recognized the tune.

Trippenstein, where are you when I really need you.

He started to run up the trail, but The Baptist had finally made his way from the house and blocked the top of the road. Milo had no doubt he could evade the headless barricade, but the possible crowd of Brotherhood men behind him wouldn't be as easy to avoid.

The air around him circled relentlessly, gaining speed and sucking the air from his lungs. Dirt and stones scoured his skin, caught in the maelstrom Salomé had created. The whirlwind closed around him as he clawed the air, battering the hail of earth and rocks that pummeled his flesh. Panic welled in his chest. He choked from within and without.

Trapped in a convergence of terror and adrenaline, instinct took control. Milo's fingers began to dance. Syllables formed in his head. He spoke them aloud, half-remembered words accompanying vague gestures. Dirt clogged his mouth and nostrils. He spat earthen paste as his voice grew louder; cleared his nose as his fingers moved faster. The roar of the microburst climbed, matched only by the bellow in his ears.

Milo stretched out his arms and the assault weakened. He opened his hands and the winds changed direction. The debris flowed around his body one more time, then followed his limbs and coalesced around his hands. He splayed his fingers and the detritus exploded across the gap, pounding into Salomé harder than any rock he could have thrown.

Milo cried aloud at the power thrumming along his body. His howl called more dirt and stones and grass from around his feet, pulling it up his legs, gathering it along his torso and flinging it down the length of his arms. Salomé's voice mingled with his own, his desperation harmonizing with Milo's triumph.

The counter attack lasted as long as Milo's vocal chords vibrated. When his voice was exhausted, the barrage ceased. Remnants of ground and gravel fell away from his arms, its momentum spent with the cessation of Milo's cry. His arms still vibrated; his legs felt rubbery. He was bruised, battered and bloody, but still standing.

Salomé wasn't.

"Basic protection spell my ass," Milo muttered. He wobbled across the road for a better look at his handiwork. His stomach immediately regretted the view, and he decorated the ground with a mixture of digestive acid and bile. The landscape didn't suffer because of his weak constitution.

Salomé had been reduced to one hundred and fifty pounds of ground beef, with a side of purple confetti. Definitely a closed-casket service, if anyone gave enough of a damn to bury the bastard. The flies had found him already. Milo was happy to leave Salomé's final arrangements to the insects.

Another collection and expulsion of saliva finally cleared his mouth of its sour and earthy aftertaste. Milo looked down at his hands. "What the hell was that?" he asked. He was still alone in his head, and Trippenstein had been AWOL for more than a day. What new fuckery had he fallen victim to?

Shit lingers, Mickey had told him. Echoes and ripples; that's what he called them. Milo risked his stomach for a final look at Salomé. *That's what echoes and ripples bought you*, Milo thought. *A terminal sandblasting.*

He hobbled back to the weeds and retrieved the *tachi*. The long sword was too valuable to abandon in the thicket. If Tajiri never returned, he'd still have one hell of a letter opener.

Gatherer!

So much for being alone in his head.

The Baptist was still standing at the top of the hill. He might have come a few inches closer, but at this distance, Milo couldn't tell. An arthritic turtle on Quaaludes moved faster than a headless psychic, even one who was pissed at the loss of his favorite lackey.

Milo pointed his hands at the remaining obstacle to his freedom, trying to generate one last echo. One more ripple.

Nothing.

He found Salomé's pants draped across the weeds and took a second to pull his rapier from its sheath. It felt just as alien in his hand as the long sword, but it was long and pointy and very sharp. Armed with two swords, maybe he'd get in a few good licks before The Baptist made his head explode or something equally messy. A few good licks might be all he could manage.

Milo trudged up the hill.

He was too tired to strategize and too sore to hurry. The long, slow walk up the road gave him time to marshal whatever reserves remained, but he had no idea what to do with them. He weaved from one side of the road to the other.

The Baptist made no effort to track him.

How did you attack a tree? Walk right up and start chopping? Sure, that sounded like the best plan, but what happened when the tree could give you an aneurism? What defense worked best against the tree convincing you to disembowel yourself?

What if the tree didn't want to be chopped?

The downside of Milo's slow approach was the time it gave his imagination to concoct all these marvelous scenarios for his impending doom. By the time he reached the middle of the hill, he'd come up with at least a dozen ways The Baptist could kill him without breathing hard, assuming a creature without a mouth breathed at all. What bothered Milo more was the realization that he might be providing his enemy with methods he hadn't considered yet.

Better to quit thinking and keep walking.

He slipped the *tachi* out of its scabbard and had to wonder how threatening he looked marching up the hill. He knew he'd be intimidated if he saw someone coming at him with two fistfuls of steel, but he had eyes, so it wasn't a valid comparison.

Keep walking.

Maybe swords weren't the answer. Milo looked around as he climbed the hill. He saw plenty of rocks, but the "Salomé boulder to the head" gambit seemed somewhat repetitious, and ultimately useless. A rock to the nuts seemed like a suitable substitution, but how could he be sure The Baptist even had nuts. He hadn't been the one boinking Mrs. Arlie, thank God, so there was no way to be sure.

Some weathered lumber lay in the grass along the road. Maybe a two-by-four would be more effective. A couple of good whaps might do the trick. Milo nearly swapped the swords for the board until he imagined the futility of swinging at a redwood. He couldn't recall the exact cartoon, but a hazy memory of Bugs, Daffy or Yosemite Sam bouncing away from an immovable object ended his flirtation with trading steel for oak.

Milo cursed his luck at finding the only militia on the planet without an account at an Army surplus store.

He reached the top of the hill. Twenty yards separated him and The Baptist. Milo whistled the first few notes of the theme from *The Good, the Bad, and the Ugly*. No reaction, which wasn't surprising. Lack of a head had to be a detriment to film appreciation. He scanned his surroundings again. More rocks and more wood. Nothing useful. He'd stick with the swords.

Then Milo realized he hadn't considered everything. There was one more item he hadn't taken into account while searching for weapons. There hadn't been one at the bottom of the road, but he saw one now, and it looked like it might be useful.

Especially hurtling towards them at forty miles an hour.

If Milo ever encountered another headless psychic…if The Baptist had an identical twin roaming the Appalachians and that twin decided to start some shit, Milo would always remember that a 2002 four-door Mazda 626 with a crazy redneck at the wheel could double as a very effective battering ram.

Milo dove to his right as the rice rocket closed in. The front bumper hit The Baptist in his calves and the car crumpled around him, wrapping him in metal shackles. The collision triggered the airbags, obscuring Milo's view of the driver and his passengers.

The Baptist teetered on his shattered legs, swaying in a circle before falling chest-first on the gravel road. He struck the ground with a solid thump.

Here was a change in altitude Milo could deal with. No longer a redwood, The Baptist looked now like a long, bloody brisket, and even a Caucasian klutz knew how to cut jerky.

Especially with an overgrown Ginsu.

Milo dropped Salomé's pigsticker, wrapped both hands around the long sword's grip and took aim. No finesse, no fancy wind-ups, just a downward stroke accompanied by the loudest scream he could coax from his wounded throat.

The *tachi* performed as advertised, passing through The Baptist's torso with hardly a hitch. Milo wrenched the blade free and hacked again, carving a slice off the upper half. He assumed he was hacking the correct area to separate the psychic from his power source, but took a few more swings to make sure.

Milo's confirmation came after the fourth strike.

A searing white light blinded him, followed by a series of *pops* in his head. At first, he thought the car had hit him too, and this was his introduction to the afterlife. There was no pain, only the absence of sight and sound. Then, as quickly as it had enveloped him, the phenomenon vanished and he found himself lying on the side of the road…

…surrounded by Maria, Etienne, Tajiri, Isadore and Kimmy.

"Oy, that looks painful," Isadore said. "These are the times I don't miss having a body so much."

Milo rolled over and groaned. "Well, anytime one of you decides they'd like to drive, be my guest. I could use the rest."

The Colony smiled, and closed their eyes. Once again, Milo felt bathed in light, but a warm, healing luminescence, not the harsh, cold flash of The Baptist's demise. When it dimmed, he felt better. Not one hundred percent, but well enough to move without screaming.

"It's good to have you back guys."

Metal groaned and Milo scrambled to his feet, thinking The Baptist had some fight left in him, but it was only the Mazda's front doors. Keith pulled himself out from behind the wheel, fighting with the side curtain airbag.

"Did you see that?" he asked. He wore a very big smile for a man who'd just totaled his pride and joy. "I mean, did you see that shit? I drove this bad boy right up that motherfucker's ass. Pow! Say goodnight Gracie."

"You hit him in the legs," Ducalion said, extricating himself from the shotgun seat. "You'd have needed a ramp to hit him in the ass."

"Nuh-uh," Keith said, patting the rice rocket's crumpled fender. "Don't diminish this shit. I took that son of a bitch out. Me and the Rice Rocket here, we took care of business."

Milo stepped around The Baptist to shake Ducalion's hand. "What are you doing here? How did you find me?"

"I got a phone call," Ducalion said, resting his free hand on Milo's shoulder. "As for the rest, you'd better ask your wife."

"My wife?"

"Hey!" Keith yelled from the other side of the car. "Where's my handshake? I just killed my car saving your ungrateful bacon. Where's my love?"

"Pucker up; I'll get to you in a minute." Milo saw Sharon and another woman in the back seat. Both looked shaken, but unhurt.

He reached through Ducalion's door to unlock Sharon's, and a moment later had the door open. Keith did the same for the other woman.

Sharon swung her legs out and ducked under the airbag. The minute her head cleared the restraint, she leapt into Milo's arms and buried her face in his chest. He pulled her closer, nuzzling the top of her head until she looked up. When she did, he covered her mouth with his, finally feeling complete.

Sharon's kiss was warmer than usual. Maybe it was the joy of reunion, but Milo lips were burning from the contact. Sharon sagged for a second in his embrace, but quickly found her footing and kissed Milo even harder.

What do you say boss, Trippenstein said in Milo's ear. *Did you miss me?*

"Trippenstein!" Milo exclaimed, pulling away from his wife to see the hippie standing with the others. He dropped his head to look into Sharon's eyes.

"I'm fine honey." Sharon pulled Milo's head farther down and whispered, "Those are some pretty amazing friends you've got there."

I told you I'd bring the cavalry, Trippenstein said, beaming. *Have a little faith.*

"I don't understand," Milo said. Sharon smiled, and the hippie explained.

I took a little trip, Trippenstein explained. It was all he had to say; their connection supplied the rest of the details. Milo saw the circuitous route the hippie had traveled, all the body hopping that had finally landed him in Sharon's "lap." It was an amazing feat, but Trippenstein was more impressed with Milo's performance against Salomé.

Looks like we've both got stories to tell. And a surprise or two.

It was Milo's turn to sag. His knees went weak from Trippenstein's revelation. He leaned back far enough to place a hand on Sharon's stomach. *Unbelievable,* he thought as the Colony began to celebrate. Trippenstein looked especially pleased, holding Milo's gaze as the others frolicked around them.

Milo looked at Sharon, who seemed puzzled. Obviously, Trippenstein hadn't told Sharon everything.

He moved his hand, trying to cover her entire midriff with his palm. Amidst the whooping and hollering of his passengers' celebration, he heard a hum. He felt a soft buzzing in the back of his brain. It was faint, but it was there. He turned back to Trippenstein, who raised his hands and shrugged.

Maybe all the news wasn't good.

CHAPTER 28

"Sounds like you had a busy week," Ducalion said. He lifted a slice of pizza from the box, flipping the errant cheese trail with a flick of his wrist.

Milo mumbled an affirmative. A mouthful of sausage and pepperoni prevented him from articulating properly, but it was enough. Camped out on the Tuckers' living room floor, the five of them had hashed and re-hashed the specifics of the last five days, Milo filling in the majority of the blanks while Sharon, Keith, Andi and Ducalion demolished three extra-large pies and drained most of a case of beer.

"It sounds pretty disjointed," Andi said. She lay stretched out on the carpet, using Keith's legs as a pillow. Milo caught Keith's eyes every chance he got and wiggled his eyebrows at the beauty lying across his thigh. Keith responded with a grim stare, but he kept his hands folded in his lap and a fresh bottle of Rolling Rock propped against his crotch.

Another fire quenched by icy suds.

Andi rolled over and rested her chin on Keith's knee. "That crazy woman at Harrifords. The kid at Bullseye. Whatever happened to you two in Huntington that Keith still won't talk about." She reached up and pinched Keith's waist. Keith slapped her hand away.

"That's a whole lot of shit," Andi continued, "but

combined, it turns into a cluster fuck of epic proportion. And that's not even counting what happened at PageSmart."

Keith smiled. He looked at Milo and then bobbed his head up and down in Andi's direction. Milo caught the message: "shit" and "fuck" in the same sentence. "Hot damn!" Keith's expression said.

Ahhh, young love.

Sharon had seen the signs as well, but didn't seem as pleased with the romance in the air. She jabbed an elbow into Milo's side, a clear warning. *Don't get too enamored with the new girl*, the poke told him. Milo didn't say anything. Keith was falling hard and fast and nothing Mama Tucker could do was going to change that.

Sharon would have someone else to mother soon enough.

"You're trying to scoop too much into the same bucket," Ducalion said. "Narrow your focus some. Not everything's connected. Jesus, what do they teach you gals in Private Eye school?"

"Not to take shit from cops," Andi said, popping Ducalion in the ass with the pointed toe of her boot. "And not to ask too many questions."

That stopped the conversation cold. Their discussion had covered a lot of ground, but Milo hadn't told them everything. There were things Sharon didn't know yet, but she would. Milo was through keeping secrets.

Except for one.

Keith would get the whole story too, in payment for sacrificing his ride. It was more than that, Milo realized. Keith wouldn't rest until he knew every chapter and verse, and he deserved them.

Then, there were questions that no one had asked.

Ducalion had taken care of the cops. He spun a complicated web for the horde of investigators that had swarmed over The Brotherhood compound. There was plenty of blood for the cops to wade through, and none of them missed the quantity of it on Milo's clothes. Ducalion had accounted for all of it, reminding the assembled authorities several times of Milo's capture of Cecil Hawkins the previous spring. The reminder served everyone well. The cops accepted the explanations, and with Milo following Ducalion's lead, they released him with nothing more than a pat on the back and an "atta boy."

If Ducalion needed any answers, he hadn't asked for them, and Milo was willing to leave it alone.

"That's my cue," Keith said, slipping his leg out from under Andi's head. "If y'all are going to talk shop, I'm going to go grab a smoke."

"You're not going to stay and protect me?"

"Hah!" Keith stood up and pulled a crumpled pack of cigarettes out of his pocket. "Just don't get any blood on the carpet. Sharon'll kill you both if you mess up her living room."

"Got that right," Sharon said. She pulled her legs in and used Milo's shoulder to push herself off the floor. "Let's get this crap out of the way before the gunfight."

"You want help honey," Milo asked, handing her the empty pizza boxes.

Sharon ruffled his hair. "I've got it. Phil and Andi can help me."

"Be glad to," Ducalion said and started collecting empty bottles.

"Count me in," Andi added.

Milo didn't feel right leaving the cleanup to Sharon and two guests, but Keith wasn't the only one able to communicate with a look. Sharon gave him a subtle nod, shifting her gaze to Keith, who had slipped out onto the patio to smoke. The conversation so far had covered *most* of what had happened; there were still stories to tell and Sharon wasn't ready to let Ducalion and Andi that far into the circle.

Milo suspected she was concerned more with Andi than Phil, but he'd leave that discussion for later. First things first.

He ducked out the sliding door and joined Keith on the small balcony.

"I was wondering how long it would take," Keith said, offering Milo a smoke.

Milo shook his head. "I guess Sharon figured we needed to talk."

"Sharon's a smart lady."

"She's pregnant," Milo said, regretting the outburst as soon as he spoke.

Keith didn't seem surprised. He punched Milo's shoulder. "Way to go chief."

Milo returned the smack. "Yeah, that's me. Manhood validated."

"When's the blessed event?"

"Trippenstein didn't say."

"Trippenstein didn't say? The hippie's a gynecologist now?"

"I sure as hell hope not."

"I promise I didn't go poking around the plumbing," Trippenstein spoke up. The balcony suddenly became a lot more crowded, in the theoretical sense.

"How's Sharon feel about all of this?" Keith asked.

"Ask him," Milo cocked a thumb at an empty space to his right.

"Sharon doesn't know yet," Trippenstein admitted.

Keith joined Milo at the railing. "Here we go again."

"No Keith, it's not 'here we go again,'" Maria said. "It pains me to admit it, but in this case I agree with Trippenstein. Sharon will know soon enough. A woman always knows. She'll figure it out and when she does, she'll tell Milo. We shouldn't steal that moment from her."

"Gawd, listening to you two is like listening to a gaggle of biddies on washday."

The patio wasn't very big. Milo and Keith took up more than two-thirds of the available room. Other than the Colony, which didn't occupy any physical space, the only other thing on the porch was a cheap, plastic deck chair that Milo and Sharon had inherited with the apartment. They'd have thrown it out long ago, but it gave Keith somewhere to park it while he smoked.

Garcen seemed pleased to have a place to sit.

"Why am I not surprised?" Milo said, nonplussed by the old man's appearance.

Keith yelped and almost dove off the balcony.

"Simmer down," Garcen said. "There's no call for getting hysterical."

Keith looked over his shoulder into the living room. Sharon and her helpers were still clearing the remnants of the carpet picnic, smiling and laughing as they worked. "I didn't even hear the door open," he said, turning back to Garcen.

"He didn't come through the door," Milo stated. His apathy amazed him. Had he been through so much that nothing surprised him any longer?

"You catch on quick," Garcen said.

"Seems as if," Milo said. "I haven't had much of a choice lately." Garcen raised an eyebrow. "That's not exactly how I see it, but you're the expert."

"Expert?" Milo replied, louder than he had intended. "That's a joke, right?"

"You tell me," Garcen said. "I know a little more than what's been in the papers, but you lived through it. How's it feel to be a killer?"

Keith gasped. Milo threw up, sending a shower over the patio rail.

Garcen leaned forward in his chair and looked at the splattered grass below. "Yep, that's about what I figured."

"A killer," Keith said.

"What else would you call it?" Garcen said, sitting back and staring up at Keith. "Damn boy, I could almost hang the same tag on you, or have you forgotten what happened to your car?"

Keith glanced at the parking lot, where his rented hatchback sat under a street lamp. No, he hadn't forgotten.

"Call it what you want, but you've both got blood on your hands. I just wanted to see how you felt about it."

Milo and Keith looked at each other. Milo assumed Keith's expression matched his.

"I'm all right with it," Milo lied, swallowing the bile that crept up his throat. "Like I said; I didn't have much choice."

"What he said," Keith said, wrestling with a mouthful of his own.

"Keep telling yourselves that," Garcen said. He pried his ass out of the chair and moved to stand between them. "Eventually you'll believe it."

"Uh-huh," Keith and Milo said, continuing to stare out into the night.

"Don't shed no tears for them boys." Garcen rested his arms on their shoulders. "They got what they had coming. If it wasn't you, it would've had to be someone else, and who knows how much damage they'd have done in the meantime."

Milo shrugged out of Garcen's grasp. "Thanks old man. That's a comfort."

"You better take it where you can get it." His voice turned harsh. "Hell son, you ain't no different than anyone else; I don't care how many folks you got crawling through your skull. You go to work every day. You settle your debts. You take care of your own. Just like every other workin' Joe on the planet."

"Oh yeah," Milo scoffed. "Everyone's got a bunch of crazies lining up to take a shot. Thanks again Garcen. I'd forgotten all about that."

"Greener grass asshole. You're standing here lookin' over the fence and getting a hard-on for the neighbor's yard. Don't fool yourself; he's got it just as hard. Sure, he might not have Crazy Amys and Eleazars and headless psychics to worry about, but then again, he don't have the same advantages you've got neither. Each according to his needs and each according to his gifts."

"Careful Milo," Keith said. "He's quoting Karl Marx. I always pegged him as more of a Groucho man."

Garcen responded with an upraised middle finger. "Here's the bird you were looking for then."

That got them laughing.

Garcen tipped them a salute, opened the sliding door and stepped through. Milo didn't bother to watch; he knew the old man would never step foot in his living room. "That's a handy talent to have," he told Keith.

"So's using people like stepping stones," Keith said. "You ever wonder how many tricks Trippenstein has in his bag?"

"I'm starting to think there's a lot."

"Hello," Trippenstein interjected. "Floating right here."

"You're probably right," Keith said, ignoring the interruption.

"It'd be nice to know how many," Milo mused.

"At least I didn't blow anything up this time," Trippenstein grumbled.

Keith looked over his shoulder. "The list of things I'd like to know is growing at an alarming rate."

Milo followed his gaze and chuckled. "I'll bet that's not the only thing that's growing."

"Blow me," Keith said. "You've already got a woman."

"I'd say you're about to join the club. You do remember what to do with one, don't you?" Congratulations offered.

"Yeah. Your mother's been teaching me all of your dad's tricks." Congratulations accepted.

They tapped fists, and that sealed the deal.

"It's a clear night." Keith craned his neck out and looked up. "Lots of stars."

The door opened again. Ducalion stuck his head through and asked, "You boys feel like some company?"

"I think there's room for one more," Milo said, sliding down the rail.

"What's the matter Phil," Keith said. "Too much estrogen in there for you?"

"They're getting friendly," Ducalion admitted. "I think Sharon's happy to have another girl around. I guess it's been a while."

"Don't you start," Keith said. He looked over his shoulder again. "She's something, isn't she?"

"She's got a hell of a rack," Milo said. "It's too soon to

tell anything else."

"Yeah, but a hell of a rack's a good place to start." Keith lit another cigarette and offered the pack to Ducalion. "I'm looking forward to finding out the rest."

Ducalion took the smoke and lit up. "So that's what you guys are doing while I'm breaking my ass in there? Talking about titties?"

"Can you think of a better subject?" Keith asked.

"We're just asking questions and looking at the stars," Milo said, staring up into the darkness.

"You boys find any answers?" Ducalion asked.

"The fault, dear Brutus, lies not in our stars but in our selves," Keith said.

"Who you calling Brutus, Popeye?" Ducalion asked, eyes twinkling in the starlight.

"That's Bluto, ya jerk," Keith said, blowing smoke in Ducalion's face.

Ducalion fanned the cloud away. "I've read Shakespeare, you know."

"Really? The comic books don't count."

"I've got your comic books, geek boy."

Milo tuned out the rest; he'd heard the song before. While Keith and Ducalion traded shots, and the Colony caught each other up on current events, Milo was content to watch the sky.

He replayed Garcen's words, concentrating less on what he had said than how he had said it. Just like their conversation in the living room, what had remained unspoken weighed heavier on his mind.

There was time.

At least another eight months.

EPILOGUE

By definition, loose ends usually come at the end, but they see no reason to wait.

Their list isn't long, but details are details, and what they don't accomplish now might be impossible later.

Well, nothing is impossible. They've proved this time after time. Maybe "difficult" is a better word.

They visit the crazy woman first. It's best to start a campaign with an easy victory, and the mental deficient with the horrendous hair provides them with their initial success. Getting next to her requires none of their carefully prepared cover stories; they only need knock on the correct door and bluff their way past the disinterested wage slave passing as a halfway house counselor.

They reward the girl by making her death quick and relatively painless.

The gangster or the other Hunter? The choice of their next target requires more consideration. The gangster is difficult to locate, but the criminal nature of his existence removes the need for delicacy. Nothing prevents them from slaughtering hundreds to guarantee the destruction of one. In addition, the carnage shocks no one, ensuring a multitude of possible culprits.

Anonymity in numbers; another time-tested axiom.

Finally, they rest their sights on the Hunter, and realize it's only fitting to have saved him for last. Matching wits against one of their own sharpens their skills. His death will be a proper challenge, an appropriate end to the preparations for their ultimate goal.

Once they dispatch the Hunter, they're ready to face the Gatherer.

In the end, all goes according to plan.

The connections are gone. They've eliminated anyone with cause to seek out their prey. The Gatherer stands isolated, his secret restored. All who remain see him only as a normal man, unworthy of note or notice. When he falls, there will be no one left to protest his demise, no ally to seek vengeance on his enemies and no peer to lay claim on his parting gift.

What they've sought will be theirs, well earned, well deserved and well hidden.

They need only wait.

They have time.

ABOUT THE AUTHOR

M. Stephen Lukac is the author of *Oogie Boogie Central, Oogie Boogie Bounce,* and *But Then Again, You'll Have This.* He lives in Southwestern Pennsylvania with his wife and children.

OTHER BOOKS BY M. STEPHEN LUKAC

Oogie Boogie Central
ISBN 978-1-929653-91-1

Footsteps echo in the darkness. We know not the passengers they carry. We cannot recognize their power, alleviate their burden, or understand their pain. We can never comprehend their sorrow, ease their loneliness, or experience their fear. The Gatherers and Hunters walk among us. They are everywhere, yet we do not know them . . .

. . . But they know one another.

Within its borders, what appears seldom is. The impossible is common. Identity is fluid. Death is not the end. Places exist not found on any maps, but they are there, known to those whose footsteps echo in the darkness . . .

. . . Welcome to Oogie Boogie Central.

Meet Milo Tucker, a quick-witted store detective, and Alex Harrison, a tragic youth who works in a bookstore. Their lives intersect when they confront Theodore Munsch, West Virginia's most notorious serial killer, and both are forced to confront their greatest doubts, their deepest fears . . .

. . . And a murderer who will not die.